THE
VENGEANCE

Also by Emma Newman

THE VENGEANCE

EMMA NEWMAN

SOLARIS

First published 2025 by Solaris
an imprint of Rebellion Publishing Ltd,
Riverside House, Osney Mead,
Oxford, OX2 0ES, UK

www.solarisbooks.com

ISBN: 978-1-83786-164-4

10 9 8 7 6 5 4 3 2 1

A CIP catalogue record for this book is available from the
British Library.

Designed & typeset by Rebellion Publishing

Printed in Denmark

MIX
Paper | Supporting
responsible forestry
FSC® C104608

For Amanda, for keeping me sane, making sure I eat, and getting me drunk since 1995. Love you, chick.

AUTHOR'S NOTE

ALEXANDER DUMAS CREATED characters and stories that I have loved for as long as I can remember. Before I was old enough to read his novels, cartoon and movie adaptations of his work shaped my idea of adventure and friendship from a very young age.

As a writer, I find myself feeling rather uncomfortable talking about the impact of adaptations rather than the original books, but I want to be truthful here as I suspect my route to discovering Dumas' work is one that is very common. If you grew up in the 80s in the UK, there's a good chance you still know the theme tune to a certain bizarre cartoon adaptation of *The Three Musketeers* (I apologise if I have just ear-wormed you!).

That cartoon, and other movies inspired by the same novel, along with the various adaptations of my favourite Dumas novel *The Count of Monte Cristo*, have given his work a special place in our hearts. How many of us picked up a stick as a child and pretended to be D'Artagnan while yelling 'all for one and one for all!'? How many of us have swooned over the lavish costumes and been gripped by the derring-do and political intrigue? How many of us have admired these stories of loyalty, friendship and revenge?

When I was asked to write a book set in the world he created, I was thrilled! I went to the novels, rediscovered the characters I had met in so many forms over my lifetime, and thought about what it was that I most wanted to pay homage to in his work.

In *The Vengeance*, I've chosen to focus on two of the themes in his work that I have loved the most: the deep bonds of friendship that can only be forged when facing death (and life) together, and revenge. The latter is a different flavour to that explored in *The Count of Monte Cristo*, as I wanted to define it in a different context. There is also the coming-of-age aspect, embodied by D'Artagnan, which I hope I have respectfully echoed in my protagonist's journey, along with a few of his other traits!

It is my hope that in reading *The Vengeance*, you feel something like I have every time I've read Alexander Dumas' work and watched adaptations thereof: the comfort of pure escapism, the delight of adventure and the thrill of the occasional, well-placed sword fight.

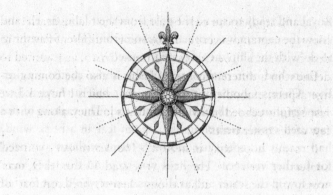

CHAPTER ONE

IF SHE HAD known that it was the last hour of her mother's life, Morgane would have done things differently. But that was the thing about a life at sea such as they had; there was no way to tell where death would come from. They all expected it at every moment, so usual a threat that it became oddly comfortable, sinking into the background like a storm front on the horizon that never quite arrived. It was going to hit at some point. They all knew it. It was going to toss everything around and potentially wreck it all, but until that day, Morgane somehow hadn't ever believed it would come for the captain of *The Vengeance*, the Scourge of the Sea.

Morgane had watched her mother pacing the deck since leaving their latest victim, a French trading ship, stricken in the water some miles back. She was finding fault with repairs, snapping at anyone who had the misfortune of needing to speak with her. Morgane was glad to be out of the way, sat as she was straddled across the bowsprit right at the front of their brigantine, her back to the sea as she sanded down the repair she'd worked on long enough to make her back ache. They were all tired and short-tempered, only a day from Port

Royal and ready to spend the gold from their labours, but she knew the captain was bothered by something else. Something to do with the ship they'd just ransacked.

There had been nothing remarkable about it, just another Four Chains Company trade ship that had surrendered to *The Vengeance*, as they all did in the end. The captain of the captured vessel, trembling like a palm leaf in a brisk wind, had readily accepted her mother's terms without any need for further violence. The haul was so good that they were now low in the water and as slow as a man who'd just feasted to the point of discomfort. There was gold aplenty to divide between them, and bundles of goods ready to be sold on for more. No one had died, and the only injury had been to Bull's left cheek, hit by a splinter. Jacques, the quartermaster and best with needle and thread, had already sewn it up.

So, what then could explain the foul temper? Her mother was usually high spirited after each victory. One more notch in the beam across her bed, a further insult to the one who'd wronged her all those years ago. She'd watched her mother run a fingertip across those notches every night before they slept, her mother in the captain's bed, herself in the hammock strung up in the corner of her cabin, as it had always been. Those few silent moments of satisfaction before climbing into bed and stretching out, hands tucked behind her head, a smile playing across her lips.

Sometimes they took a Spanish ship, just for the gold, but they didn't earn a notch in that beam, nor did any lovers. Only the taking of a Four Chains Company ship would merit one, and there were dozens of those marks in the wood. They kept a tally of her career of piracy rather than privateering, something that the captain considered a matter of personal pride. There was no letter of marque to protect her, and no bending of the knee to any king, French or not, as Anna-Marie had been known to boast when in her cups. All the crew benefitted from all the spoils, not just a portion left over after payment to the king as the privateers had.

Even if there were a king in Europe willing to sanction Anna-Marie's hatred of the Four Chains Company, Morgane was convinced that her mother would not accept any permission to do as she did. It was too personal, too important a matter to involve anyone else, and she was too proud to hide behind a piece of paper giving her permission to enact her vengeance.

Something had soured of late, though. The past few months had been as successful and as lucrative as ever, but her mother's mood had become volatile. She'd taken to brooding alone rather than drinking with the rest of them in Taverners, their favourite hostelry in Port Royal. Nothing Morgane could say or do seemed to shift those black moods that settled on her mother, just like the one setting in before her eyes. She watched her mother say something briefly to Jacques and then go below, just as the wind snatched Morgane's headscarf clean off.

"Shit and blood!" She failed to grab the scrap of fabric before it was out of reach. The sun was beating down on her scalp and she hated the way the wind was now tugging her bright blond hair free from its braid to whip her cheeks.

She finished the sanding and then scooted along the bowsprit and back onto the forecastle deck, heading for the hatch on the main deck to go below and towards the back of the ship to the cabin she shared with her mother. Over on the quarterdeck, Jacques beckoned her to join him, but she wanted another scarf, indicating that she'd only be a moment before disappearing below.

Descending into the bowels of the ship, she listened to its creaks and moans. Even if she hadn't been above all day, she'd still be able to tell how the sea lay and what the wind was doing, just from what the ship said and how she moved.

She unhooked the lantern from the top of the staircase and

then headed down the steps, needing its light after being out in the blazing sunshine.

"HONK!"

She gasped and almost dropped the lantern as a flurry of white feathers barrelled up the stairs towards her. The goose tugged at the pockets of her jacket, hoping she had a treat tucked away for him as she sometimes did when she wanted to go belowdecks without the entire ship knowing about it.

"Quiet, you noisy bastard!" she yelled at him, but he carried on honking as if his private home were being invaded – even though he usually slept up on the deck or in the bosun's hammock if it was raining. "Quiet, King Charles, or I'll chop off your head!"

His full name was King Charles the Second, out of the proper disrespect for the English king, but as long as his rank and name were spoken, he always settled. She'd never hurt a single feather on his body – she loved the stupid bird – but strangely enough, that specific threat always got him to be quiet. He settled on the top step and stared at her until she scratched the top of his head.

He nuzzled her hand with his bill and then she continued through the space filled with empty hammocks, past cannon, canvas and piles of rope, then through the open doorway partitioning off the upper storage area, the lantern light picking out the edges of the crates, bales and barrels that held the spoils of recent weeks. She picked her way through the narrow corridor left between them all to the captain's cabin door and pulled out the key she wore around her neck, only to see that it was already open, just a crack.

The hinges on the door to the cabin were well-oiled as they were both light sleepers and it meant fewer fights if either of them came in after the other had retired for the night. Morgane opened the door as slowly and silently as possible, revealing the sparsely furnished cabin. Her mother's bed was built into a nook with its own heavy burgundy velvet curtains to give her privacy. The leaded glass of the rear window allowed sunshine to cast a gridded square over the faded rug in the centre of the room. The captain's desk and chair were to the left, her hammock in the corner next to it, swinging gently back and forth, her personal chest beneath it containing her worldly goods.

Morgane froze in the doorway when she saw her mother kneeling in front of one of the chests they'd looted from the captured vessel earlier.

She watched silently as Anna-Marie picked the lock, opened the chest, and lifted out two letters that lay on top of what looked like a pile of linens. After reading the names written on them, she stuffed one down her shirt and broke the other's seal to unfold it and read the contents.

Whatever the letter said made Anna-Marie crumple forwards for a moment, before crushing the letter in her fist and slamming the chest shut. Swearing beneath her breath she stuffed that letter down her shirt, too, and then twisted round, suddenly aware of Morgane's presence.

"You spying on me?" she shouted.

"I just need another scarf, the wind took mine." She stepped inside, refusing to let her mother's baleful glare stop her from entering their cabin. "What was that letter about?"

"It's no business of yours!" Anna-Marie snapped, smoothing down her shirt as she stood.

"How could it be any business of yours, either?" Morgane asked. She wasn't trying to push back, it just made no sense to her. They'd pulled the chest off a random ship they'd raided, one of dozens of Four Chains trading vessels they'd looted over the years. Whatever the letter had said, it couldn't be personal.

Anna-Marie snatched one of her own scarves off the hook by her bed and pressed it into Morgane's chest as she pushed her back towards the door. "There! Get out!"

"Tell me what—"

A final shove and she was out of the door before she could finish. She listened to it being locked from the inside. She hammered on it with her fist. "If something is making you sore-headed enough to take it out on the crew, you should—"

"Bugger off, Morgane!"

She was about to unlock the door with her own key and have it out with her, when she heard a sharp whistle. It was so faint below deck that she fancied she'd imagined it for a moment, but then came the sound of heavy boots running overhead – Jacques heading towards the hatch down to this deck, to come and fetch the captain, she was certain – and she immediately tensed.

King Charles started honking and then Jacques appeared at the partition between the storage area she stood in and the cannons.

"She in the cabin?"

Morgane nodded.

"Ship sighted."

Morgane shrugged. "We're fully laden, we've no need to attack another ship before landfall."

He raised an eyebrow. "Are you captain now, chère?"

"Is it Four Chains?"

He nodded.

"Blood and sand." She banged on the door. "Captain! Ship sighted!"

The key turned in the lock and Anna-Marie looked past her to Jacques. As close as she was, Morgane could have sworn she'd been crying from the red blotches just beneath her eyes. But she never cried.

"Dill spotted a schooner," he said. "South by sou-east, just come over the horizon."

"One of theirs?"

He nodded. Dill, a woman so small in stature that she was often mistaken for a young boy when they were in port, had the sharpest eyes of all of them and was rarely wrong. The captain darted back into her cabin, heading for the extra pair of pistols hung beside her bed. Morgane followed her in. "You're not thinking of going for her?"

"Why would you think otherwise?" Anna-Marie slung each baldric over her head so they crossed over her chest and then settled the extra pistols into place so they didn't interfere with the pair she wore at her hips. The guns were the most elaborately decorated things she wore, not being one for fancy jackets and waistcoats, unlike some of the others in their industry. She wore plain black breeches, leather boots that went past her knees and a plain linen shirt, not unlike what Morgane preferred to wear. Practical to the last, both of them.

"Because we're already low in the water and there's no room for—"

"Surely you are not arguing for leaving them be?"

Morgane tied the scarf over her hair and tucked in the wayward blonde strands. "We've a fine haul and we're ready for port. Why—"

"Enough, Morgane. I'm taking it."

Morgane grabbed her pistols from where she'd left them in the folds of her hammock, cleaned and ready to load as she always kept them, and slung the baldric round her hips.

"It'll take us off course," she said as she buckled it and checked there was powder and shot in the pouches. "We'll be at Port Royal by morning if we—"

Out of nowhere, Anna-Marie grabbed her shirt and smashed her against the wall. "I said, enough! It's a Four Chains ship! There's no debate to be had."

"We're too slow to attack a bloody schooner!" she yelled into her mother's face. "Just think for a bloody minute!"

A pain exploded through her jaw and then, after, the

realisation that the captain had backhanded her. Her mother had never been loving, and had shoved her around all her life, but this was the first time she'd ever hit her so hard. She couldn't quite believe it. "I *am* thinking!" Anna-Marie's yelling snatched her out of the shock. "I'm thinking of what they took from me! I'll sink every one of their damn ships and ruin them for what they did to me!"

"And it won't change a bloody thing," Morgane said through the blood welling in her mouth. "You'll still be an angry bitch who hates the world."

With a guttural sound, Anna-Marie threw her to the floor, stepped over her feet and pushed past Jacques to run to the hatch.

Morgane sat up, surprised to see Jacques standing over her, offering his hand. "Anyone else and you'd be dropped off this ship faster than a wet shit."

She laughed and grabbed his hand to pull herself up. "Well, if I can't use the fortune of my birth to speak my mind, what is it even worth?"

"Your gob will be the death of you, Morgane."

"Nah, it'll be being too bloody slow to duck." She prodded her jaw gently.

"She's not herself," Jacques said quietly. "But now is not the time." He patted the top of her head gently, as he'd always done since she was tiny. For such a tall, broad man, he was very gentle. At least he always was with her. She'd seen him smash heads against masts with enough force to cave in skulls like ripe melons. But not often. Only when he needed to. Where many of the crew revelled in any violence they could find – and groaned whenever a target vessel surrendered – Jacques never did. "You ready?"

Morgane looked into his dark brown eyes, seeing nothing but concern. She took in the scar across his right cheek, the battered tricorn hat worn over the tight black curls of his hair, the dark brown of his skin. She knew his face as well as her mother's, and just like her, he'd been there on the ship for as long as she could remember. Where exactly in France he'd come from, what he'd left behind and why and how he fell in with Anna-Marie were mysteries to her, and everyone else in the crew. There were stories about how he'd saved the captain's life when Morgane had been a babe in arms, and many drunken nights of trying to get him to confirm whether this was true. But Jacques, after declaring that he would never talk about such a thing while sober, would accept all the liquor given to him before staggering off to bed with his lips still sealed. She was nineteen years old, and she'd never seen or heard of him betraying a confidence. That was why he kept several of hers, too.

"You agree with me? That we should leave that ship be and carry on to Port Royal?"

After a few moments, and a quick glance at the doorway to check the captain really had gone up on deck, he nodded. "But we'll follow her, chère, we always do, and we always profit from it."

Morgane let her frustration out with a sigh and they left the cabin together, taking care to lock it behind her.

THE CAPTAIN WAS up on the forecastle deck looking through her spy glass, *The Vengeance* altering course to intercept the schooner as Morgane and Jacques dashed to Anna-Marie's side. To Morgane's surprise, the gap between the two ships was already closing, even though a schooner should easily outrun them. They were fast, ironically often used by the trading companies in the hope of outrunning pirates, only to make their ships coveted all the more. If the schooner was at full sail, it would outrun them in this wind, especially given how laden *The Vengeance* was. But this one was limping along.

The glass was passed to Jacques and then to her. The schooner didn't seem to be very low in the water, so it wasn't as if they were burdened by an excess of cargo, and she couldn't see any damage, but then again, she couldn't see the sides of the ship at all. The masts were in place, so they were either uninterested in maximising the wind, or incapable of it. And since when were traders not interested in going as fast as they could?

"This doesn't feel right," she muttered, trying to fathom what it was that made her gut tight. "By the look of where she's sitting in the water, there's barely anything on her."

"So they've sold their wares in the Americas and are full of gold instead. Even better."

"But that's not how they work, you know that. They should be heavy with goods they're taking back to France. Something isn't right."

"Perhaps they've already run into trouble," Jacques suggested, "and someone else has had the spoils."

"They may be thin on crew, or damaged," her mother said. "We take them."

"But what for?" Morgane asked. "If there's nothing on board, what's the point of diverting and risking crew? At best it will be a ship limping home with nothing left to steal, at worst it…" She glanced back at the ship. "It could be a trap."

Her mother snorted at her. "You know nothing. We take them, we sink them if they're empty." She turned to Jacques. "Any repairs ongoing that'll get in the way?"

Jacques shook his head. Morgane had finished the repairs to the bowsprit and if she hadn't, the jib and flying jib sails at the very front of the ship wouldn't have been able to unfurl.

"I want all speed," the captain said. "Give the order."

Jacques went to the edge of the forecastle overlooking the

deck and gave a piercing whistle, making all the crew stop and look over. "Lay aloft and loose all sail!" Jacques bellowed and as if his words were a shot fired at a flock of birds, the crew scurried into action, climbing the rigging to release the last of the sails, loosening ropes and securing others, the energy of the ship changing in an instant.

Morgane looked back at her mother whose attention was singularly focused on her prey, her lips pressed tight together, all the upset caused by that letter seemingly forgotten. Then she was shoved aside by one of the crew sent fore to free a snagged rope to release the flying jib and then she was helping to heave it into place without a moment's thought.

The wind caught the extra sails and the breeze against her face picked up, too, as their speed increased. Not a huge amount, given how laden they were, but enough to feel it and enough to see the gap between the ships closing. Behind them, the crew were stowing, reeling the last coils of rope hurriedly and making sure they were in place to reduce the chance of tripping people up should a swift boarding be called for. Others were hurtling below deck to prepare the cannons, ready to give the captain whatever she called for to achieve her prize.

It was shit like this that made Morgane crave her own ship. But she wasn't stupid enough to think she was ready to form a crew and lead them on her own, even if her mother let her keep a ship they captured. A fleet of two wouldn't work, and she knew it, they both did, given how they argued about the Four Chains company. And this was a prime example of why it wouldn't work. Anna-Marie was doing the wrong thing, she knew it, so did Jacques, but they fell into line because the captain of *The Vengeance* did what she wanted and at the end of the day, everyone profited from the vendetta. The crew didn't really care that the Four Chains company had ruined Anna-Marie's life (not that anyone knew the details anyway) and none of them really cared that they'd killed the captain's sister, back when she lived in France. Not even Morgane really felt anything about that, even though it was her aunt that had been murdered. It was so long ago – before she was born – and so far away and she couldn't really imagine what it would be like to have an aunt, or a father for that matter. All the crew really cared about was the fact that Anna-Marie was usually a damn fine captain, when she wasn't out of sorts and making stupid decisions like this one, and she made them all rich.

There would be no discussion of how wise this course of action was when they were in port, deep in their cups, drinking away the plunder. Jacques was too loyal to the captain to plot against her, and besides, Morgane knew that as much as she resented it, being the daughter of one of the most feared pirates on the sea gave her advantages she couldn't yet achieve on her own. One day, though. One day she would break free, and she wouldn't do stupid shit like this.

But was it really so unwise? Now she could see that the schooner was ailing in some way, where was the harm? Most of the ships surrendered at the sight of their true colours being raised, but not all of them. And if they didn't, and it came to a fight, the captain's aim was excellent and those six shots she took into the battle would be well spent before her sword was drawn. And Morgane knew how to fight well, too. It was one of the few skills Anna-Marie had been able to pass on to her daughter.

So she busied herself – there was always a lot to do when chasing down quarry. And then, even though it had felt as though she'd been waiting for the moment to come forever, she jumped when the signal was given to raise the Jolie Rouge. She looked up at the flag replacing the trading colours, a brilliant red silk with a black heart pierced by a golden dagger.

Not for the first time, Morgane wondered how their quarry

must feel now they could see who it was. For surely that flag and *The Vengeance* were known amongst all of that company's fleet? She wondered how scared they were.

Her mother signalled for a few warning shots to be fired towards the ship, just to make their intentions absolutely clear. No formal signal of surrender was given, but slowly, one by one, each of the ship's main sails were loosened.

Morgane went to Jacques' side. "That's odd."

He nodded, watching the disorderly slowing of their prey. "Suggests they don't have a full crew," he said.

The captain, who was looking through her glass again, gave a grunt of agreement. "I only see three on the rigging, and they're moving slowly."

It pained Morgane to see the schooner's sail being left to flap in the wind instead of being hauled up and tied properly. Then a signal of surrender was raised, and her mother smiled with satisfaction.

The order was given to alter the course fractionally to enable *The Vengeance* to come to a stop alongside the vessel. And then the orders to haul down the jib and haul up the spanker made Morgane snap into action, all the nervous tension that had built up within her suddenly finding a place to go. She hauled in but didn't climb the rigging to fasten the sails that were now being loosed and raised to slow their speed. Having done something useful, she returned to her mother's side, as did Jacques.

Slowly they drew up alongside the ship. It was called *Coup de Maître* and with every inch that they approached, an unfamiliar fear took root deep in Morgane's belly. The hairs on the back of her neck were standing on end, the ends of her fingers tingling with dreadful anticipation, as death's thunderhead steadily grew.

The *Maître* was so painfully quiet, and its rigging was empty of crew, the flapping from the abandoned loose sails sounding like an eerie round of applause for an empty stage. She spotted a man slumped against the main mast, his white shirt stained brown-red around his midriff.

Jacques pointed at the chipped wood of the ship's rail and pockmarks in the hull, left by pistol shots. "They've already been done over," he said to her mother, who nodded.

"Something still feels wrong," Morgane said, making her mother tut.

"You've just never come across one of these before," she said. "If this were a trap, they'd have broadsided us by now."

Morgane scanned the side of the *Maître*, looking for any sign of the gun ports opening, but all was still. She still couldn't shake the feeling that they were missing something, though. "She's very high in the water."

"She's empty," Jacques said.

"No, too high even for that," Morgane said, but her mother was already moving down to the middle of the ship, ready to shout across to the victims who'd survived.

Jacques scanned the waterline, gave her a worried glance and then hurried after the captain.

Her mother grabbed one of the many taut ropes and pulled herself up to rest one foot on the rail, elevating her above the rest of the crew – those not manning the guns on and below the deck – who were starting to gather in anticipation behind her.

"Does your captain still live?" she shouted over.

The normal practice was to have the victims send over their captain in a boat, who would then be interrogated by her mother and always behind closed doors. Whatever she did would never last very long and then she'd come out and give the order to board and loot the vessel. Sometimes the captains were released after their ordeal, sometimes not. But the ones who survived never went back to their ships without serious injury.

A man who dragged himself up to peer over the opposing

rail looked like he was halfway to death. "No! He is dead, and all our goods taken. There is nothing left. Please be merciful!"

"How many crew are left?"

The man sagged. "Less than ten, *mon capitan*. And all injured."

"They must have resisted," her mother said to Jacques. "Well, there won't be any fight left in them then. Let's see if any among them could be useful, and whether anything was stashed too well for whoever picked them over before to find."

Morgane was doubtful. "Surely all the useful ones will have been taken already."

"If they had a cook as good as ours, they'd have left one over there," her mother said. "Let's hope they had a better carpenter's mate than we do." She twisted to point at several of the crew. "Hooks. Pull us alongside." When she noticed Morgane still watching her, she added in a quieter voice, "I don't care to waste time. This won't take long, then we'll be on our way."

They moved aside to let several members of the crew throw ropes with hooks attached across the gap between the ships and, once they were anchored against the rail, haul the ships close enough together to put down a couple of planks to form a temporary bridge.

Morgane had heard occasional jokes in the Port Royal bars about how Captain Anna-Marie boarded ships she'd taken like a visiting dignitary, rather than the more common methods of using the rigging or leaping across to the many ropes hanging off the sides and pulling oneself up. Having seen a man smashed between two ships once, when he'd miscalculated a jump, Morgane didn't mind one bit.

Even though it was clearly an empty ship, and there would be slim pickings at best, the crew was still in good spirits.

There was laughing and banter and several jokes made at the victim's expense. Listening to them, Morgane felt silly for having so many doubts, but that unbearable sense of something being off was still cramping her guts.

The moment the planks were secured her mother picked out five of the crew who'd earned first dibs and strode across them, strutting almost, and Morgane could see the grain of truth that had grown all those jokes. She was about to join the group when Jacques put a hand on her shoulder and held her back.

"Let her have her moment," Jacques said, confusing her, but she was happy to stay put.

She watched her mother speak to the man who'd answered her questions before and how he cowered beneath her boot when she placed it on his chest. The others who had accompanied her fanned out across the deck, checking the other victims, all of whom seemed to be either dead or so badly wounded that they were barely conscious.

The man said nothing that seemed to excite her mother and after glancing around and getting a sense of the state of the survivors from her own people, she headed towards the hatch that would lead below deck, the rest of her party gathering behind her as she did so.

Just as her mother grasped the metal ring and started to pull, Morgane heard a loud thud coming from somewhere lower down than she was, with no accompanying vibration through their deck. It was from the other ship!

"Captain!" she yelled, but too late. Her mother opened the hatch and a burst of light and smoke from a pistol blast erupted from below.

Her mother jack-knifed back, hitting the deck as a roar of pain erupted from her.

An instant later, there was another roar, from the hatch, that of men lying in wait below, and then the clatter of their boots coming up the steps. The first to emerge was pounced upon by Dill, who threw herself bodily at him and knocked him over, his spent pistol sent skittering across the deck.

Then they were all yelling, shouting, Morgane included, as the crew of *The Vengeance* jumped, swung and climbed onto the *Coup de Maître*. There was another pistol shot from the hatch, and another, making *The Vengeance*'s scouting group draw back and enabling the force hidden below to start pouring out like pus from a lanced boil.

Morgane fixed her sights on where her mother lay – and thankfully still moved – as she climbed up on the rail and leaped across the gap. She was vaguely aware of Jacques bellowing orders behind her and then she was on the *Maître*'s deck. There were shouts, shots, pain-filled cries and people fighting all around her, but her focus tunnelled through it all in her desperation to reach her mother and defend her from further attack.

She shoved a man out of the way when he barrelled into her path, unaware of which ship he belonged to. She ignored a glancing blow off her shoulder which must have been aimed at someone else and just as she was mere feet away from her mother, someone grabbed her headscarf and yanked her back.

Morgane fought to regain her balance and then twisted and shot the man behind her, making the scarf unravel. She hadn't even realised she'd drawn her pistol, but it had fired into his guts at near point-blank range, nonetheless. His grip on the scarf didn't weaken as he fell, though, pulling all the fabric from her head and a good clump of her hair with it. She batted the blonde mess out of her eyes and ducked beneath another man who was launching himself towards someone beside her and then she was kneeling at her mother's side.

"Shit! Shit!" her mother was gasping, clutching at her midriff, her hands slick with blood. "Is he dead?! Is he dead,

Morgane?"

Morgane scanned the violent chaos around her until she spotted Dill, tiny Dill, plunging a dagger into the shooter's chest again and again. The man had clearly died before her rage was spent. "Yes," she said, looking back at her mother.

Anna-Marie's face was shining with sweat, her lips a disturbing pale grey, but still the news that the one who'd hurt her was no more was enough to bring a smile to them.

"I told you it wasn't right!" Morgane yelled at her. "But you wouldn't listen!"

"Just get me back to my ship!" her mother rasped back at her.

Morgane holstered the spent pistol and slid her arms beneath her mother's shoulders, hooking them under her armpits so she could drag her. She'd only managed to move a few feet in the right direction before one of the enemy crew saw what she was doing and started running towards her mother with a sword.

Dumping the captain unceremoniously, Morgane drew the second of her pistols and fired it at the man just as he reached them. He went down, the sword clattering onto the deck as Morgane shoved it back into the holster and resumed pulling her mother to safety, trying her best to ignore the slick trail of blood pouring from Anna-Marie being left in their wake.

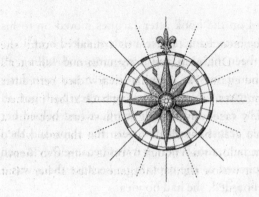

CHAPTER TWO

JEAN-PIERRE, THE CLOSEST they had to a surgeon, inspected the captain's wound as Morgane pressed herself into the corner of the cabin, feeling the reassuring strength of *The Vengeance*'s hull behind her back. Her mother moaned and writhed and swore at Jean-Pierre, but didn't interfere with his attempts to stop the bleeding.

Whatever he was trying to do, it didn't seem to be working. The captain's bed was wet with the stuff, and Morgane couldn't help but stare at the trail of it running to the open door where she'd dragged her mother. It abruptly ended at the point where Jean-Pierre had reached them and picked the captain up, he himself already spattered with blood from the fight on the other ship.

As she waited, tiny moments of that battle surfaced in Morgane's mind. At the time, she'd been so fixated on getting her mother to safety that she'd barely registered how it fared for her fellows. She had a memory of Jacques barrelling a man over who was levelling a pistol at her mother, even as she was being dragged away, and smashing his head onto a rope hook. The whites of the man's eyes flooded red, and his head remained on the hook after Jacques moved on to his next target, the body hanging like a slab of salted beef.

There had been fighting and screaming and killing all around her, but it was as if she'd been in her own little world, *The Vengeance* crew making sure they both got off the *Maître*. The cook and their best rigger had helped her get the captain across the gap between the ships and then they joined the fight, too. Whether it was because they'd seen what had happened to the captain or because there was a risk of being boarded, she had no idea.

She scratched her itching scalp and realised she'd lost the scarf her mother had given her. It was probably being trampled beneath fighting sailors. Her hair hung in filthy clumps around her face, and she swiped it back, blinking away the sweat that still ran down her face. The heat was oppressive in the cramped cabin and her heart felt like a carpenter's mallet and she wanted to stay and make sure her mother was alright, but she wanted to go and fight with Jacques, and she wanted to leap off the quarterdeck and plunge into the ocean and sink to somewhere cold and quiet and still.

Jean-Pierre glanced back over his shoulder, as if to check if she were still there, and the look in his eyes told her everything. She felt a huge sob bubble up from her guts, but she swallowed and held it down and after a few moments, she was calm. Her mother was going to die. She'd known it was likely, from the moment the pistol was fired, but somehow the effort of getting her home and handing her care over to someone else had kept the reality of that at bay.

"Oh, just say it, you soft bastard," her mother croaked, and Jean-Pierre's shoulders slumped.

"I'm sorry, captain," Jean-Pierre said as Jacques appeared at the doorway, panting. "You've not got long. I'll get what I can for the pain."

"Just get me the bottle from the cupboard over there, and Morgane."

"I'm here," Morgane said, opening the cupboard before Jean-Pierre had time to move. The bottle of cognac her mother had looted from her first ever attack was almost empty. It had been kept in that cupboard for the entirety of Morgane's life, and only brought out on the most important of occasions.

She wiped her mother's glass clean and poured as Jacques leant against the door frame, sombre.

"Go," her mother said to Jean-Pierre. "I'm not angry with you. Don't feel any guilt. You'd be better use helping the other injured."

Jean-Pierre gave both Morgane and Jacques a despairing, haunted look, and left the cabin. Jacques stepped in, now there was room for him, and closed the door behind him as Morgane helped her mother to sip the cognac.

Now she was next to her, Morgane could see the severity of the wound and how Jean-Pierre had tried to stitch it. But it was obvious that if her mother didn't die from the loss of blood, she'd surely die of the inevitable fever that a wound to the belly almost always caused. Judging from the sweat, the pallor and the rapid, shallow breathing, it looked like she wouldn't live long enough for a fever to take hold.

"How fares the crew?" Anna-Marie asked Jacques, who'd unhooked Morgane's hammock to give him the room to stand next to Morgane at the captain's bedside.

"We've taken the *Maître*," he said, with obvious pride. "The one who shot you is dead, as are several others of their crew. The rest are being held prisoner. We've lost eight, captain. Nine…"

"Nine when I go," she finished for him. "Not bad. No damage to the ships?"

"None, captain. I made sure we got below deck and

dealt with the ones manning the cannons before they could broadside us. I think they expected us to surrender after you went down."

"Idiots," she muttered and looked at Morgane. "They'll always underestimate you. Use that."

Morgane remained silent, fearful that if she opened her mouth a torrent of anger would escape. She'd known it was wrong, she'd known it, and her mother hadn't listened and now she was going to die, and she was so furious with her for it. She wanted to scream at her, not to gloat, but just to release the roiling mass of rage that she'd known better and now everything was going to fall apart, just because of her mother's pride and complacency.

"I know you're angry with me," the captain said. "And rightly so, but for the wrong reason." She took another sip of the cognac, wincing as she tried to take a deeper breath. "I know I'll soon be gone, and there's something you must know before I go to shake Satan's hand."

"I'll leave you to say what you must," Jacques said, but the captain grabbed his wrist and held him there.

"No. You stay and listen, too. When I'm gone, you... you must..."

"I understand," he said, remaining in place.

The captain's attention returned to her. "You know there are monstrous people in this world, Morgane, and I know you won't believe me, but there are... there are monsters... and your mother is one of them."

She nodded. She wasn't going to argue with that. Was she delirious?

"And I don't mean me, Morgane... because I am not your mother. I took you from that woman when you were a babe in arms, to save you from that... that... monster... She was my sister... I am your aunt, and I swear I did this to preserve your life."

Everything went silent for a moment. The creaking of *The Vengeance*, the distant yells of communication between crew members now managing two ships, all of it fell away and it was as if she was caught in some dreadful limbo between two worlds. It felt like she was leaving one that had made total sense and being dragged into a place that looked the same but had changed into something other.

Jacques' hand closed over hers and then sounds rushed in and she was staring down at the dying woman who was and wasn't her mother and she wanted to shut her eyes and cover her ears and just make it all stop for a while, just stop so she could catch her breath and let her thoughts settle but she was dying and...

And it was her only chance to discover the truth.

"You said your sister was killed. Before I was born... but she wasn't? And she was my mother? Who is she? Where is she? France?"

Anna-Marie shook her head. "Don't go looking for her. It would be the end of you. She..." A wave of pain washed away the words on her lips.

Morgane knew there was no way to make her tell her. "My father then. Who is he? Where is he?"

"Your father was my beloved, before that bitch stole him from me. We were meant to be together, but she bewitched him..." Anna-Marie's eyes welled with tears – the first time Morgane had ever seen her so close to weeping. "She took him from me."

"So you took me from her," Morgane said. "And lied... it was all lies?"

"Not all lies," Anna-Marie said, but how could she be believed now? "I couldn't leave you there... not with those monsters..."

Her face crumpled with pain, and she couldn't speak for a few moments. Morgane wanted to leave and never see or hear her again, just as much as she wanted to cling to her and beg her not to leave her. Unable to decide between the two, she ended up rooted to the spot, rigid, until she realised the glass was empty and set it aside.

"I know I've been hard on you," Anna-Marie croaked, her voice fainter now. "I wanted you to be strong. Don't go looking for them, it will be the death of you. *The Vengeance* is yours. You know how to survive. That's... that's all I wanted... for you... to... survive."

There was one last terrible, rattling breath and then she seemed to sink into her bed as all the tension flowed out of her body with her soul. For a moment it looked like the devil was pulling her down to him, body and all, but then all was still and the sense of her being there was gone. Her eyes were still open but her mother – her kidnapper – her *aunt*, was no longer there and it was so chilling that Morgane looked away as Jacques reached over to close the dead woman's eyes.

It felt like the silence was filling the cabin, pressing upon her skin, making her stumble backwards until she was back in the corner again, the strength of *The Vengeance*'s hull holding her up. Jacques lowered his head and muttered something beneath his breath. She thought he was swearing, but when he finished with 'amen' she realised he'd been saying something very different.

"There are no prayers that could save her soul," Morgane said. "Not even the Pope could keep her from Satan's claws."

"Everyone deserves a prayer," Jacques said quietly. "And it wasn't just for her."

Morgane slid down the curved hull, rested her folded arms on her knees and let her forehead settle on them, suddenly aware of how sick and exhausted she felt.

She could hear Jacques moving and the door being locked. She looked up to see him coming over to sit down on the floor in front of her. "I didn't want Jean-Pierre to come back in and see she's gone. We need to talk, before the crew know she's dead."

Morgane nodded, her mouth as dry as a deck in full sun. Her throat hurt, her head hurt, her shoulders, every bit of her was uncomfortable and telling her so. She wanted to drink three flagons of bumbo and sleep for a day and a night through, but Jacques was right.

He wanted to know how it was going to go between them, that much was clear. The crew were going to be expecting the worst and were probably already in hushed discussions over what should happen to *The Vengeance* now. It made sense to settle things between them, here and now, before going out there and dealing with fifty people whose blood was up. And no matter how much she wanted to just curl up into a ball and sob, she had to push all that aside.

"She said the ship was mine," she began, noting the way his shoulders tensed. "But she was wrong. What a stupid thing to say. She wasn't a queen, leaving her kingdom to her dau… niece." She noted his relief. "That's not how we do things. The captain is always voted in and that's how it should be."

He nodded. "I'm glad you see it that way, too."

"It's in the articles," she said with a weak smile. "And you taught me those. Not her."

"I reckon Pierre will stand."

She nodded in agreement. The bosun knew how to run the ship and he was competent. "And you, of course."

"Of course."

His gaze was steady, expectant, tense. Then she realised why.

"I won't stand against you, Jacques."

He breathed out in relief.

She smirked. "I hardly would have been a threat to your victory."

"It wasn't that," he said softly. "I… I didn't want you to

go through the process and be hurt. And there are some who would have supported you."

"Because they hold to this idea of inheritance?"

"Because they'd think that if they got you voted in, you'd be beholden to them. That you'd be easy to manipulate."

That made more sense. And with a sudden chill, she was aware that she was alone. Not that her mother – her aunt – ever made her feel truly safe – she'd been beaten by her too many times to fully relax around her – but she was aware that the rest of the crew treated her differently because of her close proximity to the captain. That protection was gone now. "You should be captain, Jacques. You'll be a better one than she ever was." She looked around the cabin, at the scant possessions her mother had held onto over the years, and thought of the chest of gold she knew was beneath her mother's bed. "I reckon the crew will agree, but the bosun is strong and he can be charming when he wants to be. If some other fool decides to stand – like Bull might – then you might not get all the votes you need."

As she spoke about the vote, she became aware of the fact that she didn't really care. She wanted Jacques to be captain, because he would be an excellent one and the ship would be in good hands. But when she tried to envisage life with him as captain just… continuing as it had before, the same yet completely different, she couldn't make it feel right. This wouldn't be her cabin anymore. Her mother lay dead and that's what she thought about? No, not her mother. Damn it! It felt like the inside of her head was being battered by a squall. Focus! Focus!

She pointed at the boards that boxed in the bottom of the bed. "There's a chest of gold in there. I'll split it with you, so you can use your half to buy off Bull and anyone else who might think they should vote for someone else. There's enough time between now and sunset to get it all arranged.

Then the vote should go your way."

He looked delighted, then relieved. "Thank you."

She sighed. "You knew about that gold all along, didn't you?"

He grinned. "I did, and no one else does. But I wouldn't have taken it. I saw it as yours. I don't agree with leaving a ship to someone, but gold is different. Thank you. How do you feel?"

She looked down at her feet and saw the blood that had soaked into the leather of her boots. It felt like half of her thoughts were happening elsewhere, maybe in the same place that she was desperately shoving all her emotions into, too.

"About what? The death or what she said before that?"

"...Both."

"I honestly have no idea," she murmured. The captain's blood was still on her hands, the floor, drips of it now drying on the wooden bed boards.

Jacques fumbled briefly and then his flask was in her hand. "Drink."

It was Cook's bumbo and it was welcome. Cook's recipe was legendary – to the extent that they'd once had to foil another crew's attempt to lure him onto their ship – and it was one he'd take to his grave. She knew from spying on him when she was younger that it contained dark rum, lemon or lime juice, a syrupy liquid that was always unlabelled, and freshly grated nutmeg. Sometimes it was cinnamon, depending on the spoils, but this batch was rich with nutmeg, which she loved. Before she knew it, the little flask had been drained dry.

"I..." It felt like she wasn't really there, in the room. "I can't think about it." It was too much, all at once. So she fell back on what she'd always known; one thing at a time. It didn't pay to think too far ahead when things were going wrong. In a storm, in a life-or-death moment high up on the rigging, she would just think of the next move up, the next rope to pull, nothing more than that. "We need to tell the crew. And you need the gold. Gold first. You've got a couple of hours before sunset."

It was stated in the articles that if the captain died or was voted out, the next captain had to be voted in by sunset the same day, or dawn if it happened at night.

She went to the loose panel below the bed, pulled it free and then used the gap to unhook the rest of the planks. It took all her strength to pull out the strong box underneath, filled to the brim with gold as it was.

With horror, she realised the key would still be in her mother's boot. No. Not her mother.

She stuffed her hands under her armpits and moved back. "The key... it's in her boot—"

He didn't need to be told which one. She looked away, unable to look at that lifeless face, pushing down the urge to cry until it went again.

At the sound of the key turning in the lock, she went back, steadfastly focusing only on the chest, and filled some pouches with Jacques. He helped her to put it all back as it was when they were done, just in case the crew came to pay their respects.

As they left and she locked the door behind them, she couldn't stop thinking about the way the cabin felt both occupied and empty, all at the same time.

THE MAJORITY OF *The Vengeance*'s crew were gathered on the deck, waiting for news, and an eerie silence descended when they emerged into the sunshine. Morgane scanned the sombre faces, still blood-spattered and sweaty from the fighting. Dill, preferring to be up high, was sat up in the rigging above everyone's heads, her feet dangling, her hands, arms and most of the front of her shirt still stained with blood.

Morgane didn't have any words in her when faced with all that expectation, so she looked to Jacques to make the announcement, fearful that she'd give away more than she wanted.

"The captain is dead," he said. "No fault of Jean-Pierre, we all saw it happen and we all know that a pistol to the guts at that range does more harm than can be sewn up."

The news was received in silence, and then those in the crew wearing hats took them off and held them over their chests. Dill's face scrunched up before she hid it in the crook of her arm and began to weep. There were several baleful glares directed at the *Coup de Maître* and Jacques read them easily.

"The one who fired is dead. I saw Dill kill him and she'll get double her share of the gold at Port Royal for her righteous act. I'll pay it." A murmur of agreement and approval rippled through the crew, a few of the men nearest to Dill reaching up to pat her boots. She ignored them.

"What now, Jacques?" Bull asked. "Do we vote on whether to kill the rest of them?"

The news of the death had united the group, but that question fractured it in an instant. Some agreed, some shouted them down, but before it could turn into a full-blown argument, Jacques raised his hands and bellowed for quiet.

"We do what it states in the articles, Bull, and that's clear. We vote for a new captain, and that vote happens at sunset on the day of the death. I reckon what we do with the *Maître* is a decision for the captain, and so we wait to see who that will be. Then we follow their orders, just as we always have."

To Morgane, it seemed like Bull had already made his first play, and Jacques had quashed it, the crew practically unanimous in their support for following the articles and then having a captain to make the decision. They all knew how those articles protected each other as well as giving them a stable life at sea. Many of them had left other ships where the whims of the captain or sometimes just the loudest members of the crew were given more weight than the articles, and it never ended well.

Then she noticed that Pierre, the bosun, was staring at her. When she gave him a quizzical look, he cleared his throat. "I agree with Jacques," he began, the rest quietening down to listen. "But I always thought Captain Anna-Marie would leave *The Vengeance* to you. She said as much to me, a few times over the years." His eyes flicked to Jacques. Was he implying that Jacques was covering something up?

Morgane had been told, many times, that telling the truth wasn't always the best policy. The trouble was, she never knew when to apply that. She couldn't tell if this was one of those occasions or not, so she settled on the easiest path. "She did."

After an almost comical chorus of gasps she added, "She said it was mine, just now when she was dying, but she was wrong. That ain't the way we do things. This ship belongs to all of us. We all work hard to keep her afloat, we all take a share of the loot, we all have a say in who the captain should be. Her wanting me to have it was just a dying woman wanting to feel like she had something to leave behind to make it easier for the one coming after her. I'm no captain and I'm no fool neither. I'll not go against the articles."

Her words were met with grunts of approval and a begrudging nod from Pierre.

"So, who's standing for captain?" Bull asked.

"I am," Jacques said.

"Aye," Pierre said, raising a hand.

A few looked at Bull. "I'm thinkin' about it," he said with a smirk.

"We meet here, at sunset," said Jacques, "and take the vote then, for captain and quartermaster, too, as written in the articles. Until that's done, I say we stay alongside the *Maître*, do nothing to her or the prisoners until we have a captain. All those who agree, say Aye."

The ayes drowned out any nays and the group drifted apart into little huddles. A few came over to put a hand on her shoulder and mutter condolences. Pierre was one of them, adding, "She raised you well. Glad you put the articles above whatever your grief might have wanted."

She just nodded, not wanting to talk to any of them and certainly not wanting to challenge any misguided assumptions they might have had about her feelings – for the former captain or for the rejected inheritance.

But she didn't want to go back below, so she found herself staring at a coiled rope without even seeing it, as flashes of the fighting, the blood, flickered through her mind.

A hand on her shoulder made her jump. Dill was reaching down from her spot on the rigging. She said nothing, just met her eyes with her own, red and tear-filled still.

"I saw what you did to the one who..." Morgane didn't need to finish the sentence, couldn't anyway. After a moment, she added, "You were fierce. Wanted to say thanks is all."

Dill wiped a green glob from her upper lip onto her shirt sleeve. "*I* shoulda opened the 'atch. Shoulda been me."

Morgane shrugged. "No way she would've let you. Was her choice."

Dill frowned at her. "Thought you'd be angry with me."

"Why? You didn't shoot her. And you killed the one who did."

"I know what they said about her in Port Royal and Charles Town and the like. They didn't like that she did things different and that she did better than a lot of them. You know she was the first to put in the articles that women can be crew? I had to hide and pretend to be a boy for years before I met her. She spotted me, in Taverners, came over and asked if I wanted to hide being a woman forever. I told her to bugger off. She hit me. I hit her back. Then she bought me a drink. I was in the crew the next day. She had that article added for me. She'd heard my eyes were the best, that I always spotted a sail before anyone else. She only picked the best, she said. I'll miss her."

In all the years she'd known her, Dill had never said so much. It felt strange, seeing her mother – no, damn it – through another person's eyes. The mark she'd left on another life.

Morgane gave an awkward smile and began to move away when Dill spoke again. "You're numb now. I know what it's like. It'll hit in a few days, when you least expect it, and it'll hit hard. It'll be like going full sail under blue skies and then a storm'll come out of nowhere and you won't be able to stop cryin' for a while. Just… be ready for it."

Morgane only nodded. Dill had no idea what had been confessed on the death bed, after all, had no inkling of the fact that there was more anger inside her now than grief. Anger at what she'd been told and anger that she'd been killed, and so stupidly, too. She drifted over to the rail on the side facing away from the *Maître*, staring out at the waves as one by one, members of the crew came over to check on her and tell her of the marks that woman had made on their lives, too, all while she tried to determine where she would settle in her own mind. Mother? Kidnapper? Aunt? None of them felt right. And what was she herself now? Daughter of one of the most feared pirates on the ocean? Her victim? Niece? None of those fitted her either. So she stood there, wishing that one of the last things she'd said to Anna-Marie in that cabin hadn't been so bloody awful, as condolences were given and bribes were paid under the heavy sapphire sky.

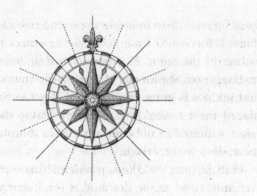

CHAPTER THREE

BETWEEN DEALING WITH the body and facilitating Jacques' efforts to dissuade anyone else from standing for captain – and in a few cases giving a good financial incentive to vote for him – the afternoon took on the quality of a dream.

Once she'd mustered the strength to do so, she went back to the cabin with a bucket of water and stood by her aunt's bedside. It took every last scrap of courage to look at her face and see the unnatural pallor, the colour leached from her lips. She cried, just a little, before something inside clamped down on it for fear of losing control. It wasn't the time for it.

She washed the face of the woman she'd only known as her mother. She covered the bloodied mess of her body with the blanket from her hammock, all of the bedding soaked beneath the body, and she couldn't bear the thought of trying to pull it free. It was a mess. All of it.

Stop. Breathe. One thing at a time.

Morgane removed Anna-Marie's baldricks and pistols and her jewellery, just so none of the crew stole them first, and put them in one of the desk drawers to deal with later.

She washed her hands in the bloodied water and went

back up on deck to invite the crew to see the captain one last time, before going back down to sit, watery legged, in the corner of the cabin. As people trailed in and stood next to the body, paying their respects in low murmurs, Morgane felt like she was floating away, tethered to her own body by only the flimsiest fishing line. Members of the crew came and went without her noticing, sometimes morphing from one to another in the strange liminal space she found herself in.

Then Jacques was there, pushing a flagon of bumbo into her hands and as she drank it, it felt like it was somehow pouring her soul back into her body again. He'd brought canvas with him. "Time to put her to rest, chère."

"Did you know?" she asked him when the flagon was drained dry. "Know she wasn't really my mother?"

"No, chèrie, no." She believed him. "All I know is that she came from France, like myself. I had a feeling something bad had happened, but she never wanted to talk about it, and I respected that. But try to forget it, no? She was your mother. She raised you. You have no idea who her sister was. Or your father. Why think about it when there's no way to find out?"

"But why even tell me?"

"She didn't want to take it to the grave. It was a terrible secret to carry all these years."

She shook her head. "This has nothing to do with guilt. She had none. If she was worried about me going to find my mother, why even raise it? If she'd said nothing…"

"She was dying, chère, she wasn't thinking it through."

Morgane shook her head. Anna-Marie had been crystal clear right to the end, in a lot of pain but not delirious like she'd seen so many when they died from fever. But then the answer came to her, as sudden as a dolphin leaping ahead of a ship's prow. "The letters!"

She scrabbled to her feet and went back to the body. Morgane didn't want to touch her, but she had to know if they were still there. She held her breath and reached beneath the bloodied shirt, finding the edges of the paper still wedged between her skin and her canvas stays.

Morgane pulled out the crushed letter and the unopened one. There was a little blood on them but none of the shot had hit them, thankfully. Morgane turned around, keeping death to her back, where it belonged.

She stared at the elegant script that covered the crumpled paper, trying so hard to decipher the words, but it was no good. She looked at the name written on the unopened one, could make out the first part of it started with an M like her own name, but that was as far as she could get. Reading was something she'd always struggled with, and this elegant cursive with its loops and slanted letters was too difficult for her to decode. Exasperated, she held the letters out to Jacques. "Will you read them to me?"

He looked at the sealed one first. "This is for someone called Marie-Louise and this one—" He smoothed the crumpled paper, and she watched his eyes skim from left to right, his eyebrows rising higher with each word.

"Who, Jacques? Read it to me!"

"Anna-Marie,

I write in the vain hope you will somehow receive this letter and that you will find charity and goodness enough in your heart to read it. It has been so long since I last saw you, and I want you to know I forgive you for what you did. It is my firm belief that you thought you were acting in my child's best interests, rather than out of a desire to wound me.

Believing that, I dare hope that you might extend that same care to my wellbeing. I do not need to tell you what circumstances I am in, for you saw it with your own eyes. You rescued my daughter from this place – do you not feel any concern for your own sister whom you left behind?

The contents of the chest are for both you and my daughter, so that you might return to France in a manner that befits your station. Speak to the captain of the ship in which you found it, and you will see how much I have done to ensure your safe return, in the hope that you will, in turn, ensure my own safety. For are we not sisters? Do you not fear for my safety as much as I fear for yours?

With the deepest love and affection,
Your sister."

Jacques looked up from the words, his gaze resting on the chest next to Morgane. "Did this come from in there?"

Morgane nodded and opened it. The scent of lavender wafted up at her and her heart raced. Beneath a layer of soft linen lay a dress of the finest silk, as dark a blue as the sky an hour after sunset. The bodice was embroidered with tiny lilac and pink flowers and embellished with beads as delicate as the drops left by fine sea mist. She lifted it out with the same care that she'd handle a day-old gosling and held the silk up to her cheek, breathing in the scent of the lavender. Beneath, nestled in the folded skirts, were several linen pouches stuffed with it, the scent now strong.

"There are fancy clothes in here," she said. "Sent by her sister?"

Jacques shuffled over to take the bodice from her, inspecting the embroidery and beading before spreading it open and examining the seams and stitching inside. "This is made by some of the finest couturiers in France."

"How do you know?"

"I just know, chèrie. This is very, very expensive." He brushed his fingertips across the linen still in the chest. "This chemise is made from the finest linen. And there's another dress in here. Her sister is very rich."

Morgane couldn't help but look at Anna-Marie's body, the

drips of her blood that had run down the side of the bed. She still felt like her mother. Deep down in her gut was a howling grief, one she was trying to keep under control as she wrestled with the anger and the confusion, too. She took the bodice from Jacques, put it back in the chest and closed it, as if she could somehow cram all the conflicting feelings in there with it.

"What about the other letter? The one to... Who was it? Marie-Louise?"

"Which is probably what your mother named you," Jacques said quietly. "When you were born."

She shook her head. "I don't know. Could be that I have a sister somewhere." Jacques looked at her like she was being stupid. She shrugged. "It's not my name. What does it say?"

He broke the seal and unfolded the piece of paper to read aloud.

"My darling daughter,

It is my heartfelt desire that this letter reaches your fair hands, even though I have sent so many to you and received no word of you in return. But just as a mother's love is eternal, so is my hope that one day, God will smile upon us and deliver this into your hands, along with the contents of this chest.

Every day I think of you and miss you desperately. If you were raised by Anna-Marie, please go to the captain of the ship who carried this chest and tell him who you are. He will know what to do. There will be nothing to fear, my darling girl. All I want is to hold you in my arms once more, God willing, and to save you from the life that Anna-Marie forced upon you.

With all my love,
Your mother"

Jacques sighed. "There has been a chest like that one on every Four Chains ship we've taken over the past year or so."

With all my love, Your mother. Morgane glanced back at Anna-Marie's body, trying to reconcile what Jacques had read aloud with the woman who'd raised her, now relegated to aunt. She'd been raised thinking that there was no one else in the world other than those on this ship that had a care about her wellbeing, and yet that letter, these gifts, those words said otherwise.

Morgane's gaze flitted between the letter in his hand and the chest. The sheer amount of wealth required to fill chests with dresses such as these and just send them out on ships in the vain hope they'd reach the people they were intended for was remarkable enough. But the fact that they were being sent out on ships that were preyed upon by pirates, and that those same pirates were the intended recipients? It just seemed ridiculously foolhardy. A triumph of hope over sense. Or perhaps wealth over fear of their loss. "Did my moth... did the captain see what was inside any of them?"

"Maybe not a couple of the early ones, but after she saw the contents of one of them, she always told me to set it aside for her. Captain's right. She never seemed to keep anything from them, but now... now I think that she took the letters and then we sold the rest."

How many times had Anna-Marie destroyed letters meant for her, from her own mother? "That was why she was so ill-tempered," Morgane muttered, her own anger starting to rise. "She was reading these letters from her own sister and just ignoring them! How could she do that?"

"We don't know what—"

"The woman who wrote these," she still couldn't bring herself to say her actual mother, "is clearly not safe!" Morgane snatched the letter to Anna-Marie up from the floor and tried to remember the words he'd read. "That's what this says, isn't it? Something about ensuring her safety? She wanted Anna-Marie to come and help her!"

"Chèrie…"

"All my life, I thought she" – Morgane pointed at the body – "was the bravest woman on the ocean. I never saw her even flinch, not once, no matter what we faced. And the whole time she was ignoring these pleas for help from her own sister? She was a coward!"

"That is not something that can be said about the captain." Jacques' voice was low, angry, as if it was a personal insult.

"There's nothing you can say to change my mind," she said, now she was certain of it. "She wasn't brave enough to tell me the truth before today, and she only did that because she knew I'd find these letters – I saw her stuff them down her shirt just before the *Maître* was sighted! She probably burned the others, but she didn't have the opportunity this time. She wouldn't have said a word otherwise, and I could have lived my whole life without knowing that she stole a babe in arms from her mother and took her to the other side of the world. She wasn't protecting a daughter, she was making sure no one could find a child she'd stolen. Why do you think she never let me out of her sight ashore? That wasn't an excess of care, it was the fear that someone would realise who I was and take me back to my mother!"

"But the letter to Anna-Marie talks of rescuing you when you were a baby!"

"From what? The same letter speaks of returning to France, so Anna-Marie must have known that my mother was still in danger and that she needs to rescue her, not just abandon her!"

"But remember what she said to you! Warning you about monstrous people and—"

"What that woman said about monsters and wanting to keep me safe was bullshit. She was just trying to justify what she did and make it into something noble. Sod her! She took me from my mother and raised me in a life more dangerous than things could ever have been in France! If we're caught, we're hanged. If she wanted to keep me safe, why not go somewhere else and live like... like..."

"Like what? People under the yoke? People who dig the dirt their whole lives and barely survive? You loved this life before you saw these letters!"

He was hurt. That stopped her. "I did. I do! I... I'm just trying to make some sense of this."

Jacques scratched the stubble under his chin. "When we were fighting on the *Maître*, none of their crew attacked you – even though you were trying to save our captain. They all went for *her*, not you, when anyone with an ounce of sense would have taken you down to finish her off at their leisure."

Morgane rubbed her temples, the heat, the foulness of the day making her head ache. "The letter to Anna-Marie talks about her coming home, but the Four Chains Company sent the *Maître* to kill the captain, to stop her from ransacking their ships."

"The company can't have any idea that these chests have contained letters to their enemy," Jacques replied.

"She always said the one who owned the company ruined her life." She chewed her lip, trying to think it all through.

"We have no way of knowing if the Four Chains company really has anything to do with your family," Jacques said "Anna-Marie hated them, but it may have been another grievance. She always said they killed her sister, but we know now that that was a lie."

"Unless there was another sister, and she was the one who stole her lover, not my mother." Morgane kicked the chest. "I don't see how it fits together! Who do I believe?"

"There's no way to know," Jacques started, but then something floated to the top of the tumult in her head.

"That letter... to Anna-Marie... it said to speak to the captain of the ship!" She jumped to her feet. "Did he survive?

The captain of the *Maître*, does he live?"

"Yes, but Morgane... I know this is overwhelming, but we cannot trust him. Remember what the captain said." He was pointing at Anna-Marie. "She——"

"I'm going to speak to the captain of the *Maître* and see if another one of these chests is there."

Jacques put a hand on her shoulder. "Morgane, just wait a moment, think this through."

She shrugged him off. "I'm going to find out who owns that ship and what their plan was."

"But you can't trust them, chèrie," Jacques said softly.

"I don't. But if they were sent by my mother to find me, then they'll want to take me back to France, yes?"

"The same people who killed our captain?" Jacques was incredulous. "Think, chèrie!"

"They won't hurt me if the captain of the *Maître* has been bribed by my mother, like the captain of the ship that these letters came from probably was. The letter said something about what my real mother has done to ensure our safe return, so——"

Jacques was on his feet in a moment. "You want to go back to France?!"

"I want to help my mother! She needs help! You read the letter!"

He grabbed her arm, "But France is not like——"

"Don't do what Anna-Marie did. Don't stop me doing what I have every right to do, dammit!"

He let go of her. "Then let me come with you when you speak to them," Jacques said. "Not because I don't think you can manage this, Morgane. As a friend. I have your back. Just like you have mine. Like always."

She moved towards the door but then saw the canvas that he'd brought on the floor. What was she thinking? "We go after... after we've put her to rest." As angry and confused as she was, it didn't seem right to just leave Anna-Marie's body there while she went to the *Maître*.

Jacques kissed the top of her head. "Yes."

He lifted up the body for Morgane to slide the canvas underneath. The watery feeling returned to her legs, but she just focused on each mechanical task in turn, be it wrapping the body, threading the needle, or holding the canvas in place as Jacques sewed it closed or cutting the thread after he'd tied off the knot. They carried the body up onto the deck, laid it out next to the others. Jacques said some words, then Bull, but all she could hear was a ringing in her ears like she'd been punched and hadn't noticed. She was given the chance to speak but shook her head, feeling like she'd forgotten how to do that. What even were words? She felt dazed, almost punch drunk, as the bodies were tipped off a plank into the sea. For the first time in her whole life, she stood on the deck of *The Vengeance* without her mother in shouting distance from her.

It was only when Jacques came over to her and said he was ready to go over to the *Maître* that Morgane felt like she was even fully in her body.

The thumping of her heart as she walked across the planks laid between the two ships was strangely reassuring, even though she was nervous. She felt focused again, present, and ready to get some answers.

"Let me speak first," Jacques said, adding, "They won't be used to our way of doing things and are likely to listen to a man more readily."

She hated it, but he was right. If the crew of the *Maître* had been pirates, it wouldn't have mattered so much, but they were traders, and she knew they didn't like women on their ships.

The prisoners were huddled together, seated on the deck, under the watchful eye of five from *The Vengeance*. There must have been about twenty, all of them with their hands tied behind their backs and looking angry and miserable in the main, apart from a couple who looked genuinely frightened.

Jacques targeted one of the latter, pointing at him and saying, "You!" in such a commanding tone that the man actually whimpered. "Is your captain still alive and among you here?"

He nodded.

"I am the captain," a long-faced man with close-set eyes said from the back of the group. He looked just as dishevelled and exhausted as the rest of them, but he did have an air of authority to him and none amongst the rest of the crew looked confused or shifty. On a few occasions prisoners had tried to hide the identity of their captain, thinking to spare him from torture, but it wasn't happening here.

Jacques walked round the group, grabbed the captain by his shirt and hauled him onto his feet to start marching him towards the hatch. Morgane hurried over to open it, seized briefly by the memory of Anna-Marie doing the same earlier that day. She pushed a flash of fear aside and hefted it open.

No pistol shot met her efforts and she climbed down the wooden stairs ahead of the men, giving her eyes a chance to adapt to the gloom. There was a lantern still lit at the end of a very short corridor which she retrieved just as Jacques pulled the prisoner down after him.

Morgane opened the only door and found herself in the guts of a ship that had clearly been stripped out for speed. The internal walls had been ripped out, along with a couple of the bulkheads, giving a large expanse of space to enable the rapid firing of the extensive array of cannon and also reduce its weight and thereby increase its speed. That was why she sat so high in the water then; she'd been given a going over like many of the frigates taken by pirates and repurposed for better use.

At the far end there was still one internal wall, however, that to the captain's cabin, she surmised. The space stank of sweat and emptied bowels, the bodies of those killed belowdecks still slumped where they'd fallen, and their mess left, too.

"Mon Dieu," the captain gasped at the smell. "Can we not conduct our business above deck?"

"No," Jacques replied crisply and marched him towards the cabin.

Morgane went ahead of them, carrying the lantern and opening the door. It was far more luxuriously appointed than the captain's cabin on *The Vengeance*, with large bay windows casting in an excess of light. She hooked the lantern up on the singular wall next to the doorway as it wasn't needed, and went inside.

Jacques threw the captain into the corner when they arrived, as Morgane went straight to the desk and admired the maps and fine brass instruments laid upon them.

"We have nothing hidden, and nothing for you to take," the captain said. "That much was true."

"You were sent to kill the captain of *The Vengeance*, yes?"

He nodded at Jacques, and then his pale blue eyes glanced at Morgane, his gaze running down the length of her hair.

"And what else?"

"Monsieur?"

Jacques loomed over him. "What else were you sent to do?"

The captain looked from him, to her, back to Jacques again, as he weighed his options. "I was told to bring the daughter of Captain Anna-Marie back to France, unharmed."

"Why? To be hanged?"

The captain looked appalled. "No, monsieur. I was told that if she was a prisoner, to free her, and if she'd been led into piracy by the scourge of the sea, to offer her official amnesty and protection from any punishment for crimes committed when under the control of that…" He trailed off, appraising Jacques' stance. "…That woman."

"Only for her?"

"Only for her, monsieur."

"And who gave you this mission?"

"I was given my orders by the manager of the fleet. Monsieur de Lombardy."

"And what does he want with Anna-Marie's daughter?"

"I have no idea, monsieur. I imagine this was an order given to him by someone else. Perhaps the owner of the company, or a friend thereof. Monsieur de Lombardy has a family and has been happily married for many years now. He has no need to take in any char—" He looked at Morgane again. "Anyone else's children, let alone have them rescued from a notoriously cruel pirate."

"And how were you to know if you'd found her?" Morgane asked.

"By the colour of her hair, mademoiselle, and I understand there is a mark that only those closest to her would know." He smiled at her, and it was a strange smile, one that combined pity and sadness and relief all at once. "Although I think that a girl willing to run into an affray and physically drag the injured captain to safety would give her identity away by her bravery and dedication to… her mother."

"This Monsieur de Lombardy, could he not be her father?" Jacques asked.

"I think not, monsieur. His father has skin the same colour as yours, and while his mother and wife are as pale as I, his children have dark hair, brown skin and eyes."

"What is this mark you speak of?" Morgane asked and the bound man shrugged.

"I was not given that information, mademoiselle. I was told to bring back the scourge's daughter, who would have hair the colour of spun gold. The mark will be checked in

France, I believe, when I take her to Monsieur de Lombardy."

Jacques and Morgane exchanged a look. Neither of them trusted him, of that she was certain. She suspected the mark was the birthmark on her back. It was disturbing that people on the other side of the world knew of the small stain that looked like someone had spilt wine on her, when only she and her mother – dammit, her aunt – had ever seen it. Other than her real mother, of course. Leaving with the *Coup de Maître* was the only chance of finding her and doing what Anna-Marie had been too cowardly for: rescuing her.

"Monsieur de Lombardy is an honourable man, and decent. I don't believe the daughter would have anything to fear. Indeed, it was pressed upon me most forcefully that she be treated as an honoured guest, to arrive in France rested, unharmed and quite well."

And de Lombardy would be able to tell her who gave him the mission to kill Anna-Marie. She would find out and then hunt them down. Even though she had lied, Anna-Marie had still raised her, and she couldn't let her death go unanswered. It wasn't enough that the man who fired the shot had paid the price for it. He'd only been following orders, after all. And if the same person who sent him was the one who was endangering her mother, all the better. Her aunt would be avenged and her mother rescued, with one simple act.

"Where are the papers detailing the amnesty?" Jacques asked, scratching the stubble on his chin.

"In my desk, monsieur, and the key is on a chain around my neck."

Jacques took the key, unlocked the drawer and rifled through its contents until he found some papers that caught his eye. He read them and showed them to Morgane, who pretended to read them. "Well, you seem to be telling the truth," Jacques said, knowing full well that she needed to be told what it meant without revealing as much.

Morgane tossed the papers onto the desk and leaned against the bed. "I see no reason to deny who I am," she said. "That much is clear. It's just a matter of trust now, I suppose."

"You have my word, mademoiselle, that you will be treated very well, and will have my personal protection. And should that not be enough to reassure you, perhaps it would be a sufficient guarantee to know that I and all of the surviving crew are to receive double our yearly wage when you are delivered unto Monsieur de Lombardy safe and well. There is no reason for anyone on this ship to harm you. Quite the contrary."

As he spoke, Jacques locked the papers away in the desk again, but gave her the key. She grinned at him as she dropped the chain over her head and tucked the key down her stays.

Jacques rubbed his chin, thoughtful. "It's up to you," he said to her softly.

She looked at the captain. "If I were to come with you, how do I know that you won't attack *The Vengeance* as soon as we part ways?"

"What would be the profit in that? They won't attack us with you on board, surely." He smiled.

Jacques winked at her before turning to face him. "What would it matter to us whether she is on board or not? She is one girl and our desire for self-preservation is stronger than any sentimentality we might have. Don't concern yourself about us," Jacques said, glancing at her with a smile. "The captain understands who we are and knows that if the *Maître* decides to use its last cannonballs on us, we'll blow her out of the water." At the captain's frown, he added, "Oh, we'll take most of your ordnance, but leave enough for you to defend yourself. Just in case any other pirates decide to pick you over on the way home."

The captain's irritation melted away. "So, she is dead then."

Jacques nodded. "If she were alive, this conversation wouldn't be happening. You'd all be in Davy Jones' locker, and we'd be well on our way." He looked at Morgane. "Any more questions for this man?"

She shook her head, looking at the captain. "No more questions, but I want your word you won't fire on *The Vengeance*, if I come with you." She didn't believe he'd keep it, should he decide to be stupid, but she wanted it, nonetheless.

"You have my word. Please believe that I have no more desire for a sea-battle than you do. If I fire, I would be putting you in harm's way, and that's just not financial good sense, is it?"

She understood that well enough. "Then it's decided. I'll come at sunset – I have things to attend to before then – and you'll stay prisoners until we part ways from *The Vengeance*."

The man smirked. "You sound like a captain's daughter."

"Oh, piss off," she snapped, and left the cabin, leaving Jacques to drag him back up above deck.

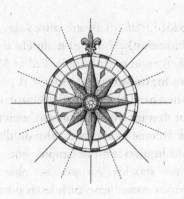

CHAPTER FOUR

In the last hour before sunset, Morgane went back to the old cabin to see if there was anything she wanted to keep. She had very few possessions and she wore most of them, aside from a couple of shirts, one pair of trousers and the trunk that was her allocated loot from the last raid.

Anna-Marie had actively discouraged her from getting attached to things. "No point hanging onto them; they'll only get lost or stolen," she'd said once, when a beautiful set of pearls that had caught the captain's eye were put in the pile of things to sell. "It's always better to have less to worry about. If you ever need to run, or if you need to leave a sinking ship, it's just weight you can't carry and then things you resent losing. Better to not form the attachment in the first place."

The only exception to this rule had been her pistols. They were laid out on the bed now. Morgane and Jacques had stared at them after taking her body above deck.

"Choose your pair," he said, and she'd looked at him, confused. "Seems only fair," he added.

"Well, that much is obvious," she'd replied. "What I don't understand is why I only get to keep two."

He'd laughed then. "Two," he said firmly. "I'm quartermaster, remember? The rest should be held for the new captain."

She couldn't argue with that, so she'd picked the pair that were worn across her mother's chest in her last fight. Morgane knew they fired well and while they were heavy, they were still slightly smaller and more elegant than the others. She liked the marquetry on the handles, too. She slung the baldrics over one shoulder for now, not able to wear them like their previous owner yet. Aside from powder and shot, there was nothing else Jacques had insisted upon splitting, and there was nothing else of value to be had. They'd agreed that the navigation instruments belonged to the ship and aside from an hourglass, that she had no desire to keep, there was only the gold in the chest which they'd already split.

There was the log, of course, still resting on the desk. She opened it and marvelled at the neatness of the hand. There was no question it should remain, and not just because it would be useless to her, so poor was her reading skill. Besides, she wouldn't be navigating the *Maître* through the waters it detailed. *The Vengeance* had never been sailed to France. No, the log belonged to the ship more than any one person. Whoever became the next captain would find far more use for it than she ever could. She brushed her fingertips over the quill, remembering the sound of it scratching across the page when she was small, sending her to sleep.

Anna-Marie had been wearing several rings when she died, and she sorted through them. None were of sentimental value; the captain used to change them with each looting, having tired of them quickly. She picked the smallest one out, a delicate gold band with a single dull garnet set into it, and pocketed that for later. The one with the largest stone that fit her, she put on, again thinking that it might come in useful if she needed more money later. The other three she tucked into her bundle, planning to sell them in France, and then stuffed that into the trunk that contained the dress sent by her real mother and her share of the gold. She and Jacques were confident that no one would resent her taking one chest from the spoils. With Anna-Marie dead, they knew she'd be moving out of the cabin now.

From the sound of boots clumping above, everyone was gathering for the vote. She stopped at the door, turning to survey the cabin for the last time.

She looked at the hammock, now hanging limply from a single hook, at the bed, stripped bare now, the bloodstains not yet sanded out and painted over as she knew they would be. She looked at the desk, seeing Anna-Marie hunched over it for the briefest moment and then the corner that she always used to huddle in when she was very small, too small to be of use in a storm, when she'd pressed herself against the hull as *The Vengeance* pitched and yawed at the mercy of the waves. How she'd trembled, curled up like a sea anemone after being prodded by a stick, praying not to God but to the ship herself to deliver them to safety.

Another sharp stab of grief briefly surfaced at the thought of leaving *The Vengeance*. She blinked a few times and took a deep breath until it passed. How could she stay and leave the one who ordered Anna-Marie's death to live out their life in peace? How could she read those letters from her birth mother and try to forget the plea for help and desperation to hold her daughter again? Anna-Marie would never have written anything like that, more likely to shove her playfully into a barrel than embrace her. It was as if she had been scared of showing anyone affection, even her lovers. Anna-Marie had had her favourites and whichever one was in port would be bought a drink and dragged willingly to one of the rooms in Taverners as Morgane was left to drink with the rest of the crew. If there was one thing that Anna-Marie had taught her, it was that men had their uses but weren't worth wasting any love on. Morgane wasn't even certain that any real love had been wasted on her either, and the contrast between that and the desperate maternal need and affection expressed in her birth mother's letters made her feel a crushing sadness and longing that was both uncomfortable and unfamiliar.

When she tried to focus on what other lessons Anna-Marie had given her, it was Jacques who came to mind. He'd taught her so many of her skills with endless hours of patient tuition. Back before he became quartermaster, when she was very small, it was invariably him who would follow her around the ship, a huge protector who guided her up the rigging safely, taught her how to thread one leg through at the top in order to anchor herself to the swaying mass of rope. He taught her the knots, and how to repair the canvas, and how to repair her clothes, too. Before his responsibilities to the ship grew, everyone brought their favourite clothes to him to be repaired, and he used those opportunities to teach her how to patch, how to sew stitches that disappeared into the fabric, how to make them strong.

He'd done his best to teach her how to read, but she'd never really taken to it. Anna-Marie never had the patience to persevere in teaching her, and besides, it wasn't as if the ship was full of books to read anyway. She learned the articles from Jacques, learned how to recognise her name and a few other key words like 'gold' and 'promise to pay the bearer' and numbers and that was it. Anything unfamiliar, or in an unusual hand, was unfathomable to her. Writing had proven impossible. She just couldn't sit still long enough to acquire the skill. With the knots and repairing clothes, she could see the benefit. When it came to scraping a quill across paper – something in short supply and often taken by the captain as first dibs – it was impossible to see its use. Without that, she couldn't apply herself. And something about that infuriated

Anna-Marie, though she'd never understood why. That was what she remembered most about the woman who wasn't her mother: the constant anger just beneath the surface.

As she reached for the door handle one memory suddenly came to mind, of a night a few years back when neither of them could sleep for some reason and they'd been lying there, Anna-Marie in the bed, Morgane in the hammock, talking. It was so rare that it happened, she could remember treasuring it at the time. The former captain was rarely reflective, and when she was, she wouldn't usually waste that mood on Morgane. They'd talked about what it was like to be captain and she'd been so happy to just have that moment of connection with a distant woman who for once didn't seem to be angry.

But it was only one good memory, mere flotsam in a cold, cold sea. Morgane left the cabin and slammed the door shut behind her.

The sky was a brilliant red when she emerged onto the deck, King Charles the Second honking loudly at the crew for having the temerity to gather near his favourite evening spot. She joined the back of the group just as Jacques and Pierre were moving to stand either side of the main mast. Bull seemed to be very settled where he was in the crowd. It looked like there were two candidates only.

Jacques held up a hand. "As quartermaster, I'm declaring the vote open for captain."

"What about the crew on the other ship?"

"If the majority is less than five, then we'll relieve them and they can add their vote," Pierre suggested. "Any objections?"

None were voiced.

"Go stand by the man you want as captain then," Jacques said.

With many of the crew illiterate, it was the easiest way to vote, and the one they'd always used. She'd heard tell of other ships with secret ballots, but it wasn't their way. Anna-Marie had always had a policy of everyone knowing where everyone stood on an issue – literally – and was always quick to punish anyone who gave another grief for the way they'd voted.

Even though she was planning to leave, Morgane was still in the crew and still had the right to vote, so she went to stand next to Jacques, and to her delight, the vast majority of the crew did the same. Bull came and stood next to her and belched loudly. Dill scrambled up the rigging behind Jacques, giving Morgane a shy smile as she settled into place above their heads.

Pierre, his shoulders sagging a little, nodded to himself and stepped forward. "I recognise Jacques as the rightful captain of *The Vengeance* and pledge my loyalty to him for as long as he serves the ship above himself."

There was a loud cheer and the last bit of tension since Anna-Marie's death rapidly faded.

Pierre was voted in as quartermaster above Bull, who took it with good humour, but she knew he would get drunk and belligerent later on. Then, as the sun began to touch the horizon, Jacques called the crew to meet below deck. It was cramped as hell, but they could all fit on the gun deck, and more importantly the prisoners held on the deck of the *Maître* wouldn't be able to hear what was said.

"There's the matter of the *Maître* to settle," Jacques said. "I've been over there, with Morgane, and the ship is bare inside. They stripped everything out for speed. There are cannon, but our ports are full. There's only powder and balls to take."

"Stripped out by the ones who took it before us?" Pierre asked. "Sounds too thorough a job for another pirate."

Jacques shook his head. "That was all a ruse. It was stripped by the owners for the purpose of hunting down *The*

Vengeance and killing our captain." As the crew muttered to each other, Morgane could sense the mood changing from one of curiosity to anger. She could see why Jacques was being open with them, but she didn't want that to lead to them deciding to torch the ship in revenge.

"May I speak, captain?" she asked, and Jacques nodded.

She stood on a crate to get some height so all could hear her. "They weren't just told to kill my mother. They were ordered to take me to France."

"Then I say we kill every last one of 'em," Bull growled.

"Wait! Wait… listen to me," she said and mercifully, they settled. "I'm going with them, back to France." At the various cries of disbelief, she held up her hands. "Not as a prisoner. A guest, so they say."

"Bollocks! They'll hang you, Morgane," Bull said. "You shot one of theirs. They'll say whatever you want to hear now, then the moment you're on land they'll clap you in chains."

"It seems a rather long-winded attempt to do that," Jacques said. "And I've seen the pardon prepared for her. The way I see it, it's up to Morgane if she trusts them or not, and it's up to us whether we're happy to let that ship go."

"I say we burn it," Pierre said, and a worrying number agreed with him. "There's nothing of value to be had, and it's the right way to honour the dead."

"If you burn it," Morgane said, raising her voice above the murmurs of assent, "then I lose my chance to find the one who sent that ship to kill my mother, and I lose my chance to avenge her."

Silence fell.

"Whether I trust them or not, it's the only way to discover who ordered her death. I want to hold a knife to their throat and tell them what they took from me. From all of us. And for all of us, I'll kill them for it. I swear I will."

One by one, the crew members nodded, a couple of those closest to her patting her on the back. "Aye, 'tis right to do so," Pierre mumbled.

"Burning the ship gives us nothing save a passing satisfaction," Jacques said. "We killed as many as they took from us, and Dill killed the one that fired the first shot. I'm not taking anything away from that by saying that man was acting under orders, and the one who gave those orders did us wrong. If we let that ship leave, with Morgane aboard, we gain the hope of her vengeance. I say we let her go with the ship and carry on to Port Royal, after we've taken most of their ordnance. Anyone who objects, speak now."

"You sure you want to go alone, Morgane?" Dill asked. "There's a lot of them and there'd be no crew behind you."

"I'm not scared of 'em," Morgane said. "I've got a brace of my mother's pistols as well as my own and I'll sleep with one under my pillow and my dagger in my hand. They'll soon learn not to bother me." As she spoke, she settled the inherited pair of pistols over her chest, baldrics crossed, just like their previous owner.

Dill gave her a mischievous grin and nodded, satisfied.

Jacques gave the crew a few more moments, and then said, "Morgane will take her share of the loot, as was portioned to her, and no more, save the best wishes of the crew and the hope that, when your vengeance is done, you might come and find us once more."

"Always a place for you with us, Morgane," Bull said. "And extra rum if you kill the one who sent that ship!"

The crew dispersed and many of them came to bid her farewell and wish her luck before going up on deck to ready the ship for departure. Dill was among them, waiting until most had said their bit before approaching her.

"Wish I could come with you," she said. "But I'm more use here and I don't want to get hanged neither."

Morgane pulled the small garnet ring from her pocket and held it out to Dill. "This was one of the rings my mother was wearing. It's yours if you want it. I'll not be offended if you don't."

Dill's eyes widened and she took the ring. It fit her thumb perfectly. She gave Morgane a long look, filled with more gratitude than words could ever express, and then rushed up the stairs. By the time Morgane made it onto the deck, Dill was up in the crow's nest, and she found herself wondering if she'd ever see her again.

Jacques and Bull were carrying her trunk over the planks and she followed them over, head high, shoulders back, determined to look like someone ready to take on the world, rather than shit through the eye of needle, as she really felt. As soon as she set foot on the *Maître*'s deck, she was suddenly filled with a desire to run back over the planks and forget about France and the chance to find her mother and righteous vengeance.

Bull patted her shoulder as he went back over to *The Vengeance* and Jacques pulled her to one side as others started to take the larger portion of the *Maître*'s ordnance over the planks. Her crew watched helplessly, still tied and under guard.

"Are you absolutely sure you want to do this? Once we part ways, there's no way I can watch over you. You'll be on your own, Morgane, for the first time in your life."

Her mouth was as dry as a beach above the tideline, but she still nodded.

He reached into his shirt and pulled out a small package that had been tucked in place against his belt, hidden from view. At first, she thought it was made of leather, but as he unwrapped it, she realised it was just a protective outer layer.

Inside was a rectangular shaped silk purse with an elaborate marque featuring a blue rose embroidered onto it.

He undid the ribbon that tied it closed at the side and opened it to reveal a small sewing kit, replete with needles, thread and a leather thimble.

"In my family, this is given as a gift when you've completed your apprenticeship," he said, tying it shut once more and wrapping it in the leather. "It proves your worth, and it enables you to find a job with any other couturier in France, England and Spain, where my extended family has many ateliers." He took her hand and pressed it into her palm. "If you ever get into any trouble… if things in France are not what you hope them to be, find any one of the ateliers – there's one in Paris, one in Lyon, and a few others, but if you go to any silk trader and ask for the nearest Couturier de la Rose Bleu, they will guide you. Present this when you find them and tell them you need help. Tell them that 'Petit Jacques' gave this to you, as a sign of his trust in you. Any of them will give you whatever help you need."

She stared at the leather parcel. "I can't take this, Jacques! It's too special."

"You can, and you will, with my blessing. It is special to me, but not more valuable than the peace of mind I'll have, knowing you can use it if you're in need. I'm captain of *The Vengeance* now, and you helped to make that happen. Take it, with my thanks."

She closed her hand around it and then threw her arms around him. There was a brief, fiercely tight embrace and then they let go of each other. Not willing to weep in front of him nor anyone in either crew, she hurried below deck to find a nook to curl up in until the ship got underway.

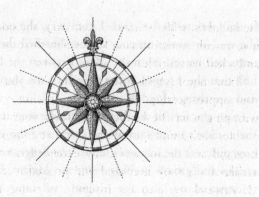

CHAPTER FIVE

"What are you doing there?"

The dagger was in her hand and pointed at the source of the voice before she even fully woke up. Morgane blinked at the captain of the *Maître* who was leaning over her, holding a lantern and looking at the blade with surprise. "Is that how you were raised to greet someone?"

"It's how I was raised to greet a stranger waking me up on a ship I don't know," she replied, not moving the dagger. "What do you want?"

"It's more a matter of what you want, my dear. Surely you don't want to spend the entire voyage back to France in this little nook?"

"Weren't no other choices."

"Perhaps if you'd spoken to me first, you'd have learned that there are. And I'd be very grateful if you could put the dagger away."

She stared at him for a few moments, trying to work out if it was a ploy to get her to lower her defences, but she could see both of his hands and he wasn't armed. And there was the matter of the financial reward for delivering her safely.

If that was to be believed. Either way, she couldn't stay as she was for weeks on end, so she sheathed the weapon and untucked herself from the space between the bulkhead and hull that she'd found in the bowels of the ship. Standing up and stretching felt good.

From the feel of it, they were underway at full sail, but she couldn't be certain of the speed and the weather, given how different the schooner felt to *The Vengeance*. There were creaks and groans coming from the *Maître*, but she didn't understand its language properly yet, and it was deeply disconcerting.

"We'll be taking on supplies in Saint-Domingue very soon, but I'd advise you to stay on the ship and out of sight."

"Why?"

"Those are my instructions, mademoiselle. To keep you safe."

"To keep me prisoner!"

"Au contraire. If you insist on going ashore, I will merely have to assign you a bodyguard or two, for your own protection, and I would rather not draw any attention to us."

"Is it that unsafe there? I've put ashore in Port Royal and Charles Town many a time. Surely your colony cannot be more dangerous than those ports?"

The captain sighed. "You may be recognised. And when word gets out of your mother's death – and it will, as soon as we put ashore – there may be some who'd like to exact revenge upon her daughter. It's a key trading post for the Four Chains Trading Company, and many a ship looted by your mother trades there. Some may even be moored there as we speak. You understand that, surely?"

Morgane reined in the instinct to rail against any sort of restrictions. She had no real desire to go ashore after all. She'd never been there, but was certain it wouldn't be like Port Royal, a place she understood and felt relatively safe in. But then she realised she'd only felt safe there because Anna-Marie rarely left her side, and the few who'd dared try anything had soon regretted their actions. It was one thing to have the woman you believed to be your mother – a pirate captain, to boot – ensuring your safety, quite another to have strangers say they'll have your back.

"I'll stay here," she said.

"You can't spend the entire trip hiding in a corner. I'd like to offer you my cabin for the voyage. Your belongings are there already."

She wrinkled her nose at the thought of stringing a hammock beside his bed, or worse, sharing it. He probably snored. Or what if he had guts like Pierre, and was able to turn any food or drink into the most obnoxious smells ever known to man? If he thought that she would exchange sex for a bed and relative privacy, he was soon to have another conversation about her knife, and it would not go the same way as the first.

The captain looked offended for some reason. "Is my offer not to your pleasing?"

"No..." She decided to test him, and not mention the implicit power imbalance between them that might make him think he could have his way with her. "I just don't know how bad your wind is and how loud you snore."

His mouth dropped open and after a shocked pause, he started to laugh, a melodic hooting sound that she couldn't help but smile at. "Oh! Oh, mademoiselle, I would not dream of sharing the cabin! I mean it is yours, alone, for the remainder of the voyage."

"Oh!" Perhaps she'd been unfair. Or perhaps he was hoping to win her over, to lull her into a false sense of security. Either way, having the cabin to herself was good, and she would wedge something under the door from the inside, just in case. "Then yes, I would like that."

He gestured with his hand to head towards the stairs up to the deck above, the one that contained his cabin. In the time since she'd come aboard, a couple of dozen hammocks had been hung back up, now their battle was over, and the smell had gone. None of the crew were there, though.

"Did I sleep the night through?"

"Yes, and the weather is fair. We're making good time. We're very low on supplies, but we'll bring aboard food and fresh water at Saint-Domingue, of course, so you'll be able to wash then."

She'd expected to not sleep a wink that night, being in such a strange place, but the day had been more exhausting than she'd appreciated.

He unlocked his cabin door and she saw the trunk brought over from *The Vengeance* in the middle of the floor, next to another of similar design. "Here are your belongings. There is brandy in the decanter, should you wish it, and hard tack in the box there. I'm afraid there's nothing more until tomorrow."

"That other chest isn't mine," she said, confused.

He smiled. "It is. I was instructed to give it to you, should we find you. It was very well hidden."

He gave her a small key and she unlocked it. The scent of lavender wafted up immediately and the top layer of linen was familiar. "A dress?"

"Yes, made of the finest silk. I have no idea if the sizing is correct. I was told the trunk contains everything you might need for your comfort."

She lifted the dress out to find a silver-backed hand mirror, along with a matching pair of brushes for her hair. She stroked the bristles, marvelling at how soft they were. She'd never used one before, but had seen a woman using one at Taverners, in one of the upper rooms. She'd been standing on the balcony, brushing her long brown hair. Their eyes had met and, in that moment, she'd felt a longing she couldn't understand. Perhaps for her beauty, or the pride she had in those long locks. Morgane's hair was always braided up and tucked underneath a scarf when in port, to stop random men touching it and commenting on how blonde it was, like she hadn't bloody noticed that herself. She hated that.

"I shall leave you to settle in," the captain said softly. "Here is the key. If there's anything you need, please come to find me above deck."

She took it. "Wait… I don't know your name, captain."

"I am Captain Etienne de Valois, at your service, mademoiselle."

"Just call me Morgane. Mademoiselle sounds strange."

He looked somewhat uncomfortable. "Morgane… what is your family name? Your mother was only known as Captain Anna-Marie, when she was not called The Scourge."

"Family name?" Morgane was stumped. "Morgane is the only one I have. None of the crew had more than one name. Bull might have had another one once, I suppose, but we only called him Bull. And we sometimes called Pierre 'Plague Arse', but I doubt that's what you mean." She knew that Jacques' family name in France had been Couture, but even though he'd been as close to a father as she'd ever have, he was not family. Besides, he never used it anymore either.

He laughed again. "Indeed. Just Morgane then. But you may need to get used to mademoiselle. I will call you that in company."

"Why?"

"Because it's polite," he replied, taken aback. "Has no one ever called you that?"

"Most people knew me in the ports, and they just called me Morgane or 'boy' if they didn't know me." She shrugged. "I never really thought about it before."

He frowned a little. "I think you are going to find France a rather strange place. But that conversation is for another day, when you are settled." He gave a small bow and left.

MORGANE WAS GRATEFUL for the cabin, and stayed inside it for the duration of the short voyage to Saint-Domingue, and during the day and night they were in the port. It was the longest she'd ever spent in a cabin while in good health. Usually, her days were filled with work, and it felt strange but also needed. She slept for a lot of it.

It wasn't just a matter of avoiding the crew who saw her as nothing but a murderous pirate – and fairly so – it was the fact she just needed to be alone for a while. The strange numbness was still there, and it felt like things had happened so fast she hadn't quite caught up with herself somehow. In the few hours that she was awake she found herself just staring into space and couldn't even remember what she'd been thinking about. It just wasn't natural, spending so much time alone and idle, but her body felt so heavy and her mind so busy, as if work of another kind was happening, but inside her head and her heart instead.

Every time she tried to settle on something to do, the desire evaporated. She slept, she pissed in the pot under the bed, she ate the food that the captain brought to her. She half expected to fall sick with a fever, she felt so strange, but it never arrived. Her thoughts slid off any attempt to focus, so she wasn't even certain what that work being done inside her was about and she'd never been the introspective type, so she just let herself sink through the numbness into deep rest.

It wasn't until they'd left Saint-Domingue, and she'd washed with the fresh water newly taken aboard and brought to her cabin by Valois, that she felt ready to open the new trunk.

Another letter, in the same hand, lay underneath the top

layer of linen. She wished Jacques were there to read it to her. But she had the one she'd taken from Anna-Marie's body, and lay it out next to the new one, trying her best to remember what Jacques had said. She knew it had begun with 'My darling daughter' and the first words were exactly the same on the second. Good!

It took an excruciating amount of effort, but she had the time and persevered longer than she ever had with any other writing she'd found, until finally, she felt she had the meaning.

"My darling daughter,
If this letter is in your fair hands, it means that Captain Lavois has found you and is bringing you home. Soon you will be in my arms once more, and your life will improve immeasurably. I have missed you desperately. I imagine Anna-Marie has said terrible things about me, but I assure you, she lied, thanks to her bitter and twisted heart. As you will soon discover, only love and the joy of being reunited once more await you. God willing, we will soon be together once more.
With all my love,
Your mother."

Morgane didn't know what 'immeasurably' or 'desperately' meant. She wasn't certain that 'twisted and bitter' were what they appeared to be either, and wished Jacques were there to confirm that she'd deciphered it all correctly. But she was confident that the woman who penned it did want her to come home, and that she would be welcomed.

But why hadn't she given her name? Even though she knew that the captain had been instructed to give the chest to her?

Feeling stupid, she realised that it was because there had been the high chance that Lavois would fail, and that Anna-

Marie would read it instead. How many of these letters had passed through her aunt's hands? It didn't bear thinking about. Then she was staring into space again, turning over old memories, as if she were trying to sift through sand in the hope of finding a gem. She couldn't remember her aunt saying anything about her previous life in France, nothing that she could hold onto as a starting point to make sense of it all. The only thing that had begun to seep in was an understanding of why she'd been so cold. She wasn't her mother. She didn't love her. Not even as an aunt, it seemed. So why steal her as a baby? It couldn't have been to satisfy a desire to have a child, as she'd always behaved as if her charge was either a burden or so devoid of value that she could barely bring herself to speak to her.

Desperate for something to take her out of the tedious circling of her thoughts, Morgane went through the contents of the new trunk.

She pressed one of the pouches to her lips, sucking the fragrance deep into her lungs. She knew the lavender pouches were probably there to keep the dress safe from moths and any mustiness that could be caused by a long sea journey, but surely it was really because it was the most beautiful scent in the world?

Jacques told her that in France there were fields of it, deep purple rows as far as the eye could see. He'd told her about running through them as a child, then later picking it for the local glove-makers who were allowed to perfume their wares with the herb. None of it really made sense to her. Why would the people who made gloves need permission to use something growing in a field? Who could stop them? Jacques was never interested in explaining things, though, not when he was in a reminiscing mood.

Morgane pulled out the skirt and laid it over her lap. What would it be like to wear such a thing?

There were ten chemises, all made of fine linen. There were several pairs of strange trousers made of the same fabric, just as voluminous as her own, but unstitched at the crotch. What use were those? Why pack half-made flimsy breeches that she couldn't wear? She stuffed those back in the trunk. Even though the contents of the two trunks differed slightly, and the dresses were different colours and the embellishments and detail of the embroidery on the stomachers were different, too, it was obvious that the same person had sent both.

Jacques was right, her mother – her real mother – was a damn wealthy woman. She'd have to be rich to send these and secure that pardon, too. Did she know that the same ship she'd used to send this trunk had been instructed to kill her sister? There was no letter for Anna-Marie in this chest, only her, which made her uncomfortable. Maybe there was a second chest for her late aunt somewhere. Or maybe she'd changed her mind and given up begging Anna-Marie to come and rescue her.

Could she have given the order to kill her? Surely not. Not her own sister, not by the sound of the letter Jacques had read to her. Morgane imagined a sad woman who looked like her aunt, packing each one with tears ready to fall, hoping her sister and daughter would receive them one day. It seemed like such a wasteful and stupid act that it could only be done by someone whose love and hope for being reunited outweighed their reason.

Even though she knew the clothes were intended for her, it felt like they were for someone else, for a young woman who bore no resemblance to her whatsoever. She'd never worn a dress in her entire life – she didn't even know the best way to get it all on, there were so many more hooks and loops and buttons than garments had any right to have. She pulled them out, admired the fine needlework and beautiful fabric, but just couldn't bring herself to put them on. These were not gifts sent with her life in mind. None of it was any use on a ship, aside from the brushes and the mirror perhaps. She couldn't climb rigging in all those layers of skirts, and in the new trunk there was a pair of stays with rigid bones stitched into them, far less supple than the canvas ones she wore.

But then her real mother wasn't going to want her stolen daughter to dress like a pirate, was she? Her real mother knew what she'd become; she'd arranged a pardon, and they were hunting for Anna-Marie's daughter, the woman known as 'The Scourge' by countless sailors. It wasn't that these dresses and gifts of perfume and powder were ill-suited, sent by a mother who didn't understand what her needs were for life on board ship. They were saying 'this is for your new life now.'

It made her more reluctant to try either dress on, but she did slip into one of the fine linen chemises as she soaked her stinking, blood splattered clothes in the leftover bathing water.

She left the dresses in the trunks. They probably didn't fit, and she would look ridiculous in them anyway. Cook had told stories about when he was apprenticed as a boy and served in a French chateau's kitchen. It had sounded like such a bizarre place, where fancy nobles had a life of ease and luxury. Was that what she was sailing towards? What was it really going to be like?

There was a knock on the door, in the style of Captain Lavois' three rapid taps. Morgane was grateful for the distraction. She unlocked it and smirked at the way Lavois took in her state of undress and flushed scarlet. "Forgive me, mademoiselle, I... I shall come back."

Morgane looked down at the linen that covered her down to her knees, wondering if there was a hole that she hadn't noticed, like the strange half-made breeches. But the chemise was voluminous and hole free and there were only a few inches more of her legs exposed to the air than when she was wearing her trousers. With all the linen just hanging down from her chest, he could see even less of her shape than before. "You're not interrupting anything. What do you want?"

"You're not dressed," he said, now turned away from the door and speaking to the hammocks hung throughout the deck.

"My clothes are filthy, so this has to do for now."

"You have a trunk full of clothes!" He looked back into the room, still steadfastly avoiding looking at her, and pointed at the fabric spilling out of the open chest.

"They're not clothes, they're... stupid fancy things. The stays are all wrong – they lace at the back and mine lace at the front, so how am I supposed to get those on? And look at this bollocks." She grabbed the breeches and opened up the slit. "Half-made! I can't wear these! As soon as I bend over my arse will be—"

"Mademoiselle!" Lavois was now a disturbing shade of puce. "Those are drawers, to be worn underneath the chemise and petticoats and dress. They are not breeches and they are not unfinished! The... the ehhhhh... the design is to make it easy for a lady to..." He glanced at the chamber pot. "To relieve herself without the need to remove her gown."

She followed his eyes, slowly deciphering the roundabout way he explained their purpose. "Oh! It's for pissing and whatnot!" She laughed. "I thought the one who made them couldn't be arsed to finish them!" She pulled them on beneath her chemise, tied the dainty cord at the waist and experimentally squatted up and down a few times. "Yeah, this works, I suppose. And nice to have a bit of a breeze down there on hot days."

Lavois looked like he was going to die. She laughed again.

He was too easy to fluster!

He rested a hand on the doorframe, stared down at the deck for a few moments as he composed himself. "Mademoiselle, I beg you to dress properly and then we can speak to one another without discomfort."

"I'm quite comfortable," she said.

"But I am not," he fired back.

She sighed. "Honest, I looked at the things in the trunk and… and I dunno how any of them things are supposed to be worn. Even if I could get those stays on, I don't know what to do with the rest. There are flat pouches with string – do I tie those around my waist? Under the stays or on top? Or on top of the dress? The stitching is so fancy on them, I think they must go on the outside, but I never saw none of the Taverners women wearing them. Not that they had anything as fancy as these, course."

The captain turned around slowly. "You've never worn a proper gown before…" he said slowly, as if it were something dawning on him.

"I've never worn any sort of gown before. I didn't know they're so complicated."

"Mon Dieu, this will not do," he muttered and then cleared his throat. "I know it isn't… proper… but would you like my assistance? I have three elder sisters and two daughters, and I have helped all of them in the past, when the maid was busy."

She didn't really see the point of putting all that paraphernalia on when they were still weeks away from their destination, but she was curious enough to agree. It was better than sitting there moping, she'd done quite enough of that.

The firmer stays were surprisingly comfortable and worn over the chemise. The pouches were pockets that were tied over the top of the stays and there were slits in the side of the petticoats and dress so she could still access them. The outfit was beautiful and quite heavy when it was all in place, but then she was used to wearing just a shirt and trousers, so it was no surprise. The boned stays and the bodice made her stand differently, straighter, with her shoulders further back. She suddenly had a décolletage to rival the women at Taverners and grinned down at it with satisfaction.

"I could rest a flagon of bumbo on these!" she said to Lavois, patting the tops of her breasts but he didn't seem to find it as entertaining as her.

The dress fit surprisingly well, with a tight, pointed bodice, a wide neckline and very full sleeves that ended just below the elbow. It was a pale blue silk and the way the light played off it was so beautiful. Whoever had guessed her size had had luck on their side. Once everything was laced and secured in place, Lavois stepped back and his eyes widened. "Mademoiselle... you are beautiful."

He wasn't leering at her like she'd seen many men leer at the women in Taverners – she would have punched him in the face if he'd shown even a hint of that, just to be sure he knew where he stood – but he was obviously seeing her differently than before. There was a reverence, almost, an awe.

He got the hand mirror from where she'd left it on the desk and held it up in front of her, so she could see her reflection. A fancy lady looked back at her, tan lines on her chest, blue eyes bright against the brown of her face, her almost white-blonde hair hanging in loose waves over her shoulders. That was her? It certainly wasn't the idea she had of herself in her head. There were no mirrors on *The Vengeance*, so she'd only seen herself when they were in Taverners and caught a glimpse of herself sometimes in the mirror that was hung near the door there. She'd never looked remarkable in any way, but then her hair had been hidden all that time. Now, seeing how it almost glowed in the lantern light, it was striking and strange.

"The ladies in France wear their hair up, of course, and often curled."

"Why?"

"It's the fashion. Wigs are popular, too." He sighed at her blank look. "Surely you braided your hair, at least?"

She nodded. "One big one, to keep it off my face. I had a scarf that I used to wrap around it and then sort of twist it and tuck it in at the back. Are the French ladies' scarves different? There wasn't one in the chest."

This time he looked confused. He shook his head. "Ladies of means do not wear scarves about their heads, mademoiselle, and certainly not with a gown such as you wear. Would you like me to teach you?"

"Will it keep it out of the way?"

When he nodded, she agreed, and then she watched what he did in the mirror.

"Do you know the name of the one who sent these clothes to me?"

"No, mademoiselle. I was simply informed that I should hide it well and give it to you should we be successful."

"By that 'Monsieur de Lombardy'?"

"Yes. But I doubt that even he could have afforded all of this." He looked at the drawers and chemises she'd piled onto the bed, the other dress, the perfume, the brush set, the delicate hose and silk slippers she hadn't even tried on yet.

"Doesn't he own the fleet?"

"No, he merely manages it. The owner is the Comte d'Artois. And from what I know of the man, he wouldn't be interested in sending gifts such as these."

"Is he rich?"

Captain Lavois laughed. "He is already married, my dear."

Morgane frowned. "I didn't ask if he was. What difference does that make to me?"

Lavois stopped, dropped his head slightly, as if

remonstrating with himself. "Forgive me. Yes, he is very rich, and a relative of the king. His wife the comtesse is a famed beauty, with golden... hair."

In the hand mirror, she watched the reflection of him staring down at the braid he was partway through. She held her breath as the pieces fell into place in her mind at the same time as his. The Comtesse d'Artois must be her mother. It was too much of a coincidence to have the same, rare hair colour of the woman who just happened to be married to the owner of the trading company Anna-Marie targeted mercilessly. And now Morgane finally understood why; the man she'd loved had abandoned her for her sister, so Anna-Marie had decided to destroy his trading empire one ship at a time.

So that meant her father was a relative of the king? The same king that so many in the crew of *The Vengeance* had cursed, and complained about? The one who was apparently just as bad, if not worse, than King Charles the Second? What did that make her?

Noble? The thought snagged in her mind for a few uncomfortable moments and then she pushed it away. It simply didn't fit. That wasn't her.

She watched Lavois swallow and then continue the rest of the braid. It had pulled the hair back from her face and was already feeling far more practical. When it was done and tied at the bottom with one of the ribbons sent in the trunk, he stepped back.

"Perhaps it would be wise to let a proper lady dress your hair we arrive. I shall leave you to enjoy your gifts," he said. "When we return to France, I'm sure all of your questions will be answered more satisfactorily by Monsieur de Lombardy."

After he left, she looked back at the two trunks and then her reflection in the mirror. The dress was beautiful, but the more she looked at her reflection, the more she realised that it really was only the dress, and that she looked horribly out of place in it. The gifts were incredibly generous. So why did she feel that she might be in more danger now than she had ever been on *The Vengeance*? Morgane tossed the mirror onto the bed and, trusting her gut, locked the door. It was only when she sat on the bed, staring down at the silk slippers, that it hit her. If the owner of the Four Chains Company ordered Anna-Marie's death, then vengeance would mean killing her own father.

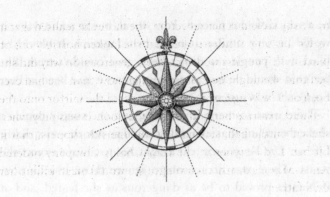

CHAPTER SIX

A DAY OUT from Saint-Domingue, Morgane woke in a panic, the first moments of consciousness filled with thinking that her mother was going to come and tip her out of her hammock for being so lazy. When the reality of being in a bed on a strange ship sank in, the panic slid into an uneasy discomfort. She didn't want to sleep the day away again, but she didn't have a list of chores or repairs to fall back on either.

She dressed in her old clothes, the dress she'd tried on before now draped over the captain's chair. She didn't like the thought of having to wear it when they arrived in France, but she liked the prospect of looking like a pirate when pulling into a French port even less. Official pardon or not, she wasn't stupid enough to invite trouble in a strange land. So she was resigned to having to wear the cumbersome outfit at least until she got to wherever her mother was, and then she'd change out of it. Not the slippers, though. They pinched horribly. At least her boots would be hidden by all those layers of petticoats and skirts.

She cast her mind forwards to what would happen when they arrived, as best she could. She knew that Nantes would be a very different place to Port Royal, but in some ways, it would be very similar. It could be dangerous. It would be filled with people she didn't know and couldn't trust. But her gold would be just as useful there as it had been in Port Royal, she was sure of it.

There were so many unknowns, and she simply couldn't shake the feeling that something could go wrong very quickly. Life on *The Vengeance* had taught her to always expect the worst. There was no reason to ignore those lessons now. If Nantes proved to be as dangerous as she feared, and at some point she had to run, she had to be able to take her gold with her. There wasn't enough room in the pockets for all the coins and her old leather pouch was even smaller. Lugging two chests around would slow her down. Morgane appreciated Anna-Marie's attitude to possessions in a new light. She needed another solution.

So she laid out the blue dress with its petticoats and the chemise she'd wear on that day and looked for places she could add more pockets. It wasn't long before it occurred to her that the copious amounts of hemline across the garments could easily be repurposed.

"Thank you, Jacques," she whispered to herself as she unwrapped the sewing kit he had given her. Those fine needlework skills he'd taught her were going to come in useful.

By the time night fell, the hems of all the petticoats and the blue dress were filled with gold and a few gems she'd prized out of the rings. It made the clothes heavier to wear, but it wasn't unmanageable and besides, the peace of mind it gave her was immense. She consolidated the remaining booty and belongings into just the one trunk. Even if the worst happened and she was robbed on the way to de Lombardy or even afterwards, at least she would always have something with which to buy herself out of trouble.

She had just put the sewing kit away when a squall hit. It took her by surprise, not being as sensitive to the slight changes she would have felt in *The Vengeance* before it hit, even below deck.

Morgane locked the cabin door behind her and raced up to the deck, needing to help rather than sit it out alone and hope these swabs were competent. Lavois was barking orders to haul up the canvas and get the *Maître* ready to ride out the storm. They were short on crew, though, and as she watched a couple of the men start to climb the rigging, she knew they'd be too slow and could lose a sail. So, she started to climb and did what she knew best, hauling the canvas with her legs wrapped around the rigging, the increasing pitch of the ship trying to throw her off as the wind whipped around her and slapped the long braid of her hair against her face.

It felt so good to be both scared and yet utterly confident of her ability. When the canvas was secured, she paused for a moment, revelling in the feeling of being so high up in fresh air after days of being stowed away like cargo. The *Maître* felt different to *The Vengeance*, lighter as she was, and she missed the sense of solidity of her old home. Then she went down the rigging, overtaking the crewmen, laughing at the howl of the wind. Damn but she felt alive again, after days and days of feeling numb.

Ropes needed to be coiled and stowed quickly, so she went to the nearest one that wasn't being dealt with and started on it herself. One of the crew was doing the same a few feet away and gave her a long stare but she ignored him. She was helping. If he didn't like it, that was his problem.

She could see a sliver of moonlight on the horizon and knew this wasn't going to be a bad one. These squalls could do a lot of damage if they weren't respected, but this one would be over in less than an hour. Lavois was clearly an experienced captain, which was reassuring to see. So, when she'd done all she could to help, she crouched down between two coils of rope in the lee of the rail to enjoy the thunder and watch for lightning. It didn't feel like there was going to be any, though. And the thunder was just an occasional rumble, nothing more, not loud enough to be felt in the belly. She was glad of that. Lightning was one of the few things that frightened her, having seen a man struck while up in the rigging when she was a child. He'd lived, and got a magnificent scar that looked like god had pressed the lightning into his flesh. Morgane had wished she had the same and couldn't understand why the man had hated it so.

What had happened to him? She hadn't thought about him for such a long time. He'd probably died on a raid or moved ship or even been killed by Anna-Marie for some slight or other. Morgane felt a brief flicker of guilt that she couldn't even remember the man's name, but she'd only been a young child.

A pair of hands grabbed her shirt, and she was pulled towards an angry face that loomed suddenly out of the storm's gloom. Before she even had a chance to swear, she was dragged towards the hatch and then manhandled down the steps to the deck below.

"I been waitin' for my chance," the man said, throwing her against the hull. "Bidin' my time."

Morgane reached for her knife and realised, with a mixture of panic and absolute fury at herself, that it wasn't there. It was still tucked into a little sheath she'd sewn into one of the petticoats earlier that evening.

The man used that moment to grab her by the neck with both hands and press her against the wood. "Don't see why you should be treated like royalty when you're nothing more than pirate filth."

"Get your bloody hands off me!" she croaked, trying to pull his arms away from her in her panic.

"You killed my friend. You shot him. I loved him, and you shot him like he was nothin'."

"He was trying… to kill… my captain…"

"So what? She was just a filthy pirate, too! She deserved it! And you'll get what you deserve as well! I'll spill your guts like you spilled his!"

Something in Morgane's mind sprang back into life and she brought her knee up as hard and as fast as she could into his groin. The hatred in his eyes gave way to shock and nauseating pain. The grip on her throat loosened. She capitalised on the moment with a solid punch to his nose, sending him staggering backwards into one of the hammocks.

She kept her fists up, as she steadily moved her way round to just in front of the cabin door, hips and knees loose as she swayed with the rocking deck, the wind howling through the open hatch.

Morgane was trying to work out whether she had time to unlock the cabin door to get her weapons when her assailant spat out some blood, more of it spilling down his upper lip, and fixed his murderous stare on her once more. She'd hoped the pain in his crotch was going to give her a bit more time, but his blood was up, and this wasn't just an average brawl. He wanted to kill her.

He moved forwards, the start of a dash to knock her over, but before he could close even half the distance between them another man was crashing down the steps fast enough to grab her attacker when he was mere inches away from her.

"Sen! Sen, for the love of God, control yourself!" the newcomer yelled. He was a big man, who reminded her of Bull with his shaved head and thick neck. But he was much taller than Bull, and his voice wasn't as deep.

"But she killed—"

"I know, I know." The big man wrapped his arms around

her attacker, pulling him away. "But if you kill her, we don't get paid."

"I don't care about the money!"

"We do!" the big man yelled back. "And killing this pirate bitch isn't going to bring him back, is it? But the money, Sen, the money will make a difference, no? Think of your family!"

"He was my family!" Sen broke down in the big man's arms and she watched him sob.

Morgane's back hit the cabin door and she wrapped her arms about herself, shaking, hating the way his pain was making her feel. She'd never seen the impact of *The Vengeance*'s attacks before; usually they struck and fled, leaving the consequences far behind. Her guts cramped as she thought of the man she'd shot, how she'd not spared a moment's thought for him or anyone who might love him. All she'd cared about was protecting her mother and her captain, only to discover that woman had only been one of those things all along.

"I'm sorry," she croaked. "I was defending—"

"Shut your mouth, scum!" Sen yelled. "When we've got our money, I'll see to it that justice is done! I'll see you hanged!"

Oh God, he hated her, with every part of him, right down to the bones and it was a horrifying thing to see. She'd seen anger, fear, disgust, all aimed at her in the past, but nothing as vicious as this. She wasn't a whole person to him, she was only what she'd done during the attack on the *Maître*. He didn't know why she'd been there, how little choice she'd had in it. She'd been so wrapped up in her own thoughts, she hadn't even stopped to think how the crew might see her. "I didn't want to attack your ship! I told her not to! But she never listened to anyone!"

"Don't waste your time!" the big man sneered. "You're a pirate, you have no care for who you kill to take what you want."

The fist she'd punched Sen with throbbed as she clenched both of them. "You killed, too, and you were paid for it – how's that any different?"

"You bitch!" Now the big man looked tempted to punch her, too. "We were defending our ship!"

"You laid a trap, you lying swab! You were sent to kill Anna-Marie and you pocketed the gold for it. Just because it comes from some rich bastard in France don't mean you're better than me or mine!" She pulled the key and its chain over her head. "We've both killed to get gold in our pockets, only difference is that I got more gold, and I didn't have to bow and scrape to no one for it!" As she yelled, she fumbled with the key behind her back, struggling to find the lock.

"Mon Dieu." The captain's voice from the bottom of the steps made the two men snap their heads round to face him. He was staring at her, taking in the scene, his gaze finally settling on Sen. "I will deal with you later, Sen. Both of you, get back up on deck and do your work." He stepped aside to allow them access to the stairs, but as they reached him, he held out a hand. "Not a word of this, to anyone, you understand?"

He didn't shout, he didn't look angry, just firm. The two crewmen nodded to him and climbed the steps.

Grateful for the distraction, Morgane unlocked the door and dashed inside, grabbing the inherited brace of pistols and dropping them into place over her chest before snatching up her sword and racing out again.

Lavois had followed the men up the steps and was just about to lower the hatch, and lock it, too, she'd wager, but she barrelled through it and jumped up onto the deck. The squall had blown out its worst and now patches of moonlight lit the deck.

"Come on then, you bastards!" Morgane yelled, kicking the hatch closed so none of them could push her through it. "I know you want to, so come on! Let's have it out right now!"

"Mademoiselle!" Lavois threw himself in front of Sen who lurched forwards. "What are you thinking? Get back below!"

"I ain't spending another minute down there, knowing you're all waiting for the chance to stab me when no one's lookin'! I ain't hiding away in that cabin, waiting for one of ya to pick the lock and gut me when I sleep! You hate me, fine! If you wanna do me in, have at me!"

She readied herself, sword in front, her left hand ready to draw a pistol if needs be. But none of them moved.

"You're worth more to us alive than dead," said a short man standing a little way away.

"He don't think so!" She jabbed the sword at Sen.

"He will control himself," Lavois said curtly, and Sen did take a step back. "Because he knows that if he gives in to any murderous desire, he'll have not only the crew to answer to, but also God."

"Oh, did God say it was fine to kill my captain and my crewmates, then?"

"You misunderstand," Lavois said, patiently. "He swore an oath to me that he will not harm you, just now, in the sight of God and witnessed by all here. Now I suggest you sheathe that sword and go back to my— your cabin."

Her heart was still pounding, and she wrestled with the desire to fight. But she could read the mood amongst the crew, even though it wasn't her own, and none of them seemed to want to face her. So she made herself sheathe it. "I ain't spending weeks in that cabin. I'll be dead from the flux before we make landfall if I stay cooped up like that."

"You are a guest. I suggest you enjoy the opportunity to rest."

"I suggest you let me work, else I'll be a bigger pain in the arse than you can handle, Lavois." She heard some muttering then, from a couple of the crew that had come closer to listen. "I know you trade sailors have got some backwards notion that women don't belong on ships, but you're wrong. I went up and down that rigging faster than two of yours, and that was in a squall, too."

"It isn't right," Lavois started.

"There ain't no right or wrong about it, you just don't feel comfortable with it. Well, I don't feel comfortable being on a ship full of people who'd see me dead if it weren't for some gold, and I have to live with that, so it's only fair, no?"

He weighed it up. "Anyone here have any objections to our guest taking first and middle watches?"

None spoke up. He was more cunning than she'd given him credit for. The first and middle watches ran from eight in the evening through to four the following morning. The latter of which was the least popular, so she'd been told by former mariners on *The Vengeance*, because it kept you from your hammock in the coldest part of the night. On *The Vengeance*, watches were less formal, and shorter, as they had a bigger crew to split them between.

He knew that there would be fewer objections if it meant they were less likely to have to fill that watch. Despite some whispers, none of the crew openly objected but one man cleared his throat, his face shrouded by the darkness. "So long as I don't have to go near her, captain."

"I don't want to be on watch with her," said another.

"You scared of me?"

"They don't trust you, mademoiselle," Lavois said softly. "I will be on every watch with our guest," he said to the crew. "The new arrangement will start tomorrow. I think there has been enough disruption for this evening."

He opened the hatch and gestured for her to go down. She gave Sen one last look, making sure he could see that she wasn't afraid of him, before she turned to go down the steps. At that moment, the clouds parted and a scrap of fabric, snagged on one of the hooks at the base of the mast, caught her eye. Her first thought was "my mother's headscarf!", before the rest came crashing in. She grabbed it and descended the steps, focusing on keeping her head held high as she did so, Lavois following.

As she reached the cabin, she turned. "Have no fear, I will stay in the cabin tonight and cause no more trouble."

"As I understand it, Sen was the one causing the trouble. I saw you go up the rigging and save that sail, and keep out of everyone's way afterwards."

"That why you agreed to let me work?"

He shook his head. "I agreed because I believe you are the daughter of the owner of this company, and I would not want your father to be disappointed with my treatment of you."

She nodded. "If they stay away from me, I'll stay away from them."

"It will not be an easy voyage for you, mademoiselle. But if you feel that would be preferable to a leisurely one, that is your decision. Good night."

Once she was inside the cabin and the door locked behind her, she looked at the sodden piece of cloth. It was definitely the headscarf she'd worn when Anna-Marie died. How hadn't she seen it before? It had probably been pulled off in the fight, blown into some corner and then dislodged by the squall.

She could remember Anna-Marie wearing it just the day before she'd given it to Morgane to get her out of the cabin. Her dark blonde hair tucked beneath it, hat on top, standing at the prow, one foot on the rail, gazing out to sea. She'd won it in a drinking contest the last time they'd been ashore.

Morgane's legs buckled as heaving sobs erupted from her. She felt like an over-ripe melon that had been dropped on the deck, her innards now spilling out of her, uncontrolled and unwanted.

Waves of grief and anger and shame were crashing through her, pouring from an ocean that had been so deep down inside her that she'd had no idea it was there until now. And it hurt, it physically hurt, in her chest, in her stomach, like it was too big for her body and would break her apart like a ship being wrecked on a reef. She drew up her knees, wrapped her arms around them and half wept, half screamed for her mother into the tiny dark space she'd created.

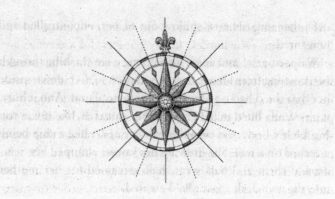

CHAPTER SEVEN

THE JOURNEY TO Europe was long and lonely. The crew avoided her, and despite her best efforts to show them she was a good sailor, not just a pirate, none of them seemed to care. She gave up on them, focusing on her tasks, revelling in the fresh air, spending hours watching moonlight on the water. If it hadn't been for Captain Lavois and his paternal instincts, she would have gone mad from the isolation. He talked to her, though, gently trying to teach her things she'd need to know in France, but none of it stuck.

What made it more difficult was the inability to even imagine what it was like there. It wasn't for lack of Lavois trying. But when he described something, like the chateau her parents lived in, all she could imagine was the largest buildings at Port Royal. They were made of wood and rough plaster, aside from a couple of ramshackle forts. He'd told her the chateau d'Artois was made of smooth stone and was higher than even Taverners, with more than two floors of living space! That they had a ballroom and servants and grand gardens. And the gardens were bigger than Port Royal, just there to look pretty.

If imagining a life like that was hard, imagining herself living it was even harder. If her parents did welcome her with open arms, as Lavois insisted they would, what would she do after that? How would her days be filled if there was no rigging to climb, no sails to mend, no wood to repair or paint? When she'd asked Lavois, he'd smiled and said that she shouldn't worry, that being a wealthy noble meant that she'd never have to worry again. It didn't quiet the fear, though. She felt like he really didn't understand her concerns and she didn't really understand why he was so convinced everything would be fine. There was no common ground between them other than life at sea, and that had nothing to do with the world she was about to enter.

One day, early in the voyage, he'd tried to persuade her to practise her handwriting, not knowing she could barely write at all. "I don't need to write anything down," she'd insisted. "I do it all in m'head." She'd watched Jacques and Anna-Marie barter all her life, so she could do rapid silent calculations.

"But mademoiselle, as a noble, you will need to correspond with others and read their replies, among other things."

"Why wouldn't I just talk to them?"

"France is a huge country, mademoiselle! You will meet people at events and then correspond with them afterwards. They may live hundreds of miles away."

"But if they're so far away, what would I have to say to 'em?"

He'd sighed heavily and after that conversation, he'd decided to teach her how to play chess instead. In the absence of drinking and dancing and taking the piss out of friends and crewmates, it was better than sitting alone in the cabin.

It grew steadily colder the further they travelled, and she hated it, needing to wrap a blanket around herself when up on deck. She'd had no idea how cold it could feel, never having left the Caribbean. The sun got weaker, too, and even the sea and sky shifted to different shades of blue. She found herself longing for the deeper blues she was used to, even for the blazing sun that she'd hated at times.

She dreamt of *The Vengeance*, of Anna-Marie, of Taverners, as if some part of her were lost and seeking them out in her sleep. Sometimes she woke crying even though she couldn't remember the dream.

And then, finally, one morning she was woken by Lavois' three knocks on the door.

"We will soon be making landfall, mademoiselle," he called through the wood. "Will you let me in?"

With a jolt, she got up and unlocked the door. "How soon?"

"Not long. I think you should dress now, as we will be busy later. I shall help you."

He meant dress in the fancy clothes.

It hit her then. This was the start of it, of her new life.

"Mademoiselle?"

Silently, she stepped back to let him in. He went to the cupboard, then to the chest. "We should have hung these... never mind. These first" – he passed a chemise and pair of drawers to her – "then this." The new stays were placed on top of the clothes resting on her hands. "I shall step outside until you are decent, call when you are ready to be laced. Mademoiselle?"

She started. "Yeah, yeah, I'll dress."

He went out and she tried to persuade her body to move, but it felt like she had frozen. She wasn't ready for this. Why had she left everything she had ever known? Why hadn't she listened to Jacques?

Her gaze fell upon the headscarf draped over the back of the captain's chair, along with the brace of pistols. The memory of blood and guts, of the woman who'd raised her, standing on the prow, then dying on her bed.

That was why she was here. Vengeance. She looked down at the clothes in her arms, sent by a woman who'd all but begged for help. She took a deep breath and a memory surfaced, from so long ago, of looking up at the rigging in a fierce storm when she was small, probably not more than seven or eight. "Go on, Morgane!" Jacques had shouted over the wind. "You know what to do. One step at a time! Hold fast!"

She dressed, feeling the determination sweep away the paralysis of fear. She'd hauled up wet canvas in storms that God had sent to sink lesser ships. She'd thrown herself into fierce brawls in Taverners to defend her friends. Hell, she'd bet more gold than she had in games of Loo with cutthroat men who'd have killed her if she'd lost but she never did. And she'd survived a few attacks when they'd been upset by that. All she had to do was find her mother, rescue her, and kill the one who sent the order to murder Anna-Marie. Only three things! Easy.

She dressed, with Lavois' help, boots on underneath the layers of linen and silk. It was heavier than the last time she'd worn it, but thankfully Lavois didn't seem to notice. He seemed tense, perhaps worried about whether he'd got the right daughter.

After he'd braided her hair and looped it up, he passed the mirror that had been left in the chest all voyage to her.

"Mademoiselle, you are beautiful."

She stared at the image in the mirror with horror. She looked close to death. The framing of her décolletage by the dress wasn't broken by the small V-shaped tan at the base of her throat that she'd had before. Her face was now just as pale as the skin on her belly, and she did not like it.

"Shit and blood! I look half-dead!"

She'd heard stories about the long trips back and forth across the Atlantic. How many fell ill and died. How many bodies the slavers tossed overboard before they reached the plantations. *The Vengeance* had several crew members who'd escaped that hell on Earth and their stories still haunted her. Her voyage had been one of relative luxury, and she was not enslaved, but she remembered the tales about the sickness and feared it could still take her, nonetheless.

Lavois chuckled. "You have merely been out of the sun. Your complexion is prized in France."

"Eh?"

"The nobility favour a clear and pale complexion."

"Why?"

"Only the peasants work the land, and the sun takes its toll. Now you look less out of place in such a gown. No one would suspect the life you have led by looking at you. Though I advise you to wear these." He'd found a pair of gloves in the chest, too, dainty things made of the softest velvety leather she'd ever touched. "Your hands do betray you."

She pulled them on, covering the callouses and stubby nails with their persistent dirty edges. The gloves were supple and comfortable, but they'd be shredded by handling wet ropes.

He smiled. "Perfect."

"Not done yet." She slung one of her baldrics around her waist, but before she'd even had a chance to buckle it, Lavois was waving his hands in mild distress.

"No, no, no, mademoiselle, what are you doing?"

"What does it look like?"

"You can't wear that!"

"I bloody well can!"

"No, no, it is impossible. Noble ladies do not wear pistols like this!"

"Then how do they wear them? Across the chest? Won't that wreck the beading?"

"No, they do not wear them at all!"

"How the bloody hell do they carry them then? In their hands?"

He pinched the skin above his nose. "They do not carry them, mademoiselle. They are not armed."

"How the shit are they supposed to keep themselves safe?"

"They… they have no need to. They are often escorted by gentlemen, as you will be. You do not have anything to fear, mademoiselle. France is not like Port Royal."

"If you think I'm leaving this ship unarmed, you're an idiot."

His stern glare surprised her. "If you leave this ship openly bearing arms you will look like a pirate in a poor disguise. You will draw unnecessary attention to us, and you will be treated with mistrust and disrespect. I cannot be clearer than that. The weapons go in the chests."

She was about to get violent, but then she realised he probably had a point. Either way, this was a problem she could solve more intelligently than losing her temper. "As you wish."

He smiled, and she let him feel he'd won. "I suggest you pack and then join me up on deck."

Morgane consolidated her belongings into the larger of the two chests, then set about hiding her weapons on her person. The inherited pistols were transferred to her old baldrick, slung low on her hips beneath the dress and petticoats, still accessible through the slits that gave access to the tied-on pockets. Not ideal, but better than leaving them in the chest. The other two pistols went in the pockets, unloaded for safety's sake, powder and shot in the pockets replacing a few handfuls of gold that went into the chest instead. She wore her sword beneath the dress and petticoats, too, tying the scabbard to her thigh. It made it possible for her to walk without it either jutting out at an obvious angle or bashing her leg, but with the cost of being much harder to access. But she had a dagger sitting within the new sheath she'd sewn into one of the pockets and another in her boot, so it would do for now.

After securing her weapons in their hiding places, Morgane took a few moments to practise walking in the gold laden, cumbersome gown and then went up onto the deck, wrestling the voluminous skirts as she ascended the steps. There was a chill in the wind, but it was sunny at least.

The captain was on the port side, leaning on the rail, and she went to join him.

He gave the same, patient smile that he had so many times over the voyage and looked back out over the water. "It will be a little while more before we reach Nantes, I'm afraid. But you're welcome to look upon the land of our birth with me, if you wish."

The land of our birth. He said the words with a strange reverence, and she could see how much it meant to him. She gazed out at the slivers of flat green land now on both sides of them, feeling no connection to the place whatsoever. But then, she'd never felt any connection to any piece of land. There was the familiarity of the ports they frequented when she lived on *The Vengeance*, but they always slept on the ship. That was the closest to belonging to a place as she'd ever felt.

"Where is the port?"

"A few miles inland. This is the estuary, where the river Loire meets the sea."

"A few miles?!"

He laughed. "Very different to Port Royal and Kingston Harbour, is it not?"

She nodded. She'd been expecting something very similar; a ribbon of land spooling out from the coast to provide a natural harbour right on the edge of the ocean. Not this.

"It's the most important port in France," he continued. "It needs to be sheltered. The cargo comes in and is transported on smaller boats on the Loire or across land by cart. It's very different to what you're used to."

"They trade in sugar?"

"Yes... among other things. I've heard rumours of more ships going to Africa first, but that's something I won't do."

She knew about the sugar and where it came from. She knew how the plantation owners lived and how the enslaved lived, too. Did any of the people in this land know?

She stayed on the deck for those several miles, watching the landscape, trying to get her head around how it was utterly unlike anywhere else she'd seen.

"Where are all the parrots?"

"Ah, the only parrots in France are exotic pets, mademoiselle."

Of all the things to make her feel utterly homesick, she hadn't expected it to be the lack of the brightly coloured birds that were as much residents of Port Royal as the people were.

The city of Nantes slowly came into view, growing like a canker on the horizon, a series of shapes that were just as alien as the trees. Was there nothing familiar here?

Two buildings dominated the shape of the port, one of which she could tell was some sort of fort. It was bigger than any she'd ever seen, but had all the characteristics of a defensible and heavily fortified building. The other was taller and spiky. Its white stone gleamed in the early autumn sunshine.

"That's the cathedral," Lavois said, noting her fascination.

"What is it for?"

"It's a place of worship, mademoiselle. But unlike anything you've ever seen, I'd wager."

She nodded. As they progressed along the river she couldn't stop admiring it. It was so big and so alien in style that it made her nervous, deep down in her belly. It was magnificent, but also intimidating.

The traffic on the river had increased, too, with other smaller boats both ahead and behind them now, all capitalising upon the favourable tide. The river was wide, but she felt it as a sudden narrowing, the freedom given by the expanse of the ocean being replaced by a sense of constriction.

It was really happening. All those times she'd wished for a different life, when angry with the captain or pissed off with sanding down a repair in oppressive heat, they all felt like childish daydreams now, ones that she wanted to take back. She ached for Jacques' reassuring voice and the familiarity of *The Vengeance*. Ever since Anna-Marie's confession, she'd fantasised about kindness and smiles, loving embraces and happy tears at the reunion with her actual mother. But now, as the city grew larger and the river narrower, she feared those fantasies were never going to become a reality.

"There is no need to be afraid, mademoiselle. Monsieur de Lombardy is an honourable man and will make sure you reach your family safely."

"I ain't afraid," she lied, and squared her shoulders to prove it.

He nodded. "My mistake," he said quietly.

The soft green banks gave way to wooden jetties owned by businesses dotted along the riverside and the countryside gave way to the city. As they approached the port she noted the change in the colour of the water, the pervasive background stink of the city. That wasn't shocking, given how unsanitary Port Royal was, but it was a stark contrast to the clean sea air she'd been used to for the past few weeks.

Lavois left her a couple of times to give orders readying the ship for docking, but he kept her in his sight. She resisted the brief desire to go and help, knowing that it wouldn't be wanted and there was nothing that she could do in this dress anyway. She watched how they were brought alongside with mooring ropes, just like in Kingston Harbour at Port Royal. And just like that place, the dockside was full of men loading and unloading cargo from several ships. Shouting and laughter in equal measure, the smells, the noise of the carts on cobbles, it was almost overwhelming after the peacefulness of a lightly crewed ship at sea. She gripped the rail and did her best to take it all in, from the timber framed houses that seemed to huddle alongside the port to the strangely shaped bread she saw a man carrying on a tray held high above the bustle.

Hundreds of little details struck her, each one making her feel like the alien she was here. Now she missed Anna-Marie and the security her presence gave her, the certainty that someone was always watching out for her, and that the people in the port wouldn't dare to interfere with her unless they were new there and didn't know better.

She looked for Lavois and spotted him handing a note to a boy who'd dashed up the newly secured gangplank. After receiving a coin, the boy touched his cap and ran back down to the dockside and darted into the bustle. The note for de Lombardy, presumably, setting it all into motion.

Lavois met her gaze and gave her a reassuring smile before instructing the crew to start unloading the cargo they'd taken on at Saint-Domingue. This captain was looking out for her, too, but it wasn't the same. She watched the crew's activity for a while, before looking back at the docks, surprised to see several men looking up at her as they walked past. A couple of them grinned, one touched his cap, another raised his rather fancy hat.

Confused, she looked behind her, to see if Lavois was standing there. He wasn't. Why were they doing that? She frowned at them, and they moved on, uncaring, puzzling her even more. Why take the trouble to acknowledge her and not care about her reaction? Did they merely seek a moment of her attention?

All of a sudden, the dress felt wrong. She started to head for the hatch to return to the cabin, desperate for her old shirt and trousers, when Lavois touched her shoulder, breaking her stride. "Is something wrong, mademoiselle?"

"I need to change my clothes."

"But we'll be disembarking soon. And this dress is just as lovely as the other."

"No, I want my old clothes. These are making people look at me funny. I don't like it."

There was a flicker of amusement before he appreciated just how uncomfortable she was. With a gentle hand on her arm, he guided her back to the rail to look out over the docks. When she went to move away, he steadied her at the elbow, indicating firmly, yet gently, that he wanted her to stay.

"Mademoiselle, please, just a moment of your time."

She sighed and waited. The same thing happened again, though interestingly none of the men doffed their hats this time. But the looks, the smiles, the lingering nature of their regard, those were all the same.

"Is it the way the men look at you?"

"I don't like it."

"But mademoiselle, they are merely appreciating the sight of a beautiful woman."

He said it like it was something to be happy about. Proud of, perhaps. "I don't like it."

"But why? To be admired is a wonderful thing."

It didn't feel that way to her. She didn't like the attention. She didn't like the way that 'admiration' felt, but couldn't explain why, not even to herself let alone Lavois.

"No one looked at me before, not like this. It's horrible. I want to put my old clothes back on."

"Mademoiselle," Lavois said softly. "Do you not understand? If you dress in the clothes you wore the day I met you, they would still stare, but not with admiration. It would be with suspicion, and hostility. Leaving this ship looking like the pirate you were would not be wise. Better to look like an elegant noble woman given passage to France on a convenient merchant vessel and accept the attention that gives. It is better than being treated like the sort of villain who is hanged before they even have a chance to meet their family."

She hated that he had a point. No one had stared at her in any of the old ports she knew, because everyone was more or less dressed the same. She blended in. Hell, for most of her life she reckoned that all of the strangers in ports had assumed she was a boy.

"I still don't like it," she muttered.

"One day, I suspect, you will feel very differently."

She gave him a sidelong glance. Captain Lavois was a kind man, and knowledgeable, too, but in this instance, she was certain he knew absolutely nothing about what she would feel in the future, nor what it was like to be suddenly very visible after a lifetime of being barely noticed.

"They shouldn't stare. They should mind their own business," she muttered, turning away from the dock and folding her arms.

"There is no harm in looking, mademoiselle."

She scowled at him. But now she was paying attention, she could see how tense he was, in his jaw, his shoulders. "You're worried."

He leaned on the rail, thinking about her question. "Yes, a little. I believe you are the most precious cargo I've ever conveyed into Nantes. I don't want to risk getting anything wrong."

She nodded. "I suppose there's a lot of money at stake."

He frowned at her. "Not just that, mademoiselle. It is my duty to see you safely conveyed to Monsieur de Lombardy. I am taking that very seriously."

"Do you think it could be dangerous?"

He rubbed his chin. "I cannot see why it would be. No

one else will know who you are, and I did not even mention you in my note. I… suppose it is the natural fear of a man walking down the street with a bag of emeralds. Even if no one else knows what he has, he still fears the cutpurse."

She felt sorry for him then, sorry for the burden her delivery was placing upon him. "If it helps… I'm good at not getting killed."

"Mademoiselle, that does not help!"

"What I mean is that I'm not just a bag of gems. I can fight. So, if anyone does try something, it might not be as bad as you fear. If some bugger grabs me, I'll punch them. Someone tried that once, at Taverners, when Anna-Marie was negotiating a deal. I punched him right in the throat, bam!" She mimed the movement just to make sure he knew how good a shot it was. "He never spoke the same way again. And I reckon he didn't grab any more girls without asking, either."

For a moment, Lavois looked utterly horrified, and then slightly impressed. He laughed a little and looked back over the water. "Monsieur de Lombardy is not going to know what to make of you, mademoiselle. Nor, I fear, will France."

CHAPTER EIGHT

THE MESSENGER BOY returned just after the last of the crates had been unloaded. Morgane watched him give a note to Lavois, who frowned at it and then beckoned over the large man who'd stopped Sen when he'd attacked her. Over the intervening weeks all she'd learned about the man was that he was called Francois and that he had five children. That was presumably why he was so keen that the bonus be earned by her safe delivery.

It was a brief exchange, but they both glanced over at her during it, so she knew it was something to do with delivering her. When it was done, Lavois came over. "I've received word from Monsieur de Lombardy. He has secured a room at an inn on the north side of the city. I know it well, it's a respectable establishment. We're to meet him there."

He didn't look happy about it. "Don't you want to?"

"It's not that," he said after a pause. "I'd assumed he would want to meet you at the company office, near to the docks. It's closer and he's usually there to pay the crew."

"Maybe he doesn't want anyone to see me going to the company office."

Lavois nodded. "That is the only explanation that makes sense to me. I suppose he has the same concerns as mine regarding your safety. There are few noble ladies who have dealings in the company offices. You being escorted into a busy and well-respected inn would not be of note, I suppose." He rubbed his chin. "I wonder if the fact that it's a coaching inn is another reason. Perhaps he has arranged swift transportation to your family." He shrugged. "It matters not. What's important is that he knows you're here and that all is well. I've asked Francois to come with us."

"Why?"

"He's big enough to deter anyone from interfering with us."

"Are you expecting trouble?"

He smiled. "Not really, but I am a cautious man. Besides, he can carry your trunk. Are you sure you only want to take the one?"

She nodded. "You have the other. They just weren't packed very well before, that's all."

"Thank you, I'll put that to good use. We'll find a fiacre on the street behind the warehouse over there. It's the main route into the centre. Are you ready to leave?"

After taking one last look at the deck, she nodded and gave him the key to his cabin. "Thank you for giving me your cabin for the journey. It did help."

He smiled. "It was my pleasure, and the least I could do, mademoiselle. We'll fetch your trunk and be on our way."

Morgane staggered the moment they left the gangplank and Captain Lavois supported her at the elbow with a gentle chuckle. "Takes a while to find one's land legs sometimes," he said with a smile.

He seemed fine, but to her it felt like they were in open sea, even though they were standing on the dock. She was expecting it; it always happened after a long stretch without layover, but the severity of it made her pause. It wasn't a good time to be wobbly on her feet. She needed to be ready for anything.

"By the time you reach your parents you'll be fine," the captain continued, steering her through the crowded dockside with Francois behind them.

Lavois seemed confident enough, striding onwards to cut a swathe through the sea of dock workers and seafarers both leaving and returning to their ships. It was noisy and chaotic, and she felt horribly unsure of herself. It wasn't just the sense of the land rolling beneath her, it was the fact she was in a dress and not amongst her crew. When *The Vengeance* moored up, it was always a big group of them that disembarked together, moving like a school of sharks. Most would go straight to Taverners, and she'd end up with either Anna-Marie or Jacques, depending on the captain's mood.

She still thought of her as her mother, even all these weeks later, even after hours and hours of stewing about it all. The mother she was on her way to meet now was nothing more than a nebulous concept, like an island she'd heard of but never visited.

The way the men stared at her as they passed, now unsettlingly close instead of being viewed at a distance from the ship, pressed in on her awareness. She reached into the side slit of her dress, through to the large pocket beneath so she could push it aside and feel for one of the pistols strapped to her thigh. She wished she'd stood her ground and worn them openly. Then everyone would know not to try anything.

But the further they walked, the more she realised they were staring because she was a novelty, rather than the way the men in Taverners looked at the women they paid for sex. She noted how few women there were – or at least women wearing dresses. Perhaps there were more here than she realised, dressed as she once did and hiding their gender, but something told her that wasn't the case. There were many in her old life, amongst the dock workers and the crews that came into Kingston Harbour. It was only the painted women in Taverners who wore dresses, the ones who earned coin for lying with men, and none of them were as fancy as the one she wore now.

Like flotsam after a wreck, a memory surfaced of when she was really small and had believed that the women in Taverners earned their coin by allowing someone to literally sleep next to them for an hour or so. The night after they'd sailed from port – after this conundrum had been stewing for some time – she mentioned over dinner that she didn't understand the appeal of paying for having a nap with a woman. *The Vengeance*'s crew had fallen about laughing, even Plague Arse Pierre had laughed until he'd cried, a first for him. Once they'd settled, they were more than happy to explain it all to her, but they'd ribbed her for the misunderstanding for years after that.

They were soon through the crowded quayside and then, after crossing a cobbled street that was strange to walk on, it was less crowded with people. Lavois led her and Francois past a couple of stone buildings, much more imposing and solid than any she'd seen before, to turn into a quiet side street.

With the sound of the crowded quayside behind them, Morgane became aware of a new set of sounds ahead, those of horses' hooves and cartwheels clattering down the thoroughfare that ran perpendicular to the one they walked down now. The side street was quieter, and darker, and even though there were far fewer people, she felt less safe somehow.

It felt like they were being watched. She scanned the windows and doorways of the buildings on either side of the street but saw no one lurking. A glance behind her revealed only Francois close behind her and the captain, rosy cheeked from carrying her trunk.

At least Lavois and Francois were armed, should her gut prove to be right. And as long as they were as sharp as she was, their defence would give her time to draw and fire her pistols, and unsheathe her sword after a few moments of fumbling.

"We will be able to hail a fiacre in that road up ahead," Lavois said, as if he sensed her tension. "Not far now. It's rather different here, no?"

She nodded, letting him believe that her nervousness was wholly due to the strange surroundings, and not just part of it. "What is a fiacre?"

"A small carriage drawn by a horse. Much faster and more comfortable than walking."

He seemed quite relaxed, but her hackles were up, and she hated how it made her long for Anna-Marie and Jacques and the life she'd abandoned. What a stupid, stupid choice she'd made! Why had she thought it was a good idea to come to such a strange place, alone, with no one there to look out for her?

Beneath the fear was an anger at herself for being so afraid. She'd thought she was brave, in her old life, almost fearless when it came to everything except Anna-Marie. But now came the uncomfortable realisation that such confidence only came from being constantly guarded by those stronger and more ruthless than she. Soon Captain Lavois would be delivering her into the care of a complete stranger, and she found herself dreading it. Now she had to be truly brave and depend upon her own skills without hiding behind the reputation of her guardians. In France, she was just a woman, not the daughter of a feared pirate. What would stop anyone who wanted to kill her?

But then they emerged onto a much wider thoroughfare with pavements and horse-drawn carriages and the comfort of the autumnal sunshine made her tension fade a little. She was just being silly. Another glance behind her confirmed how it had been her head playing tricks on her. Only Francois was there, looking slightly more bad-tempered than before. Why would anyone want to harm her here, when she was just a woman, and not a pirate? Perhaps there could be safety in that.

Lavois stopped at the edge of the pavement and held up a hand as he faced towards one of the approaching carriages. There were several coming and she wondered why the driver would stop for him. But then she saw another man further down the street do the same as Lavois, and the carriage paused. There was a brief exchange between the man and the driver who then gave a nod and the man climbed inside.

It seemed to irritate Lavois and he scowled as the carriage passed them. Another was not far behind, however, drawn by a dark brown horse controlled by a driver who sat in the open in front of the enclosed compartment for passengers. This one clattered to a stop next to them and she couldn't help but draw back from the strange contraption.

"I'll ride with you, mademoiselle," Lavois said kindly. "There's no need to be afraid." He let go of her arm to speak with the driver, another brief exchange ending with a nod and Lavois turning to Francois. "Put the trunk inside, I'll rest my feet on it," he said.

Francois did as he was asked and stepped back. There was only enough room for two passengers, and she was glad Lavois would be sharing the ride with her instead of Francois. The captain offered his hand and helped her inside the cramped compartment which rocked in a strangely reassuring manner as she did so. As she wrestled her skirts – and the weaponry hidden beneath them – into a state which allowed her to sit, she assumed that the captain would go around and climb in through the opposite door.

Just as she'd managed to get comfortable, there was the

unmistakeable soft thud and immediate 'ooof!' of someone being punched in the stomach, a sound she'd heard many times over the years, and had caused on more than a few occasions herself. She turned in time to see Francois stepping back from the captain, who was crumpling to the ground. He looked up at her, an expression of grim determination on his face, and wrapped both hands around the door frame to haul himself up into the carriage.

She had no idea why he'd struck the captain, but given that the man now lying on the pavement was the only one who'd shown her any kindness on the ship, and the one now about to climb inside the small carriage with her had struck him down, Morgane made a swift decision. She twisted around to face him, leaned back and kicked at his chest with both booted feet as hard as she could. He clearly hadn't expected that, and it sent him stumbling to slam his back against the wall of the building behind him.

Now he looked angry. She fumbled with the handle on the opposite side of the carriage, managing to open it as she felt the carriage rock from Francois jumping back up onto the step to climb inside behind her. Without looking back, she pushed the door open and jumped out onto the street.

A loud shout to her left and the loud clattering of horses' hooves made her leap out of the way of another carriage which had been driving around the parked one she'd just escaped, only to find herself in the path of a fiacre coming the other way.

She dashed forwards, barely making it to the opposite pavement in time, and risked a glance back. Francois was waiting for the carriages that had almost crashed into her to pass and Lavois was nowhere in sight, probably still lying where he'd fallen.

Francois' eyes were fixed on her and she knew he was going to come after her, so she ran, heading down the first side street to get out of his line of sight as quickly as possible, cursing her decision to sew the gold into her clothes. She gathered up the skirts in her arms and hitched them up above her knees in an effort to redistribute the weight and stop them tangling around her ankles as she ran. At least she was wearing her boots underneath; if she'd worn the slippers that had been sent with the dress she'd probably have been caught by now.

It was a short street that emerged into a huge square filled with stalls and people, a market bigger than any she'd ever seen before. There were suddenly lots of directions available and lots of hiding places, so she sprinted as fast as she could down one of the rows and then darted to the right and slowed down, dropping the skirts to let them hang normally, hoping that she would be less noticeable if she moved like the rest of the market patrons.

It soon dawned on her that she still stuck out like a badly sanded hull repair. All of the people doing their shopping wore linen and wool, with practical designs and more muted colours than the deep blue silk of her dress. Many carried baskets and wore hats, neither of which she had. And they were staring at her, like she was a parrot among geese, all brightly coloured and out of place.

She hurried along, trying to find a way out of the square as quickly as she could, panicking about where to go. She remembered Jacques' silk purse which was tucked deep in one of the pockets underneath her dress and his words about the blue rose couturiers. Perhaps they had an atelier in Nantes.

Frantically she searched for a stall selling fabric, but the goods were all meat and other foodstuffs. She reached the end of the row only to see a man selling at one of the stalls, pointing at her, with Francois standing next to him. Their eyes met and she started to run, crashing into a woman with a large basket who'd stopped behind her to buy some eggs.

The shopper stumbled back into another who fell forwards onto the goods and in moments there were smashed eggs and angry shouts. Morgane managed to keep her footing and hitched her skirts up once more to run as fast as she could, darting around the maddeningly slow shoppers as Francois closed the gap between them.

She wanted to stop and fight, rather than run, but in a new city with no one to back her up it felt like too great a risk. What if she killed him? Would she be hanged for that as well as for piracy? Shit and blood, why had she packed the pardon in the chest? Idiot!

Reaching the end of the row, she saw a way out of the square between two large buildings and headed towards it, not caring where she was going, only that she was getting away from Francois. Why was he doing this? They all wanted to be paid that bonus. Had someone else offered him more money to kill her instead? Or stop her from reaching her mother?

A man dressed in black, armed with a sword and pistol, stepped into her path ahead, interrupting her frantic speculation. He wore high bucket boots and a black capelet tied across his chest so only one shoulder and arm were covered by it. He had a moustache and tiny beard and a hat with a ridiculous plume of red feathers erupting from it. There was a flash of gold sparkling on his chest – a brooch perhaps – and he was looking right at her. She slowed, trying to determine if he was a threat, someone in league with Francois. When he put his hand on his sword, she stopped.

"Pardon me, mademoiselle, but have you recently arrived in port on the *Coup de Maître*?"

"Yes! Did Monsieur de Lombardy send you?"

He smiled. "Yes, I am to escort you to him. His crew have proven untrustworthy, it seems."

She glanced back at Francois who had only just noticed the man. "I think he wants to kill me."

The man drew his sword. "I'll dissuade him, mademoiselle."

Happy enough to have an ally, she turned to face Francois square on, reaching through the side slits in the skirts to try and pluck out her pistols from all the fabric. The man in black chuckled and stepped in front of her. "Stand back, mademoiselle, lest you be hurt. Monsieur de Lombardy will not be pleased if you are injured."

Not a little insulted by his assumption that she couldn't handle herself in a fight, she moved to one side so she could see past him. To her surprise, Francois had stopped, and his hands were patting the air as if to placate his new opponent.

"Just a misunderstanding, monsieur!" Francois said as a crowd gathered, watching in the hope of a spectacle. "I'll... I'll be on my way!"

"You poxy coward!" Morgane shouted at him, adding a gob of spit in his direction to make sure he knew just how little she thought of him, and several in the crowd gasped.

Francois' jaw clenched, along with his fists, too. The man in black took another step towards him and flipped back the cloak to reveal a blood red satin lining. When he slashed at the air a couple of times, as if he were warming up his sword arm, Francois looked at him again and stepped back. "I'll be on my way now, monsieur. Good day to you," he said and turned to hurry off back into the market throngs.

Her defender sheathed his sword before she'd managed to even free her pistols. Stupid dress! He waved dismissively at the crowd who seemed to be disappointed by the peaceful outcome and began to disperse.

The man returned to her. "Shall we go, mademoiselle?" He offered his arm, but she'd found her land legs now and just ignored it. He smiled. "Come now, I've just saved your life, surely you can be courteous with me?"

Confused, she frowned at him. "I can walk fine."

"Please, mademoiselle, allow me to escort you properly, as

a gentleman. Monsieur de Lombardy would want nothing less."

It was a manners thing, then? She hadn't realised. She didn't really want to take his arm, not knowing him, but she was lost in a foreign city, and she didn't want to look any more out of place than she already did. So, she slipped her hand into the crook of his arm and they walked out of the market together, as she tried desperately to detangle one of the pistols from its fabric prison.

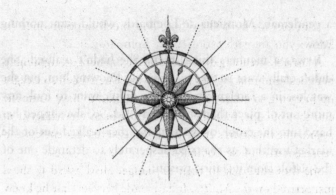

CHAPTER NINE

MORGANE WAS RELIEVED to leave the marketplace behind, and with it, the people who'd witnessed the chase and had another reason to stare at her. As they walked down the narrow street that connected to another, much wider thoroughfare, she risked a couple of glances at the man whose arm kept her close to his side.

He was very handsome. And so... clean. His facial hair was neat and his cheeks were smooth and not covered in the perennial grime that all of the men she'd met had been smeared in. But she didn't trust him. If she could just get her damn pistol out, they could have a conversation she'd have more faith in.

"Oh, my trunk!" She stopped, suddenly remembering that she'd left it behind, the pardon inside it. "It's still in the carriage. We need to go back!"

He gently, firmly encouraged her to start walking again, in the opposite direction. "The trunk can be sent on, mademoiselle. Pay it no mind."

"But what about Captain Lavois? I want to make sure he is well. And he'll be worried about me."

"I'm certain he will be fine, and much happier once he knows you are with Monsieur de Lombardy, no?"

A horrible creeping dread bloomed from her gut, tightening her chest and making her palms sweat. She'd been so caught up in trying to evade Francois, and so glad to have someone end that pursuit, that she hadn't really been very diligent in appraising this man's credentials. At least his credentials as a representative of de Lombardy.

She thought back to their exchange. He'd asked if she'd just arrived on the *Maître*. It had made her feel that he knew who she was – at least as much as one sent by Monsieur de Lombardy would have told an employee. But *he* hadn't mentioned de Lombardy's name, had he? She had asked if he'd been sent by him…

Shit.

She had no idea who he was, and felt there was no point asking, as it would be just a name to her – false or true, it would not confirm his motivations.

All she knew was that he'd been looking for a woman who'd recently disembarked from the *Maître*. She'd assumed only Monsieur de Lombardy knew of her arrival, but what if others had been waiting for her, too? Others not in the employ of her mother, or of her father's company? She had no idea why that would be so, but once the notion had taken hold, it was impossible to ignore.

As the end of the street approached, she frantically tried to think of a way to work out whether he was going to take her to de Lombardy or not. That was the only thing she knew had to happen, as without de Lombardy there was no easy way for her to find her mother. But she knew so little of the man, and indeed, the subtleties of the situation she was in, that she couldn't see a way to test her escort. Then she realised she'd been overthinking it all.

"Are we going to find another fiacre?"

"Yes. One that your pursuer has not had an opportunity to commandeer."

"And then we'll be going straight to Monsieur de Lombardy's country house, as planned?"

He looked at her and smiled. "Indeed, mademoiselle, as planned. You will simply be arriving in a different carriage, under my protection, that's all."

That wasn't the plan, and he should have known it if he'd been sent by Monsieur de Lombardy. And even if he had, why hadn't he just collected her from the ship? If de Lombardy had a man like this in his employ, and was genuinely concerned about getting her across town to him in one piece, why send her with a ship's captain? This man had no intention of taking her to de Lombardy, and she didn't want to discover what his actual plan was either.

He was clearly a capable swordsman, and strong, too, and she needed to incapacitate him as swiftly and efficiently as possible. The bloody pistol was impossible to free without lifting the dress skirts. She needed an alternative solution. "Could we stop for a moment? I... have a stone in my shoe."

He stopped, and as she hoped, he released her hand. She reached down as if to lift her hem, taking the opportunity to make sure her feet were best placed for stability. At the last moment she decided against getting her dagger from her boot, for fear he would notice and disarm her with a simple kick, instead balling her right fist and then swinging upwards to punch him in the groin as hard as she could.

He cried out and doubled over, unable to stop himself staggering back. Yet again, she mentally thanked Jacques for that trick, one he'd taught her after some unwanted attention in Taverners. He'd tried to explain how much it hurt, but struggled to find the words for it. "Just know that there is no pain like it, and that it lasts. I've seen many a man throw up afterwards, some nearly faint. Get them square on the balls with your knee, or your fist if you have to, and they'll be too busy trying to stay conscious to worry about catching you. And remember, thumb on the outside if you're punching."

Morgane hitched up her laden skirts once again and sprinted away, heading for the street they'd been walking towards in the hope that she could hail her own carriage and be away before the man in black was able to stand upright again.

When she reached the larger thoroughfare, she risked a glance back, just to check if her strike had been as painful as Jacques had claimed it would be. To her horror, she saw two new men, dressed in black just as her escort had been, stepping out from shadowy doorways and running past their presumed colleague – who was still doubled over. She hadn't seen them as they'd walked past, and it only confirmed that she'd been right to do what she had. Either way, there was only one thing to do now: get to a carriage before they got to her.

It didn't take long for her to realise that her plan was fundamentally flawed. To hail a carriage required getting the driver's attention and then waiting for the fiacre to stop. Her pursuers were closing the gap, and would easily reach her if she stopped, even for a moment. She ditched the plan and crossed the street instead, dodging fiacres and heavily laden carts to reach the other side and dash down another side street.

Of course, the plan to continue running was fundamentally flawed, too. She had no way to find the inn she was supposed to go to with Lavois and she didn't dare go back to either the fiacre or the ship, given that Francois could be there. She wasn't even sure if she could find her way back to either of them now anyway.

Another glance over her shoulder, and then she stumbled over something in her path, almost sending her sprawling. It was a heavy pan with a few coins inside that were scattered across the pavement and into the road. She hadn't even noticed the beggar, a woman with wrinkled skin, greasy hair and a ragged dress. "Sorry!" Morgane called back to her, feeling bad that the poor woman's coins were rolling all over the place because of her clumsiness.

She needed somewhere to hide until her pursuers gave up, and then when night fell, she could find the Four Chains offices and ask for de Lombardy there. Yes, that was a better plan.

A quick look over her shoulder told her that the hiding place couldn't be through one of the doorways she was running past, as her pursuers would see where she had entered. So she pressed on, lungs starting to burn a little now, and realised she was somehow heading towards the docks once more.

There was no option but to carry on, and when she reached the end of the street she turned left immediately. She was at a different point on the river, still part of the sprawling dockside area but thankfully nowhere near the *Maître*.

Panting, she scoured the dockside for a hiding place. There were many for a child playing hide and seek, but not for a woman in a stupidly impractical and brightly coloured dress. There were so many people on the dockside that even if she did pick a spot, undoubtedly someone would give her location away. So she looked at the buildings that lined the dockside instead, thinking that if she could just slip in through an open doorway, maybe her pursuers would run past.

And then she spotted something that made her heart leap: the Four Chains Trading Company logo, painted on a sign that stuck out from the building on an iron bracket. It was a big stone building with huge doors that were open. Perhaps Monsieur de Lombardy's office was inside!

Without a moment's hesitation she bolted through the

opening only to find herself in a large warehouse. There was nothing that looked like an office in there – something she'd decided must be a bit like a captain's cabin in a ship – but there were hundreds of excellent hiding places.

Bundles and bales, boxes and crates, jars and sacks piled high filled the space. She scrambled over the top of a pile of stuffed hessian sacks and dropped into the space behind them, crouching low to keep out of sight from the doorway. There was a nook between a stack of boxes and some bales of something wrapped in a coarse fabric and secured with thin rope, so she squeezed in there and tried to catch her breath without panting loudly.

The sound of footsteps by the doorway made her hold her breath.

"Merde, this is heavy!"

She smirked. It was only a man bringing in something else to be stored, probably just unloaded from one of the moored ships.

"Hey!" a second man's voice shouted from outside. "Did you see that woman run in there?"

Her heart shuddered in her chest.

"No," the man inside shouted back. "Are you fooling me again?"

"No," the other man said, and by the sound of it he'd come inside the warehouse. They were both just a few yards away with only the pile of sacks between them. "I just saw this blonde-haired woman in a blue dress run inside. She looked like a bloody noble." After a pause, he shouted, "Madame, you're trespassing! Only dockworkers and company staff are allowed in here."

She retreated further into the nook, tucking her knees as close to her chest as she could. The pistols and her sword were digging into her hips so uncomfortably, but she couldn't do anything about it.

"Madame, I dunno what you're up to, but better for you to show yourself now and be on your way."

Morgane chewed her lip.

"Why would a noblewoman come in here?" the first dockman asked.

"I dunno, but she was runnin' like the hounds of hell were at her heels. Madame!" he shouted again. "If you're in some sort of trouble, come out and perhaps we can help!"

"Maybe she's a thief."

"Don't be daft." Another pause and then a hushed conversation between the two of them that she couldn't hear well enough to understand.

"Hey!" the one who'd seen her was now shouting out of the warehouse doors by the sound of it. "Put that down and come and help me search the warehouse. We've got a trespasser!"

"Damn it," she muttered beneath her breath. They'd find her in no time! She had to move and hope she could slip back out again while they were searching elsewhere.

More footsteps and then she could hear them spreading out and starting to climb crates to look inside other nooks. Knowing there was no good time to move – it was too hard to tell whether any of them were close enough to see down into the gap she'd found – she shuffled out of her hidden nook on her backside and began to climb some stacked crates to get out. She figured it was less risky than clambering back over the hessian sacks and dropping right into the space near the entrance.

She managed to climb over the bales and onto a crate behind them. She was now closer to the wall than the open area by the doors and decided to keep heading in that direction in the hope that she could move around the edge to the doorway while they searched.

As she slowly picked her way across more goods, as silently

as she could, she became aware of new footfalls by the doorway.

"Can I help you?" one of the dockworkers called. So it wasn't one of their colleagues. Morgane hunkered down again, listening.

"We're looking for a woman in a blue dress. We heard you call your colleague in to help look for her. Perhaps we can assist you."

Morgane's throat closed up. It must be one of her pursuers. "Who are you?"

Before the answer came, she suddenly became aware of a person behind her. As she turned to look over her shoulder, there was a cry of, "Found her!" coming from high up. One of the dockworkers had climbed the highest stack of big crates on her side of the warehouse, enabling him to spot her. And worse than that, he was pointing right at her.

She didn't have time to think, she just climbed up the pile of sacks to her left in the hope that she'd be able to go over the top of them and get out of his line of sight quickly enough to throw them off her trail. But even as she scrabbled up the precarious obstacle, she knew how unlikely it was she'd be able to get out of the warehouse without being grabbed by one of the many men now keen to apprehend her.

Her efforts were in vain as one of the dockworkers vaulted over a barrel to her right to grab her ankle and pull her down to him. With nothing to hold on to without risking crushing them both with the contents of the sacks, she didn't resist, instead sliding down to him so she was better placed to elbow him in the stomach. But she swiftly changed her mind, deciding as she reached the bottom of the pile that it would actually be better to be caught by the dockworkers than the men who'd chased her. Besides, she was dressed like a fancy lady, not a pirate! Perhaps she could use it to her advantage.

"Please, help me," she said, doing all she could to appear

like a helpless, unarmed woman. "Those men are trying to kidnap me!"

The man, who was now holding her arm, was as stout as a windlass and she felt she'd made the right call when she saw his grim expression soften a little. As much as the dress and the male attention it had garnered had been annoying her, it now felt like a magnificent disguise.

"Let's get this sorted out," he said to her and guided her back towards the open area near the doors.

This time she had help as she climbed and even though she didn't need it, she accepted it, nonetheless. Better to appear to need the help if this was the approach she was going to take.

In moments they were all gathered in an uneasy group near the doorway, including the two men in their black garb, hands on their swords and looking menacing. The man who'd found her was joined by one of his colleagues, standing on either side of her. The third dockworker, older and with the air of authority to him, stood between them and the pursuers, hands on hips, frowning.

"They tried to kidnap me," she said to him. "I'm sorry I trespassed, but I had to get away from them!"

The boss frowned at her pursuers. They were both just as clean and well turned out as the man who'd lured her from the marketplace. They wore exactly the same clothes, even down to the gold brooch on their baldricks, like a uniform. They worked for someone?

"Lies," one of them replied, whose ash-blond hair was tied back in a neat ponytail. "She stole from her husband and was discovered."

"I'm not married!" she half-laughed at the absurdity of the lie. "Please, believe me. I was being escorted by Captain Lavois to Monsieur de Lombardy and we were attacked. Please take me to de Lombardy, he knows the truth!"

"I know Lavois," the dockworker on her left piped up. "He arrived on the *Maître* this morning. There was a fancy lady with him apparently."

"Yes, that was me. I was a passenger, in his care!" Morgane said in relief.

"You lying bitch!" Ash-blond snarled, hand going to the hilt of his sword. "You're a thief and you'll answer for your crimes!"

"Now, now!" The boss held up his hands, staring at the man until he took his hand off his sword. He rubbed the stubble on his chin, looking from the two men to her and then back again. "I don't want to get involved. Monsieur de Lombardy can deal with this."

"Don't be a fool, she's tricking you!"

"We'll take her off your hands and then you can just get on with your day," the other pursuer added.

"His office isn't far," the boss said loudly, cutting off any further protestations. He pointed at his colleagues. "Stay here with her." Then he pointed at her pursuers. "Wait here if you wish, but you're in a Four Chains Trading Company warehouse, and Monsieur de Lombardy has final say on what happens here, not you."

He left at a swift pace, her uniformed pursuers watching him leave as the two dockworkers looked at each other and then, after a silent agreement between them, took a couple of steps forwards to place themselves in front of her. They were going to protect her against the two pursuers! Was it really that easy to make men defend her? They didn't know her, nor did they have any loyalty to her, so why do this? Was it simply because the dress made them perceive her as a helpless woman? She'd been in several situations – usually in Taverners – where nearby members of the crew stepped in to protect her, but they all did that for each other. She herself had gathered around Bull and Dill on several occasions as those two were most likely to get into some sort of fight, the former because he was an aggressive arse and the latter because she was tiny, and people constantly underestimated her. Getting strangers to behave like this was something she'd never done before, and it made her feel almost giddy with some undefined power.

When the boss was out of sight, the two pursuers turned back to look at her, and take in the new defensive positions of the dockworkers. They were all going to fight, she knew it, without even being consciously aware of the subtle signals: the way they were adjusting their stances, the way they stared at each other. She knew this feeling, this tight, crackling moment just before violence exploded and she was ready for it, taking a couple of steps back herself to make the most of her defenders' position to give her enough time to extract her sword from the voluminous skirts of her dress. She had the feeling the dockworkers were going to be no match for these professional kidnappers and she was going to have to fight her way out of this. Pistols would be too loud, bringing more people here than she wanted to get involved.

She couldn't help but smile to herself; finally, she would be able to fight and put an end to this without crowds of people nearby to worry about. She was confident the men would underestimate her, even when they noticed she was armed, and she knew how to capitalise upon that. As the kidnappers reached for their swords, and the dockworkers launched themselves towards them in an effort to take them down before the weaponry tipped the balance against them, Morgane freed her own sword from its hidden scabbard and readied herself for the fight ahead.

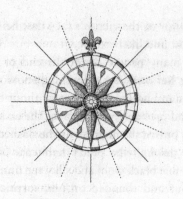

CHAPTER TEN

As THE FOUR men wrestled and punched each other, Morgane slowly made her way around the back of the fight, so she was closer to the exit if things went horribly wrong. She just had time to get behind the kidnappers when their brief, ugly fighting resolved itself faster than she'd hoped.

One of the kidnappers had been dropped by a solid gut punch that had winded him badly, leaving his opponent free to give him a kick to the head that knocked him out. At the same time the other pair had exchanged a couple of blows before the dockworker was taken down by a brutal uppercut to his jaw which had sent him toppling backwards to land heavily. The crack of his head against the hard earthen floor followed that of the punch. He was clearly out of the fight.

The remaining dockworker then launched himself at his friend's attacker, but by the time he reached him, the kidnapper had drawn his sword and merely needed to thrust it towards the man to run him through.

The dockworker slid off the metal and crumpled to the floor. She knew by the position of the blade and the immediate pallor of the victim's face that he was definitely out of the fight and likely to die.

She'd seen many people die at the end of swords, on a few occasions her own, but something about this made her pause. This man had defended her, without hesitation nor obligation, and probably wouldn't see the end of this day. A flash of anger pulsed through her as she slashed at his killer's back, slicing through the pretty half cape and sending a swathe of the fine black wool and silky red lining to the floor.

He cried out and rounded on her, surprised to see her armed, since he'd been so fixated on his other opponents. She should have run him through, but the anger had got to her and now he was angry, too. But he was bleeding, and that was as good a start as any.

"Are you sure you know how to use that sword, my dear?"

The voice was horribly familiar and came from behind her. Taking care to back away from her opponent at an angle so she could switch her attention between him and the new arrival quickly enough to keep herself safe, she confirmed the identity of the speaker.

"Oh, hello, Ball-ache," she said to the man she'd punched in the groin. "Back for more, are you?"

He laughed, but there was no mirth in it.

Her opponent, now on her right and moving, too, in order to force her to keep her back to the man in the doorway, lunged for her. He was fast, and her parry was only just sufficient to deflect the blade from stabbing her in the stomach.

"Unharmed, you fool!" Ball-ache yelled from the doorway, and she grinned.

"Oh, that must be so annoying for you," she said to her opponent. "I'd wager that cut on your back is really stinging by now."

The man's face twisted with frustration, but he resisted

the urge to strike at her, instead moving more to try to force her to turn her back to at least one of them.

She ended up with the pile of stuffed sacks behind her back and stayed there, increasingly worried about the way Ball-ache was steadily coming towards her and how hard it was to keep a close eye on both of them at the same time now. She had to take at least one of them down to have any hope of escape, so she attacked the injured one, pressing forward with a couple of swift lunges. He parried them elegantly and she was beginning to fear that he was much more skilled than she was.

A movement by the doorway stole her attention, just long enough to see a woman shuffle inside quietly. She wore a ragged dress, and was carrying a small pan, one that Morgane remembered tripping over just a few minutes before reaching the warehouse. Had the beggar woman followed her? Well, if she had come for compensation she'd have to wait.

The injured swordsman was closing in and stole her attention away from the woman, but she didn't let him intimidate her into moving towards Ball-ache, who still seemed unaware of the vagrant. Instead Morgane attacked aggressively, forcing him to be defensive rather than risk hurting her. The fact that he wasn't allowed to harm her was the best advantage she had, allowing her to keep pushing back against his efforts to force her into Ball-ache's reach.

A loud clang rang out from Ball-ache's direction, and she glanced over to see the man pitching forwards, the woman behind him completing her swing with the heavy pan. She'd struck him over the head!

A gasp from her attacker made her realise he'd been just as distracted as her – but seeing his colleague laid flat was a far more shocking development for him and it gave her the opening she needed. She slashed at his wrist, making him drop his sword, and followed up with a sharp stab to his gut.

He doubled over, crying out in pain and she darted forward to bring her knee up into his face. She felt the satisfying crunch of his nose breaking on her kneecap and then shoved him away from her.

As he writhed in pain, she wiped her blade clean on the scrap of cloak fabric that she'd sliced away earlier and hurried over to Ball-ache, the beggar woman still standing over him with a grin on her face.

"Thank you!" she said. She pinched his ear lobe to see if he really was unconscious and then knelt to cut away the purse she spotted hanging from his belt and gave it to the woman. "For spilling your coins earlier," she added.

The old woman gave her a gap-toothed grin and Morgane peered down to inspect that flash of gold she'd seen on all the kidnappers. The brooch design was of a stylised eagle, wings open, and made of solid gold by the look of it. She was just reaching to pull it free when an almighty pain erupted from the back of her head, accompanied by the same loud clang she'd heard before, and everything imploded into darkness.

FOR A FEW moments, Morgane thought she was on *The Vengeance*, hungover. She had a headache and was lying on something rocking from side to side, so it was an easy mistake to make. But then she remembered where the headache had come from and jolted into full consciousness.

The first thing she realised was that she couldn't actually move properly. Her hands were tied behind her back, and her ankles were tied, too. The second thing was that she appeared to be in some sort of large sack, judging by the feel of the fabric and the way it enclosed her completely. Only a little bit of light penetrated the dense weave of the fabric, but she could breathe at least. Then she realised she must be in a cart, not a ship, as the sound of horse hooves gently thumping along penetrated the fog of her headache. There were other things in the cart, too – hopefully just goods and not other people – and it felt like she was half buried by them.

"Shit and blood," she muttered to herself. What a bloody mess she was in. She felt stupid, and angry with herself as a result. She had no idea who was driving the cart, where they were and why they'd taken her, but she did know that whenever they stopped, she needed to be ready.

There was a moment of panic, too, when the fear surged up like a rogue wave on the ocean, so she breathed in deeply, let it out, and then took stock. She had a cracking headache, but she was awake. She was tied, but not by someone who knew what they were doing by the feel of the ropes and how much she could move. She was still fully clothed, and she could feel one of the pistols digging into her leg painfully, so whoever had taken her hadn't checked how many weapons she'd hidden on her person.

With her hands tied and the awkward, uncomfortable position she was in, it was difficult but not impossible to get her fingertips into the top of her right boot and then contort herself enough to reach down between the leather and her leg to find the small knife still in place in its hidden scabbard. Taking her time to keep her movements small, just in case someone was keeping an eye on the sack, she pulled it free and turned it around in her palm to carefully slice the binding around her wrist.

Once her hands were free, she felt much better. It was a trivial thing to slice through the rope around her ankles and then she stopped, holding the knife tight, trying to decide whether it was better to cut the sack open and just jump out and make a run for it, or to wait until they arrived and spring a surprise attack on whoever opened it.

There were advantages to both, and risks. Her pounding head didn't help. She gingerly probed the back of her skull with her fingertips and found an egg-sized lump there. If that old bitch who'd walloped her opened the sack, she'd get a fierce greeting, no mistake.

Morgane comforted herself with imagining her revenge and then realised there was no guarantee the cart driver was the one who'd hit her. For all she knew, it could be Ball-ache or one of his friends. Or Francois. Why were so many bloody people out to get her? She'd only just arrived, so it wasn't as if anyone could know who she was or have any interest in her life. She hadn't had a chance to upset anyone, nor even commit the smallest of crimes. She'd been so worried about someone finding out she'd been a pirate and being hauled in by the local governor – or whoever they had in French cities – when, in fact, that was turning out to be the least of her problems. What did they all want? The only things she could be certain of was that she hated France, and that she bitterly regretted leaving *The Vengeance*.

That deepening pit of regret sucked her inwards as she thought of Jacques and how good a captain he would be and how stupid she'd been to leave that life behind. Why hadn't she realised that it was the best place to be after Anna-Marie's death? She knew how everything worked at sea, she'd been among friends, rich, and only a day out from port and all the freedom that being without Anna-Marie would have given her – and yet somehow she'd thought it was a good idea to just strike out into the unknown with complete strangers, strangers who hated her and wished her ill. All she wanted in that moment was to have Jacques put an arm around her shoulder and let her know it was all going to be fine, and then give her a flagon of bumbo and get absolutely shit-faced drunk.

She squeezed her eyes shut, trying to contain the waves of self-hate and the tears that threatened to follow them. Such a wretched feeling, regret, one that Anna-Marie had always seemed utterly immune to. And Morgane had never felt it so keenly before – probably because she'd never had many opportunities to really make decisions for herself while Anna-Marie had lived. And then the first time she could choose what she wanted to do, she ended up in a sack on the back of cart with a thumping headache. She was the worst bloody pirate in the world.

There was no way to tell how long she wallowed in despair, but when she started to really think about that last day on *The Vengeance*, and the decision she made to come to France, the memory of what she had actually wanted resurfaced. There was still her aunt's death to avenge and her real mother to rescue, and once the drive to achieve those surfaced, the regret faded. She had a mother – and a father, though that was much harder to imagine and could be tangled unpleasantly in her desire for vengeance – somewhere in this land, who'd been searching for her all her life. A woman who must have been devastated to have had her baby taken so young, who'd spent an unimaginable amount of gold using the Four Chains Trading Company to find her and get her back.

Morgane imagined the woman who'd packed those trunks, perhaps hiding what she was doing from her own husband, who chose those dresses for the daughter she knew was out there in the clutches of a sister-turned-pirate. The care she'd shown in sending them without knowing if they'd ever reach her. Had her mother been doing that all her life? Had those same trunks in years gone by contained other gifts and dresses of varying sizes?

Surely a woman who preserved such a sense of hope and longing, and did all she could to find her child, would be a loving mother? That was just as hard to imagine as having a father.

The last remnants of regret and the bitterness of self-loathing faded. She hadn't made a stupid decision, she'd merely hit some rocks on the way. How could she have known that such a shower of bastards would be waiting to kidnap her as soon as she made landfall? Besides, she'd escaped one, then a whole other group of them and whilst she still felt a bit stupid for being laid out by the old woman, it was a perfectly understandable mistake to have made, seeing as she'd just walloped Ball-ache after seeing her being pursued by them all. And even after that error, she was still armed, no longer restrained and on the brink of escape once more. She'd get away from the cart and whoever the driver was, make a run for it and… and work it out as she went along. She had gold, she had guns, and she could punch as good as anyone else. She'd find her mother somehow, and she would rescue her. She would have her vengeance, and all of this – the fear, the pain, the constant attempts to capture her – would be transmuted into mere tales to tell over a flagon by the fire.

The cart came to a stop and Morgane's fantasy evaporated as her ears strained for any clues. Now they were stationary, she could hear other noises, mostly the calling of birds that sounded different to the ones she was used to. They were definitely not in the town anymore. And it felt colder. Maybe the day was drawing to its close. She didn't want to be running around the countryside in the cold, but if night was indeed falling, it could at least give her cover if she decided to try to escape.

"Where is she?"

It was a man's voice, one she hadn't heard before, coming from a short distance ahead.

"In the cart. In one of the sacks." That was the old woman who'd knocked her out.

"What?!" He sounded angry.

"Don't you start," the old woman replied, calm and slightly amused by the sound of it. "You didn't tell me what a brute she is. Oh, looks all sweet and fancy she does, but she fights like she grew up in barracks, not a noble house."

"Is she hurt?"

"I had to give her a little bump on the noggin. Calm yourself! I had to – I watched her fight a man, someone in the pay of a noble by the look of him. Took him down she did, with a sword and then her knee. Cracked his nose over it, and looking as comfortable as a man beating a wife as she did it, too. I'm no fool. I gave her a tiny tap on the back of the head with my pan, just to make sure there were no dramas on the way. Can't say I was happy to, mind, she seemed decent enough to the likes of me. But needs must. I've not heard a peep from her the whole journey, but she lives, don't you fret."

Morgane's desire to stab her in the gut faded. The woman had been hired to bring her to this man – yet another idiot who wanted to derail her journey, but she'd soon show him how wrong he was – and had simply chosen the most efficient way to do it. In the old woman's place, she'd have done the same.

"In the pay of a noble? Was he liveried?"

"Not that I saw. There were three of them, all in the same black clothes but no coats of arms, and a couple of dockworkers fighting over her. I just let them get on with it and picked my moment. Left them all in the Four Chains Warehouse, I did. No one saw us get her out, no fuss, no witnesses. Now pay me my money and I'll be on my way. Don't want to be in these woods at night, and you don't either, if there's any sense to you."

"I have the coin to pay you as agreed. But I'll see her first, then settle our debt."

"As you wish, friend. But mark my words, you're buying more trouble than you think. Someone's got a mark on her, someone rich enough to pay for good fighting men, and rich enough not to care about upsetting the Four Chains Company. And before you ask, those men weren't employed by the Artois family. The dockworkers were, and they were doing all they could to stop her being taken by them. One of them lost their life for their trouble an' all."

There was a pause, perhaps while the man was seeing to his horse as it seemed like there was another, too, judging by the occasional snort and snuffle coming from the same direction. Morgane made sure her blade was in a good position, gripped in her right hand and hidden below her left arm which she held behind her, so they'd think she was still tied when they opened the sack. Mercifully she was lying on her left side, so striking would be easy if needed.

Heart pounding, she listened to the sound of boots tramping through leaves and felt the cart rock as the woman climbed down from her perch, too. Morgane squeezed her eyes shut and then tried to relax, to make it look like she was still unconscious. She wanted them to be surprised when she attacked.

"You open it," the old woman said. "I'm not going near her."

Morgane couldn't deny that the woman was a sensible one. The cart rocked again as the man climbed into the back section and made his way towards her. There was fumbling around the fabric above her head and then the light level increased, bringing with it a blast of fresh air.

"Mon Dieu, she's the image of her," the man whispered, close enough for her to hear, but probably not the old woman who was staying well back.

"See, she's fine. Now I'll take my coin and be on my way."

Morgane kept her eyes shut, even though it was so hard not to sneak a peek at the man. There was a brief movement above her and then the chink of a bag of coins being caught.

"What we agreed, along with a little more to be certain of your silence, especially when it comes to our mutual friend."

"Thank you. He won't hear about it from me, you can be certain of that. But he will find out, my friend. He always does."

Morgane lay as still as she could, listening to the sound of the woman walking away, then her clicking to move another horse on. The accompanying creaks suggested she was driving another cart away.

As Morgane listened, she had the intense feeling she was being watched. When the sack was pulled down over one of her shoulders, she couldn't stay still a moment longer and opened her eyes to see a fair-haired man, older than Jacques had been but still not too old. He cried out in surprise as she sprang to life, darting back instinctively as she sliced through the sack to swing the blade round and place it between them.

"Get away from me, you bastard!" she yelled, and he toppled onto his backside in shock and then fell off the back of the cart.

The old woman, now driving an empty cart of the same size as the one filled with goods that she'd arrived in, cackled loudly from the safety of a few yards away. "I told you she was trouble!" she called out. "Bon chance, mon ami!"

Morgane ignored her, making the most of her opportunity to get the rest of the sack off her and try to bring her left arm back to life which had been numbed by the position she'd been lying in.

They were in a dense forest, populated by trees that looked very different to any she'd seen, all a world away from the dense jungles she'd experienced, and then mostly from a shoreline. The birdsong was gentle in comparison with the hoots and constant din of the island jungles she'd foraged at the edges of. In every direction there was nothing but tall trunks and leaves in varying shades of red, copper and yellow. It was absolutely beautiful, but horribly disorienting.

By the time she'd freed herself and got a sense of her surroundings, the man had got back to his feet yet remained on the ground, backing off a few paces so they could see each other. He was well dressed and somewhat dishevelled, as if he'd been up all night, and looked rather distressed. His hands were high in the air, confusing her before she realised he was trying to show he was not a threat.

"Please, please, I intend you no harm!"

"You paid that old woman to kidnap me!"

"I paid her to get you out of Nantes as quickly and safely as possible!"

"By hitting me over the head and tying me up? By giving me no choice in the matter?"

"I know, I know this isn't the way it should have been done but I had no choice either. I knew you were in danger, and I didn't have time to prepare anything better. I only found out you were arriving two days ago! Mon Dieu, I've barely slept! Please believe me, I had no idea she was going to do it this way. I only want you to be safe, I swear!"

He seemed to be telling the truth, and it threw her. She'd assumed he'd had only the worst of intentions, and that she was going to have to injure him to make her escape. But now... now she wasn't sure what to do. Her left arm was tingling painfully, her head was pounding, she felt sick and a little lightheaded, too. She was fed up of other people deciding what to do with her, without asking her first, and none of it making any sense. She scowled at him as she made her way to the edge of the cart, positioning herself so that she could leap down onto him and fight him, if needs be.

"If I am to believe you, I need to know why you've done this. And make it good, otherwise I'll slice you open and leave you for the animals."

His eyes widened at the threat. They were a dark blue, not unlike her own. This was not a violent man, but she kept her knife ready, nonetheless.

"The answer is very simple, mademoiselle. I've been looking for you all of your life. I'm your father."

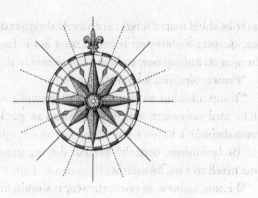

CHAPTER ELEVEN

IT WAS THE last thing she expected him to say, and it took a few moments for the words to really make sense, as if the sentiment was so far away from anything plausible that they almost sounded like a foreign language. When the meaning did finally sink in, that this man's claim made him the one who sent the *Maître*, Morgane gripped her knife tight and leaped off the back of the cart, slamming into him with enough force to knock him onto the ground again.

Winded and shocked at the distance she'd covered, he just lay there as she pinned his upper arms with her knees and held the knife to his throat.

"You sent the *Maître*?"

"Wha—" he coughed, blinking rapidly.

She pressed the blade into his flesh, just enough for him to feel its bite but not draw too much blood. "You sent the ship that killed Anna-Marie? The Scourge of the Sea, as you all call her? You did that?"

She needed to be sure she had the right man. He wasn't dressed well enough to be a comte, someone wealthy enough to be in velvets and silks, the sorts of clothes that some of the pirates she'd met in Taverners looted and paraded themselves in, like pigeons dressed as peacocks. But he'd just paid an old beggar to kidnap her, so he was probably in disguise.

"Answer me, you bastard!"

"I sent no ship to do anything!" he spluttered. "I don't have that sort of money. What I mean to say is… I am very wealthy, but I haven't any ships nor the funds to send one to do anything. Wait—" He cut off, as if something had occurred to him. "Anna-Marie is dead? Truly?"

She saw sadness in his eyes, which unsettled her. "Yes, she is, and by your hand! Who else but the owner of the fleet could send a ship and crew to hunt someone down and kill them?"

"But I am not the owner of any fleet. Please, tell me, is she dead?"

Morgane moved the blade away fractionally, confused, but still held it close enough to slit his throat if needs be. "You're not the Comte d'Artois?"

"No. Mon Dieu! I am not that despicable creature! Oh! You thought… no, no, you could not be more wrong!"

"Then who the bloody hell are you?"

"I am Jean-Baptiste Desjardins… errr, that is, I mean to say, I am… the Comte Jean-Baptiste Desjardins de Sauvineau."

"Bloody hell, that's a mouthful."

"Well, most people just call me the Comte de Sauvineau. Please could you get off me?"

She was surprised he hadn't even tried to throw her off him. She got to her feet, wrestling the dress and its layers back into place as he sat up. For a few moments he just sat there, picking leaves out of his short, light brown hair, looking rather shocked. "Why on earth would you think your father would kill your… mother?"

That pause was interesting. Did he actually know the truth? "Because I thought you were the Comte D'Artois."

He nodded slowly. "Whom you believed to be your father. I see the error."

"Are there bloody thousands of comtes in France then? Seems they're all I ever hear of."

"No, not thousands." He peered at her, eyes flicking to the knife she still held in front of her. "Are you not at all pleased to discover that the Comte d'Artois is not your father and that I indeed am?"

She snorted. "Bollocks you are," she said, backing off, glancing around her to get the lay of the land while he was still on his arse. Trees, bloody hundreds of them, as far as she could see in the dwindling light. "My father? That's just bollocks, that is."

His mouth dropped open and he looked away briefly, frowning. He got to his feet and brushed himself down. "That's… not the response I was hoping for."

She scowled back. "What did you expect? I don't know you. You've paid for me to be kidnapped—"

"Rescued!"

"*Kidnapped* from Nantes and then just announced that you're my father as if that's supposed to be some sort of, what? Justification?"

"I… thought it might make you happy to finally meet your father."

Morgane leaned against the cart, resting her aching head against one of its side boards, knife still firmly held in front of her. This wasn't what she'd had in mind either, but in all honesty, she hadn't really imagined meeting her father yet. It felt wrong, all of it, and her head was pounding worse than after three days at Taverners. There was a gentle touch on her arm, and she flinched back, bringing the dagger up. "Don't you touch me!"

The man leapt back, hands in the air again. "I'm sorry. Sorry. I merely…" He sighed heavily. "This isn't as I imagined it would be. I thought you'd be riding next to Nell, happy and..." He shook his head. "I'm a fool. Why would you believe me from my words alone?" He reached into his coat and pulled a small book from a pocket within. "I thought it may be difficult for you to believe. I cannot give any definite proof, of course, that is beyond my power. But I can prove that I knew your mother very well."

He handed the book to her, and she took it. Flipping through the pages she realised it was a sketch book, and it was old, judging by how worn and smooth the leather was on the outer binding.

There were dozens of sketches within, all of her aunt, but much younger. It was obviously Anna-Marie, but it was like looking at a dream of her, one in which she'd been a kind and happy young woman. There was none of the cruelty she knew in any of the expressions he'd captured – and captured well; if these were his drawings, he was a talented artist – and she looked younger, too.

She looked up from the pages to see him watching her, that misty-eyed hope all over his face again. "This ain't my mother," she said, handing it back to him.

His eyes widened. "You know she was your aunt?" he whispered.

"She told me just before she died."

He pressed the book to his chest, holding it over his heart. "So, it is true. Oh no... oh, Anna, no."

"Oh, spare your tears, you bastard, I know what you did. She loved you and you ploughed her sister. She blamed my mother, but I don't. If you'd kept your cock in your breeches, she wouldn't have turned into such an angry bitch."

"It's far more complicated than that," he said, tucking the sketchbook back into his jacket, as if to protect it from her anger.

Perhaps it was. She'd been so certain that the man who'd

betrayed Anna-Marie for her sister was the same man that owned the Four Chains Company. If that wasn't so, why the vendetta? How did it all fit together? But it didn't change the fact that this man, standing in front of her now, had broken her aunt's heart.

"No, it ain't complicated at all. She loved you. You got your end away with her sister. So, forgive me if I'm not weeping with joy over meeting you at last. You're just a man who couldn't control himself."

He blinked at her, varying emotions flickering across his face until one finally settled: pity. "I'm so sorry. I know what Anna-Marie became, and I imagine you've had a terrible life. And you are right, of course, I have a part to play in that."

His contrition caught her by surprise, but his pity angered her. "It was a wonderful life, in many ways, I'd have you know! I lived amongst the best people in the world!"

"They were pirates! Murderers!"

"They were the ones who taught me how to fight and how to survive and without them, I'd be dead or worse. Don't you ever speak ill of them again!"

Her furious words bounced back to her off the trees. The rage was almost overwhelming, making the knife quiver in her hand.

He was looking around them nervously. "I understand you're angry. And there is so much that Anna-Marie didn't tell you – could not tell you. All I ask is that you give me the opportunity to help you now. You're in danger, and this is not a place in which I can protect you."

"I don't need your protection!"

"Oh, but you do. Please believe me. There are forces moving around us… powerful people… this isn't the time to explain it all to you. We're only a short ride from safety and I beg you to come with me. It will be dark soon, we are many miles from Nantes, and there is nowhere else to shelter in these woods."

"Why should I believe I'm safe with you after what you paid that woman to do?"

He looked so hurt. "Because I'm your father. I'd wager that word means nothing to you, given what you've said, but in my experience, a father does everything he possibly can to protect his children, whether babes in arms or full-grown, as you are. I doubt there is anything I could say or do that will persuade you that the only thing I want is to keep you safe. I've dreamt of this day for so many years, and it bears no resemblance to the joyful scenes I imagined, and for that I am truly sorry. You've been badly treated and all I can say is that I swear to you, on my life, that I will do all I can to make your life better from this point on. I was powerless before, in more ways than you can understand, but not anymore. Please, sweet daughter of mine, please allow me to begin to earn your forgiveness."

He was unlike any man she'd met before. There was a softness to him that reminded her of Jacques when he had been drunk and mellow, but without Jacques' self-confidence. He was looking at her like a man waiting to hear if he was about to be executed or given a reprieve.

Morgane looked around the forest in the dimming light. Even though he seemed trustworthy, she couldn't be certain. But the only genuine choice she had was whether to strike out and face whatever threats could be within the trees – and a cold night with no cloak or food – or to face whatever he decided to spring upon her when her guard was down.

Between the two, he was the preferable potential threat, being merely a man, and not a very combative one at that. She'd take his offer of shelter over the prospect of a night in a cold forest and not let down her guard. It was the only sensible decision to make.

"I'll go with you, but I'll keep this knife ready, and I'll gut you if you do anything other than steer this cart to a safe place."

She watched his Adam's apple bob up and down as he swallowed, looking at the knife. "I have no intention of doing anything other than that, so I am happy to agree."

He walked round the cart to climb up onto the driver's board at the front. "Would you like to sit here, next to me?" he asked as he took up the reins.

She clambered up onto the cart, moved to the front of the arrayed goods and sat down on a plump sack behind him. "No, here is fine."

"As you wish…" He turned, looking embarrassed. "Forgive me, but I only know you as Marie-Louise… is that the name—"

"No!" she said, disgusted. "That is not my name. I am Morgane, of *The Vengeance*." The latter part tripped off her tongue as if nothing had changed, but did she still have the right to claim that she was part of its crew? No matter, Jacques had made it clear that she was always welcome to return, so that was good enough for her.

"Morgane?" He frowned. "Anna-Marie called you that?"

"What of it?"

He shook his head. "No matter. Morgane it is."

"What was your name again?"

"Well… I had hoped you'd call me Father." He took in the expression on her face. "But that may be premature. My name is Jean-Baptiste, the Comte de Sauvineau. Now, let's get out of these woods while we still have some light to see by."

THEY RODE THROUGH the woods in silence, which Morgane appreciated as it gave her a chance to take in her surroundings properly. The setting sun was casting a beautiful golden light through the trees. She thought about the pictures in the sketchbook, of what Anna-Marie was like before her heart was broken and she dedicated her life to revenge.

Morgane fluctuated between feeling sorry for her aunt as a young woman and angry that she'd allowed one stupid man to ruin her life. She couldn't understand why her mother had been the focus for her aunt's fury, why she'd been called a monster when it was the man driving the cart who'd betrayed her – if he was telling the truth about who he was. Of course, her mother could have said no, could have left him well alone and told her sister what a creature he was, so she wasn't entirely blameless, but there was something about the way Anna-Marie had gone all out to ensure her sister suffered the most that puzzled her.

Maybe it was a sibling thing. She'd never experienced that sort of relationship. Perhaps a betrayal by someone of her own family was harder to bear than that of a man she loved. After all, he was just a man and maybe it was as simple as that; a sister should have done better, and the man did only as was expected. Certainly Anna-Marie had an incredibly low opinion of men as lovers. She used them for physical pleasure and nothing more, and never lay with any of the men in her crew as she actually respected them. Until that last conversation on her death bed, Morgane had thought that it was because her aunt was so strong and independently minded that she had no need of any kind of support, let alone from a man. Now she understood that it probably was a result of being so badly hurt by those closest to her, her aunt didn't seem so strong... more scared of being hurt once more.

As she mulled over the sketches and his reaction to her knowing Anna-Marie was her aunt, it seemed more likely than not that he was telling the truth about being her father, but she retained a healthy doubt, given the kidnapping. The only thing that cheered her was the fact that if the Comte d'Artois had sent the *Maître*, she'd have no issue with killing him now, seeing as he wasn't her father. She wondered whether that would have stopped her, and couldn't really decide.

As the cart rocked and her head throbbed, she considered the vendetta against the Four Chains Company. Was it the simple fact that it was one of the things that made her real mother wealthy, and that was what her aunt had been trying to destroy? It felt less like vengeance for ruining her life and more like a petty vindictiveness. Not that Anna-Marie would have been above such a thing. But it somehow felt more squalid when Morgane considered the mariners that had been killed over those years of attacks, the captains that Anna-Marie had reduced to quivering heaps, the ones she'd killed. All because the owner of the company was married to her sister? It seemed disproportionate at the very least. Had the Comte d'Artois done something else?

The golden hue turned into a deep orange sunset and then a brilliant red as the last rays of sunlight faded in the darkening woods. She could hear howling in the distance, like that of dogs but somehow more frightening, and she shuddered at the stark chill in the air.

"Here we are," Jean-Baptiste said and pointed ahead to a pair of gates set into a stout stone wall that stretched as far as she could see in either direction, disappearing in the dusky gloom. The gates were twice the height of a man and made of stout iron rods tipped with golden spikes.

"Are you... rich?" she asked.

He smirked over his shoulder as he drew the horses to a stop. "Oh yes, very. Appallingly so!" He jumped down to go and unlock the gates with a huge iron key.

Once they were through, he locked the gates behind them and Morgane couldn't decide if that made her feel more or less safe. She made a note of which pocket he kept the key in, just in case she needed to leave later.

Within the boundary they'd just crossed, the trees were

confined to lining a wide driveway, with neatly clipped bushes framing large rectangles of equally neatly planted shrubs and the last flowers of the season. Up ahead she could see a large house, made of the same stone as the grand buildings in Nantes and with a steeply pitched roof covered in dark grey slate tiles. The windows were large, several of them casting out a warm glow. She decided this was probably safer considering how rapidly the night was falling now and hoped that the smoke emerging from a couple of the chimneys meant a good fire was to be found inside. She still wasn't used to cold nights and was not sure she would ever be fond of European weather.

He drove the cart right up to the front of the house and the door opened as he jumped down to the ground again. A man with a long, thin face and an expression that looked like he had eaten something that had soured his stomach opened the large front door. He was dressed in fancier clothes than her father, a uniform by the look of it, with a long coat and matching waistcoat in deep burgundy with black breeches and white stockings.

She carefully put the knife back into her boot, moving slowly to not draw attention to the motion as the two men greeted each other without any warmth or cheer whatsoever.

"Is she here?" Jean-Baptiste asked, and the man nodded.

"Yes, my lord, she's waiting in the salon."

Who were they talking about? Morgane clambered off the back of the cart and walked up the shallow steps.

"This is Ambillou," Jean-Baptiste said to her. "He's in charge of the staff. If you need anything, he's the one to ask."

Ambillou cleared his throat. "In the first instance, mademoiselle, ask your maid, and if she is unable to meet your needs, I will assist."

Jean-Baptiste looked a little embarrassed. "Of course, yes. And this is Morgane, Ambillou."

She noted that he didn't say anything about her being his daughter. Was he only trying to fool her into thinking she was? Or was he ashamed of her? Perhaps he just thought it was none of the servant's business.

Ambillou inclined his head to her and stepped aside so they could enter. "We're still preparing the house, my lord, my apologies for its appearance."

Everything Morgane could see was absolutely pristine, from the ornate gold chandelier and its dozens of lit candles above them to the marble floor beneath her feet. A large staircase with oak risers and balustrade had been polished until it glowed in the candlelight. There were paintings on the walls with gilded frames that caught the light, too. It was unlike anywhere she'd ever seen before.

"Oh, I understand, Ambillou, you're all doing your best. She's in the salon, did you say?"

"Yes, my lord."

Ambillou headed towards a large set of wooden doors to the left and opened them. Inside was an even more impressive space, filled with so much colour and opulence that Morgane's eyes flitted from one detail to another faster than her thoughts could keep up with.

"This is Lisette, your governess."

His words focused her attention on the young woman standing in front of the blazing fire. She was petite, looked to be about the same age as her, wearing a woollen dress that was tidy and modest. Even though the dark green bodice was cut to give the same wide neckline and full sleeves as Morgane's blue silk dress, it made her feel as if her own was somehow frivolous in comparison. Lisette's hair was dark brown, with small curls framing her face and the rest of it swept back into some sort of arrangement at the back covered by a small white linen cap.

Lisette curtsied deeply and kept her eyes downcast. There

was something so subservient and diminutive about her composure that it made Morgane feel deeply uncomfortable. She looked at Jean-Baptiste, who was smiling at Lisette. "What's a governess?"

His smile faded. Ambillou quietly withdrew, but Morgane still clocked the tiny twitch at his mouth that he tried to hide before leaving.

"Lisette is going to be your companion. She will teach you."

"Eh? I don't need a companion. I need food and, God forgive me, a wash. And a few more bloody answers, too, dammit."

Lisette's eyes, already quite large, widened at Morgane's words before her gaze flicked to Jean-Baptiste. "Who was your daughter's previous governess, my lord?"

"I've never had one," Morgane replied, irritated that the woman had asked him as if she wasn't standing right there in front of her. "What are you supposed to be teaching me?"

Lisette looked distinctly uncomfortable. "A wide variety of subjects, depending on your previous education. I had thought that we could review your Latin and take things from there, but perhaps comportment and manners would be a better place to start."

Morgane knew a put down when she heard one, no matter how dressed up it was. "You can shove your comportment lessons right up your ar—"

"Morgane!" Jean-Baptiste's voice, while not quite a shout, was stern and loud enough to drown out the insult. "I have no idea why you're not delighted by the prospect of companionship and the opportunity to receive an excellent education, but whatever the reason, I'd be grateful if you could treat Lisette with the respect she deserves."

Morgane frowned, confused, and looked back at Lisette. "Have you steered a brigantine through a storm?"

Lisette's eyebrows shot up in surprise. "I—"

"How many ways can you kill a man?"

"I beg your pardon?!"

"Morgane!" This time he did shout.

"What? I am trying to determine why she's worthy of my respect. I'm no fool, I know that smaller women can be just as deadly as the bigger ones. I just thought it would be easier to ask."

Lisette looked absolutely appalled. "My lord, you did not explain how... unusual your daughter is. I feel I have been misled." She grabbed a shawl that was neatly folded on a chair behind her and threw it around her shoulders. "I suspect another teacher would be better suited to your family's needs. Good evening."

She started to march towards the door. Morgane nodded, agreeing with the woman, but her father darted forwards to put himself between Lisette and the door. "Mademoiselle, please! If you could permit just a little more of your time, and your patience and understanding..."

"He didn't mislead you," Morgane added. "Not deliberately. We've only just met. He had no idea what I know already."

Lisette stopped, her mouth dropping open, as her father sank onto one of the over-stuffed sofas and put his head in his hands.

"Are you actually his daughter?" Lisette managed to ask.

"Maybe. I'm not entirely convinced yet."

"She is!" Jean-Baptiste yelled, back on his feet again. "You are!" he said to her. "I swear it. Why else would I have gone to all the trouble I have to rescue you?"

"Kidnap me," Morgane corrected, again, lest he forget what he actually did. "And that's hardly proof of your fatherhood; there were four other men who wanted to kidnap me, too, and none of them claimed to be my father."

"I have no idea what is happening here, but I want no part of it," Lisette declared and resumed her march towards the door.

"I feel the same," Morgane said, feeling some sympathy. "But it's cold and dark out there and if nothing else, you should have some food before you go."

Lisette looked towards the closed drapes and shuddered. "Yes... it would be better to stay until morning at least."

"Yes, of course it would!" Jean-Baptiste said and steered her back to the armchair closest to the fire.

Lisette now looked a little frightened of him, and it was one of the few things that Morgane could understand clearly. "He's not going to kidnap you, have no fear," she said, in an attempt to make the poor woman more at ease. "And I wouldn't worry, he's not got an ounce of fight in him. I could take him down again easily, if needed."

"Again?" Lisette murmured with wide eyes.

Now Jean-Baptiste's mouth was hanging open. "Do I not deserve any respect for—"

"No," Morgane replied before any more drivel came out of his mouth. "I am tired, my head hurts, I'm hungry and I hate this bloody dress. I am royally sick of being chased, being lost and being scared. I have had enough. You brought me here, to keep me safe, you say. Well, the thing I am most in danger of is fainting from hunger. I haven't eaten since I arrived in this godforsaken country, and I've done a lot of running and a lot of fighting. If you don't make food happen soon, I'll go hunting for it myself, and I don't feel like doing that when I'm stuck in this stupid dress, and I don't know what there is to be found in these woods anyway."

Jean-Baptiste put a hand over his face and dragged it downwards. "I am hungry, too," he said, wearily. "Perhaps we will all benefit from a good meal." He turned to Lisette. "Mademoiselle, please do stay for dinner, and at least one night. Your room has already been prepared."

Lisette looked from him to Morgane and back again. "I am no fool, my lord, and I do not wish to be treated like one. One night," she said after a long pause, "that is all I am willing to commit to until I understand" – she waved a hand in their direction – "*this* more thoroughly."

Jean-Baptiste's shoulders visibly relaxed. "Thank you. Good. Very well then. I suggest—"

Morgane didn't linger for whatever insipid nonsense he was about to speak. It was time to find some food before she murdered someone for it.

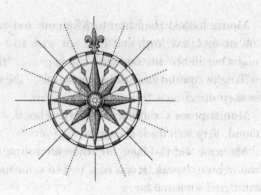

CHAPTER TWELVE

Out in the hallway it was easy to find the kitchen; she simply followed the scent of freshly baked bread. It was right at the back of the house, down a short flight of steps, filled with a huge wooden table upon which were vegetables she didn't recognise and piles of peelings. A pot hung over a large fire at the far end of the room and it was being stirred by a boy. He was rubbing his ear and glowering at a woman who was plucking a chicken and putting the feathers into a sack. Another man, the one who was peeling… something… looked at her as she entered.

He set down the paring knife and followed her gaze to the bread on the table in front of him. "Dinner will be in an hour or two."

"I'll be dead of hunger by then."

The man pursed his lips. "It is no fault of mine, mademoiselle."

"I never said it was. I haven't eaten all day."

The woman plucking the chicken sighed. "Break off some of the bread. There's some dripping there." She pointed at a shallow dish.

Morgane broke the baguette in half and looked at the dish. "What am I to do with that?"

The boy by the fire sniggered.

"It's for the bread," the woman said. "No butter until tomorrow."

Morgane took the dish and left, trying her best to ignore the sound of the child's laughter and a comment from the man about her being too fancy to know what dripping was. Too fancy? Even though he couldn't have been more wrong about her, it still annoyed her. It wasn't her fault she didn't know what dripping was. Cook never gave it to anyone to have with bread on *The Vengeance*, and they mostly ate fruit and fish when in port.

But the bread was fresh and smelt so good that she took a bite of the soft white centre as she climbed the stairs. It was heavenly. Cook's bread was thin and fried, nothing like this. She scraped the rough edge of the baguette against the dripping and took another bite. It was some sort of fat, and it tasted divine. Maybe France wasn't going to be a complete disaster, if their bread was anything to go by.

At the foot of the stairs she came across a young woman, younger than Lisette, dressed in a plain brown woollen dress and wearing a white linen cap. She seemed surprised to see Morgane, and confused by the fact she was eating the bread as she approached.

"You the maid?" Morgane asked with a mouth full of bread.

The maid nodded and bobbed a curtsey.

"Can you tell me where I'm supposed to sleep?"

"I can show you, mademoiselle."

Morgane felt distinctly uncomfortable. "Just tell me."

"Up the stairs, go to the left and it's the second door."

"And where can I find a bucket? And where do I draw water, for that matter?" The maid looked confused, so she added: "I need to wash."

"Would you like me to prepare a bath?"

Morgane shook her head, horrified by the prospect of wasting so much fresh water just for her. She'd never had a bath her whole life and she wasn't about to start now. "Just a bucket of fresh water and a linen cloth is fine. Or just tell me where to get one and I'll—"

"No, mademoiselle!" Now the maid was horrified. "I'll see to it at once!"

She hurried away, towards the kitchen. Morgane chewed on another mouthful of bread, hating the feeling of everything being slightly wrong. Dripping… the offer of a bath… the wide stairs ahead of her instead of narrow, steep steps. She felt homesick in the extreme.

She could hear Jean-Baptiste's voice through the door, but she had no desire to eavesdrop. He was probably trying to persuade Lisette that he wasn't a terrible man and that he hadn't lied to her about her job. Her head was pounding too hard to care about any of it.

She climbed the stairs, found the door and went into the room that was supposedly hers now. She took in the large four-poster bed, the gilded cheval mirror, the armoire which was more elaborately carved than any she'd ever seen, the thick and luxuriant curtains. She felt like an imposter. Was that ridiculous man really thinking this was to be her home now? It didn't feel right. None of it did. The only thing that lifted her spirits was the fact that the door had a lock, and the key was on the inside.

The room overlooked a part of the walled garden, now just muted greys in the rapidly fading light. Beyond, all she could see was forest, all the way to the horizon. She yearned for the deep blues of the sky and sea and turned away from the view.

Morgane sat heavily on the bed and polished off the rest of the bread and dripping, wishing that she'd had the wherewithal to get a drink, too. Then she removed her knife from her boot and slipped it under the pillow. At the sound of the maid's approach on the landing, she went to the door and took the bucket of water and linen from her, which the maid didn't seem to like at all. The maid followed her in to place a candle holder with a little loop as a handle on the bedside table, replete with a tall, lit candle. Morgane quelled the brief worry that the naked flame should be enclosed in a lantern, lest the wind blow it out, or it set fire to something too easily. Apparently, people who lived in houses instead of ships didn't worry about such things.

When the maid lingered, Morgane frowned at her. "Do you need something?"

That maddening look of confusion flashed across the maid's face. "Do you not need help with your dress, mademoiselle?"

"No." Morgane shooed her out of the door like she was a very tall goose and locked it behind the girl.

It was awkward, undressing alone, and involved some uncomfortable contortions to start undoing the lacing but she managed it. She washed and inspected the patches of raw skin on her shoulders where the heavy dress and petticoats had chafed her. Stupid clothes. She had to find something better to wear.

The pistols ended up beneath the pillows, too; her sword, now unstrapped from her thigh, rested at the foot of the bed. She slaked her thirst before washing herself, surprised to find a small bar of scented soap wrapped in the linen wash sheet. Soap was a rare luxury on *The Vengeance*, and she enjoyed how clean it made her feel.

There were linen shirts on the bottom shelf of the armoire, and little sachets of lavender tucked into the folds. She pulled one out and put it on. It was too big for her, but close enough to her old shirt that she didn't mind one bit. She rummaged around and found a pair of breeches made of burgundy velvet – exactly the sort of thing that Anna-Marie never let her wear. They were too big in the waist, so she moved the buttons using Jacques' sewing kit and put them on. There was enough loose fabric at the hips for her to wear the tie-on pockets. Good. She found a pair of thick woollen hose and put them on, still cold.

She felt better already, and sat on the bed to rip open the hem of the chemise she'd been wearing before. Once all the gold was out, she dumped the linen in the bucket of water, along with the hose that she'd been wearing all day and then hunted for a good hiding place for her stash of gold.

There was a loose floorboard and while it wasn't the most original of places to hide gold, it would have to do for now. She wrapped it in one of the petticoats, leaving the gold stitched into that one, and added all the gold and gems from the blue dress. She was never going to wear that damn thing again.

Satisfied, she flopped back on the bed and fell into a deep, dreamless sleep.

AN INSISTENT KNOCKING on her bedroom door woke Morgane and she sat up, disoriented and briefly surprised by the sight of the room around her. The candle was lower than before, and the shadows had deepened, the sky outside the windows now pitch black.

"What?" she called, bad tempered.

"Dinner is served, mademoiselle," came the timid voice of the maid.

Morgane's stomach growled in response. "I'll be down in a moment."

Her headache had eased a little, which was a relief, but a brief probing of the lump revealed it was still very much there and still sore. At least she wasn't wearing a dress that felt like it weighed the same as an anchor, though.

There were other candles burning in sconces along the hallway, so she blew out her own and made her way downstairs, the smell of something delicious making her stomach growl all the louder. It was quiet and she wasn't sure where to go. There was no one in the salon and only the fire providing any light, so she headed towards a glow on the other side of the hallway and found a dining room.

Only Lisette was seated at the table, its size and the grandeur of the room making her seem rather lost. There was another fire, luxurious drapes, paintings in gilded frames, but Morgane only had eyes for the small feast that had been laid out. Meat, some sort of stew, more of that bread, vegetables... she'd never seen such a spread!

With a grin, she grabbed a plate from the setting closest to her and began filling it. It was only when she had piled as much as she could onto the porcelain and sat down to tuck in that she realised her father wasn't there.

She stuffed a slice of meat – some sort of pork? – into her mouth, then tried some of the stew – so good – and then asked Lisette, "Does Jean-Baptiste know that dinner is ready?"

Lisette looked like she had swallowed a bee and was trying not to let it back out again. Morgane, uninterested in anything but the food, carried on, thinking that if Lisette had something to say, she'd say it. There was no point going hungry while she decided.

"In France," Lisette finally began, "we say a prayer before we eat."

"Oh," Morgane said through a mouthful of stew, unsure of why Lisette thought she'd find that an interesting fact.

Lisette seemed annoyed, then clasped her hands, lowered her head and muttered a string of words that Morgane ignored in favour of reaching across to dunk her chunk of bread in the stew's rich sauce.

Lisette sighed audibly and used the tongs – that Morgane had missed – to serve herself some of the pork.

"And in France, we use cutlery for our meat." She pointedly picked up her knife and a fork that was so dainty and small that Morgane had assumed it was for decoration, and began to cut.

Morgane, who had a slice of pork rolled up and held between her thumb and fingers like a fat pipe, chuckled. "Why?"

"Because it is civilised!" Lisette said, her voice louder, as if Morgane were being deliberately obtuse.

"Looks like a lot of work for little gain, to me," Morgane said, stuffing the remainder of the pork in her mouth and casting her eye over what remained.

She was aware of Lisette's expression oscillating between horror and annoyance as she grabbed the next round of food after a particularly loud and resonant belch, but she didn't care. She was hungry, so she was eating; what was there to be upset about? The food was so good, full of flavours she'd never experienced before, and she hadn't eaten this well for months.

Eventually, Lisette paid more attention to her own meal and then finally said, "Your father had to attend to a personal matter. He said he will be back by tomorrow lunchtime."

"That bloody coward!" Morgane stabbed a chunk of stewed meat with her knife and then pulled it off with her teeth.

Lisette visibly shuddered. "A messenger arrived and when he read the note, he seemed very concerned. I do think he had something to deal with."

"And very convenient for him," Morgane said. "He drags me all the way here and then buggers off before I can ask him any questions."

"He left a message for you," Lisette said, handing over an

envelope that Morgane hadn't noticed. "Perhaps some of the answers are in there."

Morgane chucked it aside.

"Do you have so little respect for your father and what he has to say?"

"Why should I respect a man I met for the first time today, after he had me—"

"Kidnapped, yes, I know," Lisette said wearily. "He explained it all to me. I understand your anger, but I do believe he did try his best in a very difficult situation."

"Well, if that's his best, he definitely does not deserve my respect."

Lisette fell silent, choosing to pour them both a glass of wine.

Morgane drank the glass dry and poured herself another. It was much smoother than the grog she was used to.

"After dinner we'll see if we can find you some better clothes," Lisette said.

"These are good."

"But hardly appropriate."

"For what?"

Lisette stared at her. "For a young lady."

Morgane sighed and tossed her knife onto the table. "Listen, I know you mean well, but I do not need you to comment on every bloody thing I do or wear. You are staying for dinner, and tomorrow you'll be gone. I will be, too. So just mind your own affairs and leave me be."

"I will not be leaving tomorrow. After your father... clarified the situation, I have decided to take up the post. That makes me your governess, and as such, it is my job to comment upon your comportment and guide you towards better behaviour."

Morgane laughed and downed the second glass of wine. "I don't want or need a governess."

"Mademoiselle, you could not be more wrong."

Morgane, losing her patience now, leaned across the corner of the table between them. "I have had enough of this shit. That barnacle of a man who claims to be my father has no idea what I need and no intention of putting things right. Hiring you, a stranger, to order me about while he sods off is not my idea of being a good father and, quite frankly, I don't care what he wants or what you think is right or wrong."

Lisette, who had shrunk back away from Morgane's intimidation, cleared her throat. "Regardless, mademoiselle, I have been engaged to do a job and I will do my best to fulfil my role."

Morgane stood. "No, you won't. Because you doing your job needs my cooperation. You'll be a shitty little captain with no crew to command. If I were you, I'd go home tomorrow and put an end to this stupidity before it wastes any more of your time."

She grabbed the wine bottle and downed half of it, belching loudly and wiping her mouth on her sleeve. Lisette looked like she was going to be sick. Morgane laughed at her, dragged the large casserole dish from the centre of the table and set upon the contents with a spoon.

As she ate, she tried to work out what to do in the morning. Was it best to just strike out in the hope of finding somewhere within a day's walk? Perhaps the cart and horse were stabled at the house; she had no idea if there were even outbuildings, having arrived at dusk in less than ideal circumstances. Even if the horse and cart she'd arrived on were still there, would she be able to use it? She'd never ridden a horse, and never driven a cart. Horses were huge and mysterious creatures that she'd never had the opportunity to handle or even get close to. The thought of trying to coax one into the right direction didn't fill her with confidence.

"I want to apologise," Lisette said, breaking her

introspection. "It was unfair of me to be so critical. Your father explained that this is the first time you've been to France and that you grew up in another country. I should have been more mindful of that, and not assumed that you knew how things are done here."

Morgane was taken aback. Anna-Marie had never apologised to her. Ever. And those in the crew who had treated her unfairly and realised it afterwards never explained why. They just handed a tankard of bumbo over and passed food to her with an apologetic smile – and even that was rare.

Morgane shrugged. "All's well. You didn't punch me or anything."

Lisette smiled tentatively. "Nevertheless, I regret the way I berated you and I suggest we start again. And instead of criticism, I shall offer answers to any questions you might have."

Morgane nodded, letting the words sink in. "I shouldn't have got so angry," she said. "You were just... trying to be something you've been asked to be, and it isn't your fault that you're not needed."

Lisette frowned slightly. "Am I to understand that you don't have a single question? Even though everything must be rather strange for you?"

"No, it's not that... it's...."

"Why not take the opportunity to have some of those questions answered? There's no harm in it, is there?"

Morgane shrugged again. "I suppose not. But you're not my governess. I don't need one of those."

Lisette smiled. "Well... how about I try to be your companion instead? That is a similar enough role to satisfy my conscience and it is hopefully more palatable for you."

"You want to be paid to be my friend?"

"That is not how I see it."

"France is stupid."

Lisette laughed. "I can imagine how it would seem so to a newcomer. Surely you have questions, Morgane?"

Morgane didn't want to admit that she did, because she didn't want Lisette to feel needed. But there was no denying that it could be useful to have some things clarified.

"What's that vegetable in the thick sauce?" She jabbed her spoon towards one of the dishes.

"Artichoke. Heavens, is this the first time you've eaten it?"

"Yeah. It's strange but good."

"I've had it many times before, because we grow it at home, but I've never had it in such a rich sauce. It was delicious!"

Morgane realised she was smiling at her and stopped, lest the captain—

She took a deep breath. Anna-Marie was dead, and her insufferable possessiveness with her. "Do we have it for breakfast, too?"

Lisette shook her head. "It may be broth, or if we're lucky, hot chocolate. We'll find out in the morning."

Morgane tried to get the measure of her, but she wasn't like any other woman she'd ever spoken to. She was so... rigid. And her voice was so soft. Lisette seemed nice enough, but she was only there because Jean-Baptiste paid her to be. They'd both claimed it was only to be her governess or companion, but was that the whole truth?

"Before I forget" – she picked up the envelope that Morgane had batted away and held it out towards her again – "your father's note."

Morgane sighed. "You may as well throw it in the fire. I can't read."

"Would you like me to read it to you?"

Morgane shrugged, not knowing whether to trust her or not. Lisette seemed to take that as enough encouragement to break the wax seal and unfold the paper. After a brief frown she read aloud.

"Dear Morgane, I am so sorry I cannot have dinner with you – I am called away on important business. I will answer your questions tomorrow, over lunch all being well, for no doubt, you have many. Your father, Jean-Baptiste."

Morgane tossed her spoon aside and stood up. "I'm not going to sit around until he finds the courage to speak to me."

"It isn't long to wait," Lisette said, reaching out to brush her arm gently. "It sounds like you had a terrible first day in France. Why not take the opportunity to rest and enjoy this beautiful house and this marvellous food?"

"Because I'm not just a piece of driftwood that washed up here! I've got things to do! Just because he says he's my father don't give him the right to have me kidnapped and brought to the middle of bloody nowhere!"

"What things do you have to do? What could be more important than being reunited with your long-lost father?"

Morgane gave her one last disbelieving look, grabbed the nearest candlestick and headed for the door.

"Where are you going?"

"If that cowardly bastard won't give me some answers, then I'll have to find them elsewhere."

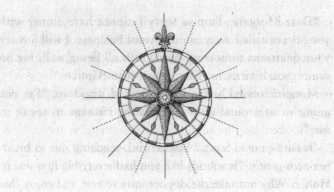

CHAPTER THIRTEEN

LISETTE FOLLOWED HER out of the dining room. "Morgane, why not just wait until he returns tomorrow?"

"Cos I'll be gone at first light. I ain't waitin' for him."

"But…" Lisette followed her into the salon where they'd first met. "But how can you want to leave so soon? Was today not the first time you've seen him? That's what he told me. That you were stolen away as a babe in arms, and he's been searching for you all his life."

Morgane scanned the room, initially looking for Ambillou, so she could quiz him instead, then looking for a desk or locked cupboard. "If that were actually true, wouldn't you want to spend time with your long-lost daughter?"

"Well, yes, but I can only assume that the business he had to attend to was of…" She trailed off as Morgane left.

There had to some way to find out more about the man. Seeing as he wasn't there to answer questions, Morgane decided that the only option was to go through his personal effects. It was always the best way to find out about a captain on a captured ship, or a new crew member that wasn't settling in and was putting people's backs up. What did this man keep in his desk? She was hoping for bills of sale, a log, hell, even just a list of things to remember would give some insights.

Room after room of stuffed animal heads mounted on walls, paintings and fancy furniture, but no desks and nothing very personal. Morgane's frustration grew with each room she went through, unable to find either the butler or anything that looked like it might contain something interesting. Lisette's slippered feet tapped on the wooden floors daintily behind her all the while as she had to half-run to keep up with Morgane's determined stride.

With all the animal heads and the dust that covered almost everything, the place had a rather morbid and melancholy feel to it. The dark corners didn't help either, the light from the candle not penetrating far enough.

She reached the last doorway on the ground floor, the one to the hallway that led to the kitchen, but Lisette put her hand on Morgane's shoulder, bringing her to a stop. "What are you looking for?"

"His captain's desk, or whatever comtes have. And that tall man would be good, too."

"I was wondering where Ambillou is, myself," Lisette added. "There doesn't seem to be a study but that's no surprise. This is only the hunting lodge, after all."

"This ain't a chateau?"

Lisette laughed. "No! My goodness, have you never seen one?"

Morgane shook her head.

"The chateau is a couple of miles from here, at the other end of the estate. It's very grand. Perhaps that's where he's been called to."

"Why not take me there?"

"He told me—"

"Don't bother, I get it. He's keeping me secret for now. This just gets better and better. Is he married?"

"Not as far as I'm aware. But there is a very good reason for—"

The door opened and both of them stepped back as Ambillou appeared, rather red cheeked, smelling of pipe smoke. "May I help you?"

"We were… errr…" Lisette faltered.

"I want to know more about the comte," Morgane said. "And whether he really did leave or if he's hiding somewhere."

Ambillou looked at her rather disdainfully. "I can assure you that the comte is not currently here, and will be back tomorrow. As for knowing more about him…" He cleared his throat. "I'm afraid I can't help you as I do not know him personally. Would you like anything more to eat, or shall I bring wine to the salon?"

"What about the others, the maid and the cooks an' all. They know him?"

He suppressed a chuckle. "Staff of their station do not interact with the comte, my… lady."

"Bloody useless," Morgane muttered, heading towards the salon. "Is there brandy?"

"Of course, mademoiselle. I shall serve it in the salon momentarily."

Morgane flopped onto one of the sofas after prodding the fire back into life, Lisette choosing the same armchair that she'd sat in before. At least the candelabras were lit, and it felt a little more cheerful. In moments Ambillou arrived with two glasses and a bottle of brandy on a tray. As he poured into both, Morgane remembered she didn't have to pay for it and said, "You can leave the bottle."

After a slight twitch of an eyebrow, he put the bottle down, stoppered it, and left.

Morgane downed her glass in one swig and poured another straight away. "Not bad, that," she said.

Lisette sipped, unsurprisingly. Morgane had downed her second before Lisette had settled back into the chair.

"What is a 'comte' anyway?" Morgane asked as she poured herself another, enjoying the warmth running down the inside of her chest. "Is it like a governor?"

"I don't know what the governors of the colonies do, I'm afraid. A comte is a member of the nobility."

"And that means being rich."

Lisette smiled. "Not necessarily. Being noble means you are elevated... that you're favoured by the king and the royal family in some way. Some are born into nobility, some are awarded it by the king."

"What about the man who claims to be my father?"

"My understanding is that your great-great-grandfather was awarded his title after many years of service to the king. The lands came with the title. His son built the chateau, I believe. That's the main house."

"So the king gave him all the money, too?"

"No, the wealth comes from the land."

Morgane looked out of the window into the total darkness outside. "What do they grow here that sells for so much?"

"No... the wealth comes from the people who live on your father's land. They all pay a portion of their income, called a tax, to him."

"Why?"

Lisette considered the question. "It's the way things are."

"The people who live on his lands must be so rich!"

"Ah... no, they're not. There are just lots of them."

"And they're happy to make him rich?"

"It's... the... it's just the way things are, Morgane. Everyone accepts it. The nobility own the land, and the vassals – the people who live on it – pay for the privilege to live on it. And to use the comte's mills and wine presses."

It all sounded very strange to Morgane. "And what does the comte have to do for the privilege to live like this?"

"He must be ready to fight for the king, whenever needed."

"And the rest of the time he… what, just pisses about being rich?"

Lisette seemed uncomfortable, but Morgane wasn't sure why. "No. A good comte will ensure his people are well cared for, that justice is done…"

"What does my father do to care for the people who make him rich?"

Lisette fell silent. "Where did you grow up, Morgane?" she asked eventually. "It must have been so very different to France."

Morgane hesitated. She couldn't tell the truth. She didn't know this woman, nor whether she could be trusted. Pirates were hanged, she knew that much, and even though it would be hard to prove, a confession would probably be accepted as evidence enough. That and the stash of gold and gems hidden in her room and clothes. The pardon sent with Lavois was in the lost trunk, because she was an idiot.

She couldn't lie and say that she grew up in one of the French colonies, because she knew nothing about how people lived there, other than their appalling treatment of slaves. At least half of *The Vengeance*'s crew had escaped that life and had told her about it. Almost all of the other half were variously made up of former trading crews, or men who'd been pressganged into serving at sea during war and those who'd been betrayed in some form or other by the people who'd had power over their lives, be them husbands, fathers, governors or other captains. The number of people who'd been happy enough in a land-based life but thought they'd be happier as pirates, she could count on one hand, Jacques being one of them. She'd had the impression he was fleeing boredom and drudgery rather than injustice. Her aunt was another. She'd known very little about Anna-Marie's life before she stole her, but she'd known it was one of at least moderate privilege, just from some of the things she'd overheard her say to others and how they'd reacted.

"I spent all of my life at sea," she said finally. It was all she knew, and she didn't have the knowledge to fake even a land-based life in the colonies. Lisette was too clever to be convinced easily.

"How remarkable!"

"Is it? There are hundreds of ships out on the seas, and thousands of people who crew them."

"Yes, but I thought that women weren't permitted aboard trading vessels."

Morgane just shrugged. "I was."

Lisette stared at her long enough to make Morgane uncomfortable, so she reached for the bottle again. "Want another?"

"Oh, no, thank you. One is quite enough for me. Has it not gone straight to your head?"

"Nope." Morgane started to refill her glass but then thought the better of it and just swigged from the bottle instead. "Are there any villages nearby?"

Lisette, wide-eyed for some unfathomable reason, shook her head. "It takes half a day to walk to my home. These woods are part of your father's estate, and no one lives in them. They'd be fools to try."

"Why?"

"The wolves... And worse."

"Bandits?"

"Yes."

"Well, he ain't a good comte then, is he, if people like you are scared of his woods?"

"There are bandits everywhere – it's too big a problem for just one comte to solve. Oh, my goodness, is that an original?" She'd just noticed one of the many ornaments on one of the bookcases and went to look more closely at it. "There are so many beautiful things here! I've always wanted to see inside this place. How lucky I am! Perhaps your father will take us to the chateau upon his return. I've heard his art collection is extraordinary."

It seemed to Morgane that wealth here in Europe was all about acquiring useless things that gathered dust, just so that other people could look at them and see that the owner was rich enough to buy them. Why exchange gold for all these dull things that brought no pleasure?

It was a world away from her old life, where money always flowed and never got trapped in useless possessions. It felt unnatural to manage the small hoard she owned now, constantly worrying about where it was and how to keep it hidden. In the past, she spent her share whenever they got back to shore, just like everyone else did, secure in the knowledge that when the money ran out, they'd go back out to sea and get more. But she had no idea where the next haul was going to come from, unused to liberating wealth on land and alone, so it had become strangely precious, in a way she didn't like.

Perhaps this was how the wealthy of France dealt with the same discomfort; instead of fretting about piles of tax coin lying around, easily stolen, they exchanged it for stupid things that no one with any sense would want to steal. She liked the idea until she realised it wasn't really solving that problem; ornaments and paintings and furniture could still be stolen and presumably exchanged back into gold again. It was just more inconvenient.

Lisette, unaware of how little any of this made sense to Morgane, pointed out the Sauvineau coat of arms and explained that all the noble families had one, and not just in France either. Apparently, it meant a great deal to people. Morgane had seen them many times, etched into some of the higher value items they'd stolen and traded on. At the time she'd thought they were merely decorative, when they were, in fact, an entire language of ownership, pride and nobility. It made her appreciate that all of this world of theirs only worked if everyone knew about it… about what everything signified. Lisette clearly did, and her deference to this new order, that Morgane intuitively disliked, reinforced its power.

"What if someone doesn't care about all this?" Lisette looked briefly confused and Morgane realised she needed to be more specific. "It seems to me that the nobles are only rich because everybody else is happy to make them so. What if someone doesn't think nobles deserve this wealth?"

Lisette's eyes widened. "Well… it depends how they acted upon their opinions. If they kept their thoughts to themselves, nothing, as long as they pay their taxes and obey the law. But if they start rallying people to turn on their lord, or the king… well… it would not go well for them."

"They'd be killed?"

Lisette nodded. "And if they were a noble, speaking against the king, and he heard about it, all their power and wealth could be stripped from them. And they could be executed, too, if they were causing enough trouble."

So that was one thing Morgane could understand; the king was like a captain. Talk shit about him, and he could kill you. Same for the other nobles, too.

"But what if the king, or a comte, is a bad one?" she asked. "What if he neglects his duties and the crew – I mean… the people of his lands – don't have a good life under his command? How easy is it for them to vote him out?"

Lisette just blinked at her. "Vote… him out?"

"Yes. Just like…" Morgane shut her mouth, realising her stupid error. The only ships that removed bad captains with a vote from the crew were pirate ships. On military or trade vessels, removing a bad captain was always seen as mutiny, no matter how justified it was.

"One cannot vote a noble in or out, Morgane. That's not how it works. It isn't like a small business, where each family member has a say in how things are run."

"Oh." At least she didn't seem to realise the error. Perhaps Lisette didn't know about how people like her lived, not really. They only knew about the violence, and the looting. Not the way a crew looked out for each other, nor paid more to those injured, nor ensured that everyone got their fair share under a good captain and could get rid of them if they were not. Morgane cast about for something to change the course of the conversation. She pointed at one of the paintings and asked where the river was that it detailed. Mercifully it was a subject Lisette was more than happy to talk about, and she set about pointing out paintings and talking to her about why they were so good. They were all much the same to Morgane. Most were landscapes. Some had rivers and lakes in them, some didn't. What she found much more interesting was the fact that Lisette had so much to say about them.

"How do you know so much?" Morgane asked after she'd talked about two paintings hung side by side and how they were clearly by the same artist because of the way the trees had been painted. "Does everyone in France learn to read and about how paintings are painted?"

Lisette blushed. "No. Not everyone is as fortunate as I am. My grandfather was a member of the guild of scriveners and believed that all his children should learn to read and write, and my mother, in turn, taught me. My father is a member of the guild of St Luke – he's skilled in illuminating manuscripts and painting for the church. He taught me everything he could, as if I were his son."

What an odd thing to say. Morgane didn't pursue it, though, because there was a look of such profound sadness in Lisette's eyes that she feared the woman would cry if she asked anything more about it.

"How did Jean-Baptiste find you?"

"Who?"

"The comte. That's one of his names, I can't remember the rest of the middle ones. Do all of them have so many?"

"I've no idea," Lisette said quietly. "My father heard the position was open," she added, but Morgane had the sense she was holding something back. "It all happened very quickly! I'm so very fortunate."

She went to the bookcase and pulled out a slim volume, flipping the pages casually, a faint smile on her lips.

"Is it useful? Being able to read?"

"I believe it is. Though there are many who would say that it is not. Most cannot read, nor write. Most people have never held a book. But I find them beautiful. Apparently, in the comte's chateau, there's a library the size of a chapel, with shelves so tall that one needs a ladder to reach all the books! Now that is something I would dearly love to see."

"Is that why you took the position?"

"No," Lisette replied, looking away briefly. "Though I confess that I was a little disappointed that we're not at the chateau, for that very reason. And it's not to hide you away, as you fear. It's because repairs are being made to the roof of the chateau. Your father explained it to me. I'd heard there were many artisans working there."

"You're absolutely certain it's not to hide me away?"

"No, of course not! I would have explained before, but Ambillou interrupted us."

Morgane folded her arms, unable to shake the feeling that something wasn't right. It was probably as simple as the fact that her father didn't want anyone to find out about her yet, not until he could be certain she wasn't an embarrassment. And judging by how things had gone so far, it was probably a wise decision.

"Sod this, I'm going to look upstairs. Maybe he has his desk in his bedroom."

"I don't think we should—"

Morgane had picked up the brandy bottle and left before Lisette finished her protestation. She took the stairs two at a time and went through the first door she came to. A bedroom, luxuriously appointed but clearly not used for some time. The bed was covered with a dust sheet, along with a chair. There was an armoire, but it only contained sheets.

"Morgane, what do you hope to find?"

"Something that... I dunno... tells me more about him."

"So you do want to know him. Why not wait to speak to him?"

Morgane went into the next room. "There's a big difference between wanting to know more about someone and wanting to know them. I don't trust him." Lisette hung back in the doorway as Morgane rummaged through another bedroom. "Do you?"

After a telling pause, Lisette finally said, "I don't feel comfortable searching my employer's rooms, and I don't think you should either."

"I ain't takin' anythin'!"

"It's the principle of the matter."

Morgane ignored her, and soon all the rooms had been checked, save for one at the far end of the hallway. It was crammed full of pieces of furniture, all covered in dust sheets.

"Oh." Lisette sounded almost relieved. "Perhaps this is a storeroom." There certainly was a lot of furniture in there, far more than could be practical. "Would you like to go back to the salon and look at the books? If anything catches your eye, I can read it to you and—"

"No." Morgane cut her off, frustrated that she was just ignoring the situation. "It's obvious he doesn't live here. Don't that strike you as odd?"

"That third bedroom is his. The bed's been made up."

"But he doesn't have any personal things there."

"It's just a lodge, not his main residence."

Morgane leaned against the doorway and swigged the last

drop out of the bottle. "If this is a place he comes to often, he'd have more things here. I'm tellin' ya, he's not to be trusted."

"I'm sure that if you wait for him to—"

Morgane waved a hand at her, and she mercifully fell silent.

It was all getting a bit too much, Lisette's steadfast unearned loyalty and the strangeness of the place. Her thoughts felt like an overstuffed sack, with not enough room to find what she wanted. She was used to spending hours doing physical work, and even on the *Maître*, when that was denied to her, she still had lots of time to herself and her own space to make her preparations. What she wanted more than anything was a really simple repair to do, some new pegs to shape and hammer in and sand down, something like that. Something she could just get on with alone and without consultation, left to her own devices as others worked around her. Solitary work without loneliness.

"Are you curious about the cutlery from dinner?"

"What?"

"I thought that perhaps if I explained what each piece is for—"

"How could anyone ever be interested in bloody spoons?! Why would you think…" Morgane sighed with exasperation. "I… I just need some time alone."

Lisette nodded. "I understand. It's all new, isn't it? Why don't we retire? Everything will seem better in the morning." She started to head back to her room and paused. "But Morgane, will you at least breakfast with me in the morning, before you leave?"

"If you're up in time to eat with me, fine. But don't get any ideas about tryin' to make me stay. It won't work."

Lisette's uncertain smile told her that she'd been right in guessing the purpose behind the request. Morgane went to her room and locked the door behind her before staggering to the bed and flopping onto it, fully dressed, letting the brandy do its work and sink her into sleep.

CHAPTER FOURTEEN

THE SUNLIGHT WAS streaming through the window when Morgane woke with a jolt. She was lying on top of the bedclothes, still fully dressed, and it took her a few moments to remember where she was. Something had woken her, she was certain.

A loud banging on the front door downstairs confirmed her suspicion. She reached under her pillow for her knife only to find that it – and the pistols – were gone!

"Shit!"

She flung the pillows off the bed, revealing nothing but crisp sheets, and realised that the bed must have been neatened by the maid while she was eating dinner the night before. Even though she'd slept on top of the sheets they were still neatly tucked in at the sides, and most definitely not how she'd left them before going down to eat with Lisette.

Panicking, she ripped off the sheets before realising how stupid that was and looked under the bed instead. Nothing. She opened the armoire and found the knife, its sheath, and the brace of pistols lying on top of her folded petticoats. Her sword was propped up in the corner.

The relief was immense. She put the knife back into her boot, strapped the pistols on and unlocked her door to open it a crack.

She could hear Lisette's voice, and she didn't sound happy, but the conversation was happening too far away for her to be able to make out the words, so she crept out into the hallway and slowly, silently, made her way towards the top of the stairs where she'd still be out of sight, but better able to listen.

"I cannot fathom why you should consider it any business of yours!" Lisette said.

"When I heard where you'd gone, I was worried – it made no sense to me!" It was a man's voice. Deep. And something in the tone put Morgane's hackles up.

"Again, no business of yours, Monsieur Laroche."

"Are you not curious about *why* I was concerned?"

"Quite frankly, monsieur, no." She sounded so irritated. They clearly knew each other.

"I understand. You're so ashamed that you've had to take employment, you don't want to talk about it."

"I am not—"

He spoke over her. "Quite why you've chosen to believe this is anything other than a farce eludes me. There is a better way to resolve this situation you find yourself in."

"I am perfectly aware of the options available to me and taking this position is – by far – the most palatable."

"You may enjoy tormenting me, but there will come a day when my patience runs out and this won't be a silly little game anymore. It may come sooner than you believe. Then you may regret being so cold towards me."

"If you have nothing of actual merit to say to me, Monsieur Laroche, then I suggest you leave."

"You would have me leave with no offer of hospitality, even after I've ridden all this way just to speak to you?"

"That was your choice, monsieur, not mine. Goodbye."

"You'll regret not listening to me, Lisette. This new situation of yours is not as it seems. But here is one last chance for you to come to your senses. I will take you back home if you wish."

Morgane was about to storm down there, pistols drawn, having heard enough of him to decide he wasn't worth the politeness that Lisette somehow managed. But then she heard the front door open, and Lisette say, "Good day, Monsieur Laroche," in a curt, no-nonsense voice that seemed to have the desired impact.

By the time Morgane reached the bottom of the stairs the front door was shut again, with Lisette leaning against it in relief.

"Who was that arsehole?"

Lisette took in the pistols, the knife, and sighed. She shook her head, perhaps as if telling herself not to bother saying anything about them, and then unpeeled herself from the door.

"No one that need concern you, mademoiselle. Merely a small man with a surfeit of power."

"Do you want me to deal with him?"

"In what way?"

Morgane drew her knife and grinned. "I've persuaded lots of men like him to stop bothering people. I'm good at it."

Lisette's eyes lingered on the blade for a few moments, and Morgane would have sworn that she was tempted, but then she shook her head. "Alas, mademoiselle, there are some problems that cannot be solved with violence."

"Nah." Morgane sheathed the knife. "Any problem involving a man can *always* be solved with violence. Violence or gold, to be fair."

"Well, that I would agree with," Lisette said sadly, and walked away from the door.

Morgane returned to her room to get her gold. The sun was much higher than she wanted it to be. Maybe that brandy had been stronger than she thought, or perhaps it was just the trials of the first day in France that had exhausted her. Regardless, she was going to be leaving much later than she'd planned.

She had no idea what Laroche had been hinting he knew, and he was probably inflating its importance to try and get Lisette to return to town with him, but nonetheless, it was a concern. He'd called it a farce, and she wasn't sure what that word meant, but from his tone she could tell he didn't believe what he'd heard about the reason Lisette was here. Why? Did he know something about the comte that she didn't? It only reinforced her sense that something was wrong here.

Morgane wondered whether to go after him and ask what he knew, but her instincts told her that would be a bad idea. Men like that loved people needing something from them, whether it was a cask of fresh water or a juicy piece of information. She wouldn't give him the pleasure, and besides, she didn't trust him to tell the truth anyway. He'd probably try to get her to persuade Lisette to leave.

None of it was her business. Finding her mother was, though, and she'd been delayed enough.

A movement outside drew her eye. She went to the side of the window and peeped out from behind the curtain to see a tall man wearing fine clothes and a long cloak looking at the house. She didn't recognise him. Perhaps he was Laroche. He looked as if he were weighing up what to do, before making a decision and heading back towards the end of the house that contained the kitchen.

Morgane didn't like the idea of leaving with that man lurking in the grounds, and she wanted to know if he was a threat. She could make a run for it, or she could stick a knife against his throat and see what he had to say for himself.

She settled upon the latter, put the loose floorboard back into place with the gold still hidden beneath it and went out into the hallway once more. Lisette's voice, sounding angry, was floating up from the lobby below. Had Laroche decided to come back for her? She paused to listen in.

"I don't understand why you think that this is acceptable," Lisette was saying. "Do you think that standards should only be maintained when the comte is in residence?"

"Mademoiselle… there's no need to make such a fuss. No one is listening." It was Ambillou.

"What do you mean by that? You should be listening to me. Breakfast is late and you failed to answer the door to a visitor. An unwelcome one at that. What were you doing?"

There was a heavy sigh. "Am I to understand that you're not happy with the quality of the staff here?"

"I do think the standards here are lower than I expected. One should always fulfil one's duties to one's employer, regardless of whether he is at home or not."

"I am tired, mademoiselle, and I think it would be much easier if you understood that there is no need to play along in this masquerade when speaking to any of the staff. I, and the kitchen staff, are more relaxed than you think we should be because the comte is in Paris."

"Regardless—"

"The comte has been in Paris for over two months now, and is likely to be there until the spring. So, you'll forgive us for not running around as if he were due to return shortly."

"But—"

"Perhaps you thought we were all oblivious to the deception and could order us about, but that is not so. I have no idea what the false comte's agenda is, and frankly, I do not care. We are all being paid very generously, and I suggest you enjoy that while you can, just as we are. Breakfast will be ready when it is ready, and I shall ring the bell so that you know when that is."

"But..."

Lisette's voice trailed off as the sound of the butler's footsteps receded.

So it was all a lie. She knew it! Jean-Baptiste was nothing more than a fraudsman, and all the staff here were in on it. No wonder Lisette had constantly been trying to placate her and encourage her to stay and listen to more of his bullshit. She was being paid to reinforce the illusion! Morgane stood there, trapped momentarily between the desire to go and beat seven shades of shit out of the lot of them or to just grab her gold and run. But then she heard Lisette's footfall on the first stair and bolted back into her room.

She had to gather her hoard and get out of there. She could defend herself from bandits, if any of them decided to have a go. Hell, she'd be tempted to join them if they seemed half-competent. They'd be more trustworthy than most of the people she'd met since making landfall.

She didn't want to wear that bloody dress again. It was too cumbersome and not a good thing to travel in nor fend off threats. So she retrieved the stash she'd hidden in the floorboards, rolled it up in one of the spare petticoats and then bundled it up to a length that she could tie and wear slung over her shoulder. She tied the pockets that she'd worn under the dress around her waist and stuffed them down the loose breeches, wanting to keep Jacques' gift and some gold on her in case the bundle had to be dropped in a fight.

A quick rummage through the armoire uncovered a thicker wool doublet that smelt musty but would be warm. A hat would be good, if she could find one, but she wasn't willing to go through the other bedrooms for it. She shrugged the doublet on, realised there was room to fit another shirt on over the one she wore as it was so oversized for her and so took it off to put on another shirt she pulled out. Good. More layers would help keep this damn European cold away from her bones. There was a large felt hat, too, a little big for her head, but with her hair braided up underneath, it fit quite well, and she would look like a young man from a distance. Given the way the French seemed to be so interested in women, she felt that would be a good thing.

She was adjusting the second shirt's sleeves, trying to make the cuffs sit comfortably over one another, when there was a knock at the door. She froze. Another knock, more urgent.

"Morgane? It's Lisette. May I come in? I need to speak to you."

"Piss off!"

"Please, it's important!" The door opened and Morgane realised with horror that she'd forgotten to lock it in her haste and anger.

Morgane grabbed the wrapped gold and stuffed it under the bed as Lisette entered and shut the door behind her. She was pale and looked distinctly uncomfortable, lips pressed tight together, as if she didn't want to speak but had to anyway.

"Morgane... I've just had a very disturbing conversation with the butler, and I think you should know..." Her hands were clasped tightly, her shoulders high with tension. "He... he said the man who brought you here isn't the Comte de Sauvineau."

Morgane stared at her. This wasn't what she'd expected. "Eh?"

"The butler just... he spoke as if I were in on the secret, but that isn't so. He called that man – your father, if he is your father – the false comte and... I took this position in good faith and... oh Morgane, I fear that both of us are being duped and I have no idea why!"

Morgane folded her arms, trying to work out what Lisette was trying to manipulate her into, but drawing a blank. "Are you telling me that you had no idea he wasn't the comte of

Sauvineau, even though you pay taxes to him and live on his land?"

"I've never seen the comte! Not in person. Not many people have. I've seen some paintings of him, and the man who brought you here has a passing resemblance to my memory of the portraits, but… I swear, Morgane, I had no idea! The butler spoke as if everyone in the house knows of this falsehood and is just playing along to earn some money and… and I'm horrified!"

She certainly seemed sincere, and Morgane felt she'd had a lot of training in working out when someone was trying to trick her, thanks to the crew's love of trying to fool each other into parting with gold after a haul. She hadn't argued with Laroche, merely dismissed his claim. What if that had been simply because she didn't believe him, rather than her just trying to maintain the lie? Ambillou hadn't given her the chance to argue… and besides, revealing the deception to her now was going to cost her the position she clearly needed.

"I knew something was wrong here," Morgane replied tentatively. "That Laroche… was he telling the truth?"

Lisette winced and covered her mouth with her hand, nodding. "Yes, my God, he was actually right… this makes it worse. He'll be even more unbearable now."

Lisette was shaking and genuinely distressed. So she had been duped, just as much as she had? That Jean-Baptiste was a piece of work!

"You know Laroche is still here? He went round the back, I reckon he's gone to talk to the staff."

"To pay them for information, no doubt." Lisette looked horrified. "Oh, Morgane, if they tell him the truth, he'll cause so much trouble! What are we going to do?"

Morgane frowned. "We?"

"We've both been tricked, and there has to be a reason why! I cannot think it would be anything good, for either of us! We're not safe, surely! What does that man who claims to be your father intend to do when he returns? Why lie to us about who he is? Why bring you here, and why employ me to teach you? I fear that the real reason for his actions may mean ill for us both!"

It struck Morgane then that Lisette seemed to be as concerned for her as for herself. And she hadn't needed to tell her what she'd discovered. There was no way she could benefit or profit from telling her the truth. She'd come to her straight away after learning about the lie because it was the decent thing to do, as if they were both in the same crew, uncovering a threat that they needed to face together.

In that moment, Morgane felt like a fist that had been clenched around her heart suddenly let go. It had been there for weeks, since Anna-Marie decided to go after the *Maître* when it was clearly a stupid thing to do. Here was a woman who, given the choice, had shared important information with her, and made it clear that the threat they now both perceived was one that should be faced together.

"I don't know what he's up to. I don't even know if he's really my father – though it's clear he's a lying swab and not a comte who owns a fancy chateau."

"Now I feel terrible for believing him over you when you said you'd been kidnapped. I'm so sorry." She sat heavily on the bed as a lone tear rolled down her cheek. "What a dreadful turn of events. I thought this was real. I thought I'd finally found a way to…" She leaned forwards and wept into her hands.

Morgane chewed her lip, wanting to be anywhere but there. She didn't know what to do. Should she leave Lisette alone, so she wouldn't be embarrassed? Or put a hand on her shoulder, like Jacques used to when she was upset?

They were in this together now, though. Lisette was crew. Morgane put a hand on her shoulder.

"I'm sorry." Lisette sniffed. "I'm being dreadfully selfish. You're the one who's been through worse. But I really thought he was telling the truth, and that I'd earn so much money that I wouldn't have to…" She broke down.

"Won't have to what?"

"Marry Laroche!" Lisette really started to cry then.

Morgane squeezed her shoulder, hating that she was so upset. "Why would earning money have anything to do with who you marry? Do you want to marry him? Is he worth sharing your spoils with, or not? Will he have your back, when you need him? Do you want him in your bunk every night? That's what it comes down to."

Lisette sniffed and looked at her with a slightly confused frown. "No… you don't understand. I hate the man! I always have. But my father is a drunken, weak-willed fool and because of his selfish ways and poor judgement, we're in debt to Mr Laroche."

"Oh." It all made sense now. "So Laroche is offering to forget the debt if you marry him?"

"That's right. And all the while he's encouraging my father to run up more. We won't have enough money to keep a roof over our head in a matter of weeks. I've sold everything I possibly could to keep us from ruin, but my damn father…"

"So that's why Laroche was so interested: so he could gloat."

Lisette nodded. "And so he could be certain that this isn't going to save me from having to accept his offer."

"This ain't right." Morgane went to the armoire and retrieved her sword. "I'm going to make sure he doesn't bother you again."

Lisette jumped up, holding her hands in front of her as if she were scared she was the target. "What are you doing?"

"I'm going to cut some sense into him."

"Bonté divine! That's not the solution!"

"It really is."

"No! He's armed and he will cut you down."

"He can try!" Morgane took a step towards the door, but Lisette grabbed her arm.

"Morgane, please, listen to me! If you even threaten him, you'll be in the most dreadful trouble. He's very rich and no noble in the land would believe you over him. You have no one to defend you, no family to rely upon… please, trust me, this isn't the way forwards!"

Morgane stopped, frustrated but not so stupid as to ignore the woman who knew this country better than she did. Reluctantly she sheathed her sword. "Then what is? What about your real comte? Will he do something about this?"

"This isn't the sort of problem one goes to the nobility about."

"Why not?"

"Because…"

"Because they don't care, that's why. Any decent captain would tell Laroche to leave you be and help you to get your father back to his senses. Or at least tell the crew to help."

"I'm not in a crew, Morgane. It's not like being at sea. I suppose family is the closest we have but my brothers have died, and my father is my only relative, and he's letting us down. The other families in the town are like other ships, all interested in their own course and their own profits."

This wasn't right. No one to help her, no chance of giving him a good scar to warn him off… it seemed like there was only one solution. Morgane knelt, reached under the bed and rummaged her way through the layers of fabric to where she'd hidden her gold. She pulled out a fistful of coins and held them out to Lisette. "Will this cover the debt?"

Lisette's mouth fell open. "Where did you…"

"It's my inheritance," Morgane said. "It's mine to do with as I please. Will this be enough?"

"More than enough! I…" She came over and plucked out a coin, examined it and looked like she might faint. "There's over fifty pistoles here! Mon Dieu, a small fortune! I would only need three of these coins, to be free of Laroche's schemes." She plucked them out, leaving the rest in Morgane's palm.

"Those can be to pay off Laroche," Morgane said, nodding towards the coins that Lisette was pressing to her chest in amazement. "And the rest is for helping your father to find a better course." She put the rest of the coins into Lisette's other hand.

Lisette looked horrified. "You can't give me your inheritance!"

"Oh, I've got more gold. I have enough. This is yours now."

Lisette burst into tears again and threw her arms around Morgane. "Oh, thank you! Thank you!"

Morgane closed her arms around her. It felt good to be in a crew again. Even if it was only a crew of two.

There was the sound of a horse neighing, not far away, and they both separated to look at each other. "I bet that's Laroche," Lisette said. "Now he's found out everything he needs to, he'll be off to cause as much trouble as possible, no doubt."

"Well, if I can't kill him, why don't we go and speak to him before he leaves?" Morgane suggested. At Lisette's nervous frown she added, "I won't draw my sword, I promise. You can pay off the debt and tell him to go bother someone else."

Lisette nodded enthusiastically. "We'll get rid of that problem, and then we'll work out what to do next."

The sound of galloping hooves made them both dash to the window to catch sight of him riding through the gates into the woods beyond.

"He's gone!" Lisette cried. "We'll never catch him!"

"He rides like demons are chasing him. Shit and blood."

Lisette leaned against the window frame, nibbling at her thumbnail. "What is he going to do, that's the question. He could tell the comte, but getting a message to Paris is expensive and slow. He doesn't like to spend his own money. He could tell the mayor, I suppose… though he hates the man and wouldn't want him to gain anything from exposing the crime."

"I'd wager that bloody maid told him about my weapons," Morgane said. "She found them and put them in the armoire."

"So he knows that there is a man pretending to be a comte whose daughter is well-armed and… unused to privilege." Lisette groaned. "I know what he's going to do. He's going to round up a small militia and come back to apprehend the false comte and potentially you, too. He'll then parade you both back into town, get you locked up and crow about being a hero. He wants to be mayor. That may well gain him enough admiration amongst the locals to get his way."

"Why would he take me, too? I haven't done anything!"

"I know that, but he won't care. It will be easy to paint you as being in on the crime. You're… clearly not a comte's daughter… you've got all those weapons… that's enough to weave a compelling story about the two of you being in on it. He'll make it sound as if the two of you are the worst brigands south of Paris, I know he will. He likes to make a drama and cast himself as the hero."

"What's wrong with being armed?"

"Well… it's not usual for a young lady who leads a god-fearing, law-abiding life to have a brace of pistols and a sword, Morgane. Not in France, anyway. Is it different where you came from?"

"Yes! It was normal… expected even. Everyone had at least the same as I, some even more."

Lisette was agog. "Extraordinary," she whispered.

Morgane shrugged. "I think more people carry weapons than you expect."

"Well, some men carry swords, I suppose. But I've never seen a woman wear a brace of pistols."

"You should try it," Morgane said with a smirk. "You might like it."

Lisette blushed a little and moved away from the window. "We're getting distracted. What are we going to do?"

"I reckon we should go. No point waiting for that lying arse to come back."

"He's not the comte but perhaps he is still your father."

Morgane shrugged. "He probably is, but it's of no interest to me. I came to France to find my mother, not him. He's done nothing and said nothing that makes me feel it's worth staying for him, and said and done a lot more to make me feel it's worth leaving him and this damn house far behind."

"But where will you go? Who is your mother? Do you know where she is?" She paused. "Who were you raised by, Morgane? I had assumed it was your mother—"

"The woman who raised me wasn't my mother, even though she told me she was, right up until she was dying and had to ease her conscience before going to hell. I have no patience for anyone lying to me, and no patience for a weak man who thought it was more important he get me under his control when I was handling everything just fine!" Morgane stopped, fists clenched tight, trying to rein in her temper.

Lisette looked horrified and confused before settling on pitying, which Morgane couldn't stand to see, so she turned away. "Oh, Morgane. You've been through so much, haven't you?"

"Leave it. It's of no matter to you." She regretted the words as soon as they filled the air between them. "I just… Sorry. I don't want to talk about it. I just want to get moving!" She pulled out the bundle from under the bed, put her boots on and checked she had all her things. "Let's go."

"We need to get back to my village as quickly as possible,

it's true," Lisette said, heading for the door. "But we need food and—" A hand bell was rung downstairs, making her smile. "Let's get some food to eat as we walk, and then we'll leave."

"But Jean-Baptiste could be back at any moment!"

"We need to eat," Lisette insisted. "Trust me, I will walk far slower on an empty stomach. When we get back to the town, I'll pay off my father's debts and make it clear to Laroche that I've left this position. I'll make him think that his words made me reflect. Then he'll feel like he has had some small victory. I predict that he'll be so set on catching the false comte that he'll leave me alone until he's enacted his plan, leaving you and I free to do what we need to, to help you find your mother. Is that agreeable to you?"

Morgane tussled with how irritatingly sensible Lisette's plan was, wanting to just strike out right now. Then she remembered the last day with Anna-Marie, how her pride, her arrogance and her refusal to listen to anyone's counsel had gotten her killed.

"I am hungry," she admitted, and followed Lisette out of the room.

CHAPTER FIFTEEN

THEY WENT DOWN to the dining room, pausing only for Lisette to collect a small bag of belongings, to find a sideboard laden with bread, butter, pastries and a steaming pan of a brown drink that Lisette squealed at the sight of. "Is that...?" She rushed over and ladled the liquid into a cup to taste it. "It's chocolate, Morgane! What a treat!"

Morgane accepted the cup that Lisette gave to her. She'd never tasted anything like it before. Even though she didn't agree with the way the French seemed very happy to make the wrong people rich, they did know a thing or two about how to make good food and drink.

"I've always wanted to try it!" Lisette gushed. "It's so expensive... I wonder if the staff want to keep us happy long enough to get paid."

Morgane drained the cup, stuffed one of the pastries into her mouth and then took two of the large linen napkins, handing one to Lisette. "We can put the food in these," she said around the pastry.

Lisette tore off a piece of bread and dunked it in the second cup of chocolate and sighed happily. "It's perfectly awful that we've been lied to, but heavens, I do think this makes up for it a little."

Morgane grinned at her. "Come on, we need to get moving."

"I'm not leaving a drop of this behind." She poured a second cup for Morgane, and then ate a pastry while dropping others onto the centre of her napkin. "I feel like a thief."

"This ain't thievin'," Morgane laughed. "They gave it to us to eat! And no one'll miss a couple of cloths."

"Napkins," Lisette corrected her.

As they ate, Lisette started to ask quite reasonable questions, like where her mother lived so she could help her to plan how to reach her. Morgane fell silent. Even though she'd decided Lisette was effectively crew, she still found it hard to be open with her. They'd banded together, yes. They were looking out for each other. But they hadn't fought together, and they hadn't faced death and not only survived, but thrived as a result. Those were the bonds that made proper crew, and she had no idea how to forge them with alternative experiences.

But silence would not get her the information she needed. She had no idea how to ride a horse, so she needed some other form of transportation. The only one she'd be happy with would be a boat, but she didn't know how big the island of France was, nor even how far away her mother lived.

"I only know her family name," she finally said. "And I know I have the same hair as her. That's all."

Lisette, who was dunking more bread into the chocolate, frowned a little. "When did you last see her?"

"I was taken from her when I was a baby." She sighed. "By my aunt."

She didn't look at Lisette, choosing to drink the remaining chocolate, rather than see any response in her eyes. But then Lisette's slender hand reached over to rest on hers.

"This aunt stole you away to the other side of the world,

and when she died and you knew the truth, you decided to come back to France to find her? Oh Morgane, I think you are the bravest person I've ever met."

Morgane looked at her then, seeing nothing but admiration. She squirmed. "Well, I had to. She needs me, I know it. And what else was I to do? I wasn't ready to be captain."

"Was your aunt a captain?"

She was giving too much away, but it was so hard to give just enough without Lisette, clever as she was, filling in the rest. She nodded reluctantly.

"My goodness, I had no idea that was even possible!"

Morgane risked a glance at her, wondering if she was finally going to work out what kind of life she used to lead, but if she had, she said nothing. "You're taking too long with that chocolate."

"It can't be rushed! This may be the only chance I'll get to enjoy it in my entire life." She stifled a belch. "It's rather rich." After a couple of sips, she asked, "Would you be happy to tell me your mother's married name?"

Morgane noted the sensitivity of the question. Lisette knew how hard all of this was for her. "All I know is that she married the Comte d'Artois."

Lisette's eyes widened. "That's one of the wealthiest families in France, Morgane."

"I know they have a trading company, that's all really."

"They have both old and new money," Lisette said, sounding almost reverential. "A very respected family."

Morgane didn't see why when their coin was minted would make a difference. "Do you know where they live?"

"In the north. Quite a long way from here. But there are coaches that travel to Nantes from my town and from there you could find transport to Paris, and from there to Artois. I imagine any driver going to the region will know where the family seat is."

"But what about their chateau?"

Lisette laughed. "That's what I meant."

Morgane digested what she'd said. The prospect of travelling for many days in a carriage did not appeal to her at all. And how would she know where to go in Paris in order to secure passage to the north of France? It felt too complicated.

But going by sea felt much better. There may even be Four Chains trading ships that went to the north of the country. Then she remembered the man she was supposed to meet, the one in charge of the company in Nantes. That made her wonder about where Captain Lavois was now. The *Maître* was probably at sea again already, and Lavois would have put it all behind him. Or perhaps he'd been sacked, having lost his most precious cargo.

The only thing that put her off returning to Nantes was the possibility of running into Ball-ache and his associates again.

"How long would it take to sail round to Artois?"

"I hadn't considered that... I've no idea. Days, if not weeks, I would imagine."

"It's a big island then." When Lisette looked confused, she added, "France... it's a big island."

"Oh! It isn't an island, Morgane. We'd have to sail up the Loire, through Nantes and then all the way round to——"

"Isn't Europe lots of big islands and France one of them?"

"Not exactly. Europe is made up of countries, not islands, and we have land borders with several of them. Perhaps one of the books in the salon has a map..."

The sound of hooves made them both stop and stare at each other before rushing to the window to see the kitchen boy leading a familiar horse and cart past them towards the stables. The front door was opening on the other side of the house.

"Shit! He came back early!"

"What shall we do?" Lisette asked, her cheeks now drained of their usual soft pink.

Morgane started to load her pistols, making the last of the colour in Lisette's lips fade away. "You're not going to shoot him, are you?"

She didn't answer, focusing on getting the shot and powder right.

"I think we need to be careful. We could slip out of the back door and make a run for it."

"I ain't runnin' from that poxy coward!"

"We don't know how he'll react, or who he really is. Please, put those away and let me talk. Whatever you do, don't provoke him. He might be dangerous."

The sound of approaching footsteps silenced both of them. Morgane raised her pistols as the door opened.

Jean-Baptiste, looking windswept and weary, opened the door and stopped at the sight of the two of them. His eyes darted from Morgane's weaponry to their faces, and back again. "Were you expecting someone else?"

"No, we were expecting *you*, you lying swab!" Morgane shouted. A faint groan of disapproval floated from Lisette, but she ignored it. "You're no comte, you snivelling rat! And there had better be a good reason for your lies or I'm—"

"Please! Please, let me explain!" he yelled, fixated on the way her hands were ready to fire the weapons. "For the love of God, allow me to come inside and have a civil conversation, rather than being threatened on an empty stomach!"

Lisette rested her hand on Morgane's arm. "Yes, come inside."

Morgane took a step back, still glowering at him, and he entered, closing the door behind him. Still keeping his eyes on her and the pistols, Jean-Baptiste made his way to the sideboard.

"Oooh, is this an apple—"

"Well?" Morgane demanded.

He abandoned the apple tart and turned to face them again with a nervous smile. "Have you both been comfortable?"

"Yes… but…" Lisette began gently.

"Why did you lie to us? Who are you really?" Morgane shouted. "Are you even my father?"

He winced. "Yes, I am. Please put those away. Let's sit down and eat together."

He was incredibly calm, considering he was unarmed. Did he simply not believe she'd shoot him? He knew where she came from, so surely he wouldn't be so stupid as to assume that? Slowly, she lowered the pistols, but didn't holster them yet.

"All I wanted was a little time and for you to be proud of me."

"A little time to do what? Convince us that you were rich?"

"No, time to complete a business deal."

Morgane felt like she'd asked someone what day of the week it was only to be told it was November.

"Please, sit down… listen… let me explain without you being so angry."

"I have every right to be angry, liar! You're wasting my time, and—"

"No, not wasting your time. I'm trying to save you!"

"From what exactly?"

He sat heavily on one of the chairs. "Your mother."

That stunned Morgane into silence. She allowed Lisette to guide her to the dining table and pulled her down to sit next to her. She placed the pistols within easy reach on the table.

"I think it may be best if you explain yourself from the beginning," Lisette said gently.

He ran his hands over his hair, trying to smooth back strands that had fallen from the ribbon at the nape of his neck. "I've been looking for you all your life, Morgane. As has your mother. I knew she was using the Four Chains Trading Company to do that. I… I have lots of contacts at the docks. I knew they'd found you after I spoke to someone who had a ship return a few days before the *Maître*, saying that he'd heard about a blonde-haired girl being hidden on board while they were alongside at Saint-Domingue. Once word of that got out, I saw people lurking in Nantes that I knew were trouble. And I knew they were there for you."

"How?"

"Because they came shortly after the rumour got out, and they watched the Four Chains warehouses and docks, day and night, waiting for the *Maître*."

"But why? I'm no one special."

"Your mother married into a very wealthy family. I can only assume they wanted to capture you, for ransom."

"So, you decided to hire an old woman to hit me over the head? What a marvel you are."

He gripped the sides of his head in his hands and almost doubled over, as if he was in pain. "No! I told you that I didn't plan for that to happen! It just happened so quickly. I had no idea they had a man on the *Maître*, it ruined everything I'd planned."

"So, you found out your long-lost daughter was returning to France, you made plans to… find her when she arrived, it didn't go entirely to plan but you were eventually reunited in the woods yesterday," Lisette said, calmly, her hand back on Morgane's arm. "What we don't understand is why you deceived us. Why you brought Morgane here and hired me."

He looked so uncomfortable. "I could see that Morgane would be in danger from the moment she arrived, so I needed to get her out of Nantes and somewhere safe as soon as I could. I have… an arrangement with the Comte de Sauvineau. He's a keen collector of certain items… paintings… pieces of art… and he… I help him to acquire them."

"You steal them?" Morgane asked.

"No! I don't steal them. I'm a dealer in rare art and…"

"Oh, you have other people steal them and then sell them to others," Morgane said, and she could tell from the look on his face that she was right. "I get it. Your contacts at the docks… finding out about cargo before it arrives… that old woman and the mutual friend you mentioned to her that you didn't want to find out about me… there's a group of you, is there? All working together to trade stolen goods?"

Lisette gasped, as though even the mere suggestion that he be involved in such activities was rude, but it was the first thing that actually made sense to Morgane. And it explained why he was so calm. It probably wasn't the first time he'd been threatened, in his line of work.

"You wanted me to think you were fancy, and rich, so I'd be so happy you'd found me. So you asked the comte for a favour… maybe promising him that you'll find him something extra special for one of his collections if he lets you stay here."

"Well, I wouldn't put it that way exactly. It's a business arrangement."

"You're a cleaner, no need to dress it up." She looked at Lisette. "I used to know lots of people like him. They buy stolen goods from whoever stole them, really cheap, and then sell them to rich people who either don't know or don't care where they came from, for profit."

Lisette looked like a woman learning far more about the world than she wanted to. She looked at Jean-Baptiste. "Is this true?"

He nodded, resigned.

"Well, at least now we understand why he lied about being a comte," she said to Morgane.

Morgane shook her head. "He was just pretending to be a different kind of thief. I don't see the point at all."

"The Comte of Sauvineau is not a thief!" Lisette said.

"He is. You just call it taxes. He takes your money and doesn't solve your problems, what else should I call him?" She glared at Jean-Baptiste. "So, you failed to greet me on my arrival, failed to have me kept safe from those men in Nantes – not that I even wanted that from you – you failed to impress me... what was all this for exactly? Why do I need to be kept safe from my own mother by a feeble liar?"

"I think that is rather harsh."

"No, it isn't," Lisette said. "You lied to me, too."

"Only because I wanted my daughter to have a companion! I couldn't give her anything before, so all I wanted was for her to have a nice young lady to help her to settle into our way of life! I feared the worst, and I was clearly proven right!" He gestured in Morgane's direction. "You were raised by a pirate and—"

"And why was Anna-Marie a pirate?! Because she was stupid enough to love you! I'm not going to make that same mistake."

"Pirate?" Lisette said in a small voice.

Jean-Baptiste's mouth was opening and closing like a recently landed fish as he struggled to find the words to argue back.

"You can take your fantasy of being a father and stuff it up your arse. You've wasted enough of my time. You pay Lisette for her time – and extra for all the bullshit you have put her through – and then we're off."

"But Morgane, you don't understand! Your mother—"

"My mother needs me and—"

"Isabeau has never needed anyone in her entire life!" His shout made Lisette jump, as Morgane thrilled at the discovery of her mother's name at last. Isabeau. "She sucks people in, chews them up and spits them out when she's bored of them! Do you know why I'm forced to sell stolen goods? Because she destroyed my life!"

Morgane shook her head. "And how did she do that? Did

she tell your actual fiancée that you were ploughing her sister? That what she did, was it?"

"She seduced me and when she fell pregnant, she accused me of rape. She turned everyone against me. I was a cabinet maker, I had a good life ahead of me, until—"

"Until you decided to fuck your fiancée's sister!" Morgane shouted. "That's where it started, you swab! If you'd stayed faithful, she couldn't have done that, could she?!"

There was a dreadful silence. "You're right," he finally said. "I never should have done that. But what she did afterwards revealed who she really was, and that's all I'm trying to explain to you."

"I don't care what you think of her, I will form my own opinion." But what he'd said had shaken her. He'd made it sound like he was the victim. She looked at Lisette. "It's time to go."

"You're right," Jean-Baptiste said. "We have to be back in Nantes by tomorrow morning."

Morgane narrowed her eyes at him. "Back to the place that was too dangerous for me? How is that a good plan?"

"It can't be helped. We'll be careful. I've booked passage to New France for both of us."

Morgane laughed. "This is a bloody jest, surely?"

He looked hurt. "No! It's not. This is what I was seeing to last night. I had to make a risky deal, pull in a couple of favours, but I—"

Morgane banged the table. "I ain't going to New bloody France! Even if I was happy to go anywhere with you – which I'm not – that's the last place I'd choose. Do you know how bloody cold and miserable it is there? I knew men who made good money selling furs there who left because of it."

"But it's the only way to keep you safe!"

She looked at Lisette. "I've heard enough from this barnacle, let's go."

"Can't you see that it's the best option – the only option – for us?" Jean-Baptiste pleaded. "Those men who tried to capture you before… they won't give up. And even if you did manage to keep away from them and get to your mother… I fear that would be even worse. You thought that Anna-Marie was cold… it's nothing compared to her!"

"I didn't betray her," Morgane said, picking up her pistols and holstering them. "You did."

"When I was a young idiot! And I paid for that mistake, a thousand times over."

The defeat and sadness in his voice almost gave Morgane pause. But then she remembered that she would probably be with her mother by now, were it not for his meddling. She stood up. "I know my mother needs me. I don't care what your opinion of her is, nor what fantasy you might have had about finding me again. I have my own path and you will not pull me from it any longer!"

He stood, too. "Listen… I will take us all back to town, to see Lisette home."

"And paid!" Morgane insisted.

"Of course, of course. We can talk on the way. If you want to leave after I've got you there safely, then… then I cannot stop you."

CHAPTER SIXTEEN

IT WASN'T LONG before the three of them were leaving the house behind them, along with the staff who'd elected to stay the night and make their own way home the next day. There were no goodbyes as no love had been lost between any of them, and Morgane was hugely relieved to see the house recede into the distance. Listening in on the awkward conversation between Lisette and Jean-Baptiste, Morgane discovered that the butler was actually an employee of the real comte, one who'd been asked to keep an eye on everything. That the comte knew about the deception had made Lisette smile for the first time since Jean-Baptiste had returned. It stole the thunder from Laroche's plans for advancement.

As they made their way through the woods, Lisette sitting at the front alongside the man who claimed to be her father, Morgane sat in the rear of the cart with their belongings. It was empty now, the goods presumably traded on in return for those useless tickets, and moved faster as a result. Still, Morgane searched for the sun's dull glow behind the clouds whenever the trees opened up a little, desperately trying to gauge how much daylight they had left. The occasional distant howl made Lisette visibly shudder.

Morgane wasn't relaxed either, but for different reasons. She found herself chewing over whether he was her father or not, and if it even mattered. He wasn't the one she'd been searching for. On the trip across the Atlantic, he'd been a fuzzy background figure, imagined as a man close to her mother but far less important. He was indeed called Jean-Baptiste, apparently sharing the same name with the comte by pure chance, although he'd accidentally given his full name when they'd met and then tried to pass it off as an absurdly long and complex noble name. She was relieved to find he wasn't a comte, given what she'd learnt about them, and his chosen profession was one she understood completely. Better a petty criminal than one who benefited from the grim spell that everyone seemed to live under here. But Lisette had talked about her mother's family wealth in awe, and she wasn't sure how she felt about that, given what she'd learned about France so far.

That was something to work out later on, though. Between the sketch book and the passion with which he'd spoken, she was starting to believe he was who he claimed to be. Why else do all the stupid things he'd done for her, a woman he'd never met? This short trip could be the only opportunity she had to speak to her father. She found herself devoid of questions, though. He'd meant nothing to her all her life. And he was utterly unfathomable. His decisions mystified her. Why think that she'd be happy to go with him to a small, barely established colony in a cold, remote location when they didn't know each other at all?

"What is a cabinet maker anyway?" she asked, reflecting upon the tense conversation in the dining room.

"An artisan who works in wood. I used to make tables, bureaus, armoires… I was very good at it. I apprenticed from the age of twelve."

"Oh! Like a carpenter. I'm good at working with wood, too. Repairs and the like. Never made furniture, though."

He twisted round to smile at her. "You must have got it from me. If you can repair ships, you can learn how to make furniture in no time, I'm sure. I could teach you."

The brief feeling of having something to connect them soured at the suggestion, like he was trying to fit her into his life without considering what she was there to do. In fairness she hadn't told him. Damn it, she'd been so angry with him for what he'd done to Anna-Marie, she hadn't given him a chance.

"Do you know why Anna-Marie hated the Four Chains Trading Company?"

"I never knew she did."

"Theirs were the only ships we attacked."

He twisted round again, genuinely interested. "Really? I cannot see why. The owner, the Comte d'Artois, saved your mother and her reputation."

"How?"

"He married her, even though she was already pregnant. I'd heard that he was going to raise you as his own, but Anna-Marie clearly had other ideas and stole you away."

"But why ever would she do that?" Lisette asked. "Why deny one's niece legitimacy and a life in the nobility?"

"I have no idea. Isabeau and Anna-Marie's parents were wealthy in their own right, but nothing compared to the family d'Artois."

"I think she wanted to hurt my mother," Morgane said quietly, and they fell into silence.

"And forgive me for asking," Lisette said after a few moments, "but why do you wish to do the same, monsieur? I'm sure Morgane's mother will be overjoyed to be reunited with her daughter. And if the comte was already prepared to claim her child as his own, it should not be an issue for her to be returned to the fold."

"I told you, Isabeau is a terrible woman. And I've heard stories about the Artois family."

"What stories?"

"That they're cruel. Even more so than Isabeau."

Perhaps that was what her mother needed to be rescued from then. Perhaps this comte, who had originally seemed like a saviour, had proven to be something terrible. Perhaps it also had something to do with the vendetta Anna-Marie had against their company.

"You've changed since then, so you claim," she said to him. "Why not her?"

He said nothing to that.

"Why New France?" she asked him.

"They speak French and it's as far away from France as we can go."

"Do you have so little affection for your home?" Lisette asked him.

"Au contraire. I love France." He glanced back at Morgane. "But I cannot see a way to keep my daughter safe here."

"I'll keep myself safe," Morgane muttered.

"Those men that tried to kidnap you in Nantes. They were highly skilled professionals. Perhaps in the employ of a rival noble family, for all I know. And if not a noble, a very successful criminal, to be able to afford them."

"I got away from them before. And if you hadn't interfered, I could have found my way to Monsieur de Lombardy and would probably be well on my way to my mother."

"Who is he?" Lisette asked.

"A man high up in the Four Chains Company. The captain of the ship who brought me here was escorting me to him when one of his own men turned on him. I suppose he was in league with those men in black."

"I don't think so," Jean-Baptiste muttered.

"You cannot really believe that so many different groups of people would want to kidnap me!"

"I can and I do. Whether it was for ransom or some other reason, that I do not know. What I do know is that they won't have your best interests at heart like I do."

"Why should I believe you?"

"Pour l'amour de Dieu! Because I am your father! Why would I—"

A deep howl in the woods to their right cut him off mid-sentence. It was much closer than the ones before. Lisette gave her a terrified glance and hunkered down further under her blanket, as if it could afford some protection.

"It's just big dogs, there's—" Morgane's ineffective reassurance was interrupted by another howl, forming a grim harmony with the first. That one sounded even closer.

Jean-Baptiste snapped the reins and urged the horse to go faster. The howls continued, three, then four, and Morgane pressed down the fear as she struggled to determine the direction they were coming from. All she could tell was that it didn't seem to be from ahead.

There was something about the howls that made her feel like she used to in the moments before boarding a targeted ship. They didn't sound like mere dogs, that's what her heart was telling her, and without even thinking about it, she fished out the pouch of fabric-covered lead balls and powder flask, just in case she needed to reload.

She drew both pistols, half-cocked the hammer on both, and then as another chorus of howls filled the air, louder, she pulled the hammer all the way back on the right-hand pistol and pointed it towards the trees behind them. As soon as she saw a movement, she would fire.

In a lull between the howling, there was the faintest sound of a man's voice, calling, but Morgane wasn't sure if she'd actually heard it. When Lisette said, "Did you hear that?"

she twisted round to face front again, making sure that the pistols were aimed away from her companions.

"Help! Help me!"

They all heard that. A man's desperate yelling from up ahead.

"It could be a trap, don't stop," she said to Jean-Baptiste.

Lisette looked horrified. "We can't just ignore him! What if the wolves have him?"

"Help!"

Lisette pointed ahead and to the left, through a parting in the trees. Morgane recognised Laroche's dark green riding coat immediately. He was high up in a tree, clinging to the trunk like it was a mast in a storm.

"It's Monsieur Laroche!" Lisette gasped. "It's no trap, please stop – we have to help him down!"

Morgane scoured the woods for any sign of Laroche's horse. It must have bolted. "Something made him climb up that tree and I reckon it was those wolves. If we stop for him, they'll make us their next meal!"

"We can't just leave him there!" Lisette insisted.

Morgane scowled at her, confused by why she was so keen to save a man who'd been making her life so miserable.

To her dismay, her father slowed the cart as they approached and Laroche noticed.

"Oh, thank the sweet Lord above," Laroche said hoarsely. "Please, help me down, before they come back!"

"Who?" Morgane shouted up at him.

"The bandits!"

"I'm telling you, this is a trap," Morgane muttered to Jean-Baptiste, but he ignored her. It was then that she realised the howling had stopped.

Somehow, the silence was worse.

"There were four of them, wearing black," Laroche was babbling as Jean-Baptiste pulled the reins and stopped the cart. It was only a few yards to Laroche's tree, but the ground was soft away from the track.

"Can you climb down?" he called up to him. "We haven't seen any bandits."

"I think the wolves scared them away," Laroche said. "I... I'll try to come down."

Morgane grit her teeth, keeping her eyes on the trees around them, and not on the idiot men. She fully cocked the second pistol, ready.

A movement drew her eyes, but was gone when she looked straight in that direction. The hairs on the back of her neck were tingling, every instinct telling her that they had to move, when she saw a flash of pale grey between the trees.

Stupidly, all she could think was 'that's no bloody dog' as the creature's amber eyes locked with hers. It was motionless, horribly beautiful and terrifying all at once. It had to be almost as tall as Lisette.

"You'd better get down from that tree, Laroche, right now, or you're going to be up there all night," she called, not taking her eyes off the creature. It was too far away for her to hit reliably, and she didn't want to waste a shot. "We need to move," she said more quietly to Jean-Baptiste.

Another movement, this time to her right. Another wolf. Closer.

"Now, we need to go now!" she said more urgently.

"Quickly, monsieur!" Jean-Baptiste yelled.

The third wolf came into view. The fourth was no doubt closing in; the pack was surrounding them slowly.

Thinking they might be like the abandoned dogs that became dangerous in big packs in Port Royal, Morgane fired the first pistol, hoping that the sudden noise would scare them off, if not give them pause.

Lisette screamed behind her, and the horse whinnied in distress, as the bark of the tree next to the closest wolf splintered. The wolf, however, didn't even flinch, instead baring its teeth slowly.

A quick glance confirmed that none of the others had been startled either. Were these creatures so used to pistol shots?

A thud made her flinch and turn, only to see that it was Laroche making a graceless landing at the bottom of the tree. When she looked back at the wolf she'd fired at, it was even closer and even bigger than she'd appreciated. With only thirty yards or so between them, it would be able to close the distance between them in moments.

She moved the loaded pistol to her right hand, dropping the spent one into her lap. Only one shot left, but if one of them leaped, it could be enough to kill it at close range. She dared not put the loaded one down to reload the other.

"Lisette, can you load a pistol?"

"No! Why would I know how to do that?!" Her words were fast and high pitched with panic.

"I can," said Laroche, clambering into the back of the cart with her as Jean-Baptiste urged the increasingly nervous horse to move.

"You're not touching my pistols," Morgane snapped at him as the cart finally lurched forwards, sending him onto his backside and forcing him to grip the wooden sides to stop himself from rolling straight back out again.

"Mon Dieu, I've never seen such big wolves!" he gasped as he spotted one. "No wonder they scared off the bandits!"

"Get down," Morgane told him as she trained her loaded pistol on the one closest to them, which seemed to be slavering in anticipation.

Thankfully, he did as she asked, perhaps because he looked almost faint with exhaustion.

The cart moved forwards in jerking lurches as Jean-Baptiste struggled to control the horse, the wolves getting closer. Morgane, filled with the pure rush of adrenaline and a perverse thrill at finally having something real to fight, switched her attention between the three wolves she could see closing in. She knew that one of them was bound to pounce into the back of the cart, and she needed to wait until the last possible moment to fire.

But pistols were unreliable, and she'd seen crew run through after a misfire when they'd banked on the same strategy. So, as she watched, she drew her knife with her left hand, just in case.

The one directly in front of her increased its speed with a sudden burst of energy and it closed the gap between it and the cart almost faster than Morgane could react to. But then it was leaping over the panels that formed the low back of the cart, its pale belly in full view, right in front of her and then she was firing and the crack of the shot made the cart lurch again with the horse's panic and there was a horrible moment when she thought she'd missed until she saw a tiny spurt of blood and heard the yelp of the injured wolf.

But it didn't collapse as she'd hoped. All it seemed to do was interrupt its attack, like it had merely been kicked, rather than shot at almost point-blank range. It landed awkwardly, half in, half out of the cart, Laroche curling into a whimpering ball inches from its front paws. The dreadful creature – bigger than a grown man – scrabbled desperately to hook its hind legs over the wood but thankfully failed and fell off the back of the cart.

Horrified, she watched it spring back onto its feet, shake itself off and resume the chase as if it wasn't even hurt. She dropped the spent pistol to lie next to the other useless weapon, not caring about reloading now. It wasn't worth the time and resulting vulnerability if they weren't stopped by each shot. She knelt instead, drawing her sword and then shifting into a low crouch, ready for the next attack.

She was so focused on the three wolves she could see that

she forgot about the fourth, right up until the horse let out a terrified noise and the cart came to an abrupt stop, knocking her onto her knees.

Snapping round to look behind her, Morgane was horrified to see the fourth wolf launch itself off the back of the horse it had just terrorised and hurl itself into Lisette. She was knocked off the cart and slammed onto the ground a few feet away, the wolf landing astride her. She was winded, face so white it looked like death was already upon her, and paralysed with fear. Instead of ripping out her throat, the wolf rested a paw on the woman's chest, effortlessly pinning her to the ground.

Morgane scrabbled to her feet and, without a moment's hesitation, planted a foot on the side of the cart and launched herself off it, sword ready to strike, her knife held as a main gauche, to land on the back of the wolf and slash at its hide. The creature roared, whether it was from pain or anger Morgane had no idea, but she didn't care, plunging her knife into its flank and raising it for a second strike.

The wolf threw her off its back and she landed badly, dropping her knife. Even though the wolf looked like it barely felt the wounds she'd given it, at least it lost interest in Lisette and was now very much focused on her instead. Then Morgane realised that the other wolf, the one she'd shot, was coming round the side of the now stationary cart, also fixated on her.

In the absence of a plan, she got to her feet as fast as she could, picking up her knife and holding both it and the sword in front of her defensively, feeling like she was holding toothpicks against an oncoming storm.

Then one of the other wolves bounded into view, heading straight for her. It snarled, but not at her, it seemed, as it looked from the stabbed wolf to the shot wolf while it padded towards her, as if it was communicating something to them.

Much to her relief, both of those wolves lowered their heads and stopped where they were. It was only a minor improvement of her situation, what with the third wolf effectively boxing her in against the cart, but at least she was still breathing.

The uninjured wolf was bigger than the other two, with streaks of sable fur that ran over its back and eyes the colour of the sky over Port Royal at dawn. Its gaze pressed her against the cart, her heart thudding so hard she could feel it in her throat and her ears.

It was close enough for her to feel the damp warmth of its breath as it plumed out towards her, despite the fact her sword was between them. And then it wasn't, knocked out of her hand with a swipe of its paw. She gripped her knife tighter and then noticed the wolf on her right growling menacingly as it stared at the hand that held it.

After a brief internal tussle, she decided to drop the knife, which settled the wolf. Neither of her weapons were going to help her. She just couldn't understand why they weren't sinking their teeth into her already.

The sable wolf stopped an arm's length away from her, and then seemed to check that the other two wolves were still before closing the last few inches. It moved slowly, not like something about to rip her throat out, but it didn't make the experience any easier.

It smelt of damp moss and a heady musky smell that made her feel sick. It sniffed at her, and then nudged her shoulder with its muzzle. Confused, she looked up to see that there was no longer a brim in her field of vision. Her hat had fallen off and the long braid of bright blonde hair that she'd twisted out of sight under it was now in full view. Was... was this monstrous wolf... recognising her?

A flash of movement behind the wolf, the evening sunlight glinted off something metallic and then the wolf roared in agony. It was so close to her face that she felt its saliva land on her cheeks, saw the inside of its throat. And then, impossibly, the muzzle started to shrink, the sheer bulk of the creature began to crumple inwards, the hair of its pelt shortening, as if being sucked into the skin it had grown out of.

It was so horrendous, so incomprehensible, that all Morgane could do was shrink back, pressing herself against the cart with such force she could feel it bruising her back. In moments, the creature was looking less like a wolf and more like a bizarre hybrid of man and beast, the roar now sounding like that of a badly injured man. Before her eyes, the sable pelt on its head morphed into blond hair and with a dreadful crackling of bones distorting, the face became one she recognised. It was the man who'd tried to lead her away from the market, the one she'd kneed in the balls, the one the old woman had knocked out in the warehouse.

And behind him was a woman, dressed in midnight blue velvet, pulling out her hands from the man's torso and revealing a set of exquisitely vicious silver claws, worn like jewellery over the tips of her fingers, dripping with blood.

Then the other wolves went for her and the blond man, wolf, whatever he was, fell at Morgane's feet and other blue clad fighters appeared, armed with the same claws, and chaos erupted.

Now fixated on killing the new arrivals, the other wolves abruptly ignored Morgane. Her panicked brain took a few moments to kick back into action. She recovered her weapons and went straight to Lisette who was desperately scooting backwards on her backside to avoid the vicious fighting.

Sheathing the sword as she reached her, Morgane held out her hand and Lisette grabbed it. She was shining with sweat, still as pale as a white pirate's arse and shaking so much she could barely stand.

Morgane had seen shock, had experienced it after her first

close call with death many years before. She slid her knife back into her boot, hooked Lisette's limp arm over her shoulder and took her weight, steering her to the back of the cart and then encouraging her to clamber into it with her help. Once her crewmate was aboard, Morgane climbed in, too, relieved to see Jean-Baptiste climbing back into place at the front. Perhaps he'd been dealing with the horse. She didn't care as soon as the cart started moving again.

Morgane settled Lisette into the corner she'd been sitting in before and then grabbed a blanket only to reveal Laroche cowering beneath it. Startled, he yelped with fear before realising that it was only her. The stench of urine was strong but mercifully none of it was on the blanket. She tucked it around Lisette and crouched next to her, hand on her arm to let her know she was safe as she surveyed the fighting around them.

It was too hard to tell who was winning, and frankly, she didn't care. Her father had managed to persuade the horse to channel its fear into escape and they were soon rattling along fast enough to leave the combatants behind. It seemed they were far more interested in killing each other than pursuing them.

Morgane sank back and put her arm around Lisette who started to weep into her shoulder. Laroche sat up and, apparently seeing Lisette's distress as an opportunity of some kind, began to move towards them.

Morgane pointed a finger at him. "Don't you bloody dare, you poxy coward. You don't deserve to even look at her. Sit in your own piss and if you say one word to me before we reach the town, I swear I will gut you and use your lungs for pillows."

He backed off and Morgane wrapped her other arm around Lisette, too.

She expected the crashing fatigue once the immediate

threat was over, but it didn't hit right away. The roaring barks of the gigantic wolfmen were still loud as the fight raged on, and she could see that glinting silver of their enemies flashing through gaps in the trees. But she could barely pay attention to it as her mind tumbled over the sight of the wolf shrinking into the form of the man who'd tried to kidnap her. Her memory cycled through the details, again and again, as if trying to force them into a shape that made sense. She squeezed her eyes shut and all she could see was the muzzle distorting, the hair disappearing, all accompanied by the crackling of the bones beneath its – his – its skin. And she knew, more than she knew anything, that she would never forget it for as long as she lived.

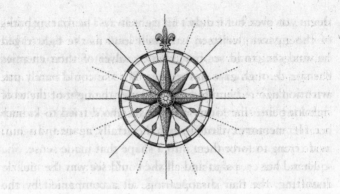

CHAPTER SEVENTEEN

THE JOURNEY TO the town was long enough that Lisette recovered her composure before they reached their destination and awkwardly disentangled herself from Morgane's protective embrace. She looked better, in that she wasn't sobbing or deathly pale anymore, but Morgane could sense how she'd been changed, too. Even though she'd mentioned the dangers of the woods so many times, actually coming face to face with them was a different matter.

But Morgane had the horrible feeling that those weren't the dangers Lisette had had in mind. Those wolves had been hunting for her, and her alone. As for those other people, who'd saved them, she was less certain. Were they simply hunting those creatures, and their small band of travellers had benefitted from it, or were they protecting her specifically from them?

She suspected it was not the latter, and that thinking so was merely the shock of seeing Ball-ache once again. As Anna-Marie had been so determined to teach her, she was not the centre of the universe.

They travelled in silence, everyone tired out and still in some degree of shock. Morgane let herself rest, only expending her energy on glaring at Laroche every time he looked like he was going to try it on with Lisette again. She didn't mind the silence, though it was strange to be sitting after a battle with no flagon of bumbo or increasingly embellished tales of fighting being shared amongst the survivors. It had been such a brief encounter, though, and mercifully no one was hurt aside from a few bruises.

There was a palpable sense of relief from her fellow travellers when they passed a stone set at the side of the road with some writing carved into it. Lisette gave her a smile. "Not long now. We're in the boundary of Mouzeil."

"That's your town?"

Lisette nodded, giving Laroche a nervous glance. She was obviously weighing something up.

"We'll take you home first, of course, Monsieur Laroche," she said, with her usual formal composure. Seeing her speak that way made Morgane appreciate just how distressed she'd been. It was like Lisette tensed up and held herself more rigidly when dealing with people she wasn't comfortable with. Watching her now, it was so hard to imagine her sobbing against her, all soft and needy, like she'd been not so long ago.

"I would appreciate that, mademoiselle," Laroche said. He, too, was trying to appear more composed than he had been, desperately trying to restore his own dignity. "You are, of course, welcome to restore yourself at my chateau if—"

"That will not be necessary, thank you," Lisette replied tersely. "Although there is a matter I'd like to discuss with you before we part ways."

The flicker of hope on his face was absolutely tragic. Morgane smirked to herself, knowing that he was going to be even more miserable before he retired to his bed.

As the sun tried its best to penetrate the thick cloud,

Morgane noted the change in the quality of the ride as the track turned into something better maintained, and then a stone surface. Lisette directed her father to go right through the town to the chateau on the far side and he gave a nod in acknowledgement. He looked very tired, from the set of his shoulders, and Morgane felt it was right to just leave him to steer the cart instead of continuing their conversation while Laroche would be able to listen in. As soon as he was deposited at his home there would be much to discuss.

They passed humble single-storey, timber-framed buildings that were far less intimidating than the stone edifices of Nantes. It was a small town, much more on a scale that Morgane could feel comfortable in. There were a couple of other roads leading out of the centre, a small square that Lisette said was for a variety of markets and public events, and a handful of stone buildings. Under Lisette's direction, her father made a couple of turnings once they were through the main part of the town and then they were approaching a set of high gates that were open, with an impressively large house at the end of a long drive. It was bigger than the lodge they'd been staying in, and looked more like a fort to Morgane.

"Right up to the door, if you'd be so kind," Laroche called ahead to her father, and the cart made its steady way through the avenue of trees.

As soon as the cart came to a stop, Lisette got to her feet at the same time as Laroche. He hastily jumped out of the cart, in part to hide the stain on his breeches, Morgane suspected. Lisette went to the edge of the cart but did not accept his hand, offered with the assumption that she was about to join him. Instead, she let him awkwardly hold it out for a few moments before he realised.

"Monsieur Laroche, I wanted to thank you for bringing your concerns about the comte to my attention," she began.

"It led me to ask the right questions and indeed, I was mistaken. The man who drove us here, after saving you from your… tree… is, in fact, a friend of the comte, who gave him permission to use his lodge temporarily. There was simply a misunderstanding on my part."

Laroche's smug expression melted into one of hard, contained anger by the end of Lisette's short speech. He glanced at Jean-Baptiste, who clearly had no interest in the conversation, and then back to Lisette. "I see. I will be sure to contact the comte to ensure that everything is in order."

"Oh, please do. As a responsible citizen, it does no harm to ask one's lord if he is satisfied with the arrangements he made without your knowledge."

Morgane couldn't help but grin. Lisette was so clever, in a way she never could be.

Laroche looked like he'd accidentally licked a sandy mollusc. As he struggled to think of something to say that would reassert his superiority, Lisette reached into her pocket.

"I'm delighted to say that this position has enabled me to secure the necessary funds to pay off my father's debt to you." She pulled out the coins that Morgane had gifted to her and held them out to Laroche. "There is enough there to cover the debt and the rent for the next six months. I trust you'll have no need to concern yourself with my family's affairs now, and that you'll be able to spend your time on more agreeable pursuits."

After blinking at her hand for a few moments, he started to reach for the coins. Lisette closed her fist around them. "I would be grateful if you could pen a note to my father, so I may reassure him that the debt is cleared. You know how much he worries about these things."

Morgane hugged her knees, watching the exchange with the same enjoyment that she used to watch Dill outwit Bull in any game he cared to play with her.

Laroche gave a single nod and went to the house. As they waited, Lisette shared a sparkling smile with Morgane, making her feel like she was caught in a single sunbeam that had burst through a clouded sky.

Laroche soon returned with a piece of paper and wearing a new coat that covered his soiled clothing. Reluctantly, he gave the note to Lisette who read it, smiled, and then gave him the coins.

"Well, I'm sure you're keen to bathe, so we won't keep you any longer," Lisette said. Her cheery words were received like a blow to Laroche's gut. He visibly crumpled at the realisation that he hadn't been able to hide his body's response to terror from her.

Lisette turned to go back to her place, when Laroche said, "Mademoiselle," as if the word had burst out of him through no intention of his own. When she looked back at him, he took in her face with an obvious longing, the thirst of a man watching the last drops drained from a barrel before he'd had a chance to hold out his cup. "I... I would very much like to... to invite you to dinner, once..."

"I think not, Monsieur Laroche," Lisette replied with a sweet smile. "Good day."

She sat down and the cart moved forwards again. Morgane felt Lisette's hand close around hers as they both watched the dejected man shuffle into his chateau without a backwards glance. The firm squeeze Lisette gave her spoke of gleeful victory shared, of the sheer happiness brought about by their collaboration to defeat a man who'd abused his power.

"Thank you," Lisette whispered in her ear and a tingle sparked down Morgane's back. She squeezed her hand back and stayed silent, wrapping the moment tightly in her heart cloth and pressing it deep into her soul, so that she might never forget its perfection.

* * *

LISETTE DIRECTED JEAN-BAPTISTE to a small house on the other side of town, not far from the market square. It was part of a row of two-storey houses and there was nowhere to stable the horse, so Lisette suggested using the communal area just off the market square where out-of-town traders put their horses on market days.

As the cart was positioned, Morgane tucked the spent pistols into her makeshift bag. Before reaching the town, she'd tucked her braid under the hat again, glad that the thing had fallen from her head as she'd leaped off to help Lisette and just landed in the cart. There were still people walking around the town, even though the day's market was over, and she didn't want anyone to notice weapons or blonde hair that might have been mentioned by the ones who had been hunting her.

Once the cart was stationary, she looped her makeshift bag over her shoulder, jumped off and went to Jean-Baptiste, wondering why he was so quiet, only to find him slumping forwards.

She knew, before she had even put a hand on his shoulder to push him back, that he was injured and was furious with herself for not taking a moment to check before. He was passing out and she couldn't stop him falling off the driver's board, managing only to slow his fall and protect his head. Laid on his side, crumpled and limp, she saw all the blood that had soaked his clothing from the midriff down. It had stained the board and from the amount and the pallor of his skin she feared he wasn't going to recover from this.

Passersby rushed over, taking her by surprise. There was a sudden flurry of activity and Lisette dashed across and took charge, directing the people who wanted to help to carry him to her house. Morgane was gently pushed back, and she found herself watching it all as if through a window, frozen, as a small tide of people swept him away.

A short woman with a wrinkled face wrapped the horse's reins around a post and gently took Morgane's arm. "Come along, young man, let's go with your father. He is your father, isn't he? I can see it. Come on now, that's it. Best to be with him now. I know it's hard, come on now."

It felt like she had to puppet her own body to make her legs move under the woman's coaxing. They followed the small crowd to Lisette's house and the old woman pushed the curious onlookers aside.

"Let us through, this is his son!" she crowed. People drifted apart, firing questions about what had happened.

"Wolves, in the woods," Morgane said, her voice sounding flat, not her own. She just wanted the questions to stop, to slake their curiosity so they would go away.

It elicited gasps and whispered exchanges. "You're of no help, you nosy sods, go home!" the old woman snapped at a particularly tight cluster blocking the door.

By the time they managed to get through into the house, Jean-Baptiste had been laid down in front of a fire, Lisette by his side, as an older man desperately pressed cloth against the wounds.

"I think the bleeding is slowing," the man said, hopefully. He'd clearly been expecting the cloth to be soaked immediately.

"No," Morgane said in that same strange, flat voice, having seen this before. "There's not enough life left in him to push it out."

"Thank you for your help," Lisette said, standing up to address the room. "Please can you give us some privacy?"

There was a change in the atmosphere, shifting from an audience taking in a spectacle to a sudden, respectful silence. The onlookers melted away, the man who'd been trying to staunch the bleeding the only one who stayed in place. Lisette didn't seem bothered by that, though, and Morgane realised it was her father.

The old woman who'd steered her in gave her a last squeeze on the arm and left, closing the door behind her to leave the four of them in their dreadful tableau.

"Why didn't you say something?" Morgane said but it came out like an angry shout.

Jean-Baptiste's eyes flickered open and fixed on her. His arm twitched, like he was trying to reach out to her, and she went to crouch at his side.

"Had to... see you safe..." he whispered. He pulled the leather pouch from his jacket and pressed it into her hands, his arm flopping away after what seemed like a herculean effort. "Morgane... don't find your... mother. She's a..."

She watched the last feeble breath escape his body and take his soul with it. His eyes lost the straining urgency of trying to speak to her and took on the glassy emptiness she'd seen so many times. But none of the men she'd watched die had claimed to be her father. None of them had died trying to save her.

Her legs wobbled and she landed on her backside, feeling like all the life was being sucked out of her, too. She barely knew the man and yet she felt such a sudden, profound sense of loss, even though he hadn't played any significant role in her life. He'd just been an irritation, a man who'd waylaid her and claimed to be acting in her best interests. But now all she wanted was to talk to him, to know him. Why hadn't she given him a chance?

She searched those dead eyes for some sort of explanation, but there was nothing to be found except a deep despair reflected back at her.

Lisette's father closed Jean-Baptiste's eyes for the last time.

"Oh, Morgane," Lisette whispered. "Oh... I'm so sorry."

She looked at the tears welling in Lisette's eyes, at how readily her new friend shared the grief she couldn't yet express. She looked back down at Jean-Baptiste's body, now being covered by a blanket that Lisette's father had pulled from a nearby chair, and then down at the pouch. It was thin leather, dark brown with an even darker, damp stain from the blood. It felt like someone else was holding it, and she was looking down on it as if through a telescope, as if she was some tiny person somehow sailing her own body like a ship.

She fumbled with the ties and opened it. There was a necklace, and a few sheafs of paper. She pulled on the gold chain first and revealed a locket. Opening it showed two tiny portraits, one of a young, innocent looking Anna-Marie before the cruelty had set on her face, the other of a young Jean-Baptiste.

She held it out to Lisette. "The woman is my aunt. As if I needed any more proof that he was my father."

"I'm sure he would have wanted you to wear it."

Morgane closed it and dropped it over her head to settle under her shirt, the heat of her body rapidly stealing the chill from the metal. Pulling the pieces of paper out revealed that the pouch had protected them from most of the blood and they were still legible. One was a letter covered with unintelligible scrawl. The other two pieces of paper were copies of each other, and looked different in their layout to a letter, but were just as indecipherable. She handed all of them to Lisette.

"The letter is from the comte," she said after a few moments. "It mentions the arrangement they'd discussed, and it gives Jean-Baptiste his blessing to use the lodge." She handed the letter back. "And these are the tickets to New France. One for him and one for you."

Morgane folded them up again and put them back into the pouch. She tied it shut and slid it inside her shirt.

Emma Newman

"I'll go and speak to the pastor," Lisette's father said. "Are you happy for his body to rest in the church before his burial?"

Morgane frowned, before realising that, stupidly, she hadn't considered what they'd do with bodies on dry land. She just nodded and watched him go.

Lisette got up, rested a hand on her shoulder briefly and then went off to another room. After an indeterminable length of time, she returned to drape a shawl around her shoulders and put a cup into her hand. "Hot milk and brandy," she said, sitting in the chair by the fire. "It will make you feel better."

Morgane sipped at it. It wasn't bumbo but it was better than nothing.

"Stupid man," she muttered, looking at the shape beneath the blanket in front of her. "If he'd just... minded his own business..."

"He wanted to be in your life."

"And look where it got him. Look what almost happened to you! What did happen!"

Lisette stayed silent.

"He should have said he was hurt. I should have asked! I just... I didn't think." Her voice cracked and she could feel her eyes welling up and hated it. "He was an idiot." She felt a tear roll down her cheek and rubbed it off her skin angrily. "I ain't cryin'!" she fired at Lisette. "Why would I be upset? I didn't even know him!"

Lisette looked like it was *her* heart that was breaking. She returned to Morgane's side. "But he was your father. And you're not crying because you lost something you had. You're crying because you have lost what could have been. You're upset because the choice of whether you let him into your life has been taken away from you, and that's terrible, and so sad."

229

"I ain't soft!" Morgane scoured another tear from her cheek with the rough wool of the doublet's sleeve. "I ain't the sort of person who cries about anything!"

"Oh, Morgane." Lisette looked like she was about to weep herself. "Where is the shame in showing you are hurting? Did you think ill of me when I wept earlier?"

"No," Morgane snivelled.

"Then give yourself the same grace. There is no one here who will mock you or punish you. Let yourself feel what you feel."

Morgane couldn't stop the tears then. They rolled down her cheeks that were hot with anger and shame, even as Lisette embraced her and held her tight, just as she had held her tight in the cart after the attack. Morgane let herself melt against her and cry. It was the first time she'd ever allowed herself to do that, that she could remember at least. It was the first time she could remember being held so tight that she felt safe, felt held in at the edges, so the centre of her could be released.

She was vaguely aware of the man returning and a brief exchange between him and Lisette. The door was still open, and the cold autumnal air made her pull away from Lisette.

"The pastor can bury him tomorrow," Lisette's father said to her. "Are you happy for his body to be taken to the church now?"

Morgane nodded and the man beckoned in a couple of younger lads who took off their hats and gave her awkward looks. She wanted to stand up, square her shoulders, look strong, but before she could muster the energy to do that they were going to the body and lifting it up and carrying it out, still covered with the blanket. Lisette's father followed them out.

"I'll be leaving as soon as he's buried," Morgane said. "I'll see it done, and then I'll be gone."

"Where are you planning to go?"

"I'm going to find my mother. I don't care what he said. She needs me. And…" She paused, worried that Lisette wouldn't understand. "And I want to find the one who sent the people who killed my aunt."

"Oh."

"To kill them."

"I see." Lisette swallowed. "Why don't you give yourself a little time to recover? You're more than welcome to stay here for as long as you need."

Morgane thought about the man-wolves. They'd tracked her from Nantes. She'd been in that cart the whole way, so surely it hadn't been a scent thing, like dogs could follow? They must have got the information from the old woman somehow. But she couldn't shake the fear that if they survived the attack by the silver-clawed assailants, they'd track them to Lisette's house somehow, putting her and her father at risk.

"No." At Lisette's questioning gaze, she explained her fear. "You saw that wolf… change, didn't you?" she added.

Lisette nodded.

"Why didn't you tell me that things like that were in France?!"

"I didn't know," Lisette replied.

Morgane remembered the state of her after the attack. "Have you not heard of anything like them?"

"No. If I hadn't seen it with my own eyes, I never would have believed it possible and" – she started shaking again – "and I never want to again. Merde… The men in black – they were the men in black from Nantes, that changed into those giant wolves?" At Morgane's nod, she said, "They followed you such a long way."

Morgane could see the fear in Lisette's eyes, fear she shared that if they survived the fight they'd fled, they'd be able to track her to this place, too. "I'm sure they're only after me. They won't bother you or your father."

Lisette nodded. "I can see why you don't want to stay." She stared down at the floor for a few moments, deep in thought, before taking her hand. "I'm coming with you."

Morgane pulled away from her. "Eh?"

"I'm coming with you to find your mother. It's so far away, Morgane. I couldn't bear to just wave you off and hope that you get there safely. And what if your father's concerns were based in truth? The thought of you going such a long way, in a country you're not used to, only to find that she isn't what you hope just…" She visibly shuddered. "No. Completely unacceptable."

"But it might be dangerous," Morgane said. "What if there are more of those… wolves?"

"How is that going to convince me that it's better for you to face those alone?"

"You can't fight, though!"

"And you cannot possibly travel so far without drawing attention to yourself if you don't have my help. Morgane, I'm sorry, but you don't know how to speak to people without showing how far from home you are. Without my help you'll only make yourself a target, whether it is a petty thief, or a fraudsman or those that hunt you." She smiled. "How about you do the fighting and I do the talking?"

"But what about your life here? Your family?"

"I've paid our debts, and I have the feeling that Laroche will leave my father alone once I'm no longer here to draw his interest." She looked at the fire. "You know, it wasn't just the prospect of earning my way out of our predicament that gave me so much joy when I was employed by your father. It was the fact that my life could be different, could be interesting and challenging. It is so boring here, Morgane. And I never really realised how little I've lived until I met you. It's as if I've been asleep all my life and have finally been woken. Yes, tonight was terrifying, but I have never felt so alive! And I saw what you did, how you defended me. Let me defend you in my own way. We can keep each other safe."

Morgane looked at her, studying her face, seeing the earnest honesty writ upon it. Lisette really was crew. She understood it, without ever having been on board ship. And she'd heard her father say she'd been a pirate, and she was still willing to do this. Perhaps she didn't really understand what that meant, though.

"You heard what my father said, before, about the life I've had?"

Lisette nodded.

"You know that I've boarded ships and taken their cargo?"

Lisette nodded again.

"You know I've killed men before?"

Lisette swallowed. "How many?"

Morgane counted them out on her hands. "Seven."

"Why did you kill them?"

"Because they were trying to kill me or my captain or my crewmates."

"Because you'd boarded their ship and were stealing their goods."

Morgane nodded. "My aunt said it was the right thing to do and I believed her. And sometimes people in the crew we'd attacked would join us, because they were treated so badly on their ship." She could see Lisette's struggle to accept what she was saying. "It's not simple, Lisette. Most of the people in my crew had no other choice. They'd been pressganged and then abandoned whenever the latest war had been won. Or they'd been enslaved and escaped a worse life. The gold that pirates steal from the Spanish was stolen from the people in the Americas. The cargo we took from the Four Chains Company was harvested or made by people who were enslaved or paid a pittance."

"Are you saying that the way you lived was acceptable?"

"Who decides what's acceptable? I didn't like killing people, but I liked being killed even less. I don't think the way you French live is acceptable, paying money to nobles who do nothing to make your lives better. Who live in houses with grounds hundreds of times bigger than the space allotted to the people who give them their wealth. That's backwards to me. We stole from those who had more than us, and we shared fairly and equally between us. We all had a say in the way things were done and agreed on the rules we lived by. We took care of crew who were injured, and we chose who led us, and if they didn't do right by the crew, then they were kicked out. Can you say the same for the way you live?"

Lisette was silent then. "Would you go back to that life, if you could?" she eventually asked.

Morgane shrugged. "It makes more sense than your life does, but I suppose that's because it's the only one I've ever known. My father thought that I'd be happy to follow him to New France, but I could never live in a place like that. I don't know where I belong yet. All I want is to find my mother. She was writing letters to my aunt, begging her to help, but my aunt was too bitter and angry to come back. I need to make sure that she is safe and that my aunt is avenged. And if you don't want to come with me, now you really know what I am... or was... then I understand."

Lisette looked away from her to gaze into the fire. "If I'd been stolen from my mother and raised by a pirate, I'm certain I would have been a pirate, too," she finally said. "What matters more" – she looked back at Morgane – "is that you were willing to attack a giant wolf, single-handedly, to save my life. And that as soon as you knew of my debts and my struggle, you gave me what I needed to free me, without a moment's thought. And you've just told me about your life, even though you knew it might repulse me, because you wanted to be sure that I knew everything I should, so I could be sure of my commitment. That speaks more to me of who you are, Morgane, rather than what you have been."

She smiled. "I'm going with you. On one condition."

"Name it."

"You let me teach you how to read along the way."

Morgane wrinkled her nose, but couldn't argue against how useful it could be. "Deal." She pulled her knife from her boot and held her left hand out, palm up. "Do you want to share blood on it?"

Lisette's eyebrows shot up. "No, no… your word will suffice."

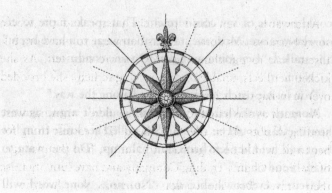

CHAPTER EIGHTEEN

MORGANE DIDN'T THINK much of land-based funerals. She wasn't allowed to sew her father into canvas and check he was really dead. He was put in a box, which made no sense to her, being a waste of good wood. The pastor said far too much nonsense and obviously thought he had an important part to play, which she couldn't fathom for the life of her. It wasn't about him, or God. It was about the man who died while getting them to safety.

Lisette and her father, a dour man called Antoine who clearly didn't like mornings, stood with her at the graveside as Morgane quietly seethed. She hated everything about it. The grey sky, the pastor's voice, the things he said. The fact that no one had a fond or funny story to tell about him. But more than anything, she seethed about the loss of a life because of her. Not that she'd asked Jean-Baptiste to do any of the stupid things he'd done, but she still couldn't shake the sense of it being her fault. She should have checked why he was so quiet. She should have kept track of the fourth wolf, the only one that could have attacked him. She should have noticed his injuries sooner.

Afterwards, when she'd paid the pastor and the whole sorry business was done, she was desperate to move on, but Lisette had to put things in order before they left. As she kicked her heels, unable to do anything to help, she brooded over Jean-Baptiste's last words.

As much as she hated to admit it, his fierce warnings were seeding doubts about the path ahead. The easiest thing for her to do would be to go back to Nantes, find the manager of the Four Chains Trading Company and have him organise their travel. But she couldn't stomach the thought of returning to that place, filled as it had been by too many men willing to resort to violence to prevent that journey. Violence that had cost her father his life. And while he had been confident that they could pass through the port without drawing undue attention, she knew it would be far harder for her to do that. She didn't have the contacts and knowledge he did, and neither did Lisette.

Her current accidental disguise as a young man could be enough to fool those that hunted her if they solely relied on witnesses and informants. But the way that those wolf-men had tracked her so far disturbed her. She knew dogs used scent to find food – what if they survived the fight and could sniff her out, disguised or not? And even if the disguise worked and she managed to reach the right man, once she revealed who she was, everything after that would be out of their control. And how could she trust him? How could she trust anyone except Lisette?

After most of a morning stewing over it all, Lisette finally appeared with two bags, ready to go. "Food, a few clothes, and blankets," she said, setting them down to tie her cloak. "I've been thinking about the journey. Let's set off for Nantes, so the locals see us going in that direction. Then once we're well out of sight, we'll take the south road down to the Loire and find a boat that can take us east. I've told my father, and everyone who's stuck their nose in, that I'm taking you to a friend of the family in Nantes and I'll be there for some time to see you settled in."

"They think I'm a boy, don't they?"

She nodded. "Yes, and too young a boy for it to be scandalous for me to travel with you. I think that could be useful on our trip."

Morgane grinned, so glad to have her. "Agreed."

"And by the time word gets to Laroche, it will be too late for his claims to the contrary to cause any problems. I have the feeling that he won't be raising that tale voluntarily either. I was sure to tell everyone that we rescued him from the woods, and that he cowered under a blanket the entire time."

"I'd have told them that he pissed himself, too."

"Oh, I told Father that. Just in case Laroche decides to become a nuisance again."

Lisette was all excited smiles when they waved goodbye to her father, who clearly was very unhappy about the turn of events. Lisette's concerns about him were allayed by the arrangements that Morgane's gold had provided; no concerns about paying the rent, and an agreement with one of the neighbours to keep an eye on him and make sure his drinking didn't get out of hand. The horse was docile enough for Lisette to coax him and the cart in the right direction, and before long the little town of Mouzeil was far behind them.

THE HOURS TURNED into days, without any sign of wolves or other hunters, and the further they got from those woods, the harder Morgane found it to believe what they'd seen there. Even though she knew it was true, whenever she tried to think about that wolf changing into a man, her thoughts merely slid off it. Somehow, she went from expecting every rustle in the trees to be one of those terrifying creatures about to pounce, to knowing it was merely the breeze. The clouds had cleared, the sun was shining, and it simply didn't feel the same as it had in that dank forest.

Once they reached the river, they travelled the track that ran close to it, heading east, and came across an elderly fisherman who had a small sailboat ideal for sailing up the Loire and no children willing to follow in his footsteps. It was in good condition and clearly well-loved. He was happy to trade it for the horse and cart and a couple of gold coins that made his eyes light up.

As soon as they were on the water, everything felt better, but a strange new sensation crept up on Morgane over the days that followed. It wasn't the relief of being competent and confident in her actions once more. It wasn't the simple joy of Lisette marvelling at her skill, nor the satisfaction of being able to teach her things she knew, instead of always being the student. It wasn't even the pleasure of seeing the beauty of the Loire Valley from the water, or of waving to strangers on the bank as they passed and how much that delighted Lisette.

It was something deeper. Almost like an absence, rather than a presence of something new. One perfect evening, after they'd dined on the last of the cheese that Lisette had packed and fresh bread bought from a baker's daughter who was smart enough to sell her wares to the traders on the river, Morgane finally realised what it was.

She was content.

There had been so many times she'd felt this way on *The Vengeance*, when the songs and laughter floated over the deck and the hold was full. When she'd staggered back to the boat after a fine evening at Taverners, or when a fight had gone in her favour. But she hadn't felt anything like it for weeks. Now, as the tension finally left her body, she was aware of how tense she'd been for all those weeks on the *Maître*. How she'd been scared and angry as she'd fled and then fought the assailants in Nantes, how unsettled and frustrated she'd been since then, punctuated by an attack in that forest that had revealed something utterly terrifying about this strange land of her birth.

But in their little sailboat, with all that behind her, contentment could stretch out like a comfortable cat on a sun-drenched deck. Even though she knew that at some point they'd have to leave the boat behind and travel north once they reached Orléans, it was not the same as constantly being on alert, waiting for the next attack.

Now, she felt not only relaxed, but safe. Lisette never snapped, or sulked or reprimanded her for anything. She got grumpy when she was hungry, but all that resulted in was less conversation and increasingly frequent questions about when they were going to stop for provisions. She was so gentle, so kind, that Morgane felt a peace when she was with her that she'd never known.

Over the two weeks it took to sail against the flow of the river to Orléans, when they weren't distracted by the business of surviving or teaching each other their most prized skills, they exchanged stories from their own lives. Morgane tucked away Lisette's anecdotes in her mind like they were gems being hoarded under her pillow. Each one delighted her, and often confused her, eliciting conversations filled with laughter as Lisette explained whatever she had misinterpreted.

And almost every story she told Lisette was met with wide eyes and a variety of emotions. Often horror, when Morgane had shared something about her life on *The Vengeance*, and sometimes a strange, morbid fascination with the tales of fights and injuries and things that had been rather commonplace to Morgane. Lisette seemed to delight in hearing about life on board the ship, the way the crew jostled along together despite the wide variety of personalities.

And Morgane made sure she didn't romanticise it, nor exaggerate her own part in what Lisette considered to be the more thrilling adventures they'd had. Somewhere along the way she'd decided she would never lie to her, just as she felt certain that Lisette had decided the same. So, she included the rotten food, the brackish water, the horrific injuries and all manner of infected wounds and unexpected maggots. But she seemed to love all of it, and Morgane discovered that she loved her reactions just as much.

The nights were cold, though, and they slept curled up together under the woollen blankets Lisette had packed for them. The tiny cabin on the boat was better than nothing, and on the nights with rain they were especially grateful for the roof, but it wasn't comfortable.

Lisette struggled with that more than she did. For Morgane, all the other joys outweighed the cold nights and lack of hammocks. She was sad when they arrived at Orléans and the river trip was over, even feeling a little choked up when they sold the boat. But she knew that they couldn't spend forever in their own little world on the river, even if there wasn't her mother to find.

It was disorienting to be back in a large town, and reliant on Lisette to navigate them instead. She was glad they barely spent a day there, just long enough for Lisette to arrange transport to Troyes. Even though there was no sign of any people looking for them, or following them, Morgane couldn't shake the feeling that they were being watched sometimes. The confrontation in the woods followed by the trip along the Loire seemed to have put an end to the hunt, but not to her paranoia. On a couple of occasions she woke in the night, thinking somebody else was in the room with them despite the door being locked – or barricaded with a chair if no lock was on the door. But there was never anybody there.

The journey settled into a new routine. Travelling as far as possible in small carriages, sometimes with strangers, sometimes just the two of them. They spent the night at inns along the way, filling the evenings with reading and writing lessons. It was then that Morgane really appreciated just how lost she would have been without Lisette. She knew who to speak to, which inns looked good enough to stay in – when they had a choice – and how to deal with the ones that didn't. She negotiated prices, found the safest coaches to travel in and worked out a route that meant they didn't need to go through Paris, which even Lisette had been rather intimidated by. As the days turned into weeks, Morgane grew more comfortable with trusting Lisette's judgement, and settled into observing and learning as much as she could from the exchanges.

Even though she was slightly taller than Lisette, the ruse of her being her younger brother seemed to be met with the total indifference they'd hoped for. It saved them money, as no one batted an eyelid at siblings sharing one room, and besides, they were used to sleeping together now.

Morgane kept her hair tucked under the large hat she'd taken from the lodge, kept her mouth shut and her weapons hidden beneath her doublet, save the sword. Occasionally, some drunkard would tease her, thinking she was a gangling youth with his upward growth outpacing the appearance of facial hair. At one inn, a busy, cramped place a couple of days south of Beauvais, one man seemed to pick Morgane out as ripe for ridicule.

Lisette had told her to wait near the door as she went with the landlord's daughter to see the last room available. Morgane lurked, hand intuitively resting on her sword pommel, avoiding eye contact and trying to look as boring as possible. But she was aware of a man sitting with three others, drunk and looking around the room for something to amuse him. She knew the type, one of those people who had nothing much in their heads at the best of times, and desperate for something to distract themselves from the state of their own life, which being in their cups made them too painfully aware of. Out of the corner of her eye, she could see his wandering gaze settle on her.

"Look at that slip of a boy wearing a sword like he knows how to use it," he slurred. "That's what I mean about the state of this country. No respect for tradition. No respect for those who earn the right to carry a sword."

They weren't wearing black, and they did not look rich. They were armed, but too drunk to fight well, she was sure of it. All had greying hair and the best of their youth far behind them. But as she examined the group, his companions started to take an interest in her, too. "That lad needs to grow a beard before he bears arms," one of them added, "otherwise people might think he's ready to fight with it."

"What makes you think I'm not?" Morgane fired at him, which delighted the first. Now he had a distraction.

"A word of advice, little boy. Wait until your voice breaks before you wear a sword."

"And some for you, grandpa: don't start a fight with someone who could stab you thrice before you could draw yours. Even if you weren't in your cups."

His companions chortled and he looked at them, the ruddiness of his cheeks deepening a little. "Show some respect for those who've defended the king's realm."

"From what? Good sense?"

He stood, barrel chested and steadier on his feet than she thought he'd be. "You pay your respect to me, boy, before you regret it."

"I only pay my respects to the dead. Will you oblige?" She partially drew her sword.

"Sit down, Claude!" one of the group said, still laughing.

"He's a child."

"No fun in beating a little boy," another said.

"I'd wager there's fun in proving an old man wrong." Morgane took a step closer. "Come on then, grandpa. Let me show you how—"

"What are you doing?"

Lisette's voice cut through the mounting tension, and she pushed through the other patrons to reach them.

"This old bastard—" Morgane began.

Lisette ignored her, stepping in front of the standing man. "Sit down, sir! Are you in the habit of taunting children until they do something reckless? Or is this a new sport for you?"

"I can take him! I can take all of them!" Morgane protested, now genuinely affronted.

"Quiet!" Lisette snapped, without taking her eyes off the man in front of her.

The man laughed, a rolling, infectious roar that made his companions join in. "Ah, no harm done, mademoiselle. Let me buy a drink for your little brother and for yourself! Come, my little friend, sit with us. You've balls enough to pick a fight with someone twice your size, let's see if that stout heart can take an ale or three!"

"I'll drink you bastards under the table!" Morgane said and lurched past Lisette to grab one of their tankards, downed it in one and slammed it back on the table. She paused to belch before reaching for a second.

One of them clapped her on the back, the man she'd been ready to fight now grinning at her. "Let's get more in. First one to pass out pays the bill!"

"I hope you have a full purse, grandpa." For the first time in days, Morgane felt at ease, comforted by the stupid banter of the men that she'd been missing, confident in her ability to hold her own. Cook's bumbo was ten times the strength of this watery slop they called ale.

There was a sudden sharp pain at the tip of her ear. "Put that tankard down!"

"Ow!" Lisette had pinched her ear and was pulling her away.

"That's quite enough of that. I turn my back for one moment and here you are, picking fights and getting into trouble. What would our mama think? Get up those stairs this instant!"

The mention of a fictional mother snapped her out of the old habits she'd fallen into, but she still drained the second tankard and chucked it towards the man as Lisette dragged her off. "Ow! That hurts!"

"Good!"

Lisette didn't let go until they reached their room and pushed her inside.

Morgane cupped a hand over her throbbing ear. "That really bloody hurt!"

"What were you thinking?"

"What? That ale is like piss! I could've—"

"You really think that's what I'm upset about? You didn't consider for one moment that picking a fight with—"

"He picked a fight with me! He said—"

"That picking a fight or getting drunk with a group of strange men is at all wise considering we agreed that drawing as little attention to ourselves as possible is the only way to reach Artois without bringing death to our door again?"

Morgane puffed a deep breath, blowing out her cheeks as she realised how stupid she'd been. "They just… they were saying these things, and it got my blood up and—"

"You don't have to prove anything here! I have no doubt that you could have drunk them all into a stupor or bested them at swordplay. I know how strong you are – both your sword arm and your stomach. There's no need to prove that to strangers who could tell anyone hunting for us about you."

"I'm sorry."

Lisette smiled. "I know it's hard not to be yourself here."

Morgane rubbed her ear again. "I think you enjoyed being an angry big sister too much."

Lisette came over, pulled her hand away and winced at the sight of her ear. "Perhaps I pinched a little too hard. But I had to make it look authentic." She leaned close and kissed the hot red skin tenderly. "There, better?"

"I think another may be needed."

Lisette laughed. "You're a big baby, for a pirate." Another delicate kiss.

"I've killed men for less than that, you know." She slid her arms around Lisette's waist, feeling the movement reciprocated.

"That may be, but I know you're actually as soft as a—"

Morgane kissed her, stealing the words away, unspoken. It was so much softer, so much more tender than the ones she'd had in the taverns of Port Royal. As Lisette responded, deepening the kiss and turning it from a tentative invitation to a deeper, firmer confirmation of mutual attraction, Morgane marvelled at how different it felt, and not just because of the absence of bristles and stinking breath. There was no other agenda beneath it, nothing like the aggressive possessiveness of the men she'd kissed before. No sense of an urgent desire to progress straight to sex, no feeling of it being a marking of territory and statement of intent. It was simply what felt right in the moment, a mutual desire to express affection and love between equals. And, she discovered, it was a much more enjoyable way to pass the time than learning to read.

Morgane started playing a new game in the evenings spent at the inns: how best to distract Lisette from teaching her. But Lisette was good at that game, too, finding ways to motivate her reluctant student with more tempting rewards.

One evening, a few days later, Morgane was lying on her

stomach and trying to decide who had won, given they both wanted to end up in bed together. She'd learned how to recognise Lisette's name, so that was definitely a win for her lover. For her, too, she supposed, because the delight when she'd picked it out from a page of handwriting had made Lisette so happy that she'd let the kissing progress without any talk of continuing the lesson.

"Have you always had this mark?" Lisette asked as she traced the outline of the birthmark on Morgane's lower back.

"Always."

"It looks like an angel spilt wine on you."

Morgane laughed. "You say the strangest things."

"No, it really does look like that. I think it's a birthmark. A cousin of mine had one on his chest, though his was larger and a darker red than yours."

"Lavois – the captain who brought me to Nantes – he mentioned a mark that would prove who I was. This must be what he was talking about. Only a couple of people know it's there, and they're back on *The Vengeance*."

"You had lovers on the ship?"

Morgane shook her head. "No. The ones who were there when I was small are who I was thinking of. I never really found anyone I liked enough to see it since then. I had some tussles, you know, like everyone does, but nothing like this. I don't reckon any of them looked at me well enough to notice it."

"You're the first lover I've ever had," Lisette said quietly.

Morgane rolled onto her side. "Maybe you've got a secret birthmark, too, and you don't even know."

Lisette giggled. "Maybe."

"Maybe I should look for it." Morgane ran a finger down her arm.

"Maybe you should."

"I shall be very thorough," Morgane murmured, and began her search.

THE CONSTANT, LOVING, playful encouragement made Morgane actually start to apply herself and make real progress. Lisette adapted to Morgane's lack of tolerance by varying the techniques she used to teach her and being endlessly kind. Every time Morgane pushed the paper away and declared she was too stupid to learn to read and write, Lisette would encourage her to keep trying, with a patience she'd never seen before. One evening, it wasn't enough.

"I know we had a deal, but you just have to accept that I'm not clever like you are!" she'd said, after failing to distract Lisette from her tuition.

"How many types of knots do you know how to tie, Morgane?"

"Lots."

"Do you remember how you learned them?"

"Not really."

"So you were born knowing how to tie them?"

"Don't be silly, of course not."

"You probably watched people. You were probably shown how to do it when you were so small you can't remember. And think about it – you don't just know how to tie them, you know where and when they should be used. Why one knot should be chosen over another. That's a lot of knowledge and you learned all of it. I simply grew up in a different home. I watched my parents write. They read to me. They showed me how to write. For me it was words, for you it was rope and knots and all the hundreds of other things you need to know to sail a ship. You know so many things I don't, Morgane."

"But sailing is easy."

"No, it isn't! I can't do it. Does that make me stupid? No. And you're not stupid, you're actually very clever. It just takes time to learn completely new things."

"I get the letters muddled up. They don't look different enough."

"Then maybe we need to get to know them like we get to know people, or animals. Let's imagine the letters sit on a wall." She drew a line across the page. "And let's imagine that one of them is a cat, sitting on that wall. Here is his little round body. And here is his tail. He likes to let it droop down, see? This is the letter g, the one from the middle of your name. You draw him."

It was silly, but the little stories Lisette started to tell with each letter helped them to stick in Morgane's memory. The 'g' became easier to recognise against the 'a' in her name because the first was the cat with his long curling tail and the second was the big fat mouse with the tiny tail. She didn't care if it was childish. It worked.

By the time they reached Troyes, she could recognise letters and write her name, and Lisette's. By the time they left Reims, she could read fifty words that Lisette had taught her. When they were on the last stretch of the journey to the town of Arras, she could, haltingly, decipher unfamiliar simple words.

Her delight at finally understanding how useful reading could be was tempered by the changes they saw the closer they got to Arras. The villages they passed through seemed less welcoming, and reluctant to sell any produce they had to travellers. People were less friendly, more suspicious and asked more questions. They both felt distinctly unsafe on a couple of occasions when the coach they were travelling in arrived at inns well after dark.

"Perhaps it's because we're closer to the border here," Lisette commented. "Perhaps they're worried about war... or previous ones have made them wary of strangers."

That didn't satisfy Morgane. It didn't feel like the fear and tension of imminent battle to her. But then again, she'd never known land-based conflict, so perhaps she didn't recognise it.

There was less laughter and less drinking in the public rooms of the inns as well. Everyone looked thinner, hungrier, and their coin was welcomed with a quiet relief by the innkeepers.

"Keep an eye on your brother," one of them said in a low voice to Lisette when she paid for their room.

"I won't cause no trouble," Morgane replied cheerily.

"That's not my concern," he said, leaning closer to the two of them. "Young men disappear from these parts, especially the sons of those travelling through, so watch your back. And you didn't hear this from me, understand?"

They kept a very low profile after that. From conversations overheard in the public rooms, they discovered that the harvest had been good, and that there was no pestilence that had blighted the area. As they travelled deeper into the region, Lisette did all she could to learn more whenever they bought food, but all she managed to winkle out of the locals was that taxes had gone up, though no one knew why. Not even the landlord of the inn they stopped at on the edge of the city knew. And he was reluctant to talk about it, even though he seemed a little better off than many they'd met.

When Lisette related their conversation to Morgane, her mood darkened. Her mother's family set those taxes and seemingly had no regard for the impact that they were having on the local people.

"I just don't understand," she muttered to Lisette later that night, neither of them able to sleep. "Why do they need all that money? What do they do with those taxes?"

Lisette sighed. "I don't know," she finally replied. "I would have said that perhaps there was war on the horizon, or a recent one to pay for, but I don't think that is so. It is different here, though – there's so much tension. Don't you feel it?"

Morgane gave a grunt of agreement. She felt it, deep in her stomach. Something was wrong here. "Why does everyone pay them, when it's doing so much harm? Why don't they just refuse to pay?"

Lisette kissed her forehead softly. "Because if they don't pay, there's violence."

"But if everyone refused, they couldn't force *everyone* off the land, or kill them all, could they?"

"Everyone just wants to survive, Morgane. You're talking about an uprising, and no one wants that, it's frightening."

"But it would help them to survive!"

"Only if everyone did it, at exactly the same time. How can people be sure of each other making a stand when the time came? People can mutter things in back rooms, but when it comes to actually taking a risk and rising up, it's much harder. It would have to be hundreds of people, scattered across towns and villages, all acting as one. It's not like the crew of a ship deciding they need a new captain."

Morgane lay there, seething about the injustice of it all, long after Lisette fell asleep against her. Before they'd reached the county of Artois, she'd started to see the appeal of living in France. The people were friendly. The food was good and, although a little cold, the weather wasn't all that bad. There hadn't been any sticky, heavy days or any of the terrifying storms that came after them. The countryside was beautiful, the sheer variety of plants and trees and birds was a constant delight. She missed the ocean, but she'd eventually stopped longing for it.

Now, though, she wanted nothing more than to dash to the coast with Lisette and find a way back to *The Vengeance*. This place put her on edge. If Lisette didn't feel the same way, she would have suspected that it was the fact that potentially, in the next day or so, she would finally meet her mother. And all the hopes and fears, held in a nebulous state, would solidify into certainty.

When she'd learned that the Artois family was one of the wealthiest in France, she'd assumed that would be reflected in the place and the people, just as a ship that worked well as a crew and benefitted from more plunder as a result had the air of success about it. But here, it felt more like something exploitative was happening, and it made her deeply uncomfortable. Perhaps her mother hated it, too, and that was one of the reasons she'd begged for help to escape. The Comte d'Artois, rich and powerful enough to keep his suffering vassals subservient, must be a cruel man indeed to ignore the impact on his people. No doubt he kept her mother just as scared. She fantasised about him confessing to sending the *Maître*, and that with one swift kill, she'd be able to avenge her aunt, free her mother and remove the oppressor of these people.

But other, more fearful possibilities crept in at the edges of these daydreams. That she'd been unwise to dismiss the things her father had said about Isabeau, about her being monstrous herself. If a place reflected those who governed it, was there not evidence mounting that his warnings were valid?

Lisette stirred and rolled over, curling herself up and pressing her back against her. The little sigh she gave as she settled made Morgane's chest swell with love. How strange that her father, who'd had no impact on her whole life, had somehow picked out a woman that she could love, and who loved her. The tickets he'd bought to New France were open, meaning that any of that trading company's ships would give them passage. They could just go, leave all of this behind, leave the hopes and fears full of potential and protected from disappointment. But Morgane knew she'd never be satisfied. Those letters penned to her aunt, all but begging for help, would haunt her for the rest of her days if she did nothing about them. She'd never forgive herself for being too cowardly to rescue her and leave her aunt unavenged.

So she turned over to curl around her lover and bury her face in her hair. She pushed aside the anger, pushed aside the fear, letting herself sink into Lisette's warmth. Tomorrow was for finding the chateau and facing her fears. Tonight was for love and rest.

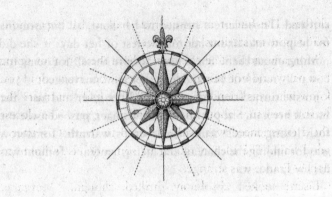

CHAPTER NINETEEN

INSIDE THE CITY walls, Arras felt different again. Instead of the sense of the quiet, gnawing hunger of the surrounding countryside's population, the city was filled with bustling streets and a palpable air of anticipation. Lisette found a tavern with a single room available and a brief conversation with the landlady revealed that the nearby chateau, the seat of the Artois family, was holding a masquerade ball in four nights' time.

The room was very small and very expensive. It was noisy and the streets smelt unpleasant and Morgane didn't like it there one bit.

"What's a masquerade ball?"

Lisette's face lit up. "Oh, the most marvellous spectacle! It's a ball, but everyone wears a mask, to hide their identity."

Morgane squinted at her. She was missing something. "A ball… how big is it? Do these masked people throw it to one another, and try to guess who—"

Lisette's chuckle stopped her. "Oh, my love, I'm sorry. I should have explained. A ball is a huge party, and there's dancing and food and drink and everyone wears their finest clothes. The fun of a masquerade ball is that everyone is made more mysterious, do you see?"

Morgane didn't. She couldn't fathom the appeal of going to a party and not being sure who was who. How could you know who was friend or enemy? Who could you trust? She wasn't even sure about the concept of a party. The closest she'd experienced was everyone deep in their cups after a good haul. The idea of going to someone else's home to dance? France was strange.

Lisette looked absolutely thrilled, though. "Morgane, don't you see? This is exactly what we need!"

"We can get drunk and dance here, if that's what you wish."

"No!" She came over and took her hands. "This is the perfect opportunity to see what your mother is like before announcing yourself to her. There's going to be dozens of people going in and out with deliveries, not to mention the guests themselves. It will be so much easier to get inside the chateau."

A large grin spread across Morgane's face. "You're right! Ah, you're a gem!"

"I haven't been to a ball, but I've been bored to death by Monsieur Laroche's account of the balls he's been to. All the guests are on a list and are announced at the door, so we won't be able to dress up and arrive like all of them. I think our best chance would be to look for a business that's due to make deliveries to the chateau. Once we've found one, perhaps we could ask for some work – they may be short-handed – and then we can go in with them. I don't know if that's realistic, but we can make a plan once we've found someone that we know is definitely going into the chateau."

Morgane pulled her close and kissed her. "I love you."

Lisette smiled. "I love you, too."

They went back out into the street with renewed purpose,

the atmosphere of the town making much more sense now. Lisette struck up conversations in the market with the friendly ease that Morgane envied. They learned that over two hundred guests had been invited, another stall holder said it was three hundred. There were tales of extraordinary commissions, ranging from gilded swans made from clay and filled with songbirds, to a fountain designed to flow with wine, rather than water. Someone said it was to celebrate a birthday, another said that he'd heard the Artois family had a grand announcement to make, a third said that the ball was being arranged simply to outdo an event held in Paris the year before, in the hope it would gain the king's favour. Given that half of the people that Lisette spoke to said the king was attending and half said he wasn't, that reason wasn't guaranteed either.

No one in the market was directly involved with the ball, however, so they carried on exploring the city, alert for any talk of making deliveries to the chateau. Just as Morgane was considering that it would be much easier to just lurk by the gates and sneak in when they were opened for someone else, she spotted a sign down a side street, hanging above an unassuming doorway. She stopped and stared at the blue rose, heart starting to race, and then pulled Lisette down the side street with her.

"Where are we going?"

"Trust me."

The door was the same colour blue as the rose, with a bell hanging beside it. "By appointment only," Lisette read from the notice beneath it.

Morgane rang the bell anyway, before Lisette decided they shouldn't.

It was opened by a middle-aged woman with grey hair and dark brown skin. She was wearing a simple woollen dress and a beautifully embroidered shawl. "Can I help you?"

Morgane retrieved Jacques' sewing kit from her pocket and untied the leather outer cover. She showed the embroidered blue rose to the woman, who looked surprised. "A friend gave this to me and said that if I ever needed help, I should bring it to one of the Blue Rose ateliers."

"And what was this friend's name?"

"Jacques. Jacques Couture. But he said to tell you that 'Petit Jacques' gave this to me, as a sign of his trust in me."

"How old was he?"

Morgane had to think about that. "Older than me, by at least twenty years… must be, he was there all my life, long as I can remember. He's still strong, in his prime. I don't know his exact age. But his birthday was at Christmas time, I know that. He said his grandmother always told him he was lucky that he was born during a time of feasting, and not of harvest. It never made much sense to me."

The woman's frown lifted, and she opened the door wider with a broad smile. "Come in, come in, both of you."

The door was closed behind them. They stood in a small receiving room with nothing but a table and chair in one corner. It was warm, thanks to a fire in the small grate. There was the sound of chattering and industry on the other side of an archway that was filled with a drawn curtain.

"I'm Morgane, this is Lisette."

"My name is Celeste. Well met. How did you come to know Jacques?"

"Do you know him? He said his family came from Paris. Jacques looked out for me, we were in the same crew."

"Were?" She looked concerned.

"Before I left. He's captain now." She grinned at the thought of it. "He'll be a fine one, too."

"May I?" The woman gestured at the sewing kit and Morgane handed it to her. "What did he tell you about this?"

"He said it was the most important thing he owned. I didn't

want him to give it to me, but he insisted. He wanted to keep looking out for me, I suppose. He said it was given to him once he finished his apprenticeship. That he could use that to find work in any of the Blue Rose ateliers. It proved his skill."

"Did he teach you?"

"Oh, he taught me a little, just how to repair things, not the fancy work."

The woman handed the little silk purse back to her, thoughtful. "Captain, you say. Even with that ear of his?"

"Eh?"

"We feared the worst when that dog near chewed it off. Hasn't held him back then?"

"That must be a different Jacques. Mine had both ears, no scarring."

The woman nodded. "Ah, yes, I am thinking of another, maybe. This Petit Jacques of yours... how could he be captain when so short?"

"He's not short! He's taller than me, by this much!" She held her hand over her head. "But he was gentle with it. It took a lot to make him lose his temper."

The woman clasped her hands and beamed at her. "My Jacques, my petit Jacques sent you to me!" She cupped Morgane's face in her hands and kissed both of her cheeks. "Forgive my questions, I wanted to be sure. A captain now, is he? A captain!" She beamed at Lisette. "Did you hear that? My son, a captain!"

She then kissed Lisette on both cheeks and beckoned them towards the curtain as Morgane carefully wrapped the purse in its leather and tucked it away again. "Welcome! Welcome! How can we help? Are you hungry? Would you like some wine? Etienne! Bring some bread and wine upstairs!"

There were over a dozen people working in a large room beyond the curtain, all either sewing or cutting fabric. Yet another room could be glimpsed through an open door to the side, which seemed to involve folding garments, perhaps preparing for delivery. Etienne was one of several young men working on the far side of the room. "Yes, auntie," he called and then they were being swept through another doorway and up a steep flight of stairs to a parlour above the work room. It was not much bigger than the receiving room, but had a cosy atmosphere and immediately put Morgane at ease.

There was a flurry of questions about the ship Jacques commanded, whether he ever spoke of home, how his health fared. Morgane answered each one as truthfully as she could without mentioning the piracy, just in case. Celeste's joy at finally having news of her son after so many years was beautiful, and Morgane didn't want to risk stealing even a mote of it from her. Bread and wine arrived, and, once Celeste had learned everything she could, she turned her attention to them.

"So, my dears, how can we help you? Are you looking for work? You're not from Arras, are you?" She directed that at Lisette, who shook her head.

"We need to get into the masked ball at the chateau," Morgane said.

Celeste frowned. "You do? Are you keen to dance with the nobles?"

Morgane wrinkled her nose. "No, it's not that." She looked at Lisette, not sure how truthful to be.

"We need to speak to one of the nobles there," Lisette said.

Morgane nodded. "There's a chance one of them may be my mother. That's the truth of it, madame. That's why I came to France. I would have stayed in Jacques' crew but... but I discovered that I was stolen as a baby and... that my mother may be here."

Celeste's hand covered her mouth. "My poor child," she muttered. "Stolen? By whom?"

"My aunt. Jacques found out the same time as I did. He

didn't want me to leave, but he understood that I need to find my mother."

"We were hoping to find someone who'd be able to help us get into the chateau," Lisette said. "Perhaps helping with deliveries for the ball."

"We just need help to get inside, that's all," Morgane added. "We thought the ball would be a good time because there will be lots of people going in and out."

Celeste nodded. "True enough, but if you think your mother is amongst the nobles, dear child, posing as tradespeople will not help you at all. The deliveries are made to staff, and the staff will keep everyone away from the guests." She leaned forwards, and all of a sudden, Morgane could see Jacques in the twinkling of her eyes and the set of her features. She looked just like her old friend when he'd had a brilliant idea. "So, the best approach would be for you to accompany us when we make our final delivery to the Artois family, to get you inside the chateau. Then you dress in costumes that would befit noble guests and hide in the chateau until well after the party has started. If you hide until all the guests have been announced, and the wine has been flowing for a while, you'll be able to slip in without being challenged. There are over three hundred guests, and the ball will span the ground floor and the gardens, if the weather holds. If your nerves are strong enough, that's the best way to get close to the nobles and approach one, if the woman you're hoping to find is amongst them."

Morgane grinned. "Yes! That's exactly what we need." She looked at Lisette, expecting to have the same excitement reflected back to her, only to see nothing but concern. "What is it? What haven't I thought of?"

Lisette considered her response carefully. "It's a huge risk... but I suppose everyone will be masked..." She looked at Celeste. "I worry that if we're discovered, it could have consequences for you and your atelier."

Celeste looked touched by her concern. "I wouldn't suggest it, if I thought the risk too high for us. I'm responsible for many livelihoods, and more beyond that. I know how busy the staff will be, how little attention will be paid to us and how easy it is to find a nook to hide in. It's simply a matter of knowing how to be invisible in plain sight, which you will be. No one will give you a second glance when you're delivering goods and no one will give you a second glance when you are masked guests in a sea of silk and pearls." She leaned back, looking at them both with concern. "Are you absolutely certain you wish to get into the chateau?"

Morgane nodded. How else would she be able to find and rescue her mother?

"I only ask because..." Celeste looked away, frowning to herself. "It's not a place I would ever want sweet young people like yourselves to go. There's a darkness there... it's not a place where God-fearing people dwell."

"What gives you that impression?" Lisette asked.

"I've been there many times, as part of my work. The nobility are a different breed. Cold. Uncaring. And there's a feeling to the place that just..." She visibly shuddered. "I never go there alone, and I never let any of my young men deliver there alone either."

"Have you met the comtesse?" Morgane asked.

Celeste shook her head. "Not properly. I've seen her, at a distance, but she commissions through her lady-in-waiting. She has the same measurements, so I do the fittings with her. The comtesse watches from the other side of the room. Never so much as given me the time of day. I'm not even allowed to look at her. And that lady-in-waiting, Cataline... she's a cold fish. But that's neither here nor there. If you're determined to get in there for the ball, I can help."

Morgane didn't like the sound of that. Why keep people so distant? Was it part of being a noble, or was the comte forcing it to be that way? If a couturier could get close to her, a message could be sneaked out, or bruises could be seen. What if it wasn't even her mother, but a stand-in? She wanted to ask more questions, but even though she was Jacques' mother, she didn't know her and besides, the more she knew, the greater the risk they could be putting her in.

Celeste stood, breaking Morgane out of her fretful thoughts. "As a friend of my Jacques, I'll provide your costumes for the cost of the materials. And if you can return them to me in good condition, I'll take only half of that. But there is a lot to do. Two costumes good enough to make you invisible with less than four days to go… that is going to be challenging. If you are both willing to help, I think we can do it."

"My sewing is only passable," Morgane said.

"As is mine," Lisette added.

"Then you can help in another way, so that my staff will be able to work on your costumes. I'll measure you first, and then we can get to work." She approached Morgane and put her hands on her hips. "Now, my friend, do you wish to have a costume that befits a young lady, or one that is in keeping with your current choice?"

Morgane blinked at her. Everyone they'd interacted with had addressed her as a young man, with no sense of mocking, just acceptance. "I… er…"

Celeste smiled. "I know they don't let girls on ships. I know you must have wanted that life very much, to live as a boy. And that doublet of yours will fool almost everyone, but not a tailor."

Morgane felt horribly awkward. Why did everyone care about being a man or a woman so much in France? On *The Vengeance*, the only thing that mattered was skill. But perhaps her aunt's ship really had been an exception. Most of the other crews they drank with at Port Royal were predominantly male. Not all of them, though, and there were other female captains, she'd met them. Not as many as the men, but there, nonetheless.

"I find dresses cumbersome," she finally said. It was the truth, after all. "So, if you can make a costume as befits a young man, I'd be grateful."

"Right you are, my friend. And Lisette, something more traditional for you, I think."

MORGANE HAD EXPECTED to be sweeping and cooking for the next four days, the sort of work that would help others to focus on their own. While Celeste wanted them to help with food, it wasn't in the way she'd expected.

Celeste's atelier played a role in the community that was far more important than the unassuming doorway tucked down a side street implied. Every day, Celeste had two of her staff take a morning out to collect and distribute food to different villages in the surrounding area.

She'd struck a deal with some of the local bakeries, guaranteeing bulk orders to keep their finances healthy in order to be able to buy more food for less money. Morgane and Lisette were assigned to help, freeing up one member of staff entirely each day and shortening the amount of time the remaining one needed to complete the deliveries.

"Make sure you have your sword," Celeste said to them, as they waited for the cart to be brought round to the shop. "And keep your wits about you."

"No need to worry about bandits." Morgane grinned.

"It's not them I fear," she replied.

"Are young men taken from the city, too?" Lisette asked nervously.

"You heard about that?" Celeste gave a grim nod. "Sometimes, though more often outside the city walls. You be on your guard. And keep an eye on Etienne for me. Never go anywhere alone, you hear?"

They nodded. "Celeste…" Morgane began, trying to decide how to ask the question that had been on her mind since they'd arrived. "We, er… we heard some stories on our travels, about wolves, big wolves, that can turn into men and back again. Have you heard about anything like that?"

"Where did you hear about that?"

"Back in the Loire," Lisette said.

"There aren't any such folk in these parts," Celeste replied matter-of-factly. "There's the cart, off you go!"

As they helped with the daily round, Morgane ruminated on her response. She hadn't laughed it off, or dismissed it as nonsense, as she would have expected. But then she was caught up in the work and once the round was done, they assisted with menial tasks in the atelier, giving the apprentices more time to work on the last-minute commissions.

Morgane enjoyed doing something useful again, even though it wasn't repairing a ship. But what she appreciated the most was being given an insight into where Jacques had learned his sense of duty. His had been devoted to his captain and crew, ensuring every single person had their share and was fairly treated. His mother was devoted to those being crippled by the high taxes imposed on the people.

None of the other local businesses were interested in helping, and yet Celeste didn't seem to resent the fact that only hers was doing something practical to help people. When Morgane asked her why she wasn't more angry, she shrugged. "What I do with my money is up to me. What they do with their money is up to them. And they give to the church and help in other ways."

"Why don't you do the same as them?" Morgane pressed.

Celeste smiled. "Because it isn't enough and because I can make sure the food gets into the hands of the people who need it most, the ones who don't have the time or the means to appeal to the churches or alms-houses, because they work the land. Those who are too proud to ask for help. The villages we take food to think that it would just go to waste if we didn't hand it out. They think there is such surplus here, because how could there not be, when they give such a high proportion of their produce in tax? They don't understand that the people in the city pay the same tithes." She set down the fabric she was stitching and looked at Morgane. "I look after my own first. We make clothes for the wealthiest, and I make sure they pay what they should. There is money left over after all the costs, after all wages, and I have no interest in hoarding it. My grandfather did that. He still died the same as everyone else. And he was far more miserable, too!"

"Why do the nobles take so much, though?" Morgane asked. "Why don't they care about the people?"

Celeste sighed. "They take what they want because they can, and because they have been raised to believe they're better than everyone else. Just as the common folk are raised to believe they are lesser."

"Someone should stop them," Morgane muttered, and Celeste laughed and kissed her cheek.

"My friend, you need to learn which battles can be fought and which cannot. Otherwise, all your anger will twist your heart and sour your soul. Besides" – she picked up her needle once more – "I've found that more good gets done when we look at how to love better, rather than how to fight harder."

CHAPTER TWENTY

CELESTE'S PLAN HAD worked perfectly. No one paid them any attention when they carried in deliveries of costumes commissioned by visiting nobles and some of the residents. When it was time to part ways, Celeste had given them both their costumes, which looked like mere deliveries, and told them about a cupboard they could hide in.

"This is your last chance to change your mind," she said, pulling them to one side. "No shame in waiting until the ball is over, perhaps finding your mother when she travels back to her home instead."

"That's not possible," Morgane lowered her voice. "She's the comtesse."

Celeste's mouth fell open. "Why didn't you tell me?! Merde! I never would have helped you!"

"Why?"

"Because she is a cruel beast of a woman," she whispered. "Had I known... oh, mes amis, come home with me, leave this all behind, I beg you!"

"But I have to help her. She's trapped here, and the comte may be keeping her prisoner for all I know."

"The comte? He hasn't been seen for over ten years! It's only the comtesse, and there are rumours that the young men who go missing are brought here! I told you it was a terrible place – why did you not listen to me?"

"I can't leave my mother in a place like this!" Morgane fired back. "I have to find her and help her!"

Celeste shook her head sadly. "May the grace of God protect you both." She reached into her pocket and then pressed something into Lisette's hand. "Wear this," she told her.

It was a small silver crucifix. Celeste reached under her bodice and pulled out the one she wore, taking it off to place the chain over Morgane's head.

"And promise me you'll wear this," she said, pressing it against her chest. "Out of sight, underneath your shirt."

Morgane frowned. "I don't believe in—"

"No matter, my dear, no matter. Wear it for me, to ease my worry. There is evil in this place, and it will protect you when you need it most."

Morgane agreed, to keep her happy. The thought of doing anything else was unconscionable, and not just because she was Jacques' mother.

"God protect you, and see you both safe into the dawn's light," she whispered, kissing them on both cheeks, eyes filling with tears.

Morgane embraced her and Celeste crushed her tight against her. "Thank you, for everything."

Tearfully, Celeste pulled away and hurried towards the cart as Morgane and Lisette went back through the servants' entrance in the throng of suppliers, finding the right moment to break off and hurry to their hiding place.

The cupboard had been emptied of supplies for the ball just that morning, and was large enough for both of them to change their clothes. A small high window provided enough light to see laces and buttons and loops for fastening.

Morgane had stitched her knife sheath into the inside of her costume's doublet, unable to even consider going to such an intimidating place without some form of weapon, and brought her sword and pistols with them in a wrapped bundle that she stashed in the corner.

"You do know that the guests will just dance and eat and drink, don't you?" Lisette said at the sight of the weapons bundle. "There won't be any fighting."

"There's no harm in being prepared," she replied. "I'll feel better if they're here than back at the inn."

The waiting was the worst part. In the dull gloom of the cupboard, huddled close together, Morgane's fears festered. She ruminated over Celeste's words. How what she said about her mother matched her father's warning. Had she made a terrible mistake? Should she have come alone? Not that Lisette would have agreed to that idea.

The fact that the comte hadn't been seen for over ten years worried her greatly. It was getting harder to cast him as the source of her concerns.

"I'm sure they were just rumours," Lisette whispered out of nowhere.

"What?"

"That the young men are brought here. Just gossip, I'm sure of it. Once someone starts a rumour, it runs away with itself."

Morgane wrapped her arms around her. "We stick together. And if we're separated, we meet at the gate that Celeste brought us through, yes?"

"Yes. Are you nervous?"

"Nah," Morgane lied. "Maybe just a little," she added after a beat. "You?"

"I'm excited, I think. Let me adjust your wig."

"Perhaps we should skip the ball. Just go looking around the chateau."

"I think that would be far more of a risk. If we go where there are other guests, we can get the lay of the land and not be out of place. If a servant comes across us in the more private areas of the house, we'll be thrown out and you may never meet her at all."

"But what if she's locked up somewhere?"

"My love, I know you're worried for her, but if she were kept a prisoner, why would they host a ball?"

"Maybe that's why it's a masked ball, to hide the fact that the real comtesse is in a dungeon!"

Lisette grasped her hands. "Morgane, how could she have written letters to you, sent chests full of gowns to you, if she was locked in a dungeon?"

"What if it wasn't my mother who sent them at all?"

Lisette squeezed her hands. "Darling, think for a moment. It may be that she is trapped in a very unhappy marriage and wanted her sister to come back, so they could reconcile and so she would have a companion. That could be reason enough for her to be desperate to bring her back, it doesn't have to be mortal danger."

Morgane tried hard to remember what exactly the letter to Anna-Marie had said, but all she could remember was the feeling it had given her, rather than the words. If only she hadn't packed it in the lost trunk!

"I know this is intimidating," Lisette continued, her voice soft and calm. "And I am nervous, too. I think we should keep the plan as we decided; we go to the ball, we listen to what people are saying and we look for your mother. When the comtesse arrives, we'll get as close to her as we can and when the moment is right, find a way to speak to her alone. That's all we can safely do this evening. If you're still concerned, we can come back, and we will know the layout of the chateau and the grounds much better."

Morgane took a deep breath, trying her best to listen

to Lisette's reasonable suggestion. They had the perfect opportunity to learn more before anything got violent, and she had to take it, so she nodded and tried to relax as much as she could as they waited for the ball to begin.

No one found them, though plenty of people hurried past, making them both hold their breath with nerves each time anyone came close. Morgane felt more confident about leaving her weapons hidden there once they decided to sneak into the ball.

She was glad that the event required masks, and that both she and Lisette had ones that covered the whole of their faces, because otherwise all the other guests would have been able to see her slack-jawed shock.

It was like they'd stepped into another world. One where clothes were decorated with more gold than could fit in a sea chest, made from fabrics that she'd never seen before. Where tables were laden with food she didn't recognise, with displays of confections and sugared fruits that looked more like art than anything edible. Everywhere she looked, there was the ostentatious displays of wealth, all set to music the likes of which she'd never heard before. The constant low hum of conversation was punctuated by laughter that sounded utterly mirthless. It felt like nothing was real at all.

Their costumes had seemed ridiculous in the atelier, but here, they fit in perfectly. Lisette's gown was a little less laden with decoration than some, but neither outfit looked like it had been put together at the last minute. They both had golden masks with only eyeholes to peer through, attached to short rods wrapped in satin ribbon. It seemed that the majority of the guests had masks that covered only half of their faces and were tied on with ribbon. Morgane envied them having both hands free. She wondered if any of the other guests wearing wigs found them as uncomfortable and itchy as she did. She didn't regret that choice, though, liking the fact that the thick brown curls that tumbled over her shoulders couldn't be more different than her real hair. Many of the men wore similar style wigs, though they also had a lot more facial hair than she did.

Now they'd emerged from their hiding place, and no one had immediately identified them as trespassers, the two of them walked arm in arm like the other couples, drifting from the edge of the ballroom to the suite of smaller rooms and then out into the formal gardens. They were lit with braziers and lanterns, making the space even more magical. Morgane cast her eyes over the trimmed hedges, the geometric shapes, the sheer mastery of nature that seemed to be so admired here. Even the plants bent to the will of the Artois family.

It was overwhelming. Morgane was starting to regret this plan. Even though the ball had made it easier to get into the chateau, it was so busy that she wasn't sure it was the best time to find her mother anyway. When she wasn't distracted by yet another roaming entertainer or a burst of false laughter, she tried to seek out the woman she'd travelled so far to find, only to find her gaze drifting from one fantastical costume to another. As her tension grew, she found herself wishing that a fight would break out, just to channel some of that nervous energy. She even started to fantasise about starting one, so she had something to do that she was good at.

"We're never going to find her," she whispered to Lisette.

"We will." Lisette's arm tightened around hers reassuringly. "I don't think your mother has arrived yet."

"How can she not have arrived? She lives here!"

"I don't think she's at the ball yet, though." Lisette steered them towards the edge of the gardens, where it was much quieter. "I've been listening to what people have been saying, and watching how they act. Everyone's still waiting for her to put in an appearance."

Yet again, Morgane found herself marvelling at Lisette. She hadn't been able to tease out anything meaningful from the exchanges she'd heard. The only insight she'd gained from watching the guests was that she could beat most of them in a fight.

"But how can you be sure? She might be pretending to be one of the guests. Maybe that's why they're having a masked ball."

"True. But from what I recall of Monsieur Laroche's experience, the host is always announced so everyone knows how they're dressed. I think it would be considered dreadfully rude to disguise oneself to listen in on the guests. And the impression I had from Laroche is that the sort of people who host parties like this tend to be announced last, so everyone is there to see their entrance. They want to be admired."

"Perhaps she was announced while we were still in the cupboard."

"Perhaps, but I don't think so. When someone more powerful than everyone else comes into a room, it changes the way everyone behaves. All the guests will want to have a chance to be acknowledged by the host, even if it's just a smile. Many will want to have a conversation with them, because that gives them social power in turn. Do you see?"

Morgane didn't. She tried to think of anything like that in her previous life. "I suppose the atmosphere would change in Taverners, if one of the really dangerous captains came in with their crew. But people would mostly stay away from them."

"You'll see, when the comtesse arrives. Watch how the guests change their behaviour. I saw it happen with Laroche, whenever there was a town meeting, or a dance. He loved it, of course. Oh, there's a seat over there."

She pointed at a stone bench positioned next to one of the ponds and they sat down together. No one else was nearby, the lack of lanterns making the area dark and uninviting for any of the legitimate guests.

"Isn't it a marvel?" Lisette asked, daring to lower her mask. "I've never seen so many beautiful things in one place."

"A marvel," Morgane replied, not wanting to douse her lover's excitement with her own discomfort.

"I don't think it feels bad here at all," Lisette continued. "Perhaps Celeste only deals with grumpy staff who give a bad impression."

"Perhaps we should try to get further into the chateau. See if we can find my mother."

"I'm sure she'll arrive soon. No one has given us a second glance, my love."

The feeling that someone was watching them sent a shudder down her back and she glanced behind them into the dark. "I just... I don't know..." She struggled to work out why she was feeling so nervous. She wished she had more than just her knife. She'd feel better with her sword and pistols.

"It is rather overwhelming, but honestly, I don't think there is a single soul here who is interested in bothering us. We'll have another walk around, and hopefully your mother will make an appearance soon."

"I suppose we should try at least one of those fancy pastries," she said, and Lisette smiled.

"That's the spirit. And remember, your mother has no idea you're here. If you see her, and you're not ready to introduce yourself, we can leave and no one will care."

"And you won't mind that I dragged you into all this and then just run away?"

"Of course not, because I wasn't dragged, I came of my own free will. I never would have seen a spectacle like this, and I won't mind leaving early as long as I can try one of those pear tarts before we leave."

Morgane took a deep breath and stood again, ready to

dive back in. Masks in place, they returned to the ballroom and lurked at the edge like many other couples. Morgane watched the dancers moving in their precise stilted way and tried to imagine them dancing a jig or the rolling, stumbling circling of pairs so drunk they had to hold each other up. What would Jacques make of all this?

The music was miserable and sedentary to her ear. One of the quartet was playing a viola like he'd never experienced any sort of joy in his life and was oblivious to how much his instrument could create. If only Bull were there to show them a tune to get cheeks flushed and feet stomping. It was as if everyone in the room were holding themselves back, afraid to actually feel any excitement.

The dance ended and the participants bowed and curtsied. Some left the dancing area, some swapped partners, but when all were ready for the next dance, the music did not start.

Instead, a man wearing the livery of the Artois family appeared at the doorway and called out, "Her grace, the Comtesse d'Artois," in a loud voice.

The waiting dancers retreated as a small entourage entered the room. Leading them was a woman with blonde hair exactly the same colour as Morgane's, arranged in ringlets that framed her face. She was wearing a deep red silk gown embellished with glittering jewels and gold trim that made everyone else's ballgowns look dull in comparison. She was holding up a full-faced golden mask, very similar to the ones that Lisette and Morgane had chosen, but its lips were encrusted with tiny rubies.

She moved the mask aside to address the room and Morgane's breath caught in her throat at the sight of her face. Her mother looked so much like the portrait of Anna-Marie in the locket her father had given her. The family resemblance was painfully clear. But her mother was beautiful in a way that Anna-Marie wasn't. She looked... flawless, as if Anna-

Marie had been a clearing of the throat and her mother was a perfectly sung note.

She was so pale and yet looked radiant, rather than sickly. Her eyes were the same blue as the ones that Morgane had stared back at in the mirror, sparkling and intense as her gaze swept the room.

"It is my deepest pleasure to welcome you all to my home," she said, sounding like Anna-Marie in those rare, soft moments. "My husband gives his apologies and hopes that I will be an adequate host for you all this evening. Now, dance, and enjoy all we have to offer!"

The players struck up the opening chords of the next song and the dancers prepared themselves. The comtesse was immediately approached by several couples who jostled for her attention as she left the ballroom and went towards one of the smaller receiving rooms. It was only then that Morgane noticed another woman in her entourage, one with blonde hair, too, though a duller shade than her mother's. A relative?

She was dressed in dark green and as she turned to leave the room to follow the comtesse, their eyes met. The woman quickly looked away and it could simply have been a chance moment, given the way Morgane was staring, but it made her feel like she'd been noticed. She didn't like it.

"The comtesse is so beautiful," Lisette whispered to her, and she nodded. "How do you feel?"

Morgane didn't know. She was shaking. Was she afraid? Excited? She didn't feel any relief, which surprised her. She'd actually found her mother, she was certain of it. So why was she just standing there and not following her out, not trying to get her attention?

The atmosphere changed again as soon as the entourage left the room. Everyone seemed to have a lot to say all of a sudden.

Morgane spotted the opportunity to raid the food display,

as everyone else was far more interested in the comtesse. It gave her something to do, a way to avoid looking so out of place. Besides, she had to get one of the pear tarts for Lisette.

She loaded two plates for them, only to realise that it would be impossible to eat anything without lowering their masks. She beckoned Lisette over to collect her plate and they retreated to a corner of the room, finding a way to hold both the plate and the mask's stick in one hand. They both nibbled on the confections, and it was a blessed relief to have something else to focus her attention on. She didn't have much appetite, but it all tasted delicious, nonetheless.

Mindful of what Lisette had said, Morgane watched the people around her and listened to them more closely. Most were looking at the door the comtesse had left through and many of them were talking about how splendid the dress was, how divinely beautiful she was and how the comte was such a fortunate man. One woman was bemoaning the fact that she'd chosen dark red for her gown and was now upstaged, others were thrilled that they had picked the same colour scheme as the most fashionable woman in France. It all seemed so vacuous. Did her mother know what was said about her? Did she enjoy all this attention? There was so much noise, so much verbal sea foam left in her mother's wake, that Morgane feared it would consume her.

"I want to go outside," Morgane whispered to Lisette, her stomach churning. She didn't want to be around these people a moment longer.

They went out onto the terrace that ran the length of the chateau. There was a different energy in the air now; everyone seemed more excited and guests who'd been in the gardens when her mother had arrived were now returning to the house. It felt like everyone had been holding their breath and now, having seen the comtesse arrive, were eager to be seen themselves.

They moved into the gardens, going against the flow of guests, until they found a corner of neatly clipped lawn that was quiet and not as well lit, allowing them to lower their masks.

"Do you feel unwell? The food was very rich."

"Yes. No. It wasn't the food. I don't know how I feel," Morgane said.

"She doesn't seem to be in need of rescue," Lisette commented.

"No."

"That's a good thing!"

"Is it? I thought she'd need me. That I would…"

"That you would sweep in and save her and that it would be easy, because you're strong and you know how to fight."

Morgane nodded. "She doesn't need me. We should leave."

"Are you certain? You've come so far, Morgane. Don't you want to meet her? You told me about the letter she sent to you, and the gifts. About the efforts she went to in order to send them to you. Surely she will be overjoyed to see you again?"

Morgane looked down at the satin shoes that were pinching her toes. She had come so far, why run now? She wasn't a coward.

But she was afraid. That woman, who was clearly her mother, seemed full of confidence and part of a world that she would never fit into. What would there be to say? What would she think of her?

How could a noble who looked like that, who spoke like she did, who held the room like her, ever want to admit to being the mother of a graceless pirate? There was such a gulf between them that could surely never be crossed. Everything about this place made her feel awkward and inferior, so how could she possibly go to that woman and tell her she was the baby that had been snatched from her? How could she survive that inevitable moment of disappointment when the comtesse looked at her and didn't see the perfect daughter she must have been hoping to find?

She felt so stupid, wrapped up in dreams of coming to the rescue when she should have focused on avenging her aunt's death.

"I'm certain," Morgane said. "She doesn't need me, and she won't want me. I don't see any merit in putting myself through the embarrassment. I never should have come. I can go back to Nantes, find de Lombardy and discover who sent the *Maître* from him. Hell, it might have been him! I thought it was the comte, but if he's sick, or in hiding, or wherever he is, it's not likely to be him." The briefest flicker of fear that her mother could have been behind the order was swiftly snuffed out. They were sisters. She'd begged her to come home. Why send letters that begged for forgiveness and for her to return, only to send others to kill her? It made no sense.

Lisette studied Morgane's face. "I won't make you stay when you have no desire to be here," she finally said. "But I don't think you can be certain of her rejection. It seems to me that by denying her the opportunity to hurt you, you're also denying her the opportunity to be what you're hoping for. Are you willing to allow your fear of being hurt to stop you from gaining a mother who could love you?"

The words stung, even though she knew Lisette was only trying to help. Morgane wanted to push her lover away and storm off, angered by the implication that she was being ruled by her cowardice. But she stayed still and silent, knowing this place wasn't safe and not wanting to abandon Lisette there either. So she chewed her lip, wrapping her arms tight about herself, feeling trapped between the fear of rejection and the fear of regret. Because she would regret it if she left now, she knew that, once they were away from the discomfort of the place and the way its opulence made her feel like an imposter.

"If you meet her, and she is not what you wished, at least you'll know," Lisette added quietly. "If she is so shallow as to reject you without knowing the value of your heart, then that is her tragedy, not yours. And if you do suffer rejection, is it still not better to have certainty, rather than spend the rest of your life wondering how it might have been?"

There was a gentle clearing of a throat behind them, and both she and Lisette raised the masks swiftly before turning to see who was announcing their presence.

The woman in the green dress from the comtesse's entourage was standing far enough away to seem polite, but close enough to have overheard them. Morgane's hand instinctively twitched for a sword that was not there.

"Pardon my interruption," the woman began. She had a soft voice and nothing in her movements suggested a threat. Her mask covered only the top half of her face, revealing her smile. "The comtesse wishes to speak with you."

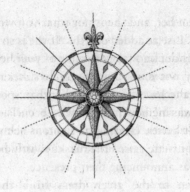

CHAPTER TWENTY-ONE

THE WOMAN'S WORDS were directed at Morgane. "If you'd like to come with me, I'll show you to her salon."

Morgane's palms began to sweat. "Why does she want to speak to me?"

The woman's head tilted fractionally, as if she were surprised by the question. "The comtesse did not share that with me. She asked me to bring you to her, so that you may meet." Morgane reached for Lisette's hand, but the woman shook her head. "Only you, young… man."

A twitch of her lips suggested she wasn't convinced by Morgane's disguise. She was about to reply that it had to be both of them or not at all, when Lisette stepped away from her. "I can wait here for you," she said to Morgane. "I don't mind."

"Have no fear, you're not in any trouble," the woman in green added. "If you were, she wouldn't have sent me."

"Go, speak to her," Lisette whispered. "I'll be here, waiting for you."

It felt wrong to leave her there, but equally wrong to say no. And Morgane could see that Lisette wanted her to accept the invitation.

In that moment, it felt more important to look brave, so Morgane nodded and started to follow the woman to the chateau. She glanced back at Lisette a couple of times, who gave her a tiny wave in acknowledgement, and then focused on what was ahead.

Morgane was nervous, but now the decision had been made, she felt better. Lisette was right, as she so often was; whatever happened next, at least she would never regret running away.

"My name is Cataline," the woman said. There was a pause, bringing with it the implicit pressure to introduce herself, but Morgane stayed silent. "There's no need to be afraid."

"I ain't afraid," Morgane retorted but Cataline's tiny smile told her she hadn't been convincing.

She was led back to the terrace, past the ballroom and several other rooms from which came the sounds of music and laughter. The dancing had started again.

They reached the far corner of the chateau and Cataline turned the corner. Morgane slowed, fearing this was a trap and giving herself some distance before rounding the corner herself. But there was no knife or assassin waiting for her, simply a lantern on a hook that Cataline was lifting off to carry. She took a moment to make sure that no one else was nearby then moved the hook upwards. With the faint sound of grinding stone, cracks appeared between some of the stonework and then a large rectangle of bricks suddenly swung inwards, revealing a secret opening to go into the house.

"It's such a crush between the salon and the ballroom," Cataline said, noting Morgane's surprise. "This way we can avoid the other guests."

And keep the summoning private, Morgane thought but didn't say. "I'm surprised the comtesse isn't dancing and enjoying the ball."

"She likes to speak with those who are lucky enough to merit her undivided attention early in the evening, when everyone is fresh. Then the guests can enjoy the ball without trying to bother her."

Morgane wasn't sure if she liked the idea of having the comtesse's undivided attention, but as she followed Cataline into the shadowy passageway, she realised that her identity must already be known. She'd given her name, but not asked Morgane for hers. Why else ask for only her and not Lisette, too? Both of them were there without an invitation, not just Morgane. And besides, if that had been a problem, surely one of the staff would have been sent to challenge them?

Cataline's words told her that this summoning, and the impending attention it brought with it, was actually a privilege. One that many of the guests at the ball were hopeful of getting for themselves. She must have been the first person sent for. Her mother wanted to meet her, but also didn't want anyone else to see her led through the public rooms. Perhaps she was just as nervous that her daughter would be a disappointment.

Out of sight now, Morgane tucked the mask into her doublet, wanting both hands free just in case. Cataline paused next to a small lever and lifted it upwards, closing the secret door behind them. They passed a couple of closed doors, then the passageway turned a corner and seemed to lead into nothing but darkness. Cataline reached up to the top right corner of the passageway and there was a soft click. A rectangle of light appeared and Morgane realised she'd opened another secret door. As she followed Cataline into the room beyond she looked for the mechanism and saw a tiny brass handle.

The comtesse was standing by the fireplace, but no fire was lit. A man, strikingly bald in a house filled with so many wearing luxuriant wigs, stood near the window. He wasn't masked and his clothes were very plain black wool with black hose. Presumably he was too humbly dressed to be the reclusive comte. His attention was fixed upon Morgane as she entered, his expression one of curiosity.

There were two other women in the room, flanking the double doors. Both were dressed in a familiar blue velvet. Morgane couldn't remember the faces of the ones who'd saved them from the wolf-men, so she had no idea if she owed her life to them specifically. Regardless, she could tell they were capable fighters, just from the way they stood and the confidence in their bearing. They were wearing dresses, unlike the fighters in the woods, but the cut of the clothing wasn't the same as the dresses she'd suffered. They were less voluminous in the skirts and the sleeves set higher in the shoulder to give better range of movement. Morgane suspected they were armed, but they simply stood guard at the doors, rather than looking actively menacing.

Cataline shut the secret door behind Morgane, and when she glanced back, there was nothing to suggest there was a door there at all. It blended into the wood panelling that covered the walls with no obvious handle in sight. The lantern was hung on a hook next to it and left lit, presumably ready for a return journey, if that was the way they were to leave again. The only normal way out of the room was through the guarded exit. Morgane's mouth was horribly dry.

She looked at the comtesse who, in turn, regarded her with an unwavering gaze. Cataline went to her side, whispered something in her ear and then stood back. The comtesse didn't react to whatever she'd been told. She merely studied Morgane's appearance, her expression inscrutable.

The silence pressed upon Morgane's chest. She hated the tension, the sense that there was probably a delicate way to handle this, one that Lisette would instinctively know but she didn't.

"I think you're my mother," she said, putting an end to

it. It was either tell the truth or hit someone, and the latter didn't feel right. Yet. "I was stolen from you, when I was a baby, by your sister."

One of the comtesse's eyebrows raised as Cataline looked like she was trying not to laugh. The bald man slowly closed his eyes, as if disappointed, as the guards at the door exchanged a glance.

"What a remarkable claim," the comtesse finally said. She turned to the guards. "Wait outside."

They left through the double doors, allowing a burst of noise into the room briefly before they were shut again.

The comtesse looked at her without warmth, without any visible reaction at all. This wasn't the reunion that she'd fantasised about! "My baby *girl* was stolen from me," she finally said.

Morgane laughed. "Oh! Piss and shit, yes!" She tore off the wig. "I'm not really a boy. This is just a disguise."

The comtesse finally smiled, but there was no joy in it. Cataline's lips were now pressed tight together, any sense of her amusement now gone.

"See, I have the same hair as you. Anna-Marie told me what she did, on her death bed. I thought she was my mother, all my life. When I found out the truth, I had to find you."

"My child was born with an extraordinary mark."

Morgane hoped that her reticence was simply a matter of not believing her. And she could understand it, she could be anyone. "It's on my back, right at the bottom of my spine." Morgane hesitated. "Do… do you need to see it?"

"What is its shape?"

"It looks like someone spilt wine down my back."

Finally, the comtesse's face was transformed by a dazzling smile. She opened her arms. "My daughter is returned!"

Morgane took a step forwards, but it was the comtesse who closed the distance between them. Her mother's embrace was strong, tight and utterly inescapable. Morgane held her, too, overwhelmed, the relief flooding through her. She'd found her mother, and she was well, and glad to see her! She squeezed her eyes shut, not wanting any tears to come, not now. But when she opened them again, still wrapped in her mother's arms, she noticed Cataline's stare. It was clear that their joy was not shared, and by the look of pure resentment on the woman's face, Morgane's return was not something to be celebrated by all.

When her mother loosened her embrace, she held Morgane at arm's length. Up close, Morgane was disturbed by just how flawless she was. There wasn't a single wrinkle, scar or spot on her skin. She was wearing make-up, but not caked on like so many of the other people she'd seen at the ball. She really was dazzlingly beautiful.

"Forgive me for being careful," she said in her sweet, soft voice. "I had to be sure."

Morgane nodded. "I understand. But you knew I was coming, didn't you? I mean… your guards…"

"I understand they helped you with some troublesome dogs. Yes, since that night I've had eyes on you. To keep you safe. You were in great danger."

"So you knew where I was the whole journey?"

She just smiled, and so did the man, Morgane noted. It felt strange to think that for the entirety of her journey with Lisette, her mother had been protecting them. She did care about her! She had done all she could to keep her safe. "Thank you. But they weren't just dogs though, in the forest," Morgane said. "I've never seen anything like them."

"They won't trouble you anymore." Her mother finally stepped away. "You're perfectly safe now."

"But those wolves that attacked us in the woods," Morgane pressed, unable to let it go. "They changed into men. Who were they? *What* were they?"

"They were Garou. An elite group, apparently. They're usually crass... bestial creatures."

"Garou?"

She nodded. "It's nothing to be concerned about. I have some in my employ. They don't change back and forth very much now, though, they're too far gone."

Morgane was horrified. "In your...?" With a creeping horror, she wondered if that was the reason for so many going missing in the region. Were they hunted down by packs of those foul beasts?

"They can be useful. My enemies were using their very best hunters to try to capture you." Another cold smile. "My guards are superior to anyone they can send."

"What enemies?"

"No one you need concern yourself with." She cupped a hand against Morgane's cheek. "Poor thing, were you very frightened?"

Morgane fidgeted, painfully aware of the attention that all three of them were focusing on her. How cold her mother's hand was. How her words expressed care but something in her eyes did not. "It was just a shock. I'd never heard of anything like them. And no one else seems to know about them."

"Well, of course they don't. The Garou are rare and well-controlled. It simply wouldn't do to have rumours and superstition run rampant through the populace." She spoke as if it were a perfectly normal thing. Morgane did not feel soothed.

"Can you dance?"

Morgane blinked at the non-sequitur. "Yes. No. I mean... I can, but not like they're dancing here."

"Do you play an instrument?"

"No."

"Sing?"

After mentally running through all the bawdy tunes she knew, and how different they sounded to what they called music here, Morgane shook her head.

"Speak any languages other than French?"

"I can tell someone they're a stinking bastard in twelve languages," she said, proudly.

Cataline covered a snigger with a gentle coughing fit.

Isabeau frowned. "Well... given what has happened to you, one can hardly be surprised."

Her disappointment stung. "I can fight." Morgane fumbled for something she was good at in the hope of impressing her. "Better than any man. And sail. I could climb the rigging faster than—"

Her mother held up a hand, looking almost pained. "My dear... you'll never need to climb rigging, whatever that is, again."

"I had to fight to make it here!"

"That was before you were in my care, my dear. Now the rest of your life will be one of ease and luxury and far less violence." She kissed her cheek. "That, I can promise you."

Morgane folded her arms. She knew she should be pleased by that, but she wasn't. Ease and luxury just sounded... boring.

"I can understand why you travelled in disguise, given you had no idea I was watching over you, but why come to the ball dressed as a boy?"

Morgane shrugged. "I wanted to be more comfortable." At her mother's stare, she added, "And I... I wasn't sure whether I might need to fight."

"Fight? Here? At the most celebrated ball of the season?" She laughed, reminding Morgane of the brittle laughter she'd heard from the guests. "Whyever would you think that?"

Before Morgane could answer there was a knock on the door. The man opened it and one of the blue-clad guards handed a note to him and whispered something in his ear. He gave them a nod and shut the door before going to the comtesse and handing the piece of paper to her. She read it and smiled a little.

"Your friend has decided to return to your inn."

Morgane frowned. She'd assumed Lisette would still be waiting for her in the garden, or by the gate as they'd agreed.

Isabeau handed the note to her. "See? There's no need for such concern, my darling, all is well."

The short note was penned in Lisette's handwriting, she would recognise that anywhere. But she needed time to decipher the words, time that she did not feel she had. She didn't want her mother – or the others – to realise she was barely literate. So she pretended to read it, her eyes skimming across the letters until she reached Lisette's name at the bottom. It read 'Lisetta', a deliberate misspelling. Lisette was trying to warn her about something – or at the very least convey that all was not well – in such a way that only she would recognise. No one else here knew her name.

Morgane kept that realisation from her expression as best she could, tucking the note at the top of her stays, beneath the shirt. "Well, I'm sure she realised that I may be some time. It was the most sensible thing to do."

Her mother nodded. "Indeed. Attending a ball unaccompanied is not the done thing, after all."

Strangely, that reassured Morgane. Perhaps Lisette had realised that she couldn't stay without drawing unwanted attention to herself. She hadn't wanted to leave, but felt she must, and so signed her name incorrectly to convey her ambivalence. There was no way to know.

"Well, despite the appalling life you've been forced into, it's clear you're certainly a resourceful and impressively determined young woman." Isabeau smiled. "You can rest now. All is well."

Morgane frowned. "But don't you want to know what happened to your sister?"

"My darling, I received news of her untimely demise some weeks ago now. I cannot tell you how many days and nights I wept for her. I was distraught, utterly distraught, was I not, Cataline?" She twisted to glance at the young woman.

"Yes, your grace." Cataline came to her side. "I was really quite concerned for you."

Morgane studied their faces, their words. Why didn't she feel convinced? Was it something to do with the way the people here comported themselves? Why did everyone seem so false?

"Of course, I'd dreaded that news from the first moment I learned of where she'd taken you. Such a spiteful thing to do, to steal my baby. I can only imagine what must have been in her heart when she did such a terrible thing. But over time, I forgave her. And my heart breaks that she cannot be with us now, that she cannot know how much I loved her, and bore her no ill will."

"Do you know who sent the *Maître*?"

"The who?"

"The ship and crew who were sent to hunt her down."

"My darling, she was a renowned pirate. All pirates are hunted. And all pirates understand the risks their choices incur."

"Sometimes that life is not a choice." Morgane tried to keep her anger in check. She had no idea, could have no idea, of all the many reasons her crewmates had gone into that life.

"No, you're entirely correct. You had no choice, after all. But as soon as you were able, you were brave enough to return to France and start a new life. A choice she could have made, had she accepted the offers of help I sent her all these years."

Morgane clenched her fists with frustration. She wanted

a person to hold responsible, the one who gave the order to kill her aunt. But from her mother's reaction, she feared that she wouldn't get that satisfaction. She spoke as if it were a standing order, just as for any of the king's ships. Perhaps all the Four Chains company ships had been instructed to kill Anna-Marie on sight, and Lavois was simply the only captain who'd been clever enough to execute that order successfully.

The bald man cleared his throat. "Forgive me, your grace, but there are many esteemed guests that crave your attention."

"Oh, how perfectly tiresome," her mother sighed. "You do understand, darling, that I must go and entertain these tedious people? You need not concern yourself with this event, however. It's clear to me that it is much better for you to go and rest after all this excitement. Cataline will show you to your room."

"My room?"

"Yes! You forget I have been expecting you! A lovely room has been prepared for you, Marie-Louise."

"That's not my name. I'm Morgane."

Her mother's nose wrinkled. "You are mistaken, my dear. What you think of as your name is merely a cruel joke on the part of my sister. Morgane was the name of the chambermaid when we were children. She was a particularly ugly and stupid girl, only good enough for emptying chamber pots and sweeping floors. I'm sure you don't want to be named after her."

Her father's surprise at her name suddenly made sense. Anna-Marie must have mentioned her, when they were together. Morgane's jaw clenched. Those were the jobs she'd hated most on *The Vengeance*, and now her aunt's insistence she do them for their cabin made bitter sense. "But Marie-Louise isn't my name."

"You'll grow accustomed to it, my dear. Cataline, show Marie-Louise to her chamber. Discreetly."

Her mother evidently had no desire for her long-lost daughter to be seen at the ball. Before Morgane could ask any one of the dozens of questions she'd saved for this very meeting, Isabeau was turning and sweeping out of the room, the man and then the guards that had been waiting outside following her. The doors were shut, leaving her alone with Cataline and a heavy silence.

Cataline stared at her, and Morgane knew that look. She was appraising an enemy. Looking her up and down, calculating where her weaknesses were and how she could do the most damage. But she knew the impending violence wouldn't be wielded with a physical weapon. Cataline was working out what to say to hurt the most. She'd seen that look on Anna-Marie's face too many times, thankfully most often directed at someone in Taverners who hadn't shown her the proper respect.

But then Cataline's demeanour changed suddenly, and she smiled sweetly at Morgane. Had she not seen the expression before, Morgane would have believed she meant her well. "How lucky you are, to be reunited with your mother at last."

Morgane could hear the tinge of unexpressed spite in her voice. "Why don't you say what you're really thinking?"

Cataline couldn't hide her surprise. "How... direct you are."

Morgane shrugged. "It makes no sense to be otherwise. Are you my sister?"

"Not by blood, no. In spirit... yes. In that the comtesse has been like a mother to me."

So that was it then. No blood to tie them, no wonder Cataline felt threatened by her arrival.

"And who was that man?"

"That's Vauquelin. He's one of your mother's most trusted advisors."

Morgane looked around the room, identifying all of the expressions of wealth that she'd learnt about at the lodge. The paintings, the ornaments, the furniture. This was supposed to be her home now? It did not feel right.

"I don't want to piss in your tankard," Morgane said to her, eliciting an uncomfortable laugh. "You have a life here, one you clearly like and… fit into." She gestured at Cataline's green dress. "I just wanted to find my mother."

"You have absolutely no idea what you've actually found here, do you?" Cataline shook her head. "I cannot believe I actually pity you. You're not what I expected at all." She rubbed her chin thoughtfully with her forefinger.

Morgane bit back a nasty response in the hope of finding some more answers. "Why did my mother's enemies want to capture me?"

Cataline rolled her eyes. "Do you have no imagination? Can you not see how they could manipulate your mother if they held you as hostage? Or turned you against her?"

"Why would anyone want to—"

"Oh, you are so unbearably stupid! To gain political power, of course. Your mother is one of the most powerful nobles in France. Had you no idea?"

"I knew she was rich."

"And why you do you think so many crave nobility and wealth? Power, of course! Influence! She has many enemies, and the most powerful amongst them wanted to use you against her."

Her words changed everything. Morgane had thought it had been an act of love to seek her, and protect her once she was in France… but was it? Was her mother simply protecting her own interests?

"Ahhhh…" Cataline's eyes glinted. "Did you think that your mother sent her best to protect you out of love? Did you think that she has pined for you, all these years, and did all she could to bring her darling daughter home?" She laughed. "You are such an ignorant savage!"

Morgane clenched her fists, filled with the instinctive urge to barrel her to the floor and give her a punch to the guts to shut her up. This stuck-up tart obviously didn't know about the chests that had been sent, the longing to be reunited that had infused the accompanying letters. But she held herself in check, knowing it wouldn't be the right way to handle such insults here. As the flare of her temper passed, shame took its place. Shame at herself for being so naive about her mother's intentions, because even though Cataline was obviously enjoying the hurt she was inflicting, it still all rang true.

Her mother hadn't seemed very interested in who she was, so maybe her efforts were simply to deny her enemies the opportunity to use her daughter as leverage against her. But she hoped, more desperately than she would ever admit, that her disinterest had been because the ball was pressing for her attention. Or perhaps it was because it didn't really matter who she was now, because her mother was planning to mould her into someone more suited for this life. A life that currently held no appeal whatsoever.

"Are you still so fond of being direct?" Cataline said, gloating at Morgane's worried introspection.

Morgane squared her shoulders, having had quite enough of feeling like she wasn't good enough for these people. "Listen. I don't give a wet shit about dresses, or balls, or dancing or who talks to who and how one rich arsehole gets power over another rich arsehole. You have your life, and I have mine, and we have different strengths because of it. If you can't be civil with me" – she leaned forwards, adjusting her stance to make it clear she was ready to punch her if needed – "I won't be civil with you. And trust me, you'll come off the worse."

"Ugh, only savages believe there's only strength in one's fists."

"I don't believe that," Morgane replied. "But I know I'm stronger than you think I am. Maybe you're not always like this, maybe you're worried that now her daughter is back, you'll be out on your ear, but for what it's worth, I ain't interested in taking away what you might have with her."

Cataline laughed. "I have no concerns about that whatsoever! I shall show you to your room. Better you wait for your mother there, rather than risk embarrassing her in polite company."

Instead of opening the double doors by which everyone else had left, Cataline unhooked a lantern from the wall containing the fireplace and opened another secret door by pressing something near her hip that was obscured by her dress. She went through the opening and for a moment, Morgane was tempted to go through the double doors and back to the ball, just to annoy her. But the thought of being there without Lisette, and the way it would irritate her mother before they'd had a chance to get to know each other, made her follow her escort into the passageway beyond.

Cataline walked swiftly, Morgane close behind her to keep within the reach of the light. She counted the handles set into the wall as they walked, all presumably ways into other rooms, before they reached a small flight of stairs and climbed them.

In the upper passageway, Cataline pulled the third handle on the left, opening a door set into the wall of a quiet hallway. After stepping out, Morgane turned immediately to see if she could see anything change when the door closed, something that might give a hint at how to open it again, but there was no clue.

She was escorted to a room at the end of the hallway, far enough from the ballroom that there was no longer the sound of music and socialising. It felt like she was being hidden away.

Cataline stood by the open door and gestured for Morgane to enter. The large room was luxuriously appointed, containing a four-poster bed, a huge armoire, an elegant dressing table and a vase of fresh flowers. The walls were covered in dark wood panelling with a few portraits of rather ugly people staring down at her. The curtains were already drawn and a small candelabra resting on the dressing table was lit. A plate of confections sat beside it and her mouth watered at the sight of them.

"They're for you," Cataline said, and so Morgane went over, plucking one from the plate. It was sticky and covered in rose petals.

She held it, ready to eat, but feeling decidedly awkward. "Am I supposed to just wait for her?"

"Yes."

Morgane shook her head. "Nah. This is bollocks. I'll come back tomorrow, once the ball is over." She turned and took a step back towards the door, but Cataline was already pulling it shut. By the time she reached it, a key was being turned from the other side.

She tried the handle, already knowing she'd been tricked as the sound of Cataline's receding laughter echoed down the hallway.

CHAPTER TWENTY-TWO

MORGANE HAMMERED THE door with the heel of her hand a few times in anger. "Shit and blood!" She kicked it twice, the stout oak too thick to break through, before sweeping the vase off the table and hurling it against the wall in rage.

"Stupid! Stupid!" she yelled at herself.

Had Cataline locked the door of her own volition, just to be certain that she wouldn't try to get back to the ball? Or had this been an order from her mother, arranged between them before Cataline had collected her? Either way, it didn't matter. She had to get out, she wasn't going to just sit there, waiting for whatever bullshit they had planned.

She didn't want to go back to the stupid ball anyway! Were they so concerned that she'd embarrass the comtesse? Why not just tell her to come back the next day? Why do this?

Morgane tossed the sweet onto the plate and went to the window, yanking the curtains open to make her escape, only to find that there was more wall behind them. It was an internal room, the curtains only there to give the impression of a window.

What had felt initially like an infuriatingly heavy-handed

way to ensure she didn't cause some sort of scandal in front of the guests now had the feeling of a terrible trap. Had those letters, those gifts, been nothing more than bait? Nothing more than a ruse to ensure that she rushed to her mother so that the comtesse's enemies couldn't use her?

But surely bringing her back to France only made that more likely? If she'd lived out the rest of her days on *The Vengeance*, Ball-ache and whomever else had designs upon kidnapping her would never have known of her existence.

None of it fit together anymore. All the way to Arras, she had held an idea of her mother in her mind, of a woman with golden hair who needed her. She'd imagined her trapped in an unhappy marriage, even held prisoner by an evil comte, but that had all evaporated this evening. Not even the nebulous hope that her mother would be overjoyed to be reunited with her and would want to know everything about her and her life up until that point had survived the encounter with her.

And worse, she had been warned, long before they'd got here, that Isabeau was not the woman she was hoping for. Her father's words, so easily brushed aside at the time, haunted her now.

But stewing over it all wasn't going to make any of it better. She'd be damned if she was going to sit there all night, waiting for her mother to spare a moment for her. She pulled out the knife from its hidden pocket in the doublet and went back to the door to see if she could pick the lock.

The blade was too wide, though, and when she tried one of the pins from her wig it snapped inside the mechanism. "Piss shit bollocks and blood!" she spat as she tried to winkle out the sliver of metal, only to hear it slip deeper into the lock. There was no way out via the door then.

Morgane slid the knife up her sleeve, ready for swift use if someone came in, and turned her attention to the walls instead, thinking of the secret passages she'd been led through. Perhaps there was one that was attached to this room, one that Cataline had forgotten about, or perhaps didn't even know of.

Meticulously, Morgane ran her hands over every visible inch of wall within her reach, hoping to feel an indentation indicating a secret door even if she couldn't see one. Nothing. She rested her head against the side of the armoire, starting to despair. Nothing like locking her in a room to make her desperate to escape it.

She noticed a trickle of water leading from the small pool that had gathered beneath where the vase had been hurled at the wall. It was running towards the armoire, disappearing behind it. With a spark of excitement, she went to the other side and saw no water there. If the water was running with the slight slope of the floorboards, why wasn't it continuing past the armoire?

For a moment, she considered that it was merely the weight of the piece, and that the water was probably pooling underneath. But when she got down on her knees to peer beneath and check, there was no water at all. She grabbed one of the candles to shine more light beneath and saw the water trickling into a gap between the wall and the floor. There was a secret entrance behind the armoire!

It was heavy, even when empty, but with her feet braced against the wall she could pull it far enough away to feel along to the place above where the water was disappearing. She could feel a tiny ridge, making her certain that something was behind there.

After several minutes of sweating, swearing and sheer bloody mindedness, she'd managed to push the armoire far enough away from the wall to squeeze in behind it. Running her fingertips over the panelling, she found a corner of one panel that pressed inwards, resulting in a thunk and then a very narrow door opening into a cold cobwebbed passageway.

The floorboards behind the armoire were so dusty that she suspected it hadn't been opened in a very long time.

She had to find her way back to the cupboard where she'd stashed her weapons, so she grabbed the candelabra and headed into the passageway. It stretched out in one direction only, parallel to the hallway Cataline had brought her down. There were no handles, so it wasn't the same one. The air was stale and the entire passageway, right up to the corner at the end, felt like it hadn't been used in years. There were probably all sorts of secrets in this chateau, and she felt no desire to learn any of them. This place wasn't for her, and she wasn't sure if she would ever come back.

Round the corner there were a few handles set into the wall, along with spy holes. She peeped through a couple of them but the rooms beyond were dark. A narrow staircase took her back to ground level and soon she could hear the music from the ball again. The passageway was less dusty, too, suggesting it was in more frequent use. She carried on until it got quiet once more, pausing only when she saw coins of light cast on to the opposing wall to look through the spy holes. She saw party guests lounging on plump sofas in various beautiful rooms, chattering and laughing, but not her mother.

At the far end of the passageway, she found the last doorway just before more steps that led down to what she presumed to be the cellar. After listening carefully, she twisted the handle to release the hidden door. She found herself at the back of the chateau, near the cupboard, and swiftly stepped out, leaving the candelabra inside the passageway. She dashed to the cupboard and, with immense relief, found the bundle where she'd left it, along with the clothes she and Lisette had arrived in. She was about to go back out the way the two of them had entered the chateau, but it was blocked by a footman arguing with one of the kitchen staff, so she doubled back. When she heard someone coming down the hallway she darted back into the secret passage, glad that she hadn't fully sealed the door, and pulled it shut.

Morgane took a moment to strap on her sword and pistols, feeling so much better for it. All she had to do was find another way out and then she could get back to the tavern and talk it all through with Lisette.

As she took a step back in the direction she'd come, hoping to find a way out through one of the empty rooms she'd passed, a sound stopped her. At first, she wasn't sure what she'd heard, but something about it made her tense. She paused, straining her ears, until there was the undeniable sound of a man, crying out in pain, coming not from the servants' hallway, but the basement stairs to her right.

Without thinking, she headed down the stairs to a lower passageway and the unmistakeable sound of someone being beaten. One coin of light could be seen on the wall ahead and as she got closer to it, the sounds got louder.

She pressed herself against the spy hole, seeing what could only be described as a cell on the other side, lit by a solitary lantern hung from a bracket by its door. A young man was being punched by one of the house staff, his face bloodied and bruised, his shirt torn. His hands were tied behind his back. The uniformed man had blood streaming from his nose, probably having been headbutted by the prisoner, and was viciously hammering his fists into the victim's stomach.

The cell door was opening then, and Morgane's stomach clenched as she saw her mother sweep into the room, a second servant behind her, pale faced and cowering.

At her entrance the violence stopped, and the young man staggered back to hit the wall, panting for breath. The servant snapped to attention at the sight of the comtesse.

"Get out of the way," she snapped at him, and he scurried into the far corner as Isabeau's gaze fixed on the victim. "You woke early, I see."

"Let me out! I done nothing wrong! Why am I here?"

Oh God, Morgane thought. He was one of the young men that had gone missing.

"Be silent. Be still." Isabeau's voice, soft and low, made Morgane shudder. She watched the young man's eyes widen, his mouth still open, the tendons in his throat straining as if he were trying to move and yet frozen.

Isabeau sighed. "I suppose a brief repast now will do no harm."

She walked up to the young man and ran her fingers through his dark brown hair, freeing it from the ponytail at the nape of his neck to play with positioning it around his shoulders. "You're really quite lovely," she murmured as he remained as still as a ship's figurehead. "Shame you're such a noisy little beast. And so dull. Always so dull."

With one hand still wrapped in his hair she pulled his head back and ran a fingernail down his throat. And then, with a movement so swift Morgane barely registered it, Isabeau sank her teeth into his neck, pulling his body close to hers and wrapping her arms around him like a terrible embrace.

Morgane clamped a hand over her own mouth, wanting to scream as she saw a trickle of blood run down to his shirt and heard a strangled cry escape from his lips. She couldn't look away, frozen in shock as she watched her mother drink his blood until his lips took on a blue tinge. She was still staring when her mother released him and he sank to the floor, the last death rattle leaving his body as he crumpled at her feet.

Isabeau gave a happy sigh, as if she had just seen a lamb playing in a field or a lovely painting, as she dabbed a fingertip at the corner of her mouth. Then she turned to the servant whose nose was still bleeding and tutted at him. "Did he hurt you?"

The man, awestruck, terrified, besotted, nodded at her, trying to cover a bulge in his breeches as blood ran from his nose.

"Well, that won't do," Isabeau replied and then held out her wrist, piercing the skin with her thumbnail until a fat ruby of blood oozed from it. "Here you are."

He leapt forward and clamped his mouth over the wound as she stroked his hair. After a few moments she grasped a handful of that hair and pulled him off her. "Greedy!" she admonished, before licking the wound.

The servant, clearly dissatisfied, whimpered a little, like a sick animal. As Morgane watched, the swelling across the bridge of his nose visibly shrank, the blossoming bruises disappeared, and the blood stopped dripping. Isabeau's blood had healed him?

"Is that how you thank me?" Isabeau backhanded him and he dropped to his knees before her.

"Thank you, thank you!"

"Clean this up," she said, sweeping out of the room. "And no more interruptions!" she called back.

The two servants dragged the body out of the room and Morgane slumped back away from the spy hole, shaking violently. She wanted to be sick, to cry, to scream and to never have seen what she had just witnessed. Slowly she dropped her hand from her mouth, ears ringing and heart pounding. She had to get out of this place and find Lisette and hold her tight and never tell her what she saw, so that she could still live in a world without that horror.

Legs trembling, she staggered a couple of paces and then ran, desperate to get out of the passageway and breathe fresh air again. One of the candles toppled from the candelabra and snuffed out as it fell but she didn't go back for it.

Morgane reached a door at the end of the passage which swung open on well-oiled hinges. She stepped out and closed the door behind her, desperate to be out of the enclosed space, only to realise she must have run in the wrong direction.

She found herself in a large open space with many pillars

holding up the floors above. There were hundreds of bottles of wine stored along the walls, along with crates of provisions. When the heavy door thunked shut behind her she jumped and looked back to see it was disguised by several wine racks. Before she could even attempt to work out what the mechanism was to open it again, a low moan stopped her.

"Ohh… what a piteous creature am I that I hope it's you. Even though all you do is torment me. Witch! Goddess! Beloved, come to me, pleeeease!"

The rasping male voice was coming from the wall on the right, behind another wine rack.

"How do I open the way in?" she called, after checking there were no servants in the cellar.

"Who is that?"

"Someone here to help," she replied. She was not going to leave another prisoner here to meet the same fate.

"Find the bottle of Bordeaux at waist height and pull on it."

Morgane searched the labels on the bottles and found one that began with a b. She pulled it and the rack swung away from the wall, revealing a short shadowy passage beyond ending with a door made of iron. There was no handle, nor lock. "How do I open this door? Do you know?"

"Push on the brick to your left, level with the top hinge."

It, too, swung open and the light from the candles revealed a small cell, divided by bars. On the other side of them was a prisoner, chained and emaciated to such a horrifying degree that his skin looked like parchment stretched over bone. He was so still, she would have thought he was dead, had she not heard his voice.

His black hair hung in filthy clumps, his dirty linen shirt fraying where it had rubbed against the manacles locked about his wrists. His breeches were a faded pale blue satin with ornate gold embroidery at the outer seams, suggesting he might have been a noble once. His stockings were grey with dirt, with no shoes in sight.

She moved closer to the bars so that the light penetrated deeper into his side of the cell. It sparkled from a necklace sporting a large ruby that still hung from his neck. She couldn't understand why it hadn't been taken from him. His cheeks were so drawn that Morgane could see the shape of his skull through them. When he moved, she jumped.

He raised his head and Morgane was struck by the brilliant green of his eyes. They were so ethereally bright in the gloom of the cell that she shuddered. "Who are you?" she asked him.

"I am the Comte d'Artois," he rasped. "Here at the comtesse's pleasure."

Was this why he hadn't been seen in public for over ten years? No wonder he looked mostly dead. "What did you do to deserve this?" Morgane asked, horrified.

He didn't answer, his attention fixated on her hair as he sniffed, loudly, like a dog catching the scent of meat from across the room. For an awful moment she feared he was one of the Garou.

"Your hair..." He sniffed again as she reached up and discovered the wig was no longer there. It had probably fallen from her head in her panicked flight down the passage. "Hell's teeth, she found you! You're her daughter!"

Morgane nodded, the panicky feeling, that had barely had a chance to subside, starting to rise again as an expression of pure horror twisted his face.

"Flee! Flee, I tell you! There is nothing but death for you here!"

"Why? Who would want to kill me? Cataline? Is she so jealous?"

"No, your mother, fool! She's been hunting you down for over ten years! You must leave, I tell you!"

Hunting her down? That had a very different connotation to a desperate search for one's long-lost daughter, one that fit disturbingly close to the predation she'd just witnessed.

"Do you not hear me? She needs your blood, and she will take it from you!"

There was a small table and stool on her side of the bars. Morgane set the candelabra down on the table and sat heavily on the stool, her legs feeling like seaweed. She thought of that poor young man, of her mother sinking her teeth into his throat. Could she do that to her own daughter?

She shook her head. "But... but I spoke with her, and she..." and then she sent her to be locked in a room until the party was over. Until she could sup on her in peace? Still, she couldn't reconcile it in her mind, couldn't even understand what she'd only just witnessed. "I saw her... there was a man, locked in the basement! I saw her bite him and..." How could she wrap flimsy words around the horror she'd witnessed? "And drink his blood!"

He nodded, as if she'd just described something utterly normal. "She's a vampire. Cursed in the eyes of God, one of the immortal undead sustained by the blood of the living. She will never age and never die. She will only grow more powerful. One of many in the nobility, but the most beautiful and cunning amongst them."

All those young men, killed by her own mother. All those families grieving, worrying, waiting for someone to come home who never would, taken by the very person who was supposed to keep them safe. And she was one of many?

"God take this wretched country," Morgane muttered beneath her breath. She took a breath, trying to wrestle this newfound knowledge into place. She still hadn't come to terms with the fact there were wolf-men, that her mother apparently kept some in her employ, let alone the fact that she herself was some supernatural monstrosity.

"You have not the time to sit there, girl! Flee, I tell you! Those young men are merely sustenance, but your blood will make her the most powerful of us and give her the strength to—"

"Us?" Morgane leapt to her feet. "*US*? You're one, too!"

She took in the unnatural intensity of his green eyes, his papery skin, the prominent veins. The fact that he was chained here – and suddenly she saw him as the architect of her family's downfall. Her mother had been a normal woman once, a woman who had borne a child. When she'd married into this cursed family, she hadn't only lost her name to this creature, she'd lost her humanity. "You did this to her!" She drew her sword. "You made her into that monster!"

"She was already a fiend! Why do you think I chose her?" he cried with frustration. "Are you so naive, so ignorant, of what she did? You fool, thinking she had a good and kind soul before my sweet gift made her monstrous. She was already monstrous."

"I don't believe you," Morgane whispered, even as her father's warning echoed in her mind, even as she tried to push away the memory of her aunt's last moments, warning her to stay away.

"There is not, and never has been, a mote of goodness in your mother," the comte said. "It's one of the many reasons I chose her, because I knew that she would have no moral objections to anything I desired of her. Do you realise how difficult it is to find someone like that, someone so beautiful, so good at appearing to be kind and compassionate, while having a heart that even Satan himself would envy?"

"But…"

"Don't you understand that you only exist because Isabeau seduced your father to break her sister's heart? And then once that feeble man was utterly besotted with her, Isabeau broke his."

"But why? Why do such a thing?"

306

"Because she wanted to. Probably because she hated that her older sister, who wasn't as pretty or clever as her, had managed to find love."

"I don't believe—"

"We laughed at their tears," he rasped. "And then when she fell pregnant by Jean-Baptiste, as we hoped she would, we were delighted. Isabeau told your grandparents that he'd raped her and saw to it that Jean-Baptiste's reputation was ruined. He was forced to abandon his business and flee. I had already positioned myself as a friend of the family and they sent her away to one of my country houses, to keep the pregnancy secret, just as we planned. During her confinement I stepped in and offered to marry her, to enable her to stay in society as a decent woman. They were so grateful. I thought I had manoeuvred everything so perfectly into place, when all the while she wrapped her tendrils around my heart and let me believe that I was the one in control."

"Why are you telling me this?"

"If you understand what a creature she was before I gave her the dark embrace, perhaps you will finally believe my warning. When you understand that you were only ever conceived to be the final nail in her sister's heart, you'll see why she will not give a moment's thought to draining the life from you." She saw the cruel glint in his eyes. "But perhaps someone as slow and weak-willed as you could not bear to know what she did. Perhaps you are more your father's daughter."

Morgane glared at him, gripping the sword tighter. She knew he was enjoying how much this hurt her, knew that he was merely goading her. As much as she wanted to slaughter him for turning her mother into that foul creature, she had to know. "Tell me."

"She sent a letter to her sister, begging for her forgiveness. She told her that she'd been forced to be so cruel. That it was all by my design. She begged Anna-Marie to come to the house where she'd spent her confinement, because she'd discovered a terrible secret and trusted no one else to hear it." He sighed wistfully. "It was a master stroke. Anna-Marie put aside her hurt and gave her sister the benefit of the doubt, riding out to visit her. I watched, from behind a spy hole, as your mother delivered a performance worthy of the Prince of Lies himself. She sobbed, she got on her knees and implored Anna-Marie to forgive her. She confided that the powerful Comte d'Artois was a vampire, and she was terrified, not only for herself, but her poor baby girl, too. 'He's going to kill my baby!' she wailed." The comte chuckled as he reminisced, like an old man thinking of long summers as a child when he was describing the poisoning of her entire family's future. "And that was my cue. I sent for a maid to go to her room, then I pretended to be crazed with hunger and drank from her throat as they watched. As we planned, Isabeau got Anna-Marie out of the room, making her think she was rescuing her. And as she had predicted, Anna-Marie returned that night to take the baby – you – to safety."

"You must be wrong," Morgane whispered. "She… she tricked you into showing Anna-Marie what you were, so she would save me! See! My mother knew she'd never be able to escape, so she—"

His laughter cut her off. "Oh, oh, how you cling to your fantasies! You were supposed to die that night! Isabeau was counting on Anna-Marie returning to rescue her and you, so she could be caught and hanged after the poor baby had been 'found smothered' by a sister gone insane with jealousy. But we both underestimated Anna-Marie. She bribed one of the stable boys and escaped with you. It was the only time your mother didn't get her own way."

Morgane thought of all those letters Isabeau had sent to Anna-Marie, begging her to come back, making it sound as if she were in need of rescue. The gifts and letters her mother had sent to her, making her think she loved her and wanted her back. All an elaborate, expensive ruse to try and lure her back. Her aunt had seen through it, because she'd fallen for it once before, and it hurt so much that she'd locked it deep down inside herself, thinking that if she kept Morgane in ignorance, she'd never know to even look for her. If only she'd had the chance to burn those last letters she'd stuffed in her shirt. Anna-Marie would have taken her secret to the grave, and the letters to 'Marie-Louise' would have been discarded, assumed to be for someone else, the dresses sold, the chests repurposed. She would still be on *The Vengeance*, thousands of miles away from this pit of misery.

Hope collapsed within her. As much as she wanted to believe that this creature was lying, she couldn't deny that it all fit with what Jean-Baptiste had told her. She'd travelled so far, been through so much, placed herself – and the woman she loved – in danger, all just to discover that he and Anna-Marie had been right all along. Even Celeste, who'd never properly met Isabeau, had warned her. But she hadn't listened, had she? She'd just stormed ahead, bull-headed and stupid, thinking that she knew better. That the terrifying, powerful woman she'd just seen drain a man of blood to the point of death needed to be rescued and that she should be the one to do it. She wanted to be her mother's saviour so badly, that she'd ignored all of them, chasing an idea of a mother who didn't really exist.

She cursed herself for being so stubborn and feeble-minded enough to have nursed that fantasy for so long. And what did she have to show for it? A dead father killed by foul creatures sent after her as part of some petty noble power game. She wanted to scream.

"The only thing that hurt Isabeau is that Anna-Marie foiled her plan to have you both killed," he spoke into the terrible silence. "She seethed about that for years. But then it turned out to be a blessing in disguise, but only for her. Listen to me! Ten years ago, she came into the possession of an old text, one written by an ancient one of our kind. It spoke of the benefit of bearing a child before accepting the dark gift. It was the reason she turned on me, and seized control of the Four Chains Company, because she could see a way of becoming more powerful than the bond between us, sire to childe.

"I languish here, starved, unable to die, unable to stop loving her, consumed by hatred for her, because she is just as bound to me as I am to her. She still loves me, as much as she hates that, but she loves herself more, just enough to give her the strength to keep me here. It's agony. Sweet, sweet agony for us both. She can't kill me, you see," he laughed, the chilling, scraping sound making her shudder. "She can't give me my final death until she has taken your blood, taken the life she gave you before her undeath, and proven to the darkness that there are no bonds she cannot break, not even the eternal bond of a mother's love for her own child. That's why she's lured you here, and why, I beg you, you must flee. Once she breaks that final bond, all others will be as nothing to her. She will be unstoppable, she will be able to overcome the bond to me, and both you and I will be dead."

Morgane staggered away from the bars, knocking the stool over, a terrible roaring in her ears, pinpricks of light crowding in at the edges of her vision, her stomach feeling like it was sinking into the bowels of the earth.

A terrible aching pain in her chest made her crumple forwards. It felt like she had been made of sand and that someone had just kicked her over, scattering her into total collapse.

Now she understood it all; where Anna-Marie's distrust and cold aloofness had come from, why Jean-Baptiste had been so desperate to get her away from this place, why he'd pretended to be more successful than he was to hide his shame, so riddled with fear and the painful memories of his life being destroyed that he couldn't trust himself to explain it all to her in a way that would make sense. Where her own flawed view of the weakness of men had sprung from, passed down as a generational wound first meted out by her own mother.

She slapped a palm against the wall, steadying herself against the dizziness that threatened to overcome her, as she saw her mother's scheme laid bare in her mind, like seeing the ribs of a ship before all the planks were hammered on. Sending out chests of gifts, letters to Anna-Marie trying to manipulate her into returning home, letters to her to portray herself as a tragic mother desperate to be reunited with her child, when all the while, all she wanted was for her to be returned to France so she could murder her own daughter.

And then the last piece fell into place, so painfully obvious now that she couldn't understand why she hadn't seen it all along. Her mother had sent the *Maître*, once she'd realised that Anna-Marie was never going to fall for the same trick twice. If her sister wasn't going to bring what she needed back to her, then she was merely an obstacle to be eliminated.

The crushing pain in her chest peaked with that realisation, only to be supplanted with a bizarre rush of euphoria as Morgane realised that all of this hurt, all of this horror, was simply the path to resolving the only other thing that had brought her to France.

Vengeance. In finding her mother, and the horrible truth, she'd also found the one she'd been searching for all along: the one who'd ordered the death of her aunt.

He'd spoken of final death, so even if they couldn't die from ageing or starvation, it seemed that the universal law that all things can be killed was one that not even the undead could disobey. Morgane straightened up, her head clearing, a cold calmness flooding her body. She turned back to face the comte. "How do I kill her?"

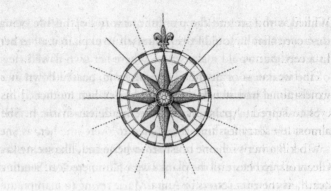

CHAPTER TWENTY-THREE

THE COMTE LAUGHED. "Oh, you are Isabeau's daughter!"

"Answer me!"

"Well… the simplest way would be to give me a little of your blood. Then I will be strong enough to kill her for you."

Morgane laughed. "If I were foolish enough to take that advice, I would deserve the death that would surely follow."

He didn't look too pleased by that. "Why should I tell you? Do you think I am so foolish as to give you the means to kill me, too?"

Morgane folded her arms. "I am going to kill Isabeau, whether you help me or not. I will find a way, and I will burn this chateau to the ground. I owe it to the people who've suffered her reign over them. You can be burned with it, or I can give you a swift death beforehand. It is your choice."

"How bold of you to assume you will be successful."

"How bold of you to assume that you will see the end of this night! If I fail, she becomes strong enough to kill you after taking my blood. If I fail but die in the attempt, before she can drain me, you stay here, tormented by her, forever. That what you want? Eternal torment or a swift death.

Which do you prefer? If you tell me how to do it, I'll see your torment ended before I leave. Then you will be free, whether I succeed or not."

He became so still then, she honestly believed that her words alone had struck the fatal blow. When he moved his eyes to stare at her, she could see the defeat in them. She almost felt sorry for him.

"To kill a vampire, one must remove the head in one strike. Clean off. No hesitation. Wounding will simply lead to your death, as their attack will be fatal."

"And that's the only way?"

"They can be killed by fire, but one as young as your mother will be able to survive anything other than a total conflagration. Old ones, like myself, are destroyed by bright sunlight, but not her. She's still young enough to enjoy a cloudy winter's day."

"Can she fight?"

"Not with a sword, but she doesn't need to. She is stronger than any man you'll face, just from the power of her blood. She'll be able to break your neck with her grip alone. Her guards are more of a threat to you. They are not vampires, but they feed on her blood. They're in thrall to her, and her blood gives them strength and vitality, too. They'll do everything they can to kill you, once you attack her. If you can."

"I can fight! I've killed before."

"She will make it difficult. She uses the power in her blood to make people do as she desires. She will put out the flames in your heart and make you docile as a lamb, should she wish it."

She remembered the young man, desperate to fight, but held still just by her words alone. She wanted to think that she could resist her, but Morgane wasn't going to make the same mistake as Anna-Marie and let arrogance be her downfall. "Is there nothing I can do to defend myself against that?"

"Some speak of the protection given by faith. I've never seen anyone of faith strong enough to stop a determined vampire. If I were you, I'd flee. Put as many leagues between you and her as you can, and resign yourself to a lifetime of looking over your shoulder. Anna-Marie eluded her for many, many years. You could, too."

It was tempting, but she knew she couldn't live like that, not knowing what she did now. She wouldn't be able to cope with the guilt of leaving all the people of Arras – including Celeste and her family – to suffer the continued rule of the Comtesse d'Artois. She'd rather die trying to free all of them, rather than live trying to save only herself.

"No. I know what I must do." She lifted her sword again. "Anything else I need to know to survive this?"

He shook his head. "Best you end me now, given you will be dead before the night is out. Pull the lever, there" – he moved his head towards the barred door of the cell and she saw a metal rod set into the wall – "to open the door."

She pulled it down, unlocking the barred door into his side of the cell. Morgane pushed it open and stepped inside, never taking her eyes off him.

She'd never executed a man. All of the times she'd killed had been in the white-hot flash of self-defence, unthinking, instinctive. This was anything but. As she got closer, mindful of keeping at least two sword's lengths between them, she began to doubt whether she could do this.

"If you restore me, there will be no need to face your mother," he said. "There is no hope for success if you try to kill her as a mere mortal girl."

"If I restore you, your first act will be to kill me. I ain't that stupid."

She stopped far enough away for him to be unable to reach

her with his mouth, yet close enough to strike at him with a lunge at full reach.

"All I ask," he said hurriedly, "is that if you survive, you never give this jewel around my neck to another living soul. It's cursed and…" He sighed. "And I would rather you throw it into the sea, than it be worn by another."

Any other jewel and she would have sold it, but with its provenance, she thought his suggestion was preferable, so she nodded and then raised her sword. He instinctively shrank back, making a clean strike to the neck without hitting the wall behind him more difficult than she wanted to try.

Keeping her eyes fixed upon him, Morgane altered the angle of her blade and sliced the top of her wrist, suspecting that if he was starved of blood, he may be unable to help himself stretching towards her.

Before a bead of her blood had even dripped onto the floor, the comte became bestial, straining at the manacles with more effort than Morgane thought he could be capable of, his lips drawn back revealing long, sharp teeth. The veins under his skin bulged, a deep blue colour, as his eyes became even brighter. He wailed with desperate frustration as he tried to break free and pounce upon her.

Fear tightened Morgane's guts, the same fear as when she'd seen the Garou change in front of her. The sure, instinctive knowledge that this was a predator, a creature that had no place in the world she knew and understood. She fought the urge to flee, forcing herself to instead raise her sword.

When her blood splattered on the earthen floor, he strained towards it, just as she'd hoped. With his neck now extended, and every instinct within her screaming for his death, it was easy to adjust her grip on the sword and cleave his head from his shoulders in one blow.

It powdered into dust mid-air, the rest of his body, even his clothes, collapsing into a scattering of ashes beneath the swinging empty manacles. The only thing that remained was the blood-red jewel, sitting on top of the dust, glinting in the candlelight.

She staggered backwards, her legs wobbling at the sight of something so desperately unnatural. "Shit and blood," she muttered, her back hitting the wall of the cell. "Shit and blood!"

Morgane hastily tore a strip from the doublet's lining, silently apologising to Celeste as she did so, and wrapped it tight around the cut. It wasn't bad – she'd made sure it wasn't too deep, nor in a place that would bleed profusely. It still stung, nonetheless. Using another strip of fabric, she picked up the jewel and stuffed it into her pocket, her instincts telling her to not even touch the damn thing. If she failed and had to flee, she'd rather take it with her than leave it for another to find.

She was about to wipe the blade clean and plan her next steps when an appalling scream coming from the floor above froze her. Her mother. Somehow, she must have sensed that the comte had met his final death.

The sound of footsteps running across the floor above sent her into a panic. There was no time to form a plan, no time even to make an escape. The only thing Morgane was certain of was her unwillingness to face her mother inside a dungeon. She dashed out into the cellar, arriving just as the door from the secret staircase flew open, spilling the bottles stored in its rack to smash on the floor.

Her mother moved so fast into the cellar that for a moment Morgane thought she flew. But then she was suddenly still, staring in shock. She clearly hadn't been expecting her daughter to be the killer. But Morgane was holding the sword and there was no reason to doubt what she saw.

"*You* killed him? Why?"

"The same reason I'm going to kill you," Morgane said as she raised her sword. "Because he bloody deserved it."

"At last, some sign that you actually have some spirit," her mother said. "I don't know how you came to talk to the comte, nor what he could have said to turn you against me, but you need to calm yourself and consider what you're doing. He was a disgusting man, who did all he could to make my life a misery. I had no choice but to lock him away, for my own protection."

"You expect me to believe that?"

"Why would you believe a deranged man over your own mother? I have only your best interests at heart, my darling. I spent so many years searching for you, and you came such a long way to find me... don't let that foul creature poison you against me."

Her voice was so soft and soothing. Morgane felt tired, heavy, like she couldn't hold on to the determination to attack Isabeau. She lowered the sword.

"There, that's better. Oh, my poor lamb, being dragged into matters that really don't concern you. Let's put this behind us, Marie-Louise, and—"

It felt like someone had just tipped a bucket of water over her. That wasn't her name! "He warned me about this... dammit!" She raised her sword again. "I know what you did! You sent the *Maître*! You sent them to kill your own sister!"

The smug twitch of her lips told Morgane she was right. "Only so that we could be reunited, my darling."

"And I know why you wanted that so badly, you disgusting creature! I know what you are!"

Her mother's face hardened. "You will come upstairs with me now."

It felt like a rope had been tossed around her waist and tugged. Morgane had to fight to stay still. "No. I don't want to do that. I found out the truth about you, and not just from him. From Anna-Marie, from my father, and from a woman better than you could ever be! That bastard just confirmed it.

If I could be sure you'd never kill me, if you'd only harmed your own family, I would have walked away, but you're like a bloody poisonous boil that will never heal. I ain't going to let you continue to starve people and steal away their sons and kill them. They can't stop you so I will."

"Drop your sword."

Morgane tightened her hold on the grip, feeling beads of sweat pop on her forehead. She didn't want to let it go, even though there was a compulsion to do so. Then she remembered the cross that Celeste had insisted she wear. Hadn't she mentioned evil being in this house? Had she known what was going on here?

The comte had said something about symbols of faith, but she couldn't quite remember what it was. As her right hand started to shake violently, she fished the cross out from under her shirt and pulled on the thin chain that held it round her neck so she could brandish the symbol at her mother.

Isabeau laughed. "Have you been listening to superstitious fools on your travels? Did they not tell you that one must have genuine faith? Not that it would work against me. I'm your mother. You must do as I say. It is the natural order of things. Drop. Your. Sword."

Morgane let the cross fall and then the sword followed with a terrible clatter. She just couldn't stop herself releasing the grip, even though it was the last thing she wanted to do.

"That's better." Her mother started to close the gap between them as four of her personal guards spilled in through the secret passageway behind her, all four of the women dressed in blue velvet armed with a pistol and a sword. "No wonder you couldn't just sit and wait in your room. You're practically feral. You're just like a dog that needs to be trained. Get down on your hands and knees and show me you're willing to be a good girl."

Morgane strained against the compulsion to obey her,

clenching her teeth so hard that her jaw sent shooting pains up into her skull. In her head she was screaming obscenities, cursing her mother and trying to force herself to run forwards, to barrel into the bitch and send her crashing into the racks behind her. But instead, she felt her knees buckling and then her palms spreading on the earthen floor, as if she had no control over her own body.

"To think I actually feared that I would find this difficult. That some vestigial motherly instinct would rear its head and make me regret what needs to be done. But now I know you're nothing more than a stupid little dog, I feel nothing. Nothing at all. Save, perhaps, the satisfaction of finally tying up one loose end."

Her footsteps were getting closer, but all Morgane could see was the floor, unable to move, even though her mother's words stoked a rage inside her like nothing she'd felt before. Powerless, the rage started to turn inwards, and she silently railed against herself. This was all her fault. Her father's death, the fact she'd brought the means for Isabeau to become even more powerful straight to her, the fact she wasn't strong enough to resist her commands. So many incorrect assumptions, so many bad decisions had led her to this point. How could she have been so stupid to think she could kill her?

But then, at the moment she realised that her stupidity was going to lead to her own death and that there was nothing she could do about it, Lisette's smile bloomed in her memory. Lisette had said she wasn't stupid so many times. In fact, Lisette had told her she was clever, and skilled, just in different ways to her. And Lisette would never treat her this way. She could imagine her lover's cheeks reddening with anger at the sight of what was unfolding here, how she'd put her hands on her hips and pull herself up to her full height and use her sternest voice to challenge what she knew was wrong.

This was wrong. Nobody should be treated this way. Not even her.

And at that moment, Lisette's note slipped from her shirt, sliding free in Morgane's prone position. It fell open and Morgane saw her lover's writing, remembered all the times she'd lovingly, patiently encouraged her to form the lines and loops of her own letters. How she'd never shouted, never got angry with her for not remembering what each letter was supposed to sound like or fumbling the sounds when two letters together changed that. Only love. Only patience. Only total belief that Morgane, clumsy, stupid Morgane, was worth the time and the effort to love.

Morgane picked up the note, only realising in that moment that she was able to move, and more than that, her mother had been continuing to talk but she hadn't even heard her.

It wasn't about faith. It was about focus!

She closed her fist around Lisette's writing as her mother's dress hem came into view. She was standing right in front of her! Morgane shook her right sleeve, all the while reciting Lisette's lessons in her head. "Put your dot on the page and move the quill up to the first tiny peak…" The dagger slid down, and its point chinked onto the floor. "Then down and to the right, like one is sliding down the hill to stop halfway down."

Slowly, slowly, Morgane lifted her right hand, allowing the dagger to slide down the tiny hill of her hand until the grip was in place.

"Then back up the next little hill, the same height as the second…"

She closed her fingers around the dagger's grip.

"And then right at the top, oh no! You fall to the bottom. And that is M. M for Morgane."

She took a deep breath.

"And M for mmm, the way your kisses make me feel. Now you write it, my love."

Morgane slashed up with the knife, thrusting forwards, using the bend at her hips to give her momentum. The knife pierced her mother's bodice and scraped upwards until it snagged on the bones in her stays.

A screech of shock from her mother as she launched herself back. The feeling of warmth as her blood slid down the blade and onto Morgane's hand. The sound of four pistols firing. Two punches in her side, the white-hot stab of shot piercing her skin.

But she was alive! She was alive, damn it, and she was on her feet before the guards arrived, able to slam her shoulder into the stomach of the first one before realising how hurt she really was.

Morgane staggered back as the other three closed in around her, Isabeau drawing back to watch, holding the front of her bodice in place. Only then did Morgane realise her sword was now out of reach.

The guards were going to kill her, there was no doubt about their intent, and no command from Isabeau to the contrary. Even though the fight was pumping fire round her veins, Morgane could feel how her movement was impeded by the wounds, and how her lips were tingling. Blood loss. Too much blood.

Blood. She remembered how Isabeau's blood had healed her servant. But wasn't there a risk that it would make her more vulnerable to her mother's manipulation?

When Morgane barely dodged the first sword attack, she knew that if she didn't take the risk, she'd be dead before she had a chance to worry about her mother. So Morgane fixed her eyes on the guard who was lining up for another blow and licked the blood from her dagger.

All of the pain in her side stopped, instantly, along with the shaking and the light-headedness. She felt like she'd downed five flagons of bumbo, but without any of the foggy thinking that came with it.

The guards all looked horrified and actually hesitated, giving her the opportunity to run at the closest one, jabbing the dagger into the guard's stomach as Morgane pushed her back. She felt the air move as one of the guards now behind her slashed at her back, and the vaguest sensation of contact, but she didn't care. If she'd been cut, she couldn't feel it.

She'd gained enough distance to get to her sword, shoving her opponent aside, her dagger still stuck in her up to the hilt. Still holding Lisette's note, Morgane grabbed her sword and then was slammed into the floor by one of them coming at her from the left.

A panicked, scrabbling, dirty fight ensued. Morgane kicked and bit and then headbutted the woman, feeling and hearing the satisfying crack of her nose breaking. As she howled, Morgane wrestled her off and immediately skewered another who was about to do exactly that to her, only missing as Morgane had twisted onto her side. She'd had too many men try to stab through her on the deck of a ship to let that happen here.

Morgane managed to get on one knee before another attack, a slash that caught her cheek and then gashed her shoulder. She pretended to be pained, then when the attacker risked a follow-up without sure footing, Morgane cut upwards from her lower position and sliced her from belly to breastbone, where her sword lodged.

As the woman fell away it ripped Morgane's sword from her hand, so she punched the last one in the face before she could bring her sword to bear, leaving all four of them on the floor as she finally got to her feet.

Her mother stood near the doorway, the stench of brandy filling the air from all the smashed bottles lying around her. "You don't want to hurt me, little dog," she said, taking a step towards Morgane, her slippers crunching on the glass. "You know how good loyalty feels now, don't you?"

A tug, like before in that Morgane was aware it was coming from Isabeau, but also different in that it felt deeper. She'd poisoned herself with the vampire's blood, and she could feel it now, like dozens of tiny threads running through her veins, running back to her mother to hold like invisible puppet strings.

Morgane tightened her grip on the note, thought about Lisette's lesson for the letter 'o', how much she'd relished forming the shape of it with her mouth. How they'd kissed. She drew one of Anna-Marie's pistols.

Isabeau laughed. "Oh, you silly creature. That can't hurt me. Put. It. Down. Before I put you down, like the stupid little dog you are."

Morgane smiled, thinking of Lisette's gasps as she'd kissed her neck during that lesson, the way her lover had dropped the quill to reach around and squeeze her backside. "I'm not a stupid little dog."

"Marie-Louise—"

"And I am not Marie-Louise. I am Morgane, of *The Vengeance*." She glanced down at the trickle of brandy, running from the pool her mother stood in to a dip in the floor just within her reach. She crouched down and pointed the pistol at the collecting alcohol. "I *am* vengeance."

Morgane fired, the flare from the powder setting the brandy alight and sending a bright flame rushing towards her mother. Morgane knew it wasn't enough to start the conflagration that she'd have liked, but the panic it caused her mother was adequate distraction for her to be able to pull her sword free from the now dead guard.

Morgane chased the flame's progress across the room, her mother twisting away to flee the fire whooshing towards her slippers and skirts that were soaked with brandy. Just as it caught the edge of her dress, Morgane swung the blade and with a grunt of effort to resist the new and terrible instinct to protect the source of her poison, sliced her head clean off.

It bounced, just the once, before crumbling to dust much more slowly than the comte's had. In moments Isabeau's collapsing body and the highly flammable dress were engulfed in the fire.

Morgane realised she was screaming, but it wasn't in terror. It was a release. It felt like all of the pain and the fear and the hurt that had been poured into her, by the deaths of her aunt and her father, by the truths she'd uncovered here, were being released with her breath, fanning the flames that consumed the one who'd started it all.

She watched it all burn and pressed Lisette's note to her lips, silently thanking the woman she loved. As the smoke filled the room, Morgane leapt over the narrowest point of the fire and dashed up the secret stairway to open the first handle she found by touch in the dark passageway.

The room beyond was empty, but a lit lantern remained by the door. Morgane grabbed it, removed the candle and then set the curtains on fire before tossing the candle onto the rug.

She barged through the doors. "Fire, fire!" she yelled at a footman walking down the hallway ahead of her. He turned, saw the smoke and began running towards the doorway ahead, through which she could see guests of the ball milling about.

Morgane turned and ran back into the room she'd set alight, satisfied that it would be very hard to put out by the time help arrived, and dashed back into the passageway, just in case any of the other guards were hunting for her.

She ran as far as she could and fumbled for the nearest handle. The sound of someone inside the room beyond helped her to find the doorway and she burst through it to find herself in a drawing room with Cataline curled up on the floor, sobbing hysterically.

"You have to leave," Morgane yelled. "There's a fire, and it's spreading."

"She's gone! She's gone!" Cataline was hysterical, but the sobbing wasn't just emotional pain. Morgane could see from the way that her hands and fingers seemed to be seized up that there was something physically painful happening, too. She was aware of a dull ache in her own chest, and wondered if there was the same cause. Perhaps Isabeau's death could be felt by those who'd drunk from her, and Cataline, her favourite, had taken more than most.

"Shit." Morgane didn't really care for her, but she wasn't willing to just leave her there to be burned alive. "Can you walk?"

Cataline didn't reply. It looked like she was in agony. Morgane slid her hands under the woman's arms and started to pull her up.

"Leave me! I cannot live without her!"

"Oh, don't be such a barnacle! Get up!"

When it became clear that Cataline wasn't capable of moving herself, Morgane shifted to picking her up and hefting her over her shoulder. Thankfully she wasn't too heavy, and after a couple of staggering steps, she found the best position for her. Cataline was too locked in her pain to protest, and Morgane suspected that any of the other elite guards still left in the house would be in the same state, so she left via the double doors leading out into the gardens and joined the throngs of people hurrying from the chateau.

Nobody gave them a second glance, and once they were far enough away, Morgane stumbled to the first patch of grass she could get to and set Cataline down.

The coolness of the air and the clumsy manner of her arrival made her look at Morgane for the first time. She took in the cut on her cheek, which was starting to really sting now, and the state of her clothes. Her bloodshot eyes widened.

Morgane cupped her face in her hands. "Yes, I did it. It was the right thing to do. Now we know who is the stronger of us. They're both gone now, and it might not feel like it right now, but you're free."

Cataline tried to reach up to Morgane's wrists, but her face twisted in pain. "I'll... I'll—"

"You owe me your life, so don't even think about coming after me. I hope you find peace."

Incapable of doing anything except feel the pain, Cataline curled back up into a ball. Morgane left her to her misery, unable to do anything more for her, and started to jog round the chateau, avoiding the main flow of guests. They were running for carriages and the main gates, whereas Morgane was keen to leave through the servants' entrance.

She passed a couple of the blue-clad guards at the edge of the gardens, both in the same state as Cataline. There could be more in the chateau, but the fire was reaching the first storey now and she wasn't willing to take the risk. There was no sign of Vauquelin, and she did not care. All she wanted was to find Lisette and make sure she was safe.

The smaller gates near the servants' entrance were open and she staggered through them. Waves of exhaustion ebbed and flowed, reassuring her that the poison of her mother's blood was long gone now. Such a tiny amount had done so much, and she suspected that if it had been much more than that, she'd be suffering like the thralls clearly were. Small mercies.

She paused, trying to remember which way it was to the inn, when the sweetest voice called her name over the chaos. "Morgane!"

She turned, looking for Lisette, to see her waving from the driver's seat of a fancy open carriage. The last of the fear flooded out of Morgane's chest, and she choked back tears as she hurried over.

Lisette jumped down and threw her arms around her. "You're hurt! Oh, my love, my darling." She kissed her and held her tight again. "I knew something wasn't right! They were so rude. And I was never going to go back to the inn like they told me to. What nonsense! Did they give you my note? When I saw the smoke, I knew something had happened, and that you were probably involved. Is it just the cut on your face? Any other injuries?"

"Shush," Morgane mumbled, and pulled herself away enough to kiss her again. "I'll be fine, just… just get us out of here. Wait… where did that carriage come from?"

"I… borrowed it," Lisette said with a half-smile somewhere between ashamed and oddly proud. "When I saw the smoke, I decided that we might need it far more than one of those stupid nobles."

"I love you." Morgane grinned.

"I love you, too. Up you go!" Lisette helped her up onto the board so they could sit together before taking her place once more and encouraging the horse to move on.

The further they got from the chateau, and the longer they went without any sign of pursuit, Morgane finally allowed herself to breathe easier. She was aware of Lisette's occasional worried glances, and the fact that she hadn't asked her what happened. Just that alone filled her with appreciation. Lisette knew her so well.

"I'll tell you what happened, I swear," Morgane said after a little while. "Just… just not yet."

"She wasn't what you hoped for," Lisette said sadly. "I understand. Take as long as you need. Where shall we go? After we've picked up our things, I mean. And returned the costumes – well, my costume – to Celeste?"

Morgane leaned forwards, propping herself up with her elbows on her knees. "How do you feel about ships?"

Lisette looked at her, reflecting back the slightly nervous look that Morgane suspected was on her own face. "Why do you ask?"

"I've been thinking. All this noble shit… all these lords and vassals and rules and stuff… It's not for me. I don't think France is, for that matter."

"I see."

Morgane reached across and put her hand over Lisette's. "Come with me. I'm going back to *The Vengeance*. I can't promise you an easy life, but it's not a dull one. And we could be together. Really together, and no one would care. And you'd get to meet Jacques, and Bull and Dill, and you'll see blues you've never seen before and—"

"And storms," Lisette said. "And blood. And pustulant wounds, maggots in the food and—" She laughed at Morgane's worried expression. "You don't need to sell it to me, Morgane. I'll take the bad with the good, however bad it gets, because it won't matter. You'll be there."

Morgane swallowed down the lump in her throat. "Really? You'll come with me, just because… you want to be with me?"

"Yes."

"Even though you'll have to meet Plague-Arse Pierre? And smell him?"

"I am willing to endure all these hardships, yes. On one condition."

Morgane groaned. "I know, I know, I will have to learn to read and write!"

"Well, that, too, but my condition is this: we have to have our own cabin." Her eyes sparkled with such lustful promise that Morgane nodded without thinking.

"Might need to take our own ship," Morgane said, after a moment's reflection. "We'll sail with *The Vengeance*, maybe start a fleet."

"I like the thought of calling you captain." Lisette grinned. "What shall we call the ship?"

Morgane leaned back to look up at the stars. "*The Triumphant*."

"No!"

Morgane sighed. "*The Victorious.*"

"No, no. Nothing like that."

"How about… *Laroche's Regret?*"

Lisette laughed. "I like it, but no."

Morgane's mind drifted to when they would have their own cabin. "*The Peachy Arse* – no, that sounds like a bad tavern."

"I have one," Lisette said quietly. "No… it's not bold enough."

"Tell me."

"*The Freedom.*"

"There's already one of those. And I don't rate the captain either."

"Damn! I thought I had it."

"Names are hard," Morgane sighed. "We might not know until we find the ship and get the feel of her."

"It doesn't matter what we name her, not really," Lisette said. "I know what she'll really be called." When Morgane looked at her, she smiled. "Home."

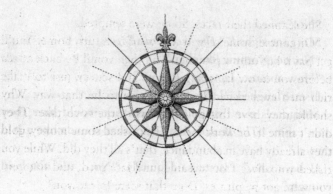

EPILOGUE

MORGANE RAISED A hand to Dill, giving her permission to send the signal to *The Vengeance*. Captain Jacques would see it and know that their quarry was under their control.

She glanced at Lisette who stood poised with her little leatherbound book, saw that she was ready, and permitted herself an appreciative look at her backside in the velvet breeches she'd taken a liking to.

They'd caught a ship bound for Spain from the Americas. Minimal casualties and the crew captured. She crossed the board from her ship to the prize and remained standing on the rail, one hand on the rigging, so she could look down on the prisoners. Bull gave her a nod, indicating he was ready to repeat her words in Spanish, for those who didn't speak French.

"Gentlemen, you have a choice to make. Either you leave with your plundered ship and go to face the wrath of your investors, or you join my crew. You'll have better pay, better rights and better grog. You'll have a say in how the ship is run, and even if I should be your captain. No such thing as mutiny in our fleet. You know why? Cos it's not needed."

She scanned their faces. Some were tempted.

"Of course, some of you will want to return home. You'll get paid, but only a pittance. And then you'll be back at sea before you know it, facing storms and scurvy, just to make rich men even richer. It doesn't have to be that way. Why should they have this gold? It wasn't theirs to take. They didn't mine it, or work for it. They risked some money, gold they already have in abundance, that's all they did. While you risked your lives. You sweated, and laboured, and dammit, you were got by pirates! Does that seem fair to you?"

She enjoyed the murmurs, the glances exchanged between them. "Those who want a new life, come with me. I can't promise it will be better, but I can promise it will be fairer. And if you don't like it, you can leave whenever we make port. But I'll tell you this. No member of my crew has ever chosen to leave. And not because they're scared of the consequences. Because they know when they got a good thing. Ain't that right, you lot?"

The crew gathered around them, and those back on her ship, all called out in agreement.

"The choice is yours. You want a new life, you give your name to my bosun." She waved a hand at Lisette. "Lisette will take your names and read the ship's articles to you. Swear to follow them, and your new ship awaits. Along with your share of the gold that you kindly delivered into our hands. You got a problem sailing with female crew, don't bother. Go back to poxy Europe and scrape in the dirt with the rest of them."

Morgane left them to it, returning to her ship with the sound of men shouting to join her crew as she crossed the boarding plank. With a grin, she went up to the prow, leaning against the rail to enjoy the heady glow of a battle well fought and won.

She thought of her aunt, and her mother, as she often did

in the quiet moments, and she pitied them. What lonely lives they'd had, trapped in their mutual hatred. They had never known the pleasure, the comfort of love, like she did.

Morgane thought of what she'd gone looking for, and how she'd found it, but not where she'd expected to. She thought of Jacques' face when she gave him the letter from his mother, and how he'd wept with gratitude and happiness at her return. She'd gone to find family, when it had been there all along. She'd gone to find a mother's love, only to realise it was never there to be found. And she'd brought back a love with her like no other.

A hand rested on her shoulder. "The new members of the crew are sworn in and waiting for you, captain," Lisette said.

Morgane nodded and went with her to the edge of the poop deck, seeing new faces and familiar ones looking up at her. Louis was hurriedly pouring bumbo into cups that had been pressed into everyone's hands. Dill dashed up the steps with cups for Lisette and Morgane.

"A toast to your ship!" Morgane said, lifting her cup once everyone had one. "*The Fearsome Heart*."

"*The Fearsome Heart*!" came the resounding response, and they all drank deep.

ACKNOWLEDGEMENTS

WITH THANKS TO Bobbu, for listening to drafts, helping me to heal and giving me the support needed to get this book written. Both you and Amanda are exemplary besties and make excellent crew. Thanks also to my son, who is the best cheerleader a mum could ever hope to have. Love you so much, Beanie.

Even though this is a historical fantasy swashbuckler, I wanted to try and get as many details correct as possible (with the occasional dollop of artistic license, of course!). I'd like to acknowledge two books that really helped: *Pirates of the West Indies* by Clinton W. Black and *Under the Black Flag, the Romance and Reality of Life Among the Pirates* by David Cordingly. Any mistakes or liberties taken are entirely mine.

Last, but not least, thanks to my editor, Amanda Rutter for the excellent feedback on the first draft and all the help since. So glad to be working with you again!

To you, dear reader, I wish you fair weather, calm seas, and the camaraderie of your own trusted crew. These are stormy times we find ourselves in, but things will get better. Hold fast.

ABOUT THE AUTHOR

EMMA NEWMAN WRITES short stories, novels and novellas in multiple speculative fiction genres. Her *Planetfall* series was nominated for the Best Series Hugo Award 2020 and individual books in that series have been shortlisted for multiple awards. She is a professional audiobook narrator, and won the Alfie and Hugo Best Fancast Awards for her podcast *Tea and Jeopardy*. Emma is a keen role-player, gamer, painter and designer-dressmaker.

FIND US ONLINE!

www.rebellionpublishing.com

/solarisbooks   /solarisbks   /solarisbooks

SIGN UP TO OUR NEWSLETTER!

rebellionpublishing.com/newsletter

YOUR REVIEWS MATTER!

Enjoy this book? Got something to say?

Leave a review on Amazon, GoodReads or with your
favourite bookseller and let the world know!